Praise for the novels of

"No one writes lip-biting sexual tensio[n]
Rhyannon Byrd." —Shayla Black, *New [York Times be]stselling author*

"An ensnaring and scalding read full of great emotional appeal, endearing and tortured characters, and a thrilling plot that leads the pair on a wonderfully written adventure culminating in an epic battle that leaves you craving more!" —*Black Lagoon Reviews*

"Steam, lust, love, loyalty . . . all these aspects and more fill the pages of this true page-turner." —*Nocturne Romance Reads*

"With a Byrd book, you know you will get plenty of sizzling sensuality as well as molten emotion." —*RT Book Reviews*

"A haunting love story." —*Publishers Weekly*

"Quite the emotional roller coaster but I had a blast hoppin' in and hanging on to what ultimately proved to be one hell of a steamy ride." —*Lovin' Me Some Romance*

"Filled with love, lust, loyalty . . . sensuality, and heady romance." —*Night Owl Reviews*

"Guaranteed to keep you reading until the very last page." —*Joyfully Reviewed*

"Delicious and hot." —*Romance Junkies*

"Not to be missed." —*Manic Readers*

Titles by Rhyannon Byrd

TAKE ME UNDER
KEEP ME CLOSER

Anthologies

WICKED AND DANGEROUS
(with Shayla Black)

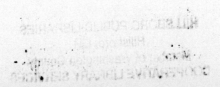

Keep Me Closer

Rhyannon Byrd

HEAT BOOKS | NEW YORK

THE BERKLEY PUBLISHING GROUP
Published by the Penguin Group
Penguin Group (USA) LLC
375 Hudson Street, New York, New York 10014

USA • Canada • UK • Ireland • Australia • New Zealand • India • South Africa • China

penguin.com

A Penguin Random House Company

This book is an original publication of The Berkley Publishing Group.

Library of Congress Cataloging-in-Publication Data

Byrd, Rhyannon.
Keep me closer / Rhyannon Byrd.
pages cm
ISBN 978-0-425-26294-8
1. Private investigators—Fiction.   2. Man-woman relationships—Fiction.   I. Title.
PR6102.Y73K44 2014
823'.92—dc23
2014000542

PUBLISHING HISTORY
Heat trade paperback edition / June 2014

PRINTED IN THE UNITED STATES OF AMERICA

10   9   8   7   6   5   4   3   2   1

Cover photograph of "couple" © Conrado/Shutterstock.
Cover design by SDG Concepts LLC.
Text design by Tiffany Estreicher.

1

As Alex Hudson waited in the shadows of the car-filled multi-story parking structure, smoking a cigarette, he silently cursed his brother for putting him in this ridiculous situation. He was a fucking private investigator, not a babysitter. He didn't, for a single moment, think there was any validity to Ben and Reese's claims that Brit Cramer's life was in danger. This was just his brother and new sister-in-law's irritating idea of playing matchmaker. The two had gotten it into their heads last summer that he and the therapist would be good together, and had done their best to make his life a living hell ever since.

It was already hard enough, having to spend so much time around the woman, without putting him through this shit. He was forced to deal with Brit's dimpled smiles and natural, in-your-face sexuality every time they were invited to the same dinners, parties, and weekend barbecues at his middle brother's beachfront home. Now that it was late spring and the weather was warming on southern Florida's gulf coast, the number of beach get-togethers was increasing, while the clothing Brit and the other women wore became practically nonexistent. The past few weeks had been absolute hell, thanks to the amount of smooth, creamy skin she'd started putting on display, and his mood was foul. Last damn thing he needed was this, being forced to watch her every night as she finally dragged herself away from her office and made it home to the two-story house she lived in alone.

And since she had no idea Ben had put him on this assignment, Alex had spent the last two evenings slinking around the parking structure attached to the medical complex where she worked like a goddamn stalker. It made him feel like the very thing he was supposedly there to protect her against, and it sucked.

It was also a serious waste of his time.

Yeah, Alex had looked over the harassment complaint Brit had filed against university student Clay Shepherd the week before, after the twenty-two-year-old had tried to force his way into her office, and he agreed with Ben that her former patient was unstable. But that didn't mean there was any credence to Ben's belief that Shepherd could prove violent. His brother might be the county sheriff here in Moss Beach, but he wasn't a fucking mind reader. No, ever since his wedding, Ben had turned into a nosey, meddling matchmaker, and a serious pain in the ass. Alex knew only too well that this was Ben's way of forcing him to pay attention to the woman he'd been trying so damn hard to avoid.

Not that avoiding her was possible. The last time they'd been invited to the same get-together, this one at Scott Ryder's house—Ryder was a friend of the family and one of Ben's deputies—Alex had tried to look right through Brit, only to nearly swallow his tongue when he saw how the dress she was wearing hugged her curves. The woman was built like a fucking pinup model from the forties, lush and tall and so damn overtly sensual he'd have wanted to eat her alive if he hadn't become a sworn woman-hater. Or at least a woman-*avoider*. But he'd finally accepted that it was physically impossible for him to ignore a woman who looked like Dr. Brit Cramer, so he'd reverted to the ol' tried and true crutch of being a dick to her.

Pathetic? Oh, yeah. Big-time. But when a guy was desperate he sometimes had to scrape the bottom of the emotional barrel. And Alex had done a stellar job of it. He still couldn't recall exactly what he'd said to her that particular night, when he'd found himself standing alone on Ryder's back patio with Brit, anger and frustration taking control of his mouth while his pulse had roared in his ears, blocking out the sound of his own voice—but it had earned him a slap across the face from the gorgeous redhead.

That had been a few weeks ago, and it was the last time he'd spoken to her.

And now he was here, pissed at his brother for pulling this crap on him, and trying hard to ignore how much he was looking forward to getting a glimpse of the doc as she walked to her car. Jesus, he really did sound like a psychotic stalker. When Ben got back from the Bahamas, where he was vacationing with Reese, Alex was kicking the guy's ass for sticking him with this assignment. He could only be thankful the woman had a quality home alarm system, or he knew his brother would have had him camping out with her, and there was no way in hell he was going there, even if she was Ben and Reese's best friend. If it came to that, their little brother Mike would have to step in.

The thought instantly made him scowl.

Knowing Mike's wild reputation, he and the doc would be screwing like rabbits within an hour of him setting foot in her house. There was no way Mike wouldn't put the moves on her, even though he'd been trying to push Alex into asking her out for months now. It was just in his baby brother's DNA. Mike might be closing in on twenty-nine, a kick-ass agent with the DEA, respected for his sharp mind and dedication to the job, but when it came to killer curves and a beautiful face, his dick could not be trusted. It was as simple as that.

The sudden vibration in Alex's front pocket told him he had an incoming call, and he grimaced when he read the name on the screen. Speak of the devil. Mike's ears must have been burning. His baby brother was recently proving to be just as big a pain in his backside as Ben, the two of them making it clear they believed Alex had wasted enough time stewing in anger after the eventful end of his marriage five years ago. Little did they know his pissy attitude these days had almost nothing to do with his bitch of an ex-wife, and everything to do with the fact that he couldn't get a particular redheaded therapist out of his thoughts.

Bracing his back against the side of his new Range Rover, Alex lifted the phone to his ear. "I'm busy, Mike. What do you want?"

"You know, it's been half a decade, Alex. People can go to college and earn degrees in that amount of time. Pop out a couple of kids. Trek through South America and set up an entire empire of llama farms. We're talking serious life changers. So don't you think it's about time you pulled your personality out of your ass and stopped acting like a prick?"

Wondering why his brothers couldn't just cut him some freaking slack, he pinched the bridge of his nose and took a deep breath. "I'm not in the mood for any of your shit tonight, Mike." Not that he was ever in the mood for it. He was an asshole, not a masochist. "So what are you calling for?"

The noises in the background made it clear that his brother was calling from his office. "I just wanted to make sure you were watching Brit," Mike replied, his slow drawl a dead giveaway that he was Southern born and raised.

"I said I would, so I am." Alex might be a dick, but he kept his promises. Even when he thought they were pointless and irritating.

"Good," Mike grunted. "I know you think this is all some sort of conspiracy against you, but Ben's really worried about this Shepherd guy. He thinks Brit was way more creeped out by him than she's letting on."

"Oh, yeah? Why's that?"

Alex had read the report, which was fairly detailed. Three years ago, Brit had been doing work for the Miami Police Department as part of a statewide program that placed a specially trained clinical psychologist with trauma victims during their police and medical interviews, the point of the program being to ease the process between victims and the officers fighting to bring them justice. That was when she'd met Ben, who had been working as a homicide detective in the city. Not long after she'd started with the program, the doc had worked with Shepherd after he'd been the victim of a violent sexual assault perpetrated by his own mother and her boyfriend.

After counseling him during the week he'd spent in hospital, Brit had passed the nineteen-year-old on to a local therapist who was meant to work with him on a permanent basis, and her association with the young man had come to an end. Until two weeks ago, when Shepherd had claimed to be the victim of another brutal attack while living on campus at Fenton, a private south Florida university in the city of Westville, located north of Moss Beach. He specifically requested a visit from Dr. Cramer when he was admitted to hospital, and being the dedicated professional that she was, she'd immediately driven up to meet with him. Two days later, after being discharged, he'd traveled down to Moss Beach for an appointment at her office, and everything had gone south after that meeting.

Though she had cautioned Shepherd several times during the appointment, he'd grown increasingly personal with her, crossing the line. When she warned him that kind of behavior wouldn't be tolerated during their sessions, he'd stormed out, only to return several days later, when he'd caused a scene with her receptionist, verbally abusing the woman. That was a week ago. Brit had immediately filed the report against him with the local sheriff's department, and made it clear to the Westville Police Department that she would no longer be seeing Shepherd as a patient. According to his attorney, Shepherd regretted his behavior and was willing to keep his distance, claiming the emotional strain he was under had caused him to act out. But Ben apparently wasn't buying it. He said there was more to the story than Brit was letting on, but Alex knew she was too smart to play with her safety.

Which meant this whole setup was nothing more than his family doing their best to yank his chain and meddle where they weren't wanted. God knew he loved them, but there were times when he wondered why he hadn't just packed up and moved to another state, putting some distance between him and their good intentions.

Despite what his brothers thought, he didn't need anything more from Brit Cramer than a hard, furious fucking that left them both wrung out and the bed in shambles. And since that wasn't something he could have, seeing as how she was so close to his family, the best thing he could do was see as little of her as possible.

"Alex!" Mike suddenly barked. "Are you even listening to me, man?"

"What?"

Mike grunted in irritation. "Fuck. Why do I even bother talking to you?"

"Damned if I know," he shot back, realizing his little brother must have been giving him a hell of a lecture while he'd zoned out thinking about Shepherd and the doc. Then he realized he'd also zoned out on watching the lobby doors of the medical complex for Brit, and a surprisingly sharp slice of anxiety knifed through him. *Shit.* "Look, Mike, I gotta go."

Without even waiting for Mike's response, Alex shoved his phone back in his pocket and started making his way between the parked cars, carrying on a silent argument with himself the entire time. He didn't understand why he was so twisted with tension when he didn't think she was in any real danger to begin with. Why was he freaking out? He was damn near running, his heart pounding as he made his way down the last row, when she emerged through the lobby doors of the clinic in a gaggle of coworkers, laughing at something one of the women had just said, and he exploded with a violent, stifled stream of curses as he jerked to a stop behind one of the parking deck's concrete columns, careful not to let her see him.

"Christ, what a fucking idiot," he muttered to himself, peeking around the column. He'd damn near given himself a heart attack, thinking he'd screwed up and missed her leaving, and there she was, looking hot and happy in one of those little designer dresses she always wore to the office, her legs appearing a mile long in a pair of fuck-me heels. The woman knew how to dress to make a man hard, that was for damn sure. He hated it as much as he loved it, seeing as how he'd made a personal vow never to lay a hand on her.

Why in God's name had he even freaked? He honestly didn't think she was in any danger from Shepherd. If he did, he wouldn't be skulking around a parking garage just to make sure she made it to her car okay each day. He'd be on her 24-7, ready to rip the throat out of any sick fuck who so much as breathed on her.

Not because it's her, he silently assured himself. *I'd do the same for any woman who was in trouble.*

"Screw this," he muttered, reaching for his cigarettes as he spun on his heel, heading back to the Rover. He could hear Mike's smoking lecture droning on in his head, and mentally flipped him off. *Cancer, emphysema, tarring his insides black.* Yeah, yeah, blah, blah. Like he gave a shit. He could no longer touch a bottle, so this was the next best thing.

He'd parked the Range Rover at the end of the first row of cars on the ground level, next to the wall, and there was enough room that he could brace his back against the driver's side door as he took a deep drag on his cigarette, holding the smoke in his lungs. With a scowl, he slowly exhaled, determined to ignore a niggling thread of unease over the way he'd turned away from Brit, letting her make her way to her car on her own, instead of under his watchful eye. She was parked at the other end of the deck, just around the corner. Odds were good one of the women she'd walked out with would be parked close by her Audi, and they could look out for each other. He didn't need to be wasting his time with this crap. He just needed to take whatever shit Ben felt like doling out and tell his brother to put one of his deputies on watch duty if he and Reese were so worried about her.

Taking another deep drag on the cigarette, Alex made the sudden decision to ring up one of the single women who lived in his condo complex to see if she was free later on. Her name was Chloe, she was blond, and she was built. She was also definitely interested, considering the way she bopped her tight little ass over to flirt with him whenever he swam laps in the community pool. He'd been putting off messing around with her, since she lived a little too close for comfort. It would no doubt come back and bite him in the ass if they hooked up, but damn it, he needed the distraction. If he had to sit around his condo by himself that night and mull over the way he'd just acted like an idiot, panicking for no reason, he'd end up driving himself crazy.

"Definitely need to make the call." Dropping the cigarette butt on the concrete floor, he ground it out with his boot and pulled his phone from his pocket again, determined to go through with it. He might wish women were something he could do without these days, but he'd always had an above average sex drive, and once he'd sobered up after his divorce, it'd refused to be completely ignored. Which meant that he might not date, but there were definitely times when he hooked up for casual sex to let off some steam. He'd just started to scroll through his contacts, hoping he could work up some decent enthusiasm for the perky dental assistant, since he needed to screw the tension he'd been carrying around for the past few days out of his system, when a strange noise caught his attention.

What the hell?

Before he could even push away from the Rover, it came again, and his gut chilled the instant he realized it was a woman's cry being choked off. *Oh, shit.* The stark sound of fear echoed in his head as he jammed his phone in his pocket and started running, his pulse roaring as fury flooded his veins. Jesus, he could be such a stupid, stubborn fuck! He wanted to keep cussing his sorry ass out, but forced it to the back of his mind, years of training sharpening his focus. By the time he rounded the concrete corner, he had his gun drawn, his gaze scanning the scene. Most of the staff at the clinic kept long hours and there were still a few dozen cars parked on this side of the parking deck. He headed straight for the doc's black Audi, but she was nowhere in sight.

No, damn it. This could *not* be fucking happening. Not after he'd been standing around, acting like a jackass.

"Cramer?" he barked, his rough voice echoing across the rows of vehicles. In a far corner he could hear a car driving off, probably one of her coworkers, but they were too far away to even hear him. "Where are you, Doc?"

Nothing but silence greeted him as he quietly moved through the cars, and then he heard it. Another muffled, choked cry, as if a woman had tried to call out before someone shoved his hand over her mouth. The sound had come from just ahead of him, on the other side of a massive Ford Excursion. Alex crept around the back of the SUV, picking up what sounded like the almost silent rustling of someone's clothes brushing against another person as they struggled against them, and he rounded the back corner with his gun raised, his stomach sinking as he took in the situation with a swift glance.

A man of slim build and medium height was wearing a ski mask and holding Brit in front of his body, and he had a fucking knife at her throat. It was small, like a pocketknife, but it didn't matter. He could still do some serious damage with it if he wanted.

The male's other hand was smashed over her mouth, her hands curled around his forearm as he jerked her backward.

"Get your fucking hands off her," Alex growled, ready to put a bullet between the man's eyes. But he couldn't take a shot when the son of a bitch was holding that knife on her.

"I've already called for backup," he bluffed, when her attacker just kept dragging her backward, toward the exit door a couple of yards behind them. "You can't make it out of here with her."

The bastard made a choked sound of frustration, his brown eyes darting from side to side. Alex was on the verge of making another threat, driving his point home, when the man suddenly shoved her away, ducking in front of the neighboring truck before Alex could get a clear shot at him. He could hear the guy making a run for it, his gaze cutting from Brit's feminine form sprawled across the ground to the shadowy recesses of the parking structure.

Shit! He hated this fucking scenario. But there wasn't any question of what he was going to do. Sure, the furious motherfucker inside him wanted to take off after that asshole and beat him to a pulp. Thrash him until he was nothing but a gruesome stain on the ground. He didn't do it, though. Instead, he shoved his gun into his shoulder holster and hurried over to the doc, taking hold of her upper arms as he helped her to her feet.

He hadn't allowed himself to look at her face before that moment, knowing he would have lost it if she'd looked terrified. But he couldn't wait to get a good long look at her now, needing to assure himself that she was okay.

"Are you all right?" He somehow gentled his touch as he pushed her auburn hair back from her face, hooking it behind her ear. "Doc, are you all right?"

She managed a nod, blinking in shock as she leaned against the Ford and touched her trembling fingers to her throat.

"Was it Shepherd?"

"What?" she croaked, pale and wide-eyed as she stared up at him.

"The asshole who had you at knifepoint. Was it Shepherd?"

"I . . . I think so. I didn't see his face, but it sounded like him."

"Fuck."

"I'm so confused." Her hair fell back in her face as she shook her head. "What's going on? What are you doing here, Alex?"

Ignoring her question, he asked, "What did he say to you?"

She pushed away from the SUV, hiked her sliding purse strap back up to her shoulder, then smoothed her hands over the bronze silk of her dress. "Seriously, Alex, where the hell did you come from?"

"Worry about me later," he ground out. "Right now, you need to tell me what happened while it's still fresh in your mind. Did he tell you what he wanted?"

"Yes. He did."

"What was it?"

She drew in a deep breath, eyeing him with a heavy dose of suspicion as she took a step back. He could tell her mind was rapidly working to come up with an explanation for why he was there. "I'd rather talk to someone from the sheriff's department."

"Tough shit," he snapped, pissed by the way she was acting, as if he was fucking diseased when he was the one who'd just saved her. "I'm here and you can damn well talk to me."

She suddenly gasped, then covered her mouth, those long-lashed hazel eyes becoming huge in her pale face. "Ohmygod!" she whispered. "He didn't. Tell me that Ben did *not* put you up to this!"

Alex held her stare with narrowed eyes, watching the shock continue to seep into her expression as everything began to click into place for her. "You want the truth or a lie?"

"Damn it! He had no right!"

Wishing like hell that every breath he took wasn't pulling her mouthwatering scent into his lungs, he forced his next words through his clenched teeth. "Cut the bullshit, Brit. Whether we like it or not, he made the right call. If I hadn't been here, watching you, you'd be in a hell of a lot of trouble. Either dead or getting carted off to God knows where, about to suffer through shit that I don't think you even want to imagine. So suck it up and act like a fucking adult."

Her nostrils flared. "You truly are an arrogant bastard, aren't you?"

"Right now, I'm the arrogant bastard who saved your ass, so try to remember that when you're breaking my balls."

"I want nothing to do with your balls!" she yelled, turning and smacking her hands down on the hood of the SUV, damn near denting the metal.

"Jesus Christ, Brittany! Calm down before you hurt yourself!"

She sucked in a sharp breath the instant he barked at her and spun toward him so quickly he was surprised it didn't make her dizzy. "You have *got* to be kidding," she whispered, blinking those long lashes. "What did you just call me?"

Despite the softness of her tone, Alex felt the hairs on the back of his neck prickle, signaling danger. "Uh, Brittany," he muttered.

"Are you *serious*? I don't believe this. Don't call me that! Ever!"

She was shouting at him again, and he lifted his hands, saying, "Whoa, okay. You're being sensitive or some shit. I get it."

"You don't get anything. I'm not sensitive," she snapped, her big eyes bright with anger. "I just expect you to get my freaking name right!"

Now *he* was starting to get pissed. "What the hell are you talking about? That *is* your name."

"No. It. Isn't!"

"Fine, whatever. I get it. You hate my guts," he snarled. "Any chance you want to explain why? I've never done anything to you. Hell, we hardly ever even talk to each other."

She went from looking pissed to stunned before Alex could so much as draw his next breath. "Do you honestly have to ask?"

He pinched the bridge of his nose, struggling for patience. "It appears so, since I can't read your mind." God, this woman drove him crazy.

"Do you even know *you*?"

"Uh, do I what?" There were times when the doc talked in fucking circles. It made his head hurt, which he could understand. What he couldn't account for was why getting screeched at by the redhead had him having to concentrate to keep his dick from getting hard. Talk about wrong time, wrong place.

She took a step toward him, her hazel eyes flashing with indignation. "I asked if you even know yourself, Alex. Because last time I checked, you were the same asshole who tried to talk his brother out of getting involved with the best damn thing that's ever happened to him!"

She was pissed at him because of something he'd done to Ben and Reese? What the fuck? Sure, Alex had made no secret in the beginning that he thought Ben was crazy for getting involved with Reese. But what did that have to do with Brit? Would he ever understand women? All this time Brit had been giving him the cold shoulder, he'd thought she'd finally clued in to the fact that he was a lost cause.

Losing his patience with the entire situation, he took hold of her arm and started pulling her toward the Range Rover on the other side of the parking deck, keeping an eye out for Shepherd along the way, just in case the idiot was stupid enough to come back.

"What are you doing? My car is over there!" she said, pointing toward the Audi.

"You're not driving your car. I'm putting you in mine so I can get you the hell out of here."

"I don't want to go anywhere with you." Even though he wasn't looking at her, he could actually feel the seething force of her glare against the side of his face. "I want to call the sheriff's department and go home."

"I didn't ask, Doc."

"I *hate* it when you call me that."

He grunted, figuring at this point that it was better to keep his mouth shut. But when she continued to glare at him, he gave in. "I made it right in the end," he pointed out. "With Ben and Reese."

She made a sharp, sarcastic sound under her breath. "And you expect to be applauded for the fact that your guilt got the better of you?"

Reaching the passenger's side door of the Range Rover, he shoved his hand into his pocket, hit the button on his key fob to unlock the doors, and slid her a dark look of warning. "I don't expect a damn thing from you other than your usual behavior. But don't act like you know me. Because you don't."

"I know enough," she shot back, her creamy complexion now flushed with color.

"Like hell you do. You know what I've wanted to show you and that's it."

She pinned him with a piercing look that lifted the hairs on the back of his neck again, that look moving over him like a physical touch. "So then it's deliberate. Is that what you're saying? You act like an asshole around me because you want me to think you're an asshole?"

"I don't want you thinking about me at all." *Lie!* "All I want is for you to shut up, listen, and do what I tell you. Nothing more, nothing less. Got it?"

"And if I don't?" she asked, arching one eyebrow as he released her arm and yanked the door open.

"You can either climb up there on your own," he muttered, jerking his chin at the seat, "or I can put you there. Either way, you're getting in, Doc."

"Such. An. Ass." She bit the words out one by one, but did as he'd told her to, damn near taking his face off when she reached out, grabbed the handle, and slammed the door shut.

Working his jaw, Alex made his way around the front of the Rover, climbed into the driver's seat, and started the engine.

Guess what? I call bullshit.

Yeah, he'd known that was coming. He could lie to everyone else, but it was damn hard to lie to your own self.

Would he do his best to see that a woman in trouble got the protection she needed? Of course he would. But he wouldn't feel driven to personally provide that protection. To put his life on hold and his body on the line.

No, there were only a handful of women he would feel the need to do *that* for. His sister-in-law. His friend Ryder's wife, Lily.

Maggie, his elderly neighbor who baked him chocolate chip cookies whenever he dropped by for a visit.

He tried to convince himself that the stubborn redhead who'd just planted her gorgeous ass in his car didn't qualify. That she didn't belong in that small, select group. But as he steered the Range Rover out of the parking deck, checking the rearview mirror to ensure they weren't being followed, Alex couldn't silence that damn know-it-all voice in his head.

You're such a fucking liar . . .

2

WHEN BEN HUDSON EVENTUALLY CAME HOME FROM HIS ROMANTIC getaway with her newest best friend, Brit Cramer figured there was a good chance she was actually going to kill his handsome ass. Sure, it would put a strain on her friendship with Reese, seeing as how she would have offed the teacher's husband, but with the way she was feeling right now, it would almost be worth it.

She couldn't believe he'd gone behind her back and stuck his damn big brother on her. Mike she could have handled. Mike was irrepressible and adorable and a blast to be around. But Alex? She honestly couldn't imagine what Ben had been thinking.

Alex Hudson might be a serious badass, and a highly successful PI, but Ben knew how much she disliked his older brother. Did she lust for every inch of his hard, ripped body and mouthwatering dark looks? Oh, without a doubt. But the man himself drove her crazy. He was broody and dour, and she was truly still pissed at him for the way he'd acted when Ben had started things with Reese last summer. Not to mention the way he'd never been particularly friendly toward her. But that she could have brushed aside and attributed to his bitterness toward most of the female gender. The thing with Ben she couldn't so easily forgive. Especially since she'd never seen Alex act all that welcoming toward Reese in the months that she and his brother had been married.

When he made a right onto Main Street instead of a left, toward her house, she turned her head to look at him. "Where are you going?"

The only response she got was a low grunt.

"Where, Alex?"

"Sheriff's station."

She groaned before she could stop herself, closing her eyes for a brief moment before forcing them open. She'd already been through hell tonight back in the parking garage, and now she was going to have to go over it all in minute detail. Not to mention the other things that she hadn't told them about Shepherd.

"What?" he muttered, cutting her a dark look before turning his attention back to the road. "I thought you wanted to talk to a deputy."

"I did. I do. I'm just not looking forward to it." She smashed her lips together, determined not to say any more. But he obviously had other ideas about how they were going to spend the drive.

Checking his rearview mirror again, he said, "We have about five minutes before we reach the station. Until we get there, I'm going to ask you some questions and you're going to give me the truth. Understood?"

She gripped the seat belt crossing her body with both hands, wondering why he always had to sound so freaking arrogant. "I have an above average IQ, so yes, I'm capable of understanding your man grunting."

He grunted again in response, which pulled a reluctant smile from her that she tried to cut off. But he must have caught it from the corner of his eye because he shook his head and snorted. Then he got right to the point. "What didn't you put in that report, Doc?"

"What are you talking about?" she hedged.

"Enough of the bullshit. There's more to this than you're letting on. There has to be."

"Hmm. So apparently you're more than just a bunch of muscles, huh? Ben's always said you were smart, but since you never really talk much around me, it was difficult to tell."

She watched his big hands tighten on the leather steering wheel. "I didn't ask for a personality profile. I just want you to answer my question."

"And you're not going to stop until I do? Is that it?" Honestly, this man could give lessons in stubborn.

"Now you're catching on," he remarked in a low rumble, still checking the Range Rover's mirrors. She knew he was making sure Shepherd wasn't following them, and she was grudgingly grateful.

Grudgingly? God, considering what he'd saved her from, she should be down on her knees thanking him. Suddenly, Brit felt petty for giving him such a hard time, and decided the least she could do was answer his questions with the truth.

Blowing out a tense breath, she leaned her head back and closed her eyes again. "He called me perfect."

She sensed the look he gave her, before turning his attention back to the road. "Go on."

Damn it, she hated this entire situation. Alex was the last person in the world she wanted to admit these things to, but after what had happened, she knew she'd made the wrong call by keeping it to herself. "When I met with Clay in my office that day, he told me that he *needed* my body to cleanse his own of the things that had happened to him. That our attraction would burn it away."

"Did he scare you?"

Opening her eyes, she stared out at the darkening sky through the windshield and quietly said, "Yes. But it was more that he made me uncomfortable as hell. His attitude was very . . . sexual. He'd never spoken to me that way before."

"And why didn't you put this in the report?"

"Because I wasn't sure why he had done it. Was it just stress? He'd just been through a traumatic experience, being raped and assaulted by an unknown male after getting drunk at a party, which meant his behavior was most likely in response to that, and could well be temporary. And what he said, it's not something I wanted to draw attention to." Crossing her arms, she rubbed her hands over her shoulders, wet her lips, and went on. "I know the guys here in Moss Beach and they're great. But they're not the only law enforcement department I work with. There are times when it's difficult to be taken seriously by some of the officers, and I've worked exceptionally hard to build a reputation as a professional. I didn't want them to . . . to—"

His tone was clipped. "You didn't want a bunch of guys standing around, making comments about your ass and tits, when you've worked so hard to get them to see beyond the porn star bod. Is that it?"

She gave him a stunned look. "I wouldn't have worded it that way, but yes."

"I get where you're coming from. I do. But it was a dumb-ass move. That guy is dangerous."

Her shoulders slumped. "I know."

"You should have trusted your instincts."

"I filed the report," she argued.

"Only after he came back and tried to force his way in to see you," he countered. "And it was a report that no one took seriously, because you held back on the details."

"Ben took me seriously!"

Brushing that off, he lowered his voice and evidently decided it was time to scare the hell out of her. "If I hadn't been there tonight, it could have been even uglier than it was. You've worked closely enough with law enforcement the last few years to know just how ugly I'm talking about."

She swallowed, then lifted her chin. "I don't need you trying to frighten me."

"No," he muttered, pulling into the sheriff's station parking lot. "What you need is to be put over some guy's knee and have that little ass of yours spanked."

Before she could think of a worthy retort to that shocking assessment—not to mention ridiculous, seeing as how her ass was *far* from little—he'd parked, climbed out of the Range Rover, and slammed his door. She followed him inside the bustling station, ready to get this over and done with so that she could get home, set her security alarm, and wash the god-awful night away with a scalding shower.

An hour later, as they left and climbed back into his car, Brit silently admitted that the sheriff's station hadn't been as crappy an experience as she'd expected. Scott Ryder had been there, which had made things easier, since she was friends with his wife, Lily. But the last thing she'd wanted to do was go over what had happened with Shepherd. She'd been doing her best not to think about it, focusing her energy on being irritated with Alex instead, since it was easier.

A bunch of the deputies had given Alex crap for not waiting at the scene of the incident, but Ryder had just given the PI a look that seemed to say he understood and approved. Why, she had no idea. It's not like she was someone important to Alex Hudson and he'd broken protocol to ensure the safety of a loved one. Yes, she was close to his family. But despite all the time they spent at the same social events, they were relative strangers.

And that was exactly how she planned on keeping it. If she had to spend any more time with him than she already did, there was a good chance lust would win out over common sense, and she could well end up making a complete and utter fool of herself. She shuddered at the thought, knowing how much Alex would enjoy lording something like that over her head.

The drive to her house on Cherry Blossom Lane was short, and anything but sweet. Brit used the time to study the rugged PI from the corner of her eye, wishing she could find something about his physical looks that she didn't like. That didn't so thoroughly do it for her. But she couldn't help thinking that the truth sucked—because the truth was that as much as he annoyed her, she'd been hung up on Alex Hudson for a long time. So long that it'd seriously started to screw with her life.

She'd tried to connect with other men since relocating to the beautiful little beach town, and had given it her best effort. She really had. But when she found herself across the table from a date in a popular restaurant, it didn't matter how good-looking or charming the guy was, she just . . . lost interest. Whatever attraction might have sparked to begin with simply faded, and she hated suspecting Alex was the reason why. Sure, there had been a few dating disasters where the supposedly great guy turned into a twit the instant he picked her up for their night out. But on the whole, the blame didn't lie with the men. It wasn't their fault they paled in comparison to the broody investigator.

Not that her luck with the male species had ever been all that stellar. But she already had enough depressing shit going on in her life at the moment without dwelling on that particular fun fact.

"Thanks for the ride," she murmured, as they pulled into her driveway. Yanking her purse strap over her shoulder, she started to reach down to unhook her seat belt before he'd even come to a complete stop, determined to get inside before they ended up in another argument.

Alex, however, obviously didn't plan to let her escape so easily. Hitting the button to activate the parental locks on the doors, he said, "Don't start, Doc. I'm going inside with you."

Struggling not to screech like a madwoman, she strove for a calm tone that was completely at odds with how she felt. "I said I would be fine. Seriously. I have an alarm and everything. Ben even made me upgrade after what happened with Reese last year. So I'm all good."

"Like hell you are," he ground out, shutting off the engine.

"Alex, listen. You're off the hook, okay? I know you don't want to be here, and I don't need you here. So go home."

Alex climbed out of the Range Rover and came around the back, opening her door while she was still sitting there, her hands clenched in her lap, looking like a pressure cooker about to blow. But he couldn't back down. Not about something this important.

"Have you even listened to a word I've said?" she asked, when she finally climbed down from her seat.

"About how you're fine and don't need any help?" He shut her door. "Yeah, I heard. I just don't care. I don't even give a shit what you want," he admitted, being brutally honest. "I saw you get attacked by some psycho asshole tonight, which means our personnel wants to have nothing to do with this situation anymore. You understand?"

He could have sworn she went a little green. "Are you trying to tell me I'm stuck with you until I hire my own bodyguard?"

Pushing his hands in his pockets after he'd activated the alarm on the Rover, Alex locked his hard gaze with hers and made himself perfectly clear. "You're stuck with me, period. There's no sense hiring someone when I can do the job better."

"Ego much?" she sputtered.

"It's only ego if I can't back it up. And since you know damn well that I can, this conversation is over."

She huffed in annoyance, but gave up the fight, apparently conceding that she wasn't going to win. He tried not to stare at her ass as he followed her to the front door of the house, but failed miserably. The dress she wore was professional, but curves like the doc had could manage to make even the classiest of outfits look like they'd been designed to make a man stiff.

Tearing his gaze off her ass, he reached down to shift his dick into a more comfortable position behind his fly, and waited as she unlocked the door. He stayed right behind her as she punched in the alarm code on the panel in the entryway, then made sure she locked the door before turning his attention to the house.

If anyone had asked him, he'd have been lying if he'd said he wasn't curious about how she lived. This was the first time he'd ever been inside her home, having only ever made it as far as the driveway before, when he'd been with Ben dropping her off. He'd hoped her taste in decorating would be loud and girlish, with too much pink and flowery shit all over the place, but should have known better, judging by the way she dressed. Yeah, she was feminine and sexy as hell, but her style was simple and sophisticated when it came to her clothes, and her home reflected that. Pale cream walls set off the dark, nearly black hardwood floors that stretched across the open floor plan. In the middle of a large antique-looking carpet, two cappuccino-colored sofas faced each other over a low, square coffee table. Oversized throw pillows in shades of cream and burgundy sat in the corners of the sofas, while a large arrangement of fresh, colorful flowers decorated the middle of the table, and a beautiful stone-faced fireplace took up the far wall.

Taking a deep breath of the citrus and clove scented air, Alex hooked his thumbs in his pockets as he made his way over to the fireplace that probably didn't see a lot of use in South Florida. The mantel held several framed photographs of Brit with an older couple he assumed were her parents, as well as ones of her and Ben, and newer ones that had Reese in them. Brit looked gorgeous in every photo, whether she was dressed up or wearing jeans, and he was surprised by the bite of jealousy he felt when he noticed the small frame on the end of the mantel held a picture of her and Mike at the Christmas party Ben and Reese had thrown last year. If he ever found out that Mike had slept with her, there was a good chance he'd have to kick the bastard's ass, no matter how much he loved him.

At the sound of the doc setting her keys down on a small table in the entryway, Alex turned around, watching as she set her purse down as well, then just stood there, staring back at him, looking a little flustered, a bit lost, and a whole lot irritated. "I'm, um, going to put on some coffee. Feel free to take a seat until I get back, at which point we're going to finish this argument." She started to head toward the archway he assumed led to her kitchen, then stopped and glared at him over her shoulder. "Don't touch anything," she warned him with a chilling stare. "I hate assholes messing with my stuff."

Thinking that she really needed to see someone about having the stick removed from her backside, Alex waited until she'd disappeared into the kitchen, then started touching all the knickknacks on the end table that was closest to him. Then he stopped and shook his head at himself. Seriously, what was he, two?

"Woman's already driving me crazy," he muttered under his breath, a scowl forming between his brows as he took a seat on one of the comfortable sofas. But he was too wound up to just sit on his ass, and by the time she came through the archway carrying a tray with two mugs on it, he'd moved back to his feet and was pacing before the fireplace. Flicking him a distracted glance, she walked over to the adjoining dining area, where a table and chairs that looked like something out of a Pottery Barn store were placed. Alex started walking over as she set the tray down on the table, watching her as she turned and flicked the wall switch that controlled the wrought iron light fixture hanging from the ceiling. A warm glow filled the space, and then she suddenly let out a startled cry.

What the fuck?

Instantly on alert, Alex was already reaching for his gun as he followed her gaze, his stomach knotting when he realized what they were looking at. The French doors leading to her patio had several splotches of a thick, creamy substance dripping down the panels of glass. Though he had no proof or forensic evidence yet to back him up, Alex was positive that he knew exactly who was responsible. He had no doubt Shepherd had come to the doc's house and jacked off all over her windows, his semen splashed across her French doors in what had to have been more than one shot. It made his blood run cold, thinking of the guy standing out there with his pants around his ankles, pumping himself off while staring through the glass into the doc's personal space.

"Son of a bitch," he growled, slipping his gun back into his shoulder holster as he moved to her side. "That sick fuck needs to be locked away."

"He's . . . ill," she whispered, her voice cracking at the end. "He needs help."

"He's dangerous, Doc. You need to stop trying to protect him and fucking accept it."

"I'm not trying to protect him. I just . . ." She took a deep breath, then looked at him with big, fear-filled eyes that were like a punch to the gut. "He was here. At my house. How the hell did he know where I live?"

"He's been following you." Alex stepped over to the doors and flicked on the outside light. The soft glow illuminated her open backyard, and he realized she probably wasn't allowed to enclose her property with fencing, as was the rule in a lot of Florida housing communities. There was no sign of Shepherd, but then it would be only too easy for the guy to hide out in the thick line of trees that bordered the back of her property. He was damn tempted to go out there and search for him, but wasn't willing to leave her alone in the house.

"This day just couldn't get any worse." She looked back over at the French doors and shuddered, an expression of revulsion sliding over her pale face. "I need to clean that up," she murmured distractedly, turning toward the archway to the kitchen.

Flicking off the outside lights, since he didn't want them being lit up like a fishbowl in there, Alex walked over and gently grasped her shoulder, catching her before she could leave the room. "You can't touch anything, Doc." Her worried, troubled gaze shot to his, her fear somehow hitting him even deeper this time. "Let's just turn the light off and head over to the sofa, okay? I need to call Ryder and get a forensics team over here."

"R-right. Sorry. I wasn't thinking."

When he had her sitting on the edge of a sofa, Alex took his phone from his pocket and scrolled through his contacts for the number he wanted. A moment later, he said, "Ryder, yeah, it's Alex. Look, I just got Brit home and that sick fuck has been to her house. No, I don't think there's any chance he got inside. Her alarm was still set when we came through the door. But he's left a hell of a mess all over her French doors from the outside." He paused, listening to the furious deputy, then went on. "Yeah, that's what I think. It looks like he went at it a couple of times, so forensics is definitely going to have some samples." Ryder started talking again, but he cut him off, saying, "No, I'm getting her out of here. If you have any questions, you can reach her at my place.

That's where I'm taking her. But this should be pretty simple for you guys. The techs don't even need to get in the house, and there's no fence blocking the back of the property. Later."

The instant he slipped his phone back in his pocket, she said, "I'm not going home with you."

Completely ignoring that statement as if she hadn't even spoken, he told her, "Pack enough to last for at least a week. If you need more, we can always come back."

She moved to her feet, and he was glad to see some color in her face again, even if it meant she was getting ready to lay into him. "Alex, please listen to me. I appreciate what you're trying to do, but it isn't necessary. I'm *not* going home with you."

He gave her a look that must have conveyed what he was feeling pretty well, because she scowled. "You're not an idiot, Doc. You know you can't stay here."

"Why not at the safe house, then?" For a moment, he wondered how she even knew about the safe house that had belonged to the county, then remembered that she'd visited Lily there last fall, when Ryder had been trying to protect the woman who was now his wife from a terrorist.

"The safe house was sold two months ago."

"Oh." She took a quick breath. "Well, I really don't think—"

"Listen," he said, stepping closer and getting right in her face. Yeah, it was rude, but he wanted her attention and for her to stop wasting time when there was only one way this was going to play out, whether they liked it or not. "Anyone else you know, this fuckhead could have seen you with. Could have easily followed you to their homes. Lily and Ryder. Ben and Reese. Your work friends. Hell, you even went to Mike's apartment for that Halloween party he threw, and we have no idea how long this guy might have been watching you before he snapped. But you've never been to my house, and I know how to make sure we're not followed. So pack a fucking bag and let's stop wasting time."

He could tell that she wanted to keep arguing but was sensible enough to know he was right. He scrubbed his hands over his face as she stiffly moved around him and started climbing the stairs, then cast another sharp glance at the now shadowed dining room. It made his skin crawl, fear slithering through his veins when he thought of that bastard being here at her house. What if he'd just dropped her off and hadn't come inside with her? What if the asshole was hiding out there in the woods somewhere, waiting for her to come home alone, after his failed attempt to nab her on the parking deck?

Cursing under his breath, Alex headed up the stairs close on her heels, needing to keep an eye on her to assure himself she was safe. He usually had nerves of steel, but they were a knotted mess at the moment, coiling in his gut, and he refused to look too closely at the reason why.

With his shoulder propped against the doorjamb, he watched her collect various pieces of clothing from her closet and a tall chest of drawers that sat on the far wall. She'd been meticulously folding and placing everything into a neat pile on her bed, when the house phone on her bedside table started to ring. The shrill sound startled them both, but Brit damn near jumped a foot.

"Hello?" she said, after taking a deep breath and grabbing the receiver. The instant she turned her head and gave him a wild look, Alex realized who was on the line. Closing the space between them, he took the phone and quietly punched the speaker function, then set the phone in her open hand.

A moment later, a clearly emotional male voice could be heard asking, "Did you hear my question, Dr. Cramer? Who was the man with you tonight?"

"He's, uh, just a friend."

"Are you sleeping with him?"

"Clay, I'm worried about you. Why . . . why did you come to see me today?"

Alex shot her a sharp look, wondering why the hell she was being so casual with the bastard, but she motioned for him to stay quiet.

"What did you expect me to do after you filed that stupid report with the sheriff's department? You left me no choice!" Shepherd made a thick, ragged sound of frustration. "The last couple of years have been so dark. The only perfect moments were when you were with me at the hospital in Miami. You were so gentle. So . . . thoughtful. I just wanted to find that again. To show you how much you mean to me."

"By pulling a knife on me tonight?"

"I need to *show* you, Dr. Cramer, to make you see things clearly, and I don't know how else to do that. Don't you understand? It won't keep eating away at me inside if you just give in. If you just love me back, everything will be okay."

Gently, she said, "Clay, I think you're hurting and that you need to talk to someone."

It sounded as if the guy was crying, but there was an unmistakable edge of rage to his next words. "Did you know that you're the only woman who has ever made me feel like a man, and not some pathetic little worm? Do you think I don't know what that means?"

Though she was shivering, Alex was amazed by how calm she sounded. "I treated you the same way I treat all my patients. I just wanted you to heal."

"I know that's what you need the others to think." Hostility made Shepherd's voice lash like a whip. "But I could tell you wanted more. You're just afraid."

"That's not true, Clay. You're confused. You need—"

"I just need *you*! Like I told you at your office that day, there is *no* other woman more perfect than you are. Your body. Your smile. The shape of your breasts and thighs and the huskiness of your voice. I dream about the things I need to do to you. The things I need you to do to me. You can make me clean again. You can burn away my sins. You can *save* me!" His voice was rising, seething with emotion. "I'll make you do it, Dr. Cramer. Whether you want to or not. You don't have any choice. I'm taking all your choices away from you. But only because I love you."

She flinched as if she'd been struck. "Is that why you defaced my home tonight? That wasn't love, Clay."

There was nothing for a moment but the heavy, erratic sound of his breathing. And then, "That was *your* fault. You made me angry when you refused to come away with me."

"Why would I go anywhere with you when you hurt me?"

Softly, he said, "I'll hurt you again."

Her fingers were gripping the phone so tightly now that Alex was surprised it hadn't cracked. "Why?"

"Because it *will* make you love me."

"No, Clay. Fear is not love. I know it might seem that way right now. But it's not. What happened to you three years ago, that wasn't done out of love."

"You're wrong. It was done to make me love her!"

"I'm sorry, but it wasn't."

Nothing but Shepherd's ragged breathing filled the line, and Alex noticed that Brit didn't mention the most recent attack that had taken place at the frat party, focusing on the abuse he'd suffered at the hands of his own mother instead. He assumed that was where she believed Shepherd's problems lay, which made sense. He didn't have a lot of the details, but from what he'd read, the abuse had been horrific.

"Clay, do you honestly love your mother? Is that what you feel when you think of what she and Hennings did to you?" she asked, prompting Shepherd to break his silence.

"No!"

"Then why do you think it will make me—"

The line went dead, and Alex took the phone from her trembling hand, setting it back in the cradle. When he lifted his gaze back to hers, he asked, "How did he get your home number?"

She was rubbing her hands over her bare arms, staring at a distant spot on the wall as if it was suddenly going to give her all the answers.

"How, Brit?"

She pulled her lower lip through her teeth, took a deep breath, and finally said, "I have a number for my patients that I can either program to a personal number, like my home or my cell, or have go directly to the clinic's answering service."

Without another word, he paced away from her and grabbed his phone from his pocket. Ryder answered on the second ring, and Alex brought him up to date on the call, telling him to get the department's tech guys to work on tracing the call as soon as possible, hoping it would give them the location where Clay had called from. Then he gave the deputy a message for Ben and Mike, told him he'd talk to him in the morning, and slipped the phone back in his pocket.

When he looked over at Brit, she was still standing there rubbing her arms, her mind a million miles away. "Just how far do you think this guy is willing to go?" he asked her, drawing her attention back to him.

"I don't know. But he's clearly in need of psychiatric care."

"I get where you're coming from. I really do. But I just don't buy it, Doc. I know there are people out there who need help. But he's not what you think he is. Not anymore."

Her eyes went wide. "What do you mean?"

With a shrug, he said, "I don't know. I'm just going from my gut."

"Well, your gut isn't going to get him well."

"I'm not interested in getting him well," he countered in a terse tone. "Just in keeping you safe."

She obviously didn't know what to say to that particular statement, because she turned away from him and started transferring the clothes she'd stacked on her bed into a brown leather duffel bag. He watched her for a moment, then forced himself to look away. His gaze unfortunately settled on the bed, and stuck. He stared at that fucker as if he'd never seen one before, unable to stop himself from imagining what she would look like laid out over the dusky purple bedding, so creamy and smooth and deliciously curved.

Finally, he rubbed a rough hand over his mouth, then made himself turn and head back downstairs. He waited at the bottom until she came down with her bag, then took it from her. After she'd reset the alarm and locked up, they made the drive to his condo in silence, while the radio played low in the background. The trip should have only taken about ten minutes, but he made a few extra turns while making sure they weren't being followed, which stretched it out to almost twenty. He had a garage around the back, but usually just parked on the curb in front of his condo for convenience. It was an upscale community with a stellar crime rate, so he didn't have any worries about leaving the Range Rover on the street.

He grabbed the doc's bag from his backseat, then led her up the walkway to the front door of his two-story unit. For some reason, he was almost embarrassed as he opened the door and flicked on a light, knowing how the condo must look in her eyes. The building itself was attractive, but the inside, while clean, wasn't anything to brag about. Decorating hadn't really been on his mind much since he'd gotten the place, which meant it was furnished for efficiency and nothing more. But he'd done well enough with his stock portfolio that the few things he had were at least good quality. A long brown leather sofa stretched across from the eighty-inch widescreen mounted on the wall, while several comfortable leather chairs sat on either end of the rustic coffee table, and there was one end table with a silver lamp on it. Several remotes sat on the coffee table, but other than that there weren't any knick-knacks. No throw pillows, or rugs, or pictures on the walls.

A small hallway branched off on the right, leading to a downstairs bathroom and his home office. Straight ahead there was an archway into his kitchen, and to the left a large alcove he used for his dining room, which had sliding glass doors that led out to his fenced-in patio.

He sensed her quietly taking it all in, then he gestured toward the stairs. "Spare room is up there."

She moved past him and climbed the stairs without comment, never looking back, which was a good thing, since he still couldn't keep his eyes off her body as he followed behind her with her bag. That heart-shaped ass of hers made his mouth water and his dick take notice every damn time it was in front of him.

When she reached the upstairs hallway, he said, "It's the one on the left."

She opened the door, and stepped into the room after flicking on the light. This room was even more sparsely furnished than his downstairs, with nothing more than a double bed, small bedside table with a lamp, and a tall chest of drawers that he stored his sweaters in. But it was clean and had its own private bath, so at least they wouldn't have to be sharing. He didn't think he could handle standing in his shower knowing that her naked ass had just been in there moments before, the citrusy scent of her soap and hair products tickling his nose.

Shit, he'd probably end up wasting all the hot water while he jacked off, which would just put him in a bad mood. He fucking hated cold showers.

"Are the sheets clean?" she asked, interrupting his thoughts with the rude question he knew was meant to insult him.

He gave her a dark look that didn't require any words.

Lifting her hands, she said, "I was just checking. From what I hear, you don't exactly go for class when you're banging out your manly needs these days."

Somehow, he kept his tone low and controlled, unwilling to verbally rise to her bait. "You're the only woman, other than Reese and Lily, who has even been in this condo, Doc. And I'm not fucking either one of them."

He hated how adorable he found her smirk. "Good to know. Their husbands would kick your ass."

"I know how to handle my brother," he told her, setting her bag on the moss green comforter that covered the bed.

"And Ryder?"

Lifting a hand, he rubbed his jaw as he slid his gaze toward hers. "He can be a scary fuck, I'll give you that."

She laughed, the look on her face telling him she was surprised he wasn't carrying around an ego so big it made him think he could take on any man, any time. He took a step back, his pulse quickening at the deliciously feminine, husky sound of her laughter, and he knew he needed to get the hell out of there.

Since they'd had pizza at the station, he didn't need to feed her dinner, so he asked, "You gonna be able to sleep?"

She nodded as she breathed out a soft, tired sigh. "I don't think I've ever been this exhausted in my life."

"Then I'll see you in the morning," he muttered, crossing the room and closing the door behind him as fast as he could without looking like he was running.

But he knew damn well that he was.

3

BRIT WAS UP AND DRESSED BY SEVEN THE NEXT MORNING, BUT ALEX was already waiting for her down in the living room, reading the news on his tablet. He had his long body sprawled in one of the leather chairs that sat perpendicular to his sofa, and was dressed in his usual work attire of jeans, black leather boots, and white button-down shirt that looked great on his broad shoulders and with his tanned complexion. His shoulder holster was already strapped on over the shirt, and there was a dark gray sports jacket lying over the back of the other chair, which she knew he'd put on to cover up the gun when they left the condo.

"Any word on Clay?" she asked, before clearing her throat. Her voice had gone a little too breathless by the end of her question, and all because Alex had looked up at her as she entered the room, his pale grayish-green eyes noticeably warming with appreciation as he checked her out from the top of her head down to her toes. She'd worn her hair loose, letting the auburn waves fall around her shoulders, and had chosen a sleeveless, fitted champagne silk sheath in deference to the heat, along with a pair of comfortable but stylish suede ankle boots with a three-inch heel. Her only jewelry was a pair of silver Tiffany hoops in her ears that Ben and Reese had given her for Christmas, a silver ring, and matching silver bangle.

"Alex?" she prompted, when he just continued to sit there, staring at her.

He shook his head as if to bring himself out of a daze, then answered her question about Clay. "They're still looking for him. It won't take long before they uncover the rock he's hiding under. Guy's not thinking straight."

"That doesn't mean he can't be clever."

"True. But it also means that he's more likely to make a mistake." Setting the tablet on the coffee table, he moved to his feet. He was tall, like his brothers, a few inches over six feet, and it was hard as hell not to stare at the way his jeans molded over his long, muscular thighs. "You ready for some breakfast?" he asked her, drawing her gaze back up to his.

"You're cooking?"

A smirk twisted his killer mouth at the sound of her surprise. "I'm trying to keep you alive, Doc, not kill you. But I can manage toasted bagels and cream cheese."

"Oh, um, thank you. That sounds great."

Bemused and more than a little uncertain, feeling as if she'd awakened in some kind of alternate reality where Alex Hudson wasn't a total ass, Brit followed him into the kitchen. He denied her offer to help, telling her to take a seat at the small pine table situated in the cozy breakfast nook. He gave her a cup of coffee doctored with cream and sugar, just the way she liked it, then started on the bagels. Sitting back in her chair, Brit used the moment to simply watch him as he moved around the small but clean kitchen.

She honestly didn't think she'd ever seen a more beautiful male. He was lean and hard and obviously well-hung, if the bulge in his jeans was anything to go by. And he was so damn gorgeous it was hard to breathe when she looked at him. He was that freaking incredible, possessing every rugged, masculine thing that she loved about the opposite sex.

Biting her lip, she realized that she'd probably made the wrong decision. Last night, when she'd been putting the last few things into her bag, she'd been tempted to grab her vibrator and bring it along. *To vibe or not to vibe?* That was the question that had run through her head, and she snorted to herself, wondering if the stress was taking its toll on her mind. She was worried about Clay, worried about herself, worried about spending so much time with Alex. The guy was as mercurial as, well, mercury. Okay, so the analogy wasn't all that original, but she was tired, damn it. Not to mention under a tremendous amount of stress. She really couldn't *stress* that point enough, even if she was repeating herself.

In the end, she'd decided it was best to leave the vibrator behind. But now, given the panty-soaking view, she was pretty sure she'd made the wrong call.

Needing to get her mind onto another topic, she took a drink of her coffee and asked, "So what's the plan for the day? I'm guessing you have cases right now that need your attention. You can't drop everything just to keep an eye on me. That's ridiculous."

"I won't need to drop everything," he murmured, standing with his back to her as he took the bagels out of the toaster. "I'm going to have a talk with the security guards at McNamara when I take you into work. I'm assuming you have appointments all day with your patients, right?"

"Today, yes. The same for tomorrow."

"Then you'll be safe at the office during the day. I'll pop by from time to time to check on things, but he isn't going to make a move on you there in broad daylight, and you won't be driving yourself." He shot her a hard look over his shoulder. "And no leaving the office with anyone during the day. If your friends go out for lunch, have them bring you something back. I don't want you out and about town unless I'm with you."

"So I wait at work all day like a good little girl, until you come to pick me up. And then what? How long do you think we can do this before killing each other?"

He muttered something under his breath that she couldn't quite make out, but didn't offer her a response.

"I'm serious, Alex. You can't just put your life on hold because some woman you know has a problem. No one expects that of you. If this is about Ben and what he expects you to do, then tell him he's crazy. I certainly plan to."

"I don't care what anyone expects. Never have, and I'm not about to start now. And you're not just *some woman I know*, Doc. You're close to my family. That makes it different."

She was glad he didn't try to claim they were friends or anything equally ridiculous.

"I'm just not comfortable with this, Alex. It's incredibly unfair to you. At least let me pay you or something. Whatever rate you would normally charge your clients."

He went completely still, gripping the edge of the counter with his big hands. She listened as he exhaled deeply, then he slowly turned around, arms crossed over his chest as he leaned against the countertop. His brows were pinched, and his voice was gritty. "Don't be so goddamn insulting. I don't need your money. And I'm not taking it."

"All right," she murmured, twisting her hands in her lap in a nervous gesture that was completely unlike her. "I apologize for insulting you. It wasn't my intention."

He gave one of those low, irritating grunts in response, but she bit her tongue instead of calling him on it. The guy was feeding her, not to mention turning his life upside down to help her out, so she figured she could let the grunting thing slide. For the moment, at least.

"So, I have a question," he said, after setting two plates down on the table and taking the chair across from her.

She took another sip of her coffee, surprised by how good it tasted, and nodded for him to go on.

Smearing cream cheese onto half of his bagel, he asked, "What do you have against the name Brittany?"

The genuine confusion in his deep voice was almost endearing enough to make her smile. "I don't have anything against the name Brittany."

His dark brows knitted together in a priceless look of bafflement. "Then why did you bite my head off last night when I used it?"

She finished chewing her bite of bagel, swallowed, and said, "Because it's not my name, Alex. You've known me for how long now? Have you ever heard anyone call me Brittany?"

"No, I don't reckon I have."

"Well, there you have it."

He'd managed to finish off both his bagel and coffee before his frustration got the better of him. "All right, I give. If your name's not Brittany, then what is it?"

Flicking her gaze to the clock that hung on the wall, she murmured, "Wow, look at the time. I really need to be getting to work."

He leaned back in his chair, studying her with a heavy-lidded stare. "You're not going to tell me, are you?"

Brit smirked, cut him a *where would be the fun in that?* look, and carried her dishes to the sink.

"Christ, you make my head hurt," he muttered from just behind her, brushing against her right side as he set his own dishes in the sink, and she gasped from the rush of awareness that shot through her when his body touched hers. Quickly stepping away, she grabbed a paper towel to wipe her hands off as she stood beside the table, willing her stupid pulse to slow before he mistook her reaction for fear.

Fear? Hah! She was so sexually primed for this broken, arrogant male she could probably orgasm if he so much as breathed on her.

When he turned around to face her, his arms were crossed over his chest again, his fine ass resting against the edge of the counter once more. He watched the way she rubbed her upper arms, frowned, then locked his pale gaze with hers. "Look, I don't want you to get the wrong idea about what's going on here. If that's what's worrying you, don't let it."

Her hands stilled. "Meaning what, exactly?" she asked, her tone careful and subdued.

He scrubbed one of his big hands over the top of his head, then gestured between them. "You don't have to worry about . . . this. Yeah, we'll be living here together for a time. But you'll have your own space. I won't be trying anything with you. It won't be like that."

With wide eyes, she returned his stare, and tried to decide if she was touched that he wanted to put her at ease . . . or insulted that he apparently wasn't at all interested in going to bed with her. The silence started to get uncomfortably heavy, and then she heard herself say, "To be honest, I didn't imagine that would be an issue. Seeing as how you hate me and all. I just don't like feeling like an imposition and a serious suck on your time."

She couldn't miss the way his own eyes widened at her words. "I don't hate you."

Brit gave a sarcastic snort. "Seriously? You're the biggest

woman-hater I've ever known. And considering what I do for a living, that's really saying something."

His gaze got glacial, narrowing with anger. "I do not hate women."

"Couldn't prove it by me," she murmured.

He started to respond, then stopped himself. Cocking his head a bit to the side, he studied her as he pushed away from the counter, then calmly asked, "Did I miss something? Because it suddenly feels like you're trying to start a fight."

Hell. She knew her hurt feelings were taking control of her mouth, which was never a good idea, but there didn't seem to be a damn thing she could do about it. "Who's fighting? I'm simply stating a fact. One that's held by the majority of the people who know you."

His sensual mouth flattened into a hard line. "You don't know shit, Doc."

"I know this is a bad idea. I know you're one of the rudest, coldest, most hardheaded men I've ever—"

"You just never learn when to shut up, do you?" he growled, cutting her off. It only took him two steps to close the distance between them, and then she was having to crane her head back to hold his glittering, smoldering glare.

"I'll shut up when I feel like— *Oomph!*"

One second she was screeching, completely losing her shit as all the stress from the past night crashed down on her, and in the next Alex Hudson had his big hands in her hair, holding her head still as he crushed his lips against her own. She gasped, reeling, more shocked than she'd ever been in her life, and he went in for the kill, sending his tongue inside to slide against the tender, intimate recesses of her mouth, stroking them like he knew her secrets. Oh, God. Oh, *hell*. That shouldn't feel so right, but it did.

It felt freaking incredible, as if everything she'd ever known about kissing had just been a warm-up for the main event.

He took her mouth like he owned it. Like he wanted to violate and possess it in every way known to man. Take whatever he wanted from it. From her. It was *that* aggressive. That outrageously devastating. If he fucked like he kissed, she was surprised women weren't lining up around the block from his condo, begging for his attention. But then, she knew that if ever there was a guy who could bed a woman, blow her mind to the point she didn't even remember her own name, and then give her the cold shoulder, it was most likely this one.

He growled against her lips, the way he held her head and the rigidity of his tall body against hers telling her he was just as into this as she was. Not to mention the hungry, ravaging nature of the kiss, as if he couldn't get enough of her taste. Her nipples tightened, and she was wet as hell between her legs, the feel and flavor and scent of him sending her spiraling toward a release that would be beyond horrifying, considering this had *started* because he'd been trying to shut her up and teach her a lesson. To show her that he had the upper hand and could use his lethal sexuality on her whenever he chose.

Whew. He might not like women all that much, but he sure as hell knew how to make one melt. Her hands were sliding up his chest, tingling from the solid feel of his muscles, and Brit knew if she didn't put a stop to this now, she would soon be begging him for more. To finish her. And there would be no living that down.

"Enough!" she gasped, reaching deep for the strength to break away from the kiss and his unbelievable mouth.

She could have sworn she heard him mutter, *"Not nearly,"* under his breath, but couldn't be sure. He had her hormones so jacked up, she was probably hearing things.

"We can't do that," she said huskily, smoothing her hands over her dress as she backed away from him. "You can't kiss me."

He worked his jaw, a muscle pulsing under his skin, looking as though he wanted to ask her why. But he didn't. Instead, he closed down right in front of her eyes, going glacial and cold as he stepped past her and headed into the living room.

It was a physical effort not to turn and run after him, throwing herself on him, begging him to finish what he'd started. His decadent taste was in her mouth, her lips trembling from the remembered feel of his possession, and she had to clench her teeth together to keep from making a sound.

Damn it, she could do this. She could be smart and resist him. But she *would* have him take her home for more clothes in a day or two. And when he did, she was doing the smart thing. The only thing she could think of that might at least make the ache he'd ignited manageable, before she embarrassed herself.

As soon as she had the chance, she was grabbing the damn vibrator.

AFTER GETTING BRIT TO THE MCNAMARA CLINIC AND WALKING HER to her office, Alex went in search of the security office and spoke with Carl Stevens, the department's director. Then he made the thirty-minute drive to Mike's office at one of the statewide DEA buildings.

He said hello to a few people he knew as he made his way up to Mike's third-floor office, sinking into one of the chairs in front of Mike's desk while his brother typed something into his computer. Mike looked tired, his dark hair even shaggier than usual, dark circles under his green eyes, and Alex wondered if his brother had been working a case late into the night . . . or a woman. Knowing Mike, it could have well been both, his brother often working off an adrenaline rush after a hard night at work with one of his numerous fuck-buddies. Women flocked to the guy like flies to honey, charmed by his good looks and charismatic personality, each of them hoping they'd be the one to tame his bad boy ways. But so far, none of them had even gotten close.

"Where's Barnes?" Alex asked when Mike finally lifted his head, jerking his chin in a silent greeting. David Barnes was the agent who shared Mike's office and a friend of his baby brother. He was a nice enough guy, but Alex preferred to have some privacy at the moment.

Reading his mind, Mike said, "We've got the office to ourselves for a while. Barnes is out on a coffee break with the receptionist he's currently boning."

Alex lifted his brows. "I thought he was seeing a nurse."

"He is," Mike muttered, his tone flat. For all Mike's womanizing, he always made sure that he made his intentions clear and never led a woman on, or let her believe they were exclusive when they weren't. From his brother's tone and expression, Alex could tell that Barnes wasn't exactly following that code.

"Damn," he murmured, letting Mike know he understood.

"Yeah, he's a jackass. What can I say? I've warned him it's all going to come back and bite him in the ass one of these days. If he isn't ready to settle down, then he shouldn't let a woman think he is."

Bracing one boot on his opposite knee, Alex asked, "And what did he say to that unsolicited bit of wisdom?"

"He told me to fuck off."

Alex choked out a laugh. "That sounds like Barnes."

Mike snorted, then slid him a curious look. "So how's Brit this morning?"

"Prickly as ever, but she isn't cowering. She's with patients at her office right now."

Pinning him with a knowing stare, Mike rocked back in his chair. "And let me guess. You've come over here to beg me to slide in and take your place. Am I right?"

Unwilling to rise to his brother's bait, Alex forced a calm reply, though his jaw was tighter than he would have liked. "I can't see how that would work. We both know you'd be too busy trying to nail her to actually be able to protect her."

Mike whistled, then grinned like a jackass. "Wow, you sound jealous."

"Just get Ben on the phone, so we can get this over and done with. I'm assuming Ryder has already brought him up to date, like he did with you, right?"

Reaching over to his desk phone, Mike said, "Yeah, he called both of us last night." He looked at Alex with a wry smirk lifting the corner of his mouth. "Ben wasn't too happy about you not getting in touch with him yourself. According to Ryder, you didn't want him bothering you."

His jaw still tight, he picked at a frayed patch on the hem of his jeans. "I didn't want to get into it with either one of you in front of Brit."

"Uh-huh," Mike murmured, sounding like he was trying not to laugh.

Alex scowled. "Just make the damn call and stop acting like an asshole."

Mike dialed Ben's cell phone number, engaged the speaker function on the phone, and within seconds they were listening to the middle Hudson brother ask, "How's Brit doing? I tried to catch her at her office this morning, but she was already in with a patient."

"She's doing good," Alex replied.

Ben's low voice was edged with frustration. "I told you I had a feeling about this guy."

"Yeah, I should have listened to you."

"You're damn right you should have." Ben took a sharp breath, cursed, and then slowly exhaled. Though his next words were still rough, they sounded a bit calmer. "But the point is that you were there when it mattered, man. That's what counts."

"So exactly how messed up is this guy?" Mike asked, rocking back in his chair with his fingers laced behind his head this time, his biceps bulging against the seams of the black DEA polo he was wearing.

"I listened in when he called her last night," Alex said, scrubbing his hands over his face, and then bracing his elbows on his spread knees as he leaned forward in his chair. "He spouted a lot of psycho-sounding bullshit about proving he loved her by making her hurt. To be honest, it made my damn skin crawl. Brit pointed out to him that he was talking about trying to do the same thing to her that his mother did to him, which I'm sure I don't have to tell either one of you is going to lead to the motherfucker's death if he tries. No way in hell we can let him pose that kind of a threat to her."

Mike frowned. "His mom was like something from the Manson family. It can't be good that he's drawing on his experience with her and using it to justify his obsession with Brit."

"No shit," Alex growled. "She told me on our drive to the clinic this morning that she had a chat a few days ago with the therapist Shepherd was referred to back in Miami. Apparently, Shepherd had been doing well enough when he quit his therapy sessions that the doctor hadn't felt the need to contact anyone in regards to his mental health. So he was free of any watching eyes up in Westville."

"What do you think set him off?" Ben asked.

"Who knows? My gut tells me that he's been carrying a torch for Brit for a long time. Maybe college life didn't work out the way he thought it would, and it pushed his obsession into something darker."

"And the attack on him a few weeks ago?" This time the question came from Mike.

Alex rubbed his jaw. "I'd like to talk with the detectives up in Westville. There's something about that whole thing that just doesn't sit right with me."

"Yeah, I've been thinking the same thing," Ben agreed.

"Can you get something set up for me with them?" Alex knew that while a lot of police forces were open-minded about working with private investigators, there were still some who got bent out of shape when they felt like someone was butting into their territory. With Ben's assistance, he'd probably get a hell of a lot more cooperation out of the cops than he would on his own.

"I'll take care of it. And I just want you to know that I appreciate you looking out for her last night, Alex. I've got a call into one of the security guys I know in Miami. His name is Hank Smith and he's one of the best. If he's free, I'll get him to head over and step in for you."

Alex grunted in response, already knowing there was no way in hell he was leaving her personal security up to some paid protection. Fuck that. He might hate it, the constant back and forth between them, not to mention the physical struggle he'd be going through to keep his hands off her—to not give in and touch her again—but he wasn't leaving something this important up to someone else.

"You not happy with that plan?" Ben's deep voice held a curious edge.

Alex shifted in his seat. "He doesn't know her. She wouldn't be comfortable."

"If you want her comfortable, then it should be me watching out for her," Mike cut in with a lazy drawl. "She loves my cute ass."

"Shut up, Mike."

His baby brother just grinned like a jackass again. "Guess it's possible she could love yours, too. I mean, you've kept yourself in good shape for a guy who'll be pushing forty in the not too distant future. You should go for it."

"This isn't about fucking her. It's about keeping her alive."

Mike lifted his brows. "And you can't mix business with pleasure?"

"Jesus, what is it with you? I thought you considered this woman a friend."

"I do."

His next words burst from his throat in a guttural snarl. "Then why the hell would you want her messing around with a guy like me?"

"Because you're not nearly as much of an asshole as you want everyone to think you are. And I think Dr. Gorgeous might be just the thing to thaw that lump of ice you've had wedged up your ass for the last five years. If she can't melt you down, no one will."

"You're full of shit, Mike. Hell, she doesn't even like me."

Mike snickered. "You wouldn't say that if you'd ever caught the way she stares at you when you aren't looking."

Whoa. Alex *really* didn't need to be thinking about that. Or about how fucking incredible that kiss they'd shared had been. Clearing his throat, he said, "Even if that were true, this isn't the time. This Shepherd guy is seriously fucked in the head."

"I'm not saying he isn't. I'm just saying that you're missing a golden opportunity here. All it'll take is a little multitasking."

"I'm not going to compromise her damn safety."

"I agree," Ben rumbled, breaking into the argument. "Alex knows what he's talking about, Mike."

Alex felt the pull between his brows as he stared at the speakerphone, wondering what the hell his brother was up to. Had Ben changed his mind about getting the two of them together? Or was this some kind of new reverse psychology on his brother's part? Before he could figure it out, Mike interrupted his train of thought.

"Sure, he knows what he's doing when it comes to work." Mike's low voice had lost its teasing tone, the serious edge making Alex prepare for the coming verbal blow. "But he doesn't know shit about taking a chance on someone. He never did."

"Why chance something that I already know will end in shit? I'd rather save myself the trouble."

Mike lowered his arms and shook his head. Alex didn't like the way the guy was looking at him. "Fuck. I get it now. You're scared."

"Back off, Mike. And stay out of it."

Ignoring him, Mike matched his quiet tone. "The sad thing is, I don't think you're running because you don't want her. I think you're running because of how badly you do. You're just panicking, you pathetic jackass."

"Running? I said I'd protect her."

"Not from this situation. I'm talking about running from your emotions."

"I'm done with this shit," he snapped, suddenly moving to his feet. "Ben, I'll call you in the morning with an update. But don't bother contacting Smith."

Without waiting for a reply, Alex turned and got the hell out of there, thankful that Mike knew better than to come after him. He spent the rest of the morning and afternoon working on a few cases that he had in the works, then eventually made his way back to the McNamara Clinic. His mood had turned from foul to deadly as the day wore on, the conversation with Mike making his teeth grind every time he thought about it. Which had been often.

Nodding a hello to Brit's receptionist, who he'd been introduced to that morning, he took a seat in the upscale waiting area and pulled out his phone. He had about an hour before he reckoned Brit would be ready to head home, and figured he could use the time to read through some e-mail. He started glancing through a report a cop out in Arizona had sent him regarding one of his current cases, but couldn't seem to give it his full attention, his gaze repeatedly cutting toward the doc's office door, waiting for it to open.

Jesus, he hadn't been this uptight about a woman since Judith, and God only knew that couldn't be a good sign.

Hell, it was more like a sign of the freaking apocalypse.

For a long time after his divorce, Alex had carried his wounds inside, where they were crusty and deep, seething with rage, eating at him like a cancer. But they hadn't been invisible. His family had seen them. Even when he'd been trying to numb the pain by drowning himself in liquor, they'd known. But they'd never understood. They'd thought he was heartbroken. Hurting because of the wreck of his marriage. But that hadn't been it. Any feelings he'd ever held for Judith had been killed the moment he'd found her taking it up the ass from one of the other detectives in his department. The speed with which those feelings had died had been a testament to just how shallow his connection with her had been. Or maybe by that time the connection had simply eroded, broken down after the months of arguing about every aspect of their life together because there didn't seem to be anything else to say to each other.

So, yeah, it was pretty clear to him that a broken heart hadn't been why he'd lost himself at the bottom of a bottle.

Still, the emotion driving him to self-destruct had been strong, as well as violent, and it'd nearly killed him. He didn't need to be making any more mistakes that were going to land him in that same shit pile. Which was why he'd been living in survival mode ever since. He might want Brit Cramer so badly he could taste it, but even if it turned out that she felt the same—and that was a *huge* if—there was no way he could give a woman like her what she deserved. He'd locked down parts of himself so tightly, the need could no longer sink beneath his skin. It simply remained surface and physical. A desire to nail her fine ass until his body was used and spent and drained. Until he'd slaked himself in her, drowning himself in hours of hard, raw, relentless fucking. Then he'd be done and move on, as cold inside as ever.

Mike might think differently. But Mike didn't know what the hell he was talking about. Because there were some things that could never be thawed, no matter how much heat they were exposed to.

Just then, the door to her office opened and she came out with a middle-aged woman and a little girl. The little girl turned and gave the doc a quick hug, burying her face against her middle, and he watched as Brit ruffled the child's golden curls and gave her a gentle smile. The moment clicked in his mind like a lock breaking open on a vault, and he knew in an instant that all he'd been doing was spouting a bunch of bullshit. He wasn't going to keep his hands off the doc because he didn't have enough to offer a woman like her. He was going to do it because Mike was right—this was goddamn self-preservation. He was afraid. Scared shitless, actually, that his lust for this woman wouldn't be so easily satisfied if he tried. And all he could think about was trying.

Damn it, he never should have kissed her. Never should have given himself that brief taste, because it was screwing with his head. Jacking him up. If he didn't take the edge off, there was a good chance he wouldn't be able to keep his hands *off* her. Or his tongue. Or his dick. And that was a scenario that would only lead to trouble.

Kissing the woman had cranked him up higher than any of the one-night stands he'd had in a long time. God only knew what fucking her would do. Going down on her. If her pussy was anywhere near as soft and sweet as her mouth, he wouldn't be able to get his head out from between her thighs. He'd end up staying there forever, wallowing in that juicy secret flesh, licking her, eating her, swallowing her hot girl juice down his throat until he was full of it.

And forever was something he did not, and would not, ever do. It didn't matter how incredible her little cunt tasted. Or how good it felt wrapped around his dick. It wasn't ever going to happen, which meant he needed to do the right thing, and do it now. Tonight. Before it was too damn late.

Pulling up a new screen on his phone, Alex scrolled through his contacts until he found the number he wanted.

"Hey, Alex," chirped a cheerful voice that immediately grated on his nerves. "What's up?"

Dropping his head against the wall, he closed his eyes and forced himself to ask the question burning in his throat.

"What are you doing tonight?"

4

AFTER A LONG, STRESSFUL DAY OF WORRYING ABOUT SHEPHERD AND working with her patients, Brit had grabbed a glass of wine and headed up to the guest room to soak in a hot bath. Afterward, she'd put on music while sorting through her things, picking out her clothes for the next day, then stretched out on the bed and watched a show on the TV set that Alex had moved to her room, trying not to wonder about what he was doing downstairs. They'd seemed to be acting on some unspoken truce from the moment they'd left her office that afternoon. He'd given her an update on the search for Shepherd, she'd told him she hadn't heard anything new from him, and they'd stopped by the store. She hadn't felt like eating when they'd arrived at the condo, and he'd taken his dinner back to his office, leaving her on her own.

It'd been a dull evening all the way around, but she knew it was for the best. The less they had to do with each other, the better it would be for her emotions. She needed to be careful, because she could all too easily see herself making more out of his determination to protect her than it really was. She'd spoken to Reese on her cell for only a few minutes that day, but it'd been enough to realize that Alex hadn't thought there was anything to Ben's worries about Shepherd. He'd been watching her with a great deal of reluctance, and no doubt didn't like that he'd been wrong. So he was most likely only trying to right what his alpha male mind saw as a mistake. It had nothing to do with *her*, specifically, and she'd be smart to remember it.

So then why did it bother her so much?

And why was it so much freaking easier to look at other people's problems than to delve into her own troubled psyche?

Though she had an outgoing personality with her friends and coworkers, Brit had never found it easy to just be herself with a man she was attracted to. She wasn't shy with men, but then neither was she brazen. She just . . . she just always felt as if they saw her surface and nothing more. As if they watched her mouth, thinking about what she might eventually do with it, never really listening to what she was saying. The feeling had started in junior high, when she'd begun to develop, and had become worse as time went on.

That was the odd thing about Alex. Even when he'd been trying hard to give the impression he was ignoring her, she'd often had the feeling that he'd been secretly listening, studying her, trying to figure her out. He might not *want* to get involved with her, or even like her all that much, but it was intensely seductive, knowing there was some part of him that was drawn to her. Even if it was a draw he didn't want. One that had sent him into hiding for the night.

To say that the guy had baggage would be putting it lightly. It sucked, but she didn't blame him for it. Like she'd told him on the parking deck after he'd rescued her from Shepherd, her anger toward Alex Hudson came from the way he'd been so against Ben and Reese's relationship. Not anything that he'd done to her personally—except for the shitty things he'd said to her that night on Ryder and Lily's patio. But, hell, as much as his words that night had stung, she could chalk them up to a bad mood and stress. She didn't plan to go around carrying a grudge about them. The slap across the face she'd given him that night had been enough to soothe her raw feelings.

But where did that leave her now? Was she going to ignore him? Try to build a friendship with him? Would a friendship even be possible, when she wanted him so badly?

She didn't have the answers, and as tired as she was, she wasn't going to find them tonight. Now that the wine was gone and it was getting late, all she wanted was a bottle of water from the kitchen before she headed to bed.

As she made her way down the stairs and across the living room, Brit wondered if Alex was still working in his office. She was trying to decide if she should go back and say good night, when a noise outside the sliding glass doors made her jump. Swinging her gaze in that direction, she blinked, unable to believe what she was seeing. Alex was outside . . . and he wasn't alone.

Oh, shit.

She reeled back like she'd just been shoved hard in the chest, wishing she could look away, but her damn eyeballs were glued onto the scene with a hold she couldn't seem to break. It was like goddamn emotional superglue. Painful and completely indestructible.

Alex was standing on his patio facing her, shirtless, barefoot, the faded pair of jeans he'd changed into when he'd gotten home hanging around his thighs, while a tiny blonde knelt on the ground before him, between his tall body and the glass. He had his dick in the woman's mouth, but he didn't appear to be that into it. His head was tilted back a bit, eyes closed, and he looked kind of . . . bored. Maybe a little tired. Even frustrated.

His lips moved with what looked like a soundless curse, and he shifted position, leaning forward to brace his hands against the glass, his abs rippling with movement as he fucked the woman's mouth. Brit realized she must have just made some kind of sound, because his head suddenly shot up, his pale gaze immediately locking hard with hers. Her heart jolted, and her pulse roared in her ears. She felt the connection crackle between them with startling force, same as it always did . . . even when another woman was sucking him off.

He scowled as his gaze drilled into her, then reached down with one hand, as if he was going to pull the woman off. But the blonde wasn't having it. She gripped his hips with both hands and started bobbing her head enthusiastically, obviously giving it everything she had. His ferocious scowl deepened, the cords in his neck visible as he clenched his jaw, his nostrils flaring. He held Brit's gaze the entire time, and she watched as sexual heat finally filled his piercing stare. His chest started to heave, lips parting for his ragged breaths. The bastard was going to come down that skank's throat while he was visually locked onto *her*, and she felt a wave of nausea roll through her.

Damn it. No matter how badly she wanted to deny it, this hurt. It fucking sucked!

Disgusted with him, and with herself for just standing there and watching, Brit was only seconds away from jerking herself out of the magnetic hold he had on her . . . and running away. But then his face tightened as if he was in pain, the big hands he'd pressed against the glass again curling into fists, and she knew he was coming. He kept his dark, heavy-lidded gaze locked on her the entire time, and she crossed her arms over her chest, suddenly determined to wait and see what he would do when it was over. What his next move in this strange tableau would be.

She didn't have to wait long. As soon as he could, he jerked back, looking down at the woman as he said something to her that Brit couldn't hear. The blonde's shoulders dropped in a gesture of disappointment, but she didn't slap his face when she moved to her feet. Instead, she leaned up on her toes and gave him a brief kiss on the lips, then let herself out through his patio gate, all without ever noticing that Brit was inside, watching the entire thing. The woman hadn't even noticed that Alex's attention was focused on someone else, and not on her.

But it was. It had been, from the moment he'd realized Brit was standing there.

He stood alone now in the muted glow of the outside light, jeans hanging below his hips, giving Brit a clear shot of his heavy testicles and his still erect dick. And, God, was it a sight. Why couldn't he have a tiny prick? Some sad, shriveled-up little thing? But no, he had to be as breathtaking *there* as he was everywhere else. Dense, dark hair curled around the thick root, and it was a view of pure masculine perfection, the shaft long and broad, the dark skin crisscrossed with heavy veins, the head fat and plum-sized. She'd never, ever, in all of her thirty-one years thought of a guy's cock as being beautiful before, but Alex's was. Somewhat brutal and intimidating, yes. But definitely beautiful.

She swallowed the lump of lust in her throat, her breath quickening, and all she could think was, *He's standing there with his junk hanging out and I really want to kill him. But I want to jump on him, too. And I hate myself for feeling this way. I need to despise him, damn it. For what he's done, I need to detest the freaking sight of him.*

Was it an irrational reaction? Probably. There was no commitment between them. None whatsoever. All they'd ever shared was a kiss. But that didn't mean it hadn't hurt.

As she watched him pull up his jeans, partially buttoning the fly, then reach over and open the door, she had a startling rush of clarity. In that moment, she knew *exactly* what this had been. What Alex had been trying to achieve. And it'd worked. She wouldn't be making another mistake like she'd made that morning. No more kissing him back if he put his mouth on hers. No more . . . anything. She would talk to Ben when he got home about finding someone else who could provide security for her, and then she would put Alex Hudson out of her mind. For good.

The energy in the room actually changed as he stepped inside, her skin prickling with physical awareness, making her shiver. He closed the door behind him, locked it, then turned to face her. When she realized she was staring at the dark happy trail that led south from his navel, disappearing into the open top of his fly, she jerked her traitorous gaze back to his face, cursing her damn hormones.

He lifted a hand, rubbing the back of his neck, then finally ended the uncomfortable, silent stare down. "I'm sorry I didn't notice when you came down. I had to . . . talk to a neighbor."

"Oh, really?" Brit couldn't help but give a brittle laugh as she slowly arched a brow. "Is that what you call it? *Talking?*"

He grunted, then pressed his sensual lips into a flat line.

"You know, Alex, you could have just gone to her place. Spared me the disgusting picture show."

"I didn't want to leave you here alone." His nostrils flared as he pulled in a deep breath, his jaw rigid. "And I thought you'd gone to bed. I didn't ask you to watch."

"No, but you didn't try to be discreet, either."

Another grunt. And it was seriously starting to get on her nerves.

In what was undoubtedly a childish attempt to pluck at his own nerves, she asked, "Why do I get the feeling you didn't exactly enjoy that little sexual episode?"

His gaze went flinty and cold, the rasp in his deep voice giving it a raw edge. "Be a bitch if you need to. But don't play shrink on me, Doc."

Brit smirked. "It wasn't a professional observation," she said lightly. "It was a female one."

He was starting to look pissed. "I came, didn't I?"

"You ejaculated. But that wasn't a climax. There wasn't any real pleasure involved in it for you."

"And you stuck around to the bitter end, didn't you?" This time he was the one with the sardonic smile on his lips. "You get off on watching?"

She debated with herself for several seconds, and then decided what the hell? She might as well give him an honest answer. It wasn't like anything would come of it, considering he'd just shot his load down another woman's throat. "I liked watching *you*. You're a prick, but any woman who says you aren't nice scenery is lying. So was that meant to teach me a lesson, Alex? Put me in my place?"

Shoving a hand back through his short hair, he cursed under his breath. But the only explanation he gave her was a gritty, "I've had a shit week."

"Yeah, well, mine's been just peachy."

His eyes slid closed as he pulled in another deep breath, then his lashes lifted as he slowly exhaled. He opened his mouth, but nothing came out, so he closed it again. And she took that as her cue to go.

"I just hope she was worth it," she tossed back at him, turning on her heel.

"Brit, wait!"

She looked over her shoulder. "What?"

For the first time since the awkward as hell conversation had started, there was a flush of color burning across the tops of his cheekbones. "I wasn't trying to embarrass you. I swear. I just needed to . . . take the edge off."

With a sharp smile, she said, "And any willing mouth would do, huh?"

She could have sworn he flicked a dark look at her own lips, before scrubbing his hands over his face. "Something like that."

Needing to get away from not only him, but also the entire depressing situation, she looked ahead and started walking away.

"Where are you going?" he asked, when she started up the stairs.

"To bed," she replied in a low voice, feeling his hard gaze follow her every step of the way. When she finally had the bedroom door closed behind her, she flipped the lock and threw herself on the bed. Rubbing at the center of her chest, she wondered why she was such a fool, actually hurting over what she'd seen when she knew he didn't want her. She was just being overly emotional, because of everything that was going on in her life. But the longer she gave herself the pep talk, the deeper the pain in her chest kept digging.

She felt like a pathetic idiot. And she hated that she'd let him get to her.

Rolling onto her side, Brit punched one of the stupid pillows on her bed and closed her eyes, trying to put him out of her mind. But all she kept seeing, over and over, was the sight of him pounding his dick into the blonde's mouth, until a tear actually spilled from the corner of her eye.

That's it. That does it, she thought, swiping furiously at her damp face.

She wasn't going to cry over him. Instead, she was going to get a grip and stop acting like a crushed-out teen. Which meant she needed to keep her head on straight, and not let her stupid hormones play haywire with her emotions.

Taking a deep breath, she crawled under the covers and turned out the light, determined to think of anything but the man downstairs. In fact, she was going to devote her mental energy to his meddling brother, who needed to have his ass kicked for doing this to her.

And who should have known better than to ever ask Alex Hudson to watch over her in the first place.

5

Alex had been in some awkward situations in his life, but this morning took the prize. When he finally dragged his tired ass downstairs, just after seven thirty, Brit was already in the kitchen making omelets for breakfast. He cast a wary glance at her back when she told him to grab a cup of coffee and a seat at the table, hoping she wasn't going to poison him.

Wondering what the hell he was going to do about her, he slipped into a chair with the mug he'd just filled for himself and tried to keep his gaze focused on the tabletop. But it was pointless when she was standing at his stove in a fucking silky green dress that seemed to flow over her curves like water. And when she came to the table, setting a mouthwatering omelet in front of him, the front shot of her damn near made him drool. It wasn't just the perfect tits and hips and long legs. It was the goddamn wavy red hair and creamy skin and smoky eyes with eyelashes that looked about a mile long. The silver hoops in her delicate ears and the pulse fluttering like mad at the base of her pale throat.

"So what's up with the breakfast?"

Her shoulders lifted in a careless shrug. "I just like to cook when I'm tense."

He noticed there were faint smudges under her eyes, which meant she'd probably slept about as badly as he had. But she didn't seem so much pissed at him as she did . . . uninterested. And that stung, damn it. The omelet tasted delicious, but he could hardly enjoy it with this sour feeling pumping through his veins. Then he noticed the little hungry, sideways glance she stole at him, and his tension increased for an entirely different reason.

Jesus, that look had just made him ten times harder than Chloe's mouth had done last night, and the woman wasn't even touching him.

Chloe . . . *shit*. What the hell had he been thinking? She was nothing but fluff. It sounded cruel, but it was the God's honest truth. And he'd taken advantage of it. Had come in her mouth because he knew she'd let him, and he'd been feeling desperate. But it'd been a mistake. Hell, he hadn't even been that into it until he'd looked up and seen Brit standing there in the middle of his living room, watching him with those wide hazel eyes. He'd noticed her flinch, and knew a classy woman like her had been mortified by the situation. Yeah, it'd been awkward, getting caught with his pants down and his cock buried between another woman's lips. But even with her pissed and embarrassed, having the doc's eyes on him had been what set him off.

He looked up at her now, after taking a drink of his coffee, and the fucking air nearly crackled with sparks as their gazes connected. Then hers quickly skittered away.

Christ, this was screwed up. He might not like it, but there was no denying that the intensity of the attraction between them was unlike anything he'd ever come across in his personal experience. He'd lost his virginity at fifteen, and could honestly say that despite his crap marriage, the years before he'd met Judith had seen him having some damn fine sex. Fun, gritty, raw. He'd more than enjoyed finding a woman who could take his level of intensity and making her come until she was worn out and sated. Had fucking *loved* it.

But Alex had never craved another person like he did this one, and it'd been that way for a hell of a lot longer than he wanted to admit. All the doc had to do was walk into the same room as him, and you could feel something simmering in the air. It was that damn chemistry or whatever you wanted to call it that Reese had picked up on, and then run with it, convincing Ben that they needed to figure out a way to get the two of them together.

But what his brother and sister-in-law didn't know was that Alex had nothing to give a woman past what he'd shared with Chloe last night. And somehow he didn't see a gritty sexual affair as being something that the doc would agree to, even if he could have survived one with his sanity intact.

"I need to be at the office early this morning," she murmured, after setting down her fork. "I was thinking that I could call Mike and ask him for a lift on his way in to work. That way you can get on with your day."

"No. I'll take you."

She gave him a guarded look. "Alex, you don't need to—"

"I said I'll take you," he ground out.

And that was the end of the conversation.

Just as they were getting ready to step out the front door, her cell phone started to ring. She answered it after taking it from her purse, and he immediately knew from her body language that it was Shepherd again.

"Try to get him to meet you," he mouthed to her, shutting the door again. "Somewhere in town, if you can."

BRIT GRIPPED THE PHONE TO HER EAR AS SHE STARED AT ALEX, wondering if he'd lost his mind. Or maybe he was just so desperate to get her out of his life that he was willing to put her in a risky situation. Whatever the case, she would be willing to do it to help her patient. Not the asshole watching her with those damn unreadable eyes.

Turning her attention to the call, she listened to Clay's choked voice wobble as he said, "I know you're not at home, Dr. Cramer."

"Clay, you sound very troubled. You need someone to talk to, and I'm . . . I'm sorry I wasn't there for you before. Why don't we . . . meet somewhere in town today so that we can talk about how you're feeling?"

For a moment there was nothing but the erratic sound of his breathing, and then he snapped, "So you can set me up? Pick a time and place so you can sic the cops on me? I don't think so, Dr. Cramer. That won't work."

"Clay, listen . . ."

"I just wanted you to know that I know you went somewhere with *that* man, and I'll figure it out. You won't be able to hide from me much longer."

The call ended, and she took a deep breath as she slipped the phone back into the inside pocket of her purse.

"What did he say?"

Biting her lip, she flicked a worried look up at Alex, who was still standing right in front of her. "Just that he suspects I'm staying with you, and he's determined to find out where."

Some of the cold rigidity seemed to ease from his expression, the look in his eyes almost . . . caring. "Don't worry, Doc. He won't. He's not getting anywhere near you."

Seriously? "You wanted me to meet him someplace, Alex."

Pulling the door open again, he said, "Only because I would have been there, along with Ryder and the others, to take him down."

She gave him a distracted reply as she followed him out the door, glad for the call, if only to be reminded of what the real problem was here. She had a patient who was hurting, who could very well hurt others, and who wanted to hurt her. In light of all that, Alex's actions the night before meant nothing. She had no business wasting mental energy or emotion on the man. She just needed to stay focused and alert, while working on a way to reach Clay Shepherd before it was too late.

Unfortunately, they'd learned from Ryder that his calls were coming from prepaid cell phones, or burn phones, which made tracing his location difficult.

Still lost in her thoughts, the last thing Brit expected to see when she and Alex arrived at her work and walked into her patient waiting area, other than Clay himself, was the clinic's founder and director, Ray McNamara, lounging with his hip perched on the corner of her receptionist's desk, apparently waiting for Brit to arrive. Despite being in his early fifties, he could have easily passed for forty. He kept in shape, had a thick head of sandy-colored hair, and was considered a bit of a heartthrob by most of the nurses at the clinic. But Brit had always felt that his looks were a little too polished. He was probably the kind of guy who had his teeth regularly bleached and visited a spa for his weekly pedicures. Not that she had anything against a man taking care of himself, but there came a point when it was just a bit too much.

"Ray, it's good to see you," she murmured, wondering what had brought him down from his seventh-floor office. They usually only interacted at company events or staff meetings. In fact, she didn't think she'd seen him for nearly two weeks.

Ray cut a narrow look toward Alex as he moved to his feet. It was clear from the expression on his face as he shook Brit's hand that he didn't like the PI, and she was trying to reason out why when Ray shocked her by leaning down and pressing a kiss to her cheek.

"Ray?" she croaked, completely confused as he pulled back and gave her a grave look of concern.

"I've been so worried about you since Director Stevens told me what was happening with your patient, Brit. Are you all right? Is there anything I can do to help?"

He was still clasping her hand, and she stood there with a stupefied look on her face, feeling as if she'd somehow stepped into yet another alternate reality the minute she'd walked into work. McNamara was acting odd. But he'd recently gone through an ugly divorce, and he was probably worried about any negative publicity the Shepherd case could bring the clinic. It didn't have anything to do with *her*, she kept telling herself. But the calculating gleam in his ice-blue eyes as he stared down at her was making her extremely uncomfortable.

"I'm fine," she murmured, thankful for the chance to take the focus off herself as Alex came to stand by her side. "Ray, I'd like to introduce you to Alex Hudson. He's a . . . friend of mine." She flicked a glance at Alex, startled to find him staring at her boss with a cold, measuring gaze. "Um, Alex, this is the clinic's director, Ray McNamara."

Ray finally released her hand as he looked at Alex. "Director Stevens mentioned you when I spoke to him, Mr. Hudson. I wasn't aware that private investigators were in the business of providing personal security," he remarked in a condescending tone that made her cringe.

What on earth was Ray doing?

She half expected Alex to just come right out and call the guy a jackass. But he didn't. He simply responded with a crooked, satisfied smile she had a feeling was meant to goad the hell out of the other man. "This is personal, not professional. The doc is a really *close* friend of mine and my family."

"Hmm," Ray murmured, shifting his attention back to her. "Brit, you know if you ever need a place to stay, I have plenty of room."

"Oh, uh . . . thank you. That's very . . . kind," she practically choked out, nearly jumping out of her skin when Alex placed his hand on her lower back. He kept it there, softly stroking the silk of her dress with his thumb, and McNamara's gaze narrowed with annoyance.

"Call me if you need me," he told her, taking her hand again and giving it a final squeeze before making his exit without a word to Alex, and she didn't know whether to laugh at their strange behavior, or pinch herself to see if she needed to wake up from this bizarre dream.

"So that was your boss?" Alex asked, after they'd walked into her office and he'd shut the door behind him.

Stopping in front of her desk, Brit set her purse down beside her phone and turned back around to find him propping his shoulders against the door. "In a roundabout way, I suppose. He's the clinic's director, as well as the founder."

"Have you ever fucked him?" he asked in a low, almost silent voice. But she'd heard him. She just couldn't believe he'd had the audacity to ask her such a personal question.

"Excuse me?"

"You heard me, Doc."

She drew herself up to her full height and lifted her chin. "That's none of your damn business, Alex."

Pushing away from the door, he came a few steps closer, crossed his arms over his wide chest, and regarded her with a breathtaking intensity that was causing her pulse to race. "Not true. At the moment, everything you do is my business."

"Well, then, since I'm currently *living* with you, I think it's safe to say you would know if I was sleeping with him."

"I didn't ask if you screwed him last night. I'm asking if it's *ever* happened."

"You know, I get that this might come as a shock to you, but believe it or not, I've never needed to use sex to advance my career!" she yelled.

"That still doesn't answer the question."

Exhaling a sharp, bitter breath, she said, "No, Alex. I have *never* had sex with Ray McNamara. Is that clear enough for you?"

His expression hardened. "But he's tried, hasn't he?"

"He's a married man," she snapped, trying not to flinch under the raw force of his gaze. "Or at least he was, until recently. But that's a line I never cross."

"So then he's made his move, but you refused. Good." His eyes gleamed with satisfaction. "I hate the thought of his slimy hands being on you."

"I don't want you thinking of any man's hands on me!"

Quietly, he said, "Too late, Doc."

She could tell from his wry expression that he'd guessed the exact moment she figured out he was talking about himself, and how it'd affected her. She watched him with a wide, startled gaze as he walked over to the door and flicked the lock. When he turned back to her, he leaned his back against the door again, evidently waiting for her to say something.

"You must be fucking crazy." She didn't use the f-word often. But this was definitely the time to throw that baby out there.

He lifted his brows. "You telling me you haven't thought about it?"

"I haven't!"

Giving her a crooked smile, he called her on the lie. "Bullshit. I saw the look on your face last night."

"You mean the one of disgust when I found you getting sucked off by the blonde?"

His smile disappeared, replaced by a steady look of resolve. "You might not have liked the situation, but you got off on the view."

She bristled with irritation. "You are so bloody arrogant!"

"I've also had enough of this pointless game we're playing," he growled, pushing off from the door and heading right for her. "So lose the fucking dress."

She wet her lips and blinked, getting the feeling that he'd just shocked himself as much as her when those particular words had come out of his mouth. When she could finally form a response, her voice was whisper soft, thrumming with emotion. "What did you say?"

He stopped a few feet in front of her. "I think you heard me just fine."

Her mouth started to tremble, her skin tingling with awareness. "Are you . . . are you asking me to get naked for you?"

He gave a brief, curt shake of his head. "I'm not asking. I'm telling. Big difference."

She took a quick, unsteady breath, and knew he could see the confusion roiling through her. The part that wanted to slap his face and keep her distance battling against the part that was ruled by animal lust. They both knew it was a mistake to give in to whatever this crazy, volatile thing was building between them—a mistake that would only lead to trouble—but they were breaking beneath its inexorable pull. "I see."

Her voice was huskier than before, and his mouth kicked up at the corner. "Good."

She glared at his smirking lips, then slowly lifted her gaze back to his. "And you think I'm going to make a fool of myself over you why, exactly?"

Softly now, he told her, "Because you want it as badly as I do."

She started to shake her head, but he stopped her with nothing more than a look. "Don't even try it, Doc. You might not like me all that much, but your body has a mind of its own." He flicked his gaze down to her breasts, then back up again. "Your nipples are already hard."

She fought the urge to cover her chest like a coward. "Yes, well, my body doesn't make the decisions around here."

He stepped closer, and she enjoyed the soft puffs of breath from his mouth as he lowered his face over hers. "I get it," he said in a raw, gravelly rumble. "I really do. And while we might not like it, we *both* know how this is going to play out. It's not going to just go away. I tried to shove it aside last night, and you saw how well that went. So we can either ignore it and be miserable, or deal with it once and for all."

So many emotions fired through her, it was difficult to tell which one was going to win out over the others. Shock? Anger? Desire? "You mean get it out of our systems?" she finally whispered, feeling the effects of them all.

Lifting his hand, he cupped her jaw, his thumb settling against the corner of her mouth. "I don't want you finding someone else to watch over you. It would drive me bat-shit. And I can't claim to completely understand why that is. All I know is that I *need* to know that you're safe. But you keep me on edge, and that led to what happened last night. Which, believe it or not, I *am* sorry that you saw. Hell, I'm sorry it even happened in the first place."

She pulled in a shaky breath. "Me, too."

"So the way I see it, the easiest solution is to simply do what feels right."

A notch formed between her brows as they drew together. "And the two of us? That feels *right* to you?"

"I can ignore you when I have to, Doc. Keep my distance when things get too intense. But not like this. Not when I see you every morning and every night. We need to deal with it."

There was a part of Brit that felt an immense sense of relief that he was admitting to feeling the same intense attraction that she did. That agreed with what he was suggesting. But there was a part that was also dreading how badly it might backfire on them.

Stroking his thumb across the heat in her cheek, he went on. "There's nothing to be embarrassed about. You're the one with the fancy degree, so I'm sure you understand how it works even better than I do. Sometimes there's no explanation for chemistry. Whether you want it or not, you just have to deal with it before you can move on."

God, why did it hurt so badly to hear him say out loud what she knew was nothing more than the truth? That he didn't want any part of this attraction that existed between them. And yet, there was something in his eyes and expression that was impossible to resist. Something that made her feel more *seen* and *needed* than she'd ever felt with any other man, and it was intoxicating. A lush, mesmerizing drug that was pulling her completely under its spell.

Under *his* spell.

It didn't make any sense, considering this was Alex Hudson and she knew enough of his history to know how he felt about women. And whether she wanted to admit it or not, last night had shown her that there was more to her interest in Alex than just an avid appreciation of his good looks. The way she'd felt when she saw him with the blonde had made that pretty clear. So the real question was how much of a risk to her emotions was she willing to take in exchange for the pleasure he was offering?

She stood there before his magnificent body, unable to take her eyes off him as she carried on the silent debate inside her head, and finally came to a decision. God help her, she was going to do it. Even knowing she would most likely regret it later, she wasn't going to let this fleeting moment of madness slip away from her without first wringing it of every ounce of pleasure that she could possibly get.

Not wanting to give herself the time to change her mind, she started to lift her arms around his neck, but he shook his head and stepped back, lowering his hand to his side. At her questioning look, he said, "Clothes first, Doc."

Oh, God. The delicious rasp of his deep voice combined with the hungry gleam in his eyes had her pulse thrashing, her body going hot and wet and soft. He was the kind of man who was built to fight and fuck, his body lean and ripped and battle-honed, the provocative way he moved as powerful as it was seductive. And she wanted him so badly it was a physical ache that pulsed inside her.

"Right here?" she asked, the breathless sound of her voice catching her by surprise. "You want me to strip for you in my office?" The far wall of windows was specially treated to make it impossible to see inside, but the feeling was still one of . . . exposure. Of course, she was going to feel even more naked beneath Alex's searing gaze than she would if she was standing in the middle of a crowded courtyard.

"You trust me?" he asked her.

She pulled her shoulders back. "Yes. I mean, to a certain extent. I know that you won't hurt me."

"Then take off the dress."

His rough words vibrated with that low, husky tone of command that was starting to sound not only familiar, but intoxicating, and Brit couldn't resist. She knew it was insanity, but she was drawn to him like lightning to metal. And yet, there was one thing she needed to make clear before this went any further. "I'm not willing to have sex with you."

Not yet. Maybe not ever . . .

Instead of getting angry, she could have sworn there was a spark of humor in his heavy-lidded gaze. "I won't put my dick in you, Doc. We don't have enough time right now, and I have the feeling that once I got inside you, I wouldn't want out. So relax."

She choked out a laugh. "Relaxing isn't something that I usually do when you're around."

He gave her another one of those crooked, sexy smiles. "Then this'll be a first."

She started to reach behind her, then paused. Catching her lip in her teeth, she locked her gaze with his. "Alex, are you sure this is a good idea? It's going to—"

"Stop overthinking it," he said, cutting her off as he slipped out of his jacket. He tossed it onto a nearby chair, and she loved the way he looked in the crisp white shirt and shoulder holster. "You know we both want it. I'm man enough to admit that I *need* to get my hands on you, Brit. I'm not going to be able to think straight until I do."

AND HELL NO, IT'S NOT A GOOD IDEA, HE THOUGHT, KEEPING THAT LAST bit to himself. But Alex wasn't going to let that stop him. His eyes fucking burned as he watched her reach behind her back, lowering the dress's zipper with a sibilant, metallic hiss. He reached down to rearrange his dick, his shaft so hard he had to grit his teeth against the savage urge to rip his fly open and sink inside her right then and there. Then she pushed the dress off her shoulders, letting it slide down her body to puddle on the floor, and he forgot about anything else in that moment but drinking in the sight of her standing before him in nothing more than a cream-colored bra and matching panties. They were lacy and sexy as fuck, and his damn hands shook as he settled them on her waist, lifting her up onto the edge of her desk.

"Lie back," he growled, quickly gripping her thighs and pushing them wide as she lowered her back to the desktop. Forcing himself not to rush, he ran his hands up the smooth insides of her thighs, then leaned down and pressed his open mouth to the damp gusset on her underwear, her incredible scent making his head spin.

She gasped as she reached down, touching his face, and he was glad that he'd shaved that morning. Her skin was so delicate, he'd have to be careful not to scratch her. "You said hands," she murmured, sounding a bit scandalized as he coasted over the humid panel of lace with his lips.

"What's that?" he murmured.

"You said you were going to get your *hands* on me."

Ah. His lips quirked as he glanced up at her crimson face. "Mouth, too, Doc." He nuzzled his nose against the skimpy lace covering her auburn curls, and pulled in a deep breath. "Definitely my mouth," he groaned. "You taste half as good as you smell, and it'll be the sweetest thing I've ever gotten under my tongue."

"Oh, God," she moaned, just as he moved the soaked panel of lace aside and took a moment to take a good long look at her pussy. And, fuck, she was beautiful. Pink and puffy and already slick with her juices. He could have leaned over her and held this position forever, memorizing every explicit, erotic detail, but there was too strong a chance he might keel over from hunger if he didn't hurry up and get his damn mouth on her.

"Hold these to the side," he ground out, his deep voice rough with need as he grabbed her hand, placing her fingers where he wanted them so she could keep the lace out of his way. Pulling her swollen lips wide with his thumbs, opening her up like a juicy peach, he didn't waste any time, quickly burying his face against her and letting his tongue take what it wanted. And, holy fuck, did she taste delicious. Nothing but hot, sweet, syrupy perfection.

He was going to make her come so hard, this moment right here would be all she'd ever be able to think about when she sat down at her desk, instead of that sly-faced asshole who owned the place. McNamara's smarmy style had made his skin crawl, and Alex knew the son of a bitch had been planning on using the shit with Shepherd as a way to get Brit in his bed.

No way in hell was he letting that happen.

Licking her from her ass all the way up to her throbbing clit, he gave the tiny bundle of nerves a firm, tugging suckle that had her gripping his head with her free hand and shoving that sweet cunt even harder against him. "Tastes even better," he murmured, surprised by the raw sound of his voice.

"What?" Her own voice was breathless and dazed, and he couldn't help but smile.

"Your pussy. It tastes even better than it smells, and it smells incredible. Mouthwatering, even. You know what that means?"

"No," she gasped.

Alex looked up at her over her glistening mound, his lips moving against her slippery folds as he spoke. "It means you are so fucked, Doc. Because now I'm gonna be getting my face between your long legs as often as possible, tonguing your pretty little cunt twenty-four/seven."

"Damn it," she groaned, covering her eyes with her hand. "You're trying to embarrass the hell out of me, aren't you?"

"Naw. I'm just telling it like it is."

When he pushed his long index finger into her creamy sheath, she arched, gasping again, so fucking gorgeous it made his chest hurt. And she was so deliciously snug, her plush inner muscles clasping him in a breathtaking grip, that it damn near had his eyes rolling back in his head at the thought of what she would feel like on his dick.

"How many fingers can you take?" he rasped, working a second finger alongside the first. She was stretched so tight around him he had to reach deep and stroke her sweet spot, getting her even wetter, before he could start giving her a proper fucking with the long digits.

"That's perfect," she moaned, and he almost started to talk her into taking a third, since it would make it easier for him to get his dick inside her. But he stopped himself, determined to be unselfish for once and make this about her and not him.

He just hoped he didn't cause himself any kind of permanent damage in the process, his cock throbbing so hard he would have grit his teeth against the ache if he didn't have something so perfect under his mouth.

When he started to feel the tight vibrations that signaled her coming orgasm, he pulled his fingers back and went at her like he'd been dying to from the start, all lips and tongue and teeth. He fucking consumed her, the taste and texture of her tender flesh and slick juices making him feel like a starved man who'd suddenly been seated at the most decadent feast he'd ever seen. Then she let out a soft, keening cry that she tried to choke back, considering where they were, and a primitive growl broke from his throat as he pulled her open with his thumbs again and thrust his tongue inside her as deep as it would go, determined to feel every ripple and pulse, swallowing down as much of her as he could. He shoved his face against her even harder and all he could think was *Oh, fuck*. When she came, her sweet taste got even richer. Hotter. Who needed alcohol when a man could get strung out on this? Talk about addictive. He was latched on to her, licking as deep into her snug pussy as he could get, tonguing her like his fucking life depended on it. Like he needed those sweet juices to survive. And that's how he felt.

When she was finally too sensitive to enjoy it, he forced himself to stop lapping his tongue over those drenched, swollen folds, and lifted himself up on straight arms that were braced on either side of her waist. He took a moment to catch his breath, then stood and used his hand to wipe his wet mouth, irritated that he couldn't just keep his face buried between those silky thighs, wallowing in all of that warm, slippery cream.

She took a few deep, languid breaths, then lifted herself into a sitting position, her chest and face rosy with color, hazel eyes dark with passion, and Alex knew he'd never seen a more beautiful woman. Christ, there wasn't even a close second, and touching her had been even more mind-shattering than he'd always suspected it would be—and he'd suspected *a lot*.

When she reached for his belt, making it clear that she planned to reciprocate and blow *his* mind, he was so damn tempted it was almost impossible to resist.

"Can't," he somehow managed to scrape out with a sharp jerk of his head, followed by a step back. At the look on her face, Alex winced, then reached down and rearranged his hard-on. It throbbed like a fucking toothache, his balls drawn so tight he figured he'd probably go off with a single stroke. But even more than his lack of control at the moment, it just seemed fucking *wrong* to let her put his cock in her mouth when he'd been ramming it down Chloe's throat the night before. Even he wasn't that much of a bastard.

"Why not?" she asked with a soft note of confusion.

"I'm not trying to be a dick. I just . . . I'm barely keeping it together here."

With a playful smile on her beautiful mouth, she said, "That's why I'm offering to help. I believe in being fair."

Trying not to notice how the creamy mounds of her breasts were being pushed up by the lacy bra, jiggling with her every breath, he shook his head again. "I'd love to take you up on that, Doc. But right now you're going to have to trust me when I say it's a bad idea."

Her elegant brows pulled together, and she bit her lip, clearly wanting to ask him for an explanation.

He opened his mouth, ready to say something more, to try and make her understand without scaring her off, but his phone started ringing in his pocket. She slid off the desk, grabbed her dress off the floor, and turned away, giving him a moment to take the call. It was a lawyer he'd been working with in conjunction with a case, and he was needed at the county courthouse.

While he made arrangements to meet the lawyer, Alex watched Brit slip her dress back on, then make her way over to her private bathroom. He was just slipping his phone back in his pocket when she came out looking smooth and refreshed, the heat in her cheeks concealed by some kind of translucent powder that women wore, her hair brushed into place, and something inside of him rebelled. It was like she'd erased what had just happened between them, looking calm and unaffected, while his dick was still aching and her taste lingered on his lips. Every time he took a breath, he could smell her mouthwatering scent, and he flicked his tongue across his lower lip again, wanting more of her flavor.

He waited for her to ask about the call, but when she didn't, he told her, "I need to head over to the courthouse to meet with a lawyer about one of my cases."

"I hope everything's all right."

"It's fine. We just need to file some paperwork, and it's complicated because the client's wife is living out of the country."

She raised her brows. "He hired you about his wife?"

Mouth twisted in a wry grimace, he said, "More like he hired me to find the ten million she ran off with."

She immediately winced. "Ouch."

"No kidding."

"Well, then, let me walk you out."

The smooth, unruffled persona she was throwing in his face after she'd been blown wide open for him only moments before set Alex's teeth on edge. His hand shot out over her shoulder, holding the door shut as he lowered his mouth to her ear. "Are we going to talk about it?"

She stiffened, so still he didn't think she'd even drawn her next breath. "I think it's probably best if we don't." She looked over her shoulder and gave him a tight smile. "Don't you?"

He jerked his chin toward her face. "I wish you hadn't tidied up so quickly."

A delicious rose color stained the crests of her cheekbones. "I can't very well walk around my office looking like . . ."

When she trailed off, he said, "Like you just came all over my face?"

"Yes," she admitted with a strained laugh, the slight softening of her posture making him want to pull her close and just . . . hold her. Her bright eyes lowered to his mouth, and he liked the way her long lashes fluttered as she lifted her hand, rubbing her thumb against the corner of his lip, where he must have still had a smear of her girl juice.

He placed his hand on her waist, curving it over her hip. "Brit, I—"

"Alex, really, I'm fine. We can . . . we can talk later. But you need to go, and I need to get ready for my first appointment."

She opened the door, forcing him to move away, and he hesitated before stepping into the empty reception area, knowing he should say *something*, but no idea what it was. In the end, he simply settled on, "Be careful today."

"I will."

He nodded, swept one last look over her, then forced himself to turn and walk away. Just before she closed the door, he turned back and said, "Hey, Doc?"

Standing in the narrow opening, she lifted her gaze to his. "Yes?"

He was scared shitless by what was happening to him, but damn it, it wouldn't kill him to try being nice to her for once. "I was an ass not to mention it before, but you look beautiful today."

She blushed clear to the roots of her hair, which made him laugh. "Um, thanks."

He flashed her a quick grin, then headed out.

By the time he'd made it out to the parking deck where he'd left the Range Rover, the morning heat was already oppressive, and Alex had decided that as far as mistakes went, that one had been monumental. The kind with proportions so epic, he couldn't even wrap his mind around them.

Instead of slaking his need, working it down, his taste of Brit Cramer had made one thing unnervingly clear, and he'd have been lying through his teeth if he'd said it didn't scare the fuck out of him.

It was stupid. Doomed. And bound to break them.

But he needed *more*.

6

BY THE TIME ALEX PULLED UP IN FRONT OF HIS CONDO THAT EVENING, it felt like days had passed since he'd last seen Brit. He climbed out of the Range Rover and spoke with the deputy he'd asked Ryder to send over to keep an eye on the place until he made it home, then sent the guy on his way. Things had taken a lot longer at the courthouse than he'd expected, and he'd finally had to call Mike, who had keys to his place, and ask him to give Brit a ride from the clinic to his condo.

She'd given Ryder the key fob to her Audi on Wednesday night, and he'd had two deputies go back over to the clinic to pick it up, then bring it back to the sheriff's station. No way in hell would anyone mess with it there. And Alex had liked that it kept her from doing something reckless, like deciding she could drive herself home if he couldn't be there to get her.

It'd bothered him, even more than he'd thought it would, when he'd had to call Mike and ask him to play chauffeur. Of course, his brother had been only too happy to help out, and Alex had spent a good ten minutes lecturing him on how important it was that he spend less time flirting with her and more time making sure they weren't followed. The last thing he wanted was Shepherd finding out where he lived, because it would mean having to move locations, and for some uncharacteristic reason that he didn't completely understand, he actually *liked* having her under his roof.

Under his body would be even better, but he figured he had better play it by ear and see how she acted when she saw him.

The moment he stepped inside the condo, he heard soft music coming from his kitchen, and a grin twitched at the corner of his mouth just as the spicy scent of something Mexican filled his nostrils. His stomach rumbled with approval, while a different kind of heat spread through his system at the fact that Brit Cramer was in his kitchen, cooking for him again.

A week ago, if someone had told him this would be happening, he would have laughed his ass off at them and said they were screwed up in the head. But now that he was living it, he'd have been lying if he'd said there wasn't something incredibly satisfying about knowing he was going to walk into his kitchen and set eyes on her. He hated the danger she was in from Shepherd, and had bitched Ryder out over the phone the entire drive home for not making more progress in tracking the psychotic son of a bitch down. But that didn't mean his pulse wasn't quickening as he set his keys and gun on the end table in the living room, then made his way over to the kitchen archway.

He'd already been sporting a semi, just from the thought of seeing her, but the instant she came into view, his damn dick shot as solid as a fucking rock. The lust and need and hunger hit him so hard, blasting through him like a shock wave, that he knew he didn't have a chance in hell of fighting it.

He stood in the archway, hands hanging loose at his sides as he leaned his shoulder against the wall, and simply drank in the sight of her, wanting it permanently inked into his brain like a tattoo. She had music playing on the radio, something jazzy and full of sax, while she swayed her hips to the rhythm and stirred something in a bowl on the counter. She'd changed when she'd gotten in, because she was now wearing a loose, short, simple cotton sundress, the deep blue color looking amazing with her hair and complexion, her slender feet adorable and bare, toenails painted a dark red.

She obviously hadn't heard him when he came in, and even though it probably made him a voyeur, Alex decided to just chill and enjoy the view. It was one of the sexiest damn things he'd ever seen, the natural sensuality of her movements as she lost herself in the music, and his already overheated body temp spiked even higher. He stripped his shirt off, letting it drop to the floor, and when he looked up, she was standing in the middle of the kitchen, her wavy red hair falling around her shoulders, her lips glossy and pink, her creamy skin flushed with color.

And she was staring right at him, her beautiful eyes smoky and hot.

Ah, hell. A fresh wave of need shot straight to his dick, and if he'd ever been this painfully stiff before, he'd blocked it from his memory. All the reasons that had kept flicking through his head that day about why this was such a bad idea—his past, his baggage, the intensity of their chemistry, not to mention her relationship with his family and the situation with Shepherd—started banging around again. But he didn't give a shit. With a silent snarl, he told them all to go to hell, no longer giving a damn about what he *should* do. He just wanted to focus on what was going to happen. Right now. Because unless she told him no, he was going to be so deep in this woman she'd be tasting him at the back of her throat for days. He wanted his scent all over her. Inside of her.

Wanted every man who looked at her to know that she'd been ridden long and hard and deep, and that he was the one who'd done it.

He just hoped to fuck she didn't say no.

Please. Please just let me have this . . .

Wondering if his heart was going to actually blast its way past his sternum, Alex felt her gaze move over his bare chest, and some of the tension in his gut relaxed. He might be shit when it came to dealing with women these days, but that wasn't the look of a woman who wanted to tell him to fuck off. It was the look of a woman who wanted him to fuck her. And the shadow of caution in those beautiful eyes meant she wasn't an idiot. She knew damn well what she was getting into with him. What he was willing to offer her, and what he wasn't. Which meant they were free to indulge until she eventually decided to kick his ass to the curb.

The key was to stay as detached as he could, so that he didn't have to worry about what condition he'd be in when that time finally came. Because he didn't have a choice. As gun-shy and wary as he was, he couldn't turn away from her. Not anymore. With or without the Shepherd problem, he'd had a taste of her, and he needed another. He'd been hooked by the first sip of her lips, then he'd gone down on her, and her mouthwatering flavor had been more addictive than any of the alcohol he'd drowned himself in after his divorce.

So, like the pathetic bastard he was, he was going to glut himself on her until he was forced to go cold turkey. And it might make him sound like a dick, but he wasn't nearly as concerned about the condition she'd be in when they crashed and burned. Yeah, she hadn't liked the dick move he'd made with Chloe, but he wasn't stupid. The doc was as classy an act as they came, and he knew the odds were strong that he'd never really touch her on an emotional level. And that was fine. He just wanted to make sure that when she finally walked away, her body felt his presence all the way down in her bones.

That he wasn't going to be a part of her life that was too easily forgotten.

The song on the radio ended, blending into something even sultrier, both of their chests rising and falling with a rhythm that matched the deep, sexual beat. She lowered her smoldering gaze to his boots, then slowly ran it up his body, taking her time, taking him in, and bit her lip when she got to his crotch, the denim of his jeans bulging as it tried to contain his erection. She lingered there for so long he started to sweat, his muscles twitching, and then she made her way up to his abs, and he thanked God for every grueling hour he spent working to keep his body in shape. In that moment, they were worth it, just to see the rich appreciation that made her hot gaze even hotter.

Shoving a hand back through his short hair, he hissed, "Jesus, Brit."

She cocked her head a bit to the side, as if she didn't know what to make of the raw edge in his voice. "Alex?"

He gave a quick, hard shake of his head, and straightened away from the wall. "Don't say anything, unless you need to tell me to get lost. Otherwise . . ." His breathing was getting deeper, making a harsh, rasping sound as it rushed past his lips. "Otherwise, just keep looking at me like that."

He braced himself for her to laugh in his face and tell him to take a hike. But he should have known not to try and predict what she would do. Instead, her eyes got a soft, molten look that made him want to roar. That made him want to throw her down on the nearest available surface and pound himself so deep inside her, it obliterated everything but the feel of her silky, curvy body. No past. No future. Just the mind-shattering feel of Brit Cramer's deluxe little cunt wrapped around him, sucking him dry, hurtling him into paradise.

"I want more. More of *you*." His voice was low and hard-edged, the words scraping from his tight throat. "But I can't . . . I can't give you more than this."

She lowered her lashes, shielding whatever emotion must have just flashed in that smoky gaze. No woman liked to hear that she was just sex, even if she was too good for the guy. But the doc didn't turn away from him. She took a quick breath, then lifted her lashes and looked right at him. "I didn't ask for more."

"We're good?"

A small, nearly imperceptible nod. Then a whispered, "We're good."

And that was all the fucking permission he needed.

He didn't remember crossing the space between them. He just knew that one second he was standing in the archway, and the next he had his hands on her. All over her. He ripped the dress open, tearing it down her shoulder on one side, taking the cup of her bra with it, and his mouth latched on to her breast as he gripped her ass, lifting her off the floor. He sucked hard, the pressure probably just shy of pain as he carried her out of the room, setting her down on the dining room table after he kicked a chair out of his way.

He pulled back, his gaze roaming over every inch of her upper body, his mouth wanting to be everywhere at once as he ripped at the buttons on his jeans, in such a hurry he nearly tore one off. Shoving them over his hips with his boxers, he heaved a ragged groan of relief when his dick sprang free, swollen nearly to bursting and almost embarrassingly brutal-looking, with its thick veins and ruddy coloring, more than ready to bury itself in what was sure to be its newest favorite place. His damn fingers had been tingling all day whenever he thought about how sweet she felt inside. God only knew what she was going to do to his cock.

Needing to see every beautiful inch of her naked and ready, Alex ripped the rest of her dress away, dropping the ruined pieces on the floor, then gave the same caveman treatment to her lacy panties. And, fuck, she was stunning. He was thankful as hell that she'd pulled the blinds over the sliding glass doors when she'd gotten in, because he didn't think he would have had the strength to walk away from her to do it himself.

"Wait!" she gasped, when he put his hands on the insides of her thighs and started to push them as wide as they'd go.

"Why?" he ground out, thinking there was a good chance he might actually bawl like a fucking baby if she'd changed her mind. But her next words damn near made him come then and there.

With her heavy-lidded gaze locked on his dick, she breathed out, "I want to touch it first."

He hissed a curse through his teeth, then groaned her name, wondering why everything felt so different with her. So . . . raw and exciting, when he'd thought he'd already experienced everything there was to experience when it came to sex.

"Please," she whispered, his damn heart nearly stopping as she reached out and grasped him with both hands, pulling the rigid shaft away from his body. "It's gorgeous and I want to hold it for a moment."

Alex stared, jaw hanging, not sure how he felt about hearing a woman refer to his dick as being gorgeous. It was weird as hell, but then, it was also fucking hot. No denying that. He was so turned on he was creaming the plum-sized head, pre-cum leaking all over her feminine hands as she gripped him. She was petting him, tracing the thick veins with the delicate tip of her finger, then testing the girth to see if she could wrap her fingers around him, which she couldn't. And, Christ, that only made him thicker, seeing how huge he looked in her delicate grip. Yeah, he knew his dick was bigger than a lot of women had seen, but he'd never had a woman who looked as if she so thoroughly appreciated the way he was built. Not just the size, but the whole fucking package. Literally.

Of course, it didn't mean shit in the long run. Hadn't kept

Judith from spreading her legs for his coworkers. But he was going to use every God-given inch to make this something that blew the doc's mind. He wanted her ruined with it. Screaming and clawing and fucking begging him for more.

Pulling her hands away from him, he growled, "I can't wait, Doc. You can play with it later."

She exhaled deeply as she leaned back, propping herself on her elbows, the provocative position doing downright sinful things to the thrust of her breasts. If he weren't on the verge of desperation to get inside her, he would have taken a moment to jack himself off all over those perfect, pink-tipped tits, making sure he got the thick little nipples nice and drenched.

Whoa, man. Focus! Shaking his head, he reached down and grasped his dick, squeezing hard, hoping the pain might help him gain a measure of control. Pointing himself toward her, he slid the head through the slippery cream coating her smooth slit, wringing a curse from his lips. He hadn't come inside a woman in so long, it was undoubtedly going to be a shitload of spunk that he shot inside her. And he wanted her feeling its heat. Wanted her soaked in it. But he wasn't so much of a bastard that he would make the decision for her. So he made himself ask, "Do I need a condom?"

"I'm on the pill. But . . ."

"But what?"

"Well, they're not 100 percent."

"They're close enough," he grunted. "And I'm clean. It's been years since I've done this without suiting up."

She'd been staring at him coating the head of his dick in her slippery juices, but his confession had her glancing up at him through her long, russet-colored lashes. "Then why now?"

Bracing his free hand on the table beside her hip, Alex let go of his dick and sank two fingers inside her tender opening. His body shook, and he pressed his damp forehead against hers, his deep voice guttural with lust. "Because you have the hottest, juiciest, snuggest little cunt I've ever felt," he told her, curving his fingers so that he could rub against the rough, sensitive spot deep inside her that made her breath hitch. "It's perfect, Doc. Cushioned and tight and slick. I want to feel you on my skin. Want to feel you from the inside out more than I've ever wanted any goddamn thing in this world. And I swear I'm not feeding you a line. I mean every word." Lifting his head so he could see her face, he asked, "So you with me? Or do I need to grab my wallet?"

For a moment, she stared back at him as if to say this was total madness. But then her lips parted, and he heard her murmur, "No, I'm . . . I'm with you."

"Good." He pulled his fingers back and aimed his cockhead right for her swollen, slippery vulva. "Because I'm about to fuck you so hard, I don't think a rubber could have taken it."

Her breath caught as he pushed the first inch inside, and though he felt like he was burning with fever, she was even hotter. And so fucking tight. He started to work his hips in careful back and forth lunges, determined to get inside her sweet little body without hurting her. Each time he pulled back and then pushed back in, he gained a bit more of that fist-tight sheath, his mind blown from how snug and wet and fucking soft she felt. But there was still a hell of a long way to go.

When she bit her lip and moaned, *"God, Alex,"* there was a genuine thread of panic in her voice, and he couldn't help but want to soothe her.

"Shh. Just let me in and relax. It'll be okay. *Better* than okay."

She gave an adorable laugh that was choked. "That's easy for you to say. You're not the one getting crammed full of a massive penis right now."

He lowered his forehead to hers again, his shoulders shaking. "Fuck, Brit, don't do that. Don't make me laugh."

"You don't like laughing?"

"Time and place, Doc. Time and place."

Before she could say anything else to make him lose it, he leaned down and used his teeth to pull down the other cup of her bra, exposing the firm, pale breast. Damn, she was beautiful. Needing to feel her against his tongue, he took the newly exposed, tight pink nipple into his mouth, sucking and tonguing it until he could feel her clenching pussy start to give way a bit for him. She was still mind-blowingly tight, but he was gaining ground now, pumping a little harder . . . a bit faster, and oh, fuck, it was going to feel so unreal when he was finally buried so deep he was hitting the end of her.

"Here we go," he groaned, lifting his head so that he could watch her face when it happened. "That's it, Doc. All the way now."

BRIT STARED INTO ALEX'S PALE GREEN EYES, AND LET OUT A THROATY cry as he finally slammed every thick inch of that amazing cock of his into her body. Her mouth fell open as wild, breathless sounds tore from her throat, the incredible sensation of holding all of him inside her almost too much to bear. Then he started to move, and it got even better. He held her hips and ground her against him on every downstroke, making her take every inch of him, until there wasn't even a sliver of space between their bodies. They were wet and hot and slick, skin glistening with sweat, their groins slapping against each other as he pulled back and then slammed into her again, giving it to her so hard she cried out from the jarring shock of pleasure-pain. The table legs were screeching as they got shoved across the tiled floor, and she couldn't do anything but hold on for dear life.

Oh, God. Talk about backfiring. She thought she'd be able to dive into this experience with him and enjoy it for the pleasure, like a naïve little ninny traipsing through the flower fields of lust, tra-la-la and isn't this nice, getting a bunch of lovely orgasms from the surly, but gorgeous Alex Hudson. *Hah!* She couldn't have been more wrong. Oh, the pleasure was un-fucking-believable, but there was nothing casual about what was happening. She was clawing him, for God's sake. Sinking her nails into his powerful shoulders, silently demanding he fuck her harder. *Deeper.* She was completely losing it, her usual inhibitions gone, and she couldn't help but be a little freaked out.

Then she was suddenly coming, convulsing around that thick, beautiful stalk that was powering in and out of her body, and she couldn't do anything but throw her head back and scream, completely destroyed by the pleasure. Somewhere in the middle of her out-of-control orgasm, she must have lost all awareness of the outside world, completely consumed by what was happening inside her, because the next thing she knew she was no longer even lying on the table. At some point Alex had pulled her up into his arms as he straightened, because his hands were now under her ass, moving her sensitive pussy over his burgeoning cock as he braced his feet apart and worked her down on him over and over with a violent, brutal force that felt so good she had to lean down and sink her teeth into his muscular golden shoulder, and it shot him over the edge right along with her. With a savage shout, he slammed her against him in short, jarring thrusts, the tendons in his neck straining beneath his skin as his hot semen started blasting inside her, the blistering surges drenching her until she could feel herself overflowing.

Um, wow. There wasn't anything in the entire world that could have prepared her for *that.*

They were both shaking, muscles tremoring with little aftershocks of pleasure, when he finally set her back on her feet, his hands gripping her upper arms to help keep her steady as she swayed.

"Huh," he grunted. "Look at that."

"What?" she wheezed, concentrating on not falling on her ass.

There was a deliciously raw, husky edge to his voice as he said, "The floor is wet. My cum's dripping out of you."

"Oh, God." He was right, it was. And it was so freaking sexy.

She didn't think she would have thought so with another man. No, she would probably be worrying about what he thought of her, or how it looked, letting her head get in the way of appreciating the moment. But there was no way to look at the sight of Alex's cum dripping out of her as anything other than hot as fuck. Maybe it meant she wasn't nearly as refined as she'd thought she was, but she didn't care. She felt more desirable in that moment than she ever had before, and she would have thanked him for it if she'd had the ability to do anything more than pant.

Her gaze lifted to his cock, and she licked her lips as she watched it grow thicker, harder, the head so succulent and ripe, gleaming with their combined juices. She wanted nothing more than to lean over and taste him. But Alex had a different plan, because he suddenly turned her around, putting her back to his front, and bent her over the table. She felt his rock-hard erection brush against her ass, and jolted with surprise.

"Already?" she asked.

"Brace yourself." He gripped her hips and leaned over her, pressing his lips to the middle of her spine. She felt the intimate touch of his tongue to her skin, the soft drag as he licked his way up to her nape, and her insides clenched so hard she actually whimpered.

His voice sounded savage as he said, "No way I can see something like that and not want to just blast you full of more."

"Caveman," she breathed out, knowing he could hear the smile in her voice.

He reached under her, using two of his callused fingertips to work her clit, and she nearly screamed. "Maybe," he murmured into her ear, biting the lobe. "But while I might fuck you raw, Doc, I promise I won't leave you hanging. I'll make you feel good."

"You do. You make me feel incredible. I think maybe you have a magic cock or something. What's your secret?"

His chest rumbled against her back as he laughed, and she almost cried when she felt him press a tender kiss against the damp skin at her nape. Softly, he said, "I think it's you, Doc. I think it's *all* you." Then she felt the weight of that succulent cockhead nuzzling inside her swollen vulva, and he pushed himself back inside her, making them both moan low and deep in their chests.

She was even tighter now, her inner tissues even plumper after his previous possession, and he was careful to work her carefully until some of the tension in her muscles eased. The air filled with the wet, slick sounds of their bodies moving together, and he picked up the pace, making her breath catch.

"Can you take it harder?"

"I can take anything you can give me. *Anything.*"

He groaned, the sexy sound low and male, telling her how much he liked her response. Her lips started to curl with another smile, until she felt him pulling the cheeks of her ass apart, completely exposing her to his gaze. She gave an embarrassed squeal that made him chuckle, the wicked sound blending into another throaty groan.

"Um, Alex?" she choked out, peering over her shoulder. "What are you doing?"

"I'm looking at you," Alex growled, pulling her lush ass cheeks even farther apart. He was mesmerized by the painfully erotic sight of her tiny pink asshole, and beneath it, the breathtaking view of her juicy cunt being stretched and reamed by his greedy cock. "Jesus, Doc. I can't stop. I can't stop watching your sweet little pussy when I'm fucking it. It's so goddamn beautiful. The view back here is incredible."

"Mmm." She suddenly sounded as caught up in the moment as he was. "I wish I could see it."

"Aw, shit, you're killing me," he muttered, knowing he couldn't hold back. Moving one hand to her chest, he squeezed a plump nipple while he reached around her hip with his other hand, pushing two fingers against her clit again. "I need you to come now, baby. Right the fuck now!" he roared, his head going back as he started spurting blast after blast of his cum inside her, her lusty cunt squeezing down on his cock in tight convulsions, milking him for everything he could give her. Every single fucking drop.

He didn't know how it was possible, but he was unloading even more into her with this second release than he had with the first one, and as he dropped his head forward, Alex stared in shocked amazement at the sight of his milky semen squeezing out around his thick root, spilling down her silky thighs.

What the fuck was happening to him? He'd never come like this in his life. Was his body trying to kill him? He wasn't eighteen anymore, damn it. Not that he'd ever felt this kind of gut-clawing need at that age. In fact, he'd *never* felt it like this. Not until Brit. And that should have had him running hard and fast for cover. But it didn't. Instead, he pushed a little deeper inside her, enjoying the combined slick of their cum soaking his shaft, her snug, muscular cunt clasping him like a hungry mouth. She was still pulsing, still trying to draw more out of him, and his eyes nearly rolled back in his head when he gave another hard spurt that drained him dry.

Son of a bitch, he thought, collapsing over her in utter exhaustion. His chest felt like it was on fire, heart beating so hard he probably needed medical attention, while every inch of him was drenched with sweat. Panicked, he pulled back so suddenly it actually hurt his dick, and he winced, hoping like hell he hadn't hurt her as well. The curve of her spine was beyond graceful as she pushed herself up, her gleaming hair falling over the side of her face as she turned her head and looked at him over her shoulder, a question in her beautiful eyes over why he'd pulled away from her so abruptly.

He opened his mouth, but nothing came out. In that moment, he couldn't have found the right words to say to save his life.

She waited, breath held, plush lower lip caught in her teeth. It was painful, seeing that worried, fragile hope in her eyes that he knew she wouldn't want him to recognize. All it would take was a few simple words to make things right. *Stay with me. Sleep with me. Let me hold you.* But he couldn't seem to find the way to get them out. Wasn't even sure that he *wanted* to say them, when there was a good chance he might fall apart.

Finally, she lowered her flushed face and knelt down to pick up the ruined remnants of her dress. She clutched them against her chest as she stood, as if she needed to shield herself from his view, one shaky hand lifting to tuck her gleaming hair behind the delicate shape of her ear.

She shot him a wistful, pained, regretful smile, then turned and walked away. He listened to her light footsteps on the stairs as he hiked up his boxers and jeans and dropped into a chair, elbows braced on his knees as he lowered his head into his hands.

He didn't know if he'd just saved himself or made another colossal mistake.

But whatever it was, she'd made her mark on him.

And he was so fucked—so *desperate* for her—he didn't even care.

7

When he was finally done with sitting on his ass and worrying about how he was going to make things right with the doc after the silent brush-off he'd just given her, since it sure as hell wasn't going to solve anything, Alex pulled off his boots and socks. Then he jumped up, went into the kitchen to wash his hands, and started working on finishing dinner. His stomach growled when he found cheese-covered enchiladas cooking in the oven, and the ingredients for a killer salad set out on the counter. The timer on the oven showed that the enchiladas had another fifteen minutes to cook, so he started dicing the veggies for the salad, hoping like crazy that Brit was planning on coming back downstairs to eat with him.

Of course, once she did, he was probably going to have to do some serious groveling in order to get back in her good graces. *Not that I've ever actually been in those,* he thought with a grimace. She hadn't fucked him because she cared about him, or even liked him. That had been about nothing but good old-fashioned lust.

And he would use it. Exploit it. Press it to his advantage, and thank any higher powers who might be out there listening for the chemistry that allowed him to experience being inside her.

God knew his personality couldn't have gotten him there. Hell, it probably couldn't even get her through his front door.

She came back down a few minutes later, fresh from a shower, her wet hair gleaming like red silk as it curled over one shoulder, her curvy body dressed in a slouchy pair of sweats and hoodie that she probably thought would hide her gorgeous figure from him. But it was a pointless try. Every inch of her beautiful, mouthwatering form had been burned into his brain like a brand. It was so fucking perfect he'd probably be seeing it on the back of his eyelids when he took his last breath.

And while her choice of clothing said a lot about how she was feeling at the moment, he was relieved she wasn't trying to avoid his company, joining him in the kitchen instead. They spoke in murmurs, neither commenting on what had happened between them.

She seemed surprised to find him helping out with dinner, but she didn't try to shoo him off. It was a nice change, after living with Judith, who had always been such a control freak. If he'd tried to cook something that wasn't to her specifications, she would rant and bitch until he finally just let it go and stopped helping. But Brit seemed happy to give him free rein, and even went so far as to compliment the salad he'd put together. Her praise made him go a little hot around the ears, and he was thankful as hell that Mike wasn't there to see his ridiculous reaction. His brother would have been a total douche about it, and then Alex would have had to kick his ass, and dinner would be ruined. And it smelled too damn good to go to waste.

Thinking it might be awkward sitting at the dinner table, after they'd just fucked each other's brains out on it not thirty minutes ago, Alex suggested they sit in the living room and watch something on television while they ate. Once they were settled with heaping plates and ice-cold glasses of tea, he switched on the TV. An episode of his favorite crime drama was starting, and he almost set the remote back down, before realizing this was probably something Brit wouldn't want to watch. Judith had always given him hell whenever he tried to watch anything with the slightest bit of bite to it. But he should have known not to expect the usual from the surprisingly easygoing doc. She curled up on the opposite end of the sofa with her dinner, and started watching right along with him.

All in all, it was a pretty fine way to spend a Friday night.

Fuck, who was he kidding? Even with all the questions and worries crowding his head, between the mind-blowing sex and her company, this was the best damn night he'd had in . . . Hell, he couldn't even remember the last time he'd felt this good. This . . . excited about what might happen next. There suddenly seemed to be a sense of . . . of possibility that hadn't been there before, and he liked it. Probably more than he should have, but he still had all those damn endorphins running through his system, and for the moment he was determined to just sit back and enjoy himself.

The food turned out to be as delicious as it smelled, and he went back for seconds, refilling her tea for her before sitting back down for the rest of the show. When it ended, they went to work on cleaning up the kitchen. While they washed and dried the things that wouldn't fit in the dishwasher, they talked about his case that had kept him busy that afternoon, as well as the lack of progress being made in the search for Shepherd.

She was frustrated, like he was, but worried about the bastard in a way that Alex couldn't quite get his head around. Yeah, he knew from Shepherd's case history, which he'd had Ryder e-mail over to him, that the guy had been through some serious shit. At nineteen, Shepherd's mother and boyfriend had kept the teenager tied to a bed for two days, during which time they beat and sexually assaulted him more than a dozen times, before a neighbor finally heard his screams for help and called the police. Shepherd was taken to a local hospital, and his mother and the boyfriend both killed themselves in their jail cells a few days later. When questioned by the police, Shepherd had told them that his mother claimed the attack had been her way of proving to him that she loved him and was the only woman for him, after she'd discovered he was secretly dating one of the girls in their neighborhood.

The woman had clearly been a psychotic bitch who deserved to fry. But as awful as Shepherd's history was, any sympathy Alex might have felt for the guy had been killed when he decided to endanger Brit's life. That was something Alex couldn't, and wouldn't, get past.

And the fact that he was really twisted up inside over what she was going through, instead of just protectively concerned, was something he didn't readily have an explanation for.

In fact, he figured it was something he'd be better off not even thinking about.

The cynic in him wanted to say that if anything, Clay Shepherd's story showed that love was something men were better off not knowing . . . or even looking for. But he knew that was bullshit. What had happened to that kid had nothing to do with love. That was just pure, fucked-up evil. The kind of thing you could never really wrap your head around if you were sane. That could seriously mess you up if you thought about it for too long. About why things like that happened. About why men and women carried the capacity for that kind of insane madness inside them to begin with.

But it had *nothing* to do with anything good and pure. With the kind of love that Ben and Reese shared. Or Ryder and Lily.

He wondered if the doc had ever felt like that about someone. If she'd already found the great love of her life, but lost him. Or if she was still looking, thinking he would come along one day. It made him scowl, thinking of her with some faceless jackass who swept in and wrapped her around his little finger, giving her everything she'd ever wanted. Everything a woman like her deserved.

When the kitchen was clean and the dishwasher started, she set down the dish towel she'd used to do the drying up and gave him a long look that had unspoken words jamming up in his throat again. The feeling was definitely one he was getting familiar with. It occurred to him that they'd stopped talking some time ago, probably when he'd gone off in his head, and had been finishing up in silence. There was a new sense of tension in the air, but he didn't know if it was coming from him, or her, or hell, maybe it was coming from both of them. She gave him time to finally make a stand and tell her what he wanted—where he wanted the night to go from there—but when he just stood there without saying a word, she turned her back on him and headed upstairs.

The entire scene was strangely reminiscent of what had happened just a few hours ago. But this time, Alex was actually thankful for the momentary reprieve. He was so raw at the moment, there was no telling what might have slipped past his lips if they'd started that particular conversation. They were probably both better off not knowing.

He smoked a cigarette while he sat out on his patio and answered a couple of e-mails on his tablet, before hooking it up to charge in his office. This whole time, he was still thinking his silence had been the right choice. That it'd been his *only* choice. But when he eventually made his way upstairs to his room, he couldn't ignore the fact that the sight of his empty king-size bed irritated the hell out of him.

Damn it, it just seemed wrong to sleep by himself when there was a hot, willing, incredible woman right across the hall. A woman who had given him the most intensely erotic sexual experience of his life downstairs on his dining room table. An experience he needed to repeat, *badly*.

He stood in the middle of his bedroom, shoving his hands back through his hair, his breaths quickening as he let his imagination go a bit wild, thinking of how it would be if he went to her. Then the panic set in, and he started trying to convince himself that some space for the moment would probably do him some good. If he wasn't careful, he was going to get in even deeper than he already was with her, right? And there was no way in hell he was letting *that* happen.

Too restless to stay still, he started pacing at the foot of his bed, fingers laced behind his head, every muscle in his body tensed with strain, while his brain just wouldn't let it go.

The way he saw it, he could continue to fuck her, and if he was careful, he could also share a certain level of friendship with her. But that's where it needed to stop. Anything more would be venturing into territory he would fight tooth and nail to avoid. When it came to relationships, he figured he'd been there, done that, and it sucked so bad he didn't even want the souvenir T-shirt. He just wanted it left in the past, where it belonged, and to get through the rest of his life in as whole a piece as he could manage. Judith had chipped away anything extra he'd ever possessed to give to another person, which meant things would be better for them all if he just stuck to what he knew and didn't venture outside of his comfort zone.

Stopping at the foot of his bed, Alex lowered his arms, rolled his neck across his shoulders, and exhaled slow and deep, forcing himself to chill the fuck out. Pacing a hole in his floor wasn't going to solve anything. And he'd reached the answers he knew he needed to accept.

Hell, there'd never really been any question of what he should do, had there?

Throwing his discarded jeans over a chair, he climbed into bed wearing his boxers and stretched out on the cool sheets, enjoying the slight chill from the air-conditioning vent as it blew across his tension-drawn body. Staring up at his shadowed ceiling, Alex couldn't help but laugh at himself when he realized where his thoughts had taken him. Here he was going on about what he was willing to give her, as if Brit were begging him for more, when that sure as hell hadn't been the case. Sure, she probably would have enjoyed some sort of show of affection after the sex, as well as a few nice words tonight before they went to bed, but what woman wouldn't have? That was simply the way they were programmed. It didn't mean she wanted more from him than he'd given her. For all he knew, she liked his big dick, but felt the rest of him was barely tolerable.

Shit, given the way he'd acted around her the past couple of years, why *would* she feel any differently? It wasn't like he'd ever made any kind of effort to show her who he was, because it'd been safer just to keep as far off her radar as possible.

But now that he'd touched her, he knew he'd been wrong in thinking sex would be the answer to his problems. It was his goddamn theme at the moment, since he just kept making one dumbass mistake after another. He'd been counting on this incessant craving he had for her to at least fade a bit after such a hot, thorough fucking. Two of them, actually. But it hadn't. If anything, it'd only made it worse, sharpening the ache until it throbbed like a wound under his skin.

Without a doubt, his entire strategy had blown up in his face, and now it was too late. He was already hooked in even deeper. Completely addicted.

And wondering how long he would have to wait before he

could get his hands on her again. Not to mention a whole bunch of his other body parts.

He must have finally dozed off at some point, because he woke up just after 5 a.m., drenched in sweat, his heart pounding. Sitting up at the side of his bed, he scrubbed his hands down his face as pieces of the weird-ass dream he'd been having began coming back to him.

He'd been treading water in the middle of a dark, violent ocean, trying to reach Brit's lifeless body as she was tossed about in the waves, her auburn hair streaming like skeins of blood in the churning sea. He kept shouting her name and trying to reach her, only to have a swell pull her farther away whenever he grazed her cold skin with his fingertips.

It'd been a harrowing, gut-shredding nightmare, and he had to take a moment to shake his head and laugh at himself when he thought about what the doc would make of it. There was no doubt some deep-seated psychological meaning to the dream, and no way in hell was he laying *that* in her lap. She already thought he was screwed up enough as it was.

Figuring he might as well get dressed and get in an early morning workout, since he knew he wouldn't be able to fall back asleep, he'd just reached out to turn on his bedside light when his cell phone started ringing on his nightstand. Knowing it had to be important for someone to be calling so early, Alex quickly grabbed for the phone, puzzled when he didn't recognize the number.

"Hudson," he said in a clipped voice. "Who is this?"

"Mr. Hudson, this is Director Stevens at the McNamara Clinic. We've had a problem here at the center. Dr. Cramer's office has been vandalized. One of our officers noticed the damage when he was doing his rounds and put the call in. I came down here to see for myself before notifying you, and it isn't pretty. I'm thinking this was definitely that Shepherd guy we talked about on Thursday."

Squeezing the bridge of his nose so hard that it hurt, he cursed under his breath. "What's he done?"

"Trashed the hell out of everything, and from the looks of it, jacked off on a photo she had on her desk of her and some friends."

Son of a bitch, he thought, scrubbing his hand over his mouth as his head dropped back. He knew that photo. He'd seen it yesterday, around about the time when he'd had her beautiful body spread out on her desk and his tongue buried deep in her cunt. It was a photo that had been taken after Ben and Reese's rehearsal dinner, all of them standing and laughing on the beach. Brit was wearing a sleeveless gray dress, and she looked phenomenal. The idea of Shepherd staring at that happy smile on her face while touching himself made bile rise in the back of Alex's throat, while a cold, sickening fear slithered through his veins.

"Was it just vandalism," he scraped out, "or does it look like he was searching for anything?"

Stevens thanked someone for a cup of coffee that must have just been handed to him, then answered the question. "One of my tech guys is going over her computer. He says that someone did an extensive search of her non-password-protected files about two hours ago, and that they also accessed most of her contact information for friends and family. He seems to have been searching for personal information about her."

Shit! The fucker was probably trying to get his hands on the addresses of her relatives, thinking she might be staying with them.

"Anything else?"

"He left a scrawled note on a piece of paper," Stevens replied. "Most of it's fairly illegible, as if his hand was shaking when he wrote it, but we've been able to make out a few phrases about how he'll keep looking for her, waiting for her. Typical stalker bullshit. Then there's something about how he's going to make her pay for not wanting him the way he wants her. That he'll, quote, 'kill the dark-haired fucker' he saw her with here at the clinic. That sounds like you, Hudson. You should be on your guard."

"I can take care of myself. It's Cramer I'm worried about."

"We all are. I've known Dr. Cramer for over a year now and I've always liked her. Just keep taking care of her, and I'll handle things here. One of my guards is currently putting a call in to the sheriff's department so that they can get their forensics team out here. Then I'll arrange for a cleaning crew to come in and do a heavy-duty job on the place. Should have everything back to normal for her by Monday morning."

Alex thanked him and ended the call, staring blankly at the far wall as he worked everything over in his head.

The bastard was getting desperate, and Alex was no longer comfortable with the idea of Brit being at her office without him there to watch over her. Damn it, he wasn't comfortable with her being out in the open at all in this town. Which led him to wondering how hard it would be to convince her to lay low there at his place with him until Shepherd was caught.

Better yet, he wanted her out of town altogether, at least for the weekend, and he suddenly knew exactly what would work. He had a buddy in Miami who had been asking him to come over and talk to a woman about a potential pro bono case, which Alex sometimes did for women who were in trouble. Thinking this could be the perfect way to get Brit away for a few days, Alex scrolled through the contacts on his phone until he found Diaz's number, then gave him a call.

The next call he made was to Ryder. Alex kept it short and brief, letting the deputy know what had happened at Brit's office, that he was taking her out of town for a few days, and that he wanted every last resource the department had searching for Shepherd. Ryder was cool about the whole thing, saying he knew where

Alex was coming from, and considering what had happened last fall with Lily, he figured the guy probably did. Hell, Ryder had been in love with Lily when her life had been put on the line, which must have made the entire situation even more intolerable.

He couldn't imagine how he would be reacting if he were in a similar circumstance with the doc. Even though they were only friends, and not very close ones at that, fury was nowhere near a strong enough word to describe how he felt about the way this fucker was messing with her life. The way he'd slunk in right under their noses and touched her things, violating her privacy. Her sense of safety. The idea of Shepherd being in her personal space, jacking off over her desk, made him want to howl with outrage and go for the guy's blood.

He was giving Ryder the weekend to find Shepherd, and then he was going to deal with the problem himself. Ryder had warned him on Wednesday night, when he'd taken Brit in to give her statement at the station, that he needed to stay back as much as he could and let them handle the situation. But so far they hadn't managed to handle shit, and he wasn't going to stand around doing nothing when her safety was hanging in the balance.

The more he thought about it, the more he realized Miami was a fucking brilliant idea. Shepherd's tenacity was worrying the hell out of him, and Alex just wanted her someplace safe. He knew it was a knee-jerk reaction, but he wanted her out of this damn town, if just for a few days. Needed to get her away, on his own, where they could take a moment to unwind without feeling like someone was breathing down their necks, watching them from the shadows, taking note of their every move.

Grabbing a quick shower, he threw on a clean T-shirt and pair of jeans, then walked across the hall to the guest bedroom, where Brit was sleeping. She'd closed the door, but hadn't bothered to lock it. The light from the hallway spilled into the shadowed room as he opened the door, and he could easily make out her sleeping form on the near side of the bed, her red hair gleaming against the white pillowcase.

Careful not to startle her, Alex sat down on the bed near her hip and reached for her shoulder, intending to gently jostle her awake. But just as his fingers grazed her skin, she cried out, throwing her arms up, as if she wanted to hold someone away from her, or shield herself.

He'd have thought she would shout Shepherd's name, if she was frightened, but that wasn't what she gasped. No, it'd sounded like she'd cried for someone named Jason to leave her alone.

What the hell?

"Damn it, Doc, it's me," he said in a low voice, as she scrambled back from him. "It's Alex."

"Ohmyg-god," she stammered, moving up against the headboard as she struggled to catch her breath. She blinked rapidly, as if trying to convince herself she was awake. "I'm so sorry. I didn't mean to freak out on you. I just . . ."

"What the fuck was that about?" He winced at the harshness of his question, his voice little more than a snarl, but the direction his thoughts were taking was seriously pissing him off.

"N-nothing."

"Don't," he warned her, shaking his head. He reached over and turned the bedside lamp on to its lowest setting, illumining the room in a muted glow. "Don't even think about it."

She stiffened at his tone, sliding him a worried look as she lifted her hand and pushed her hair out of her eyes. "It was nothing," she murmured, obviously trying to sound convincing. "I was just having a bad dream."

"About some guy named Jason?"

"Um, yeah. I guess." Her eyelids flickered, and he knew she was lying to him.

"Cut the bullshit, Doc." He rubbed his hand over the unshaven edge of his jaw. "Who is he?"

"Who is who?"

Protectiveness, along with a shocking dose of possessiveness, had his voice sounding even huskier than usual. "This Jason guy. Who the hell is he, and why did you try to protect yourself when you thought I was him?"

Tugging self-consciously at the hem of her short blue night-gown, which barely reached the tops of her thighs, she said, "Alex, it's the middle of the night and I'm half asleep. Why are you even in here?"

"It's not the middle of the night, Brit. It's almost six in the morning. And we're not discussing anything until you answer my question."

"You are so freaking stubborn!"

His tone was flat, but firm. "So says my ex-wife and pretty much anyone who knows me. So get on with it."

"He was just a guy that I knew," she said with exasperation. "We dated for a while. End of story."

His brows pulled together, creasing his forehead. "I don't remember you dating anyone named Jason."

She shot him a curious look, no doubt wondering why he'd been keeping track of the guys she'd dated since they met. "It was before I moved to Moss Beach," she explained, her tight voice making it clear that she didn't want to be sharing any of this with him. "He was a detective who worked with Ben in Miami. That was actually how I met him."

"What happened?"

When she started to look away, he reached out and gently grasped her chin, letting her know with his touch that he was prepared to sit there all damn day until she finally gave him the truth.

"He had issues with his temper," she finally murmured. "Ones I *should* have seen before things got out of hand."

He swept his thumb against her soft skin. "He hit you?"

"Only once," she admitted, staring at his chin while her face flushed with heat. "But once was enough."

His thumb stopped moving the instant she answered his question. He took a deep breath, forcing himself to stay calm as he lowered his hand. Very softly, he asked, "Where is he now?"

She lifted her wide eyes to his. "It doesn't matter."

"It matters to me."

She shook her head. "Leave it, Alex. He isn't worth your time."

"He's worth a hell of a lot more than my time, Doc. He deserves to have his motherfucking ass kicked."

Her lips slowly curled with a smirk. "I won't argue with that," she murmured. Then her mouth flattened, and she added, "But not by you."

He didn't say anything in response, and she pulled the sheet over her legs as she brought her knees to her chest, wrapping her arms around them.

"It's okay, you know. I wasn't seriously injured or anything, Alex. I got the hell out as soon as I could and never had anything to do with him again. I might be stubborn, but I refused to be a victim."

"Did Ben know?"

Her eyes went wide again. "God, no. He would have killed him."

Alex couldn't help but snort. "And you think I won't?"

"Yes."

"And why's that?"

"Because," she said quietly, staring back at him with those big, beautiful eyes, "it's one of the few things I'll ask of you."

He grunted, wondering why it was so easy for this woman to get under his skin. It was more than just the fact that she was incredibly gorgeous and sexy as hell. There was just something about her. About the way she smiled and laughed and looked at him. And when she looked at him like she was right now, he was damn tempted to do whatever she wanted him to.

Placing his hand on her knee, he gave it a light squeeze. "I'm sorry for scaring you."

"Don't be. I lo— I mean, I *like* the way you touch me." She blushed so hot he figured he would have been able to feel the heat against his fingertips if he touched her face again. The idea of anyone ever marring that tender, delicate skin or raising a hand to it in anger, whether it was Shepherd or some other asshole, made him livid.

And now he was more determined than ever to get her to agree to go away with him.

He noticed the way her chest rose as she took a deep breath, her breasts pressing against the silky material of her gown or nightie or whatever women called them. Then she scooted over a little, and pulled back the sheet. "Do you want to lie down with me for a while and get some more sleep?"

Now was the time to tell her about her office, but he held his tongue. He wanted to get her away so that she could enjoy herself, and that wasn't going to happen if he brought up the break-in and vandalism. She'd be too concerned with getting over to the clinic to check on everything, potentially putting herself in more danger, not to mention the upset he knew seeing her office in that kind of shape would cause her. Deciding to keep the information to himself until they got back, Alex reached over to flick the lamp to a higher setting, and said, "It's actually time to rise and shine, Doc. We've got to hit the road."

"The road?" she murmured, blinking against the brighter light. "What are you talking about?"

"That's why I came in here," he rumbled, pushing his hand

back through his hair, the gesture always a sure sign of his nerves. "I wanted to know if we can call a truce?"

She looked surprised, and then her lips twisted with a crooked smile. "Are we at war or something, Alex?"

He could feel the color rising in his face, and realized he was botching the entire thing. He felt like an idiot. "No, of course not."

She didn't respond, simply waiting for him to explain, and in a moment of panic he found himself wondering again if this was a good idea. Was it?

Fuck it. Of course it wasn't. The more time he spent with her, the deeper he was going to get. He knew it as surely as he knew that Mike was a player and his ex-wife was a bitch. But he still couldn't stop himself from saying, "I was, uh, hoping we could let everything go for a few days and just . . . get away. Something's come up and I need to head over to Miami today, and I don't want to leave you."

"Oh. Um, that's okay," she murmured, tucking a glossy strand of hair behind her ear. "I'm sure I can stay with Ryder and Lily or something. I'll be fine."

Fighting against the knee-jerk impulse to back down and save face, he moved to his feet and kept his gaze locked on hers. "But it wouldn't be fine with me. I need to know that you're safe, Brit." A wry grin ghosted his lips. "And I'm arrogant enough to believe that I'm the best person for the job."

Her beautiful mouth twitched in response to his husky admission, her eyes bright as she looked up at him. "I wasn't trying to say that you aren't. Ben thinks you are. And I happen to agree with him."

"Then can you get someone to cover your calls and come with me?"

She looked surprised again. "Why would I need to have my calls covered?"

He rolled his shoulder. "I think it would do you some good to take a break from it all while we're gone. No cell phones. No worrying about when the next call from Shepherd might come in. I was thinking we could stay overnight and make a weekend of it."

She chewed on that plump lower lip for a moment, which made him want to sink his teeth into it, too. "I *could* set my calls to go through the clinic's answering service and have Margaret Chin, one of my colleagues, keep an eye on them for me," she said after a long pause. "But I would need to leave an emergency number in case there was a problem with one of my patients."

"You can use my cell. I'll have it with me at all times in case Ryder needs to get in touch with us."

Giving him a small smile, she said, "Then I'll call Margaret when it's a bit later. I don't want to wake her up."

Before he could respond, she added, "So now that that's settled, are you going to snuggle up with me for a few hours?" She patted the mattress beside her.

Christ, talk about an invite. Alex didn't think he'd ever seen anything so completely . . . *enticing.* But he knew there wasn't any chance he'd be able to lay down with her on that damn bed and not have his dick inside her within a minute. It was as sure a thing as turkey on Thanksgiving and tears at a wedding.

Backing toward the door, he said, "I'll snuggle all you want in Miami. But right now I want us to get on the road."

"Now? Alex, the sun isn't even up yet."

"I know. We'll miss most of the traffic. So come on."

She groaned as she swept her long legs over the far side of the bed, running her fingers through her sleep-tousled curls. Looking over her shoulder, she asked, "Can we stop by my place on the way out of town? I don't even have a bathing suit with me. And everyone knows you can't go to Miami without a bathing suit."

"Don't worry. We'll hit a mall in Miami."

She gave him an arch look. "What makes you think I want to go shopping?"

He blinked. "You're a woman, aren't you?"

"Having a vag does not automatically mean I'm a shopaholic," she stated, rolling her eyes at him. "The two aren't synonymous any more than having a dick means a guy has to like football."

"Any guy who doesn't like football isn't really a guy. Unless maybe he's an ice hockey fan," he argued. Then he lifted his hands up and shook his head. "But I'm sorry for assuming. If you don't want to shop, I'll do it for you."

"Actually, I love to shop," she offered with a smirk. "I was just making a point."

Shit. He couldn't help it; he laughed. "More like busting my balls."

"Well, someone has to."

Hands braced on his hips, Alex gave her a mock glare from his side of the room. "You've been spending too much time with my brothers."

Brit snuffled a soft laugh under her breath, enjoying their playful banter. This was a side of Alex that she'd never really seen, since he was usually so quiet when she was around him and his family. She saw so much of Ben and Mike in him when he was like this, and it just made her want to crawl over the mattress and hug him. Of course, the hug would be followed by throwing herself at him, and as odd as it sounded, she didn't want sex to ruin the moment they were having.

"That's probably true, but at least I've got good taste," she drawled in response to his comment, moving to her feet and slipping into the short robe she'd left on the foot of the bed. "If a woman's going to hang out with a bunch of guys, she couldn't find a better-looking bunch than the Hudsons. You're all gorgeous and you know it."

He looked as if he'd gone a bit warm as he returned her smile, his color high. Then he shook his head again and snorted. "Whatever you do, don't let Mike hear you say anything like that. He's already got it in his big head that you think he has a cute ass."

"Can't deny that," she said wistfully. Then she winked at him. "But yours is cuter."

He dropped his head forward as a sinful laugh rumbled up from deep in his chest, and rubbed the back of his neck. She wondered if he was avoiding her gaze because her compliment had embarrassed him, her suspicions growing when he started to turn toward the door, clearly wanting to make his escape. But then he stopped and looked back at her, his green eyes difficult to read. "Hey, Brit?"

"Yes?"

He suddenly looked a little pained. "I just wanted to say that I'm, uh, sorry for the way I acted last night. What happened between us . . . It was . . ."

"It's okay," she murmured, hating to see him struggle. "You don't have to do this, Alex."

With a wry twist of his lips, he said, "If I want to fuck you again, I have a feeling I do."

She laughed, caught off guard by his honesty. It was blunt, but refreshing. Whatever else he might be, Alex Hudson wasn't a man who would ever lie to get what he wanted or sugarcoat the truth.

He pushed his hands in his pockets and held her gaze. "Anyway, what I was trying to say is that it was . . . incredible. I should have told you that last night. But you, uh, kind of fried my brain."

She tried not to smile, but wasn't very successful at it. Her lips tilted up at the corners, and she knew her damn dimples were showing when he slid his gaze over her cheek.

"I haven't had nearly enough of you," he went on to say in that deliciously deep, husky voice that was causing chills to sweep over her skin. "Not even close. So I'm hoping like hell that you feel the same way." He paused, searching her expression, then cleared his throat and added, "No one will need to know. It's none of their damn business anyway, what we do together."

He must have instantly picked up on her disappointment, because he quickly said, "Or tell them. I don't care. Just . . . do what feels right. It's up to you. Just, *please* forgive me for being an ass."

Brit knew she was making one of the classic female mistakes, giving this gun-shy man the opportunity to draw her in even deeper, but it was the damn "please" that did it. She would have bet everything she owned that it was a word Alex hadn't said to a woman in years.

"All right," she whispered, unable to say more. But it was enough for him. He gave her a breathtaking smile that was impossibly sexy, full of hunger and heat . . . and maybe even a little bit of relief, and then he turned and left her alone so that she could get ready.

As she headed into the bathroom to grab a quick shower, Brit was fully aware of what she'd just gotten herself into. That she had agreed to go away for a no-holds-barred weekend of decadent sex with a man she found impossible to resist. A man she was also starting to like . . . and even enjoy. Which meant she was only setting herself up for an even bigger letdown when it all ended.

But other than her worry about her own emotional state, what was stopping her from enjoying him while she had the chance? They were both single. They wouldn't be hurting anyone. And, damn it, she deserved it. Now that she knew just how incredible he could make her feel, she'd have argued until she was blue in the face that she deserved the hell out of it. It might sound bizarre, considering everything that was happening, but this felt . . . right.

Felt as if she was doing precisely what she was *meant* to be doing, and even with the Clay Shepherd nightmare hanging over her head, it felt unbelievably good.

She had no great tragedy in her life. She was an only child, and her parents were fine. Not overly attentive, but she'd never gone hungry or without the physical things that she needed. Other than Jason and Clay, no one had ever crossed a line with her, either personally or professionally. Her existence was just . . . there. All very neat and tidy and status quo. She threw herself into her work not only because she loved it, but because there had been times when she felt as though it was the only thing that defined her. That without it she would somehow slip away, disappearing into the background until no one even saw her anymore.

And, yes, she knew that while she was self-conscious about the size of her breasts and ass, she had a figure that made men take notice every now and then. But they seldom wanted more. She'd dated, but knew when a guy was only going out with her because he wanted to get laid, which meant it wasn't going to happen. And even when she did like a guy enough to go to bed with him, it seldom lived up to expectations. His or hers.

Now in her early thirties, Brit had actually started wondering if maybe there was some fatal flaw in her when it came to sexual relationships. If they fizzled out so quickly because the men had sensed that there was always a bit of herself that she held back. She wasn't a prude, but she'd never found it easy to just let go with a man, either.

Until Alex. And on a physical level, it had been incredible. Better than she'd ever truly believed it could be, as if he knew precisely how to create and mold and build her pleasure. Like a freaking expert—like it came as easy to him as taking candy from a baby—and she wanted to return the favor and make him feel good, as well. She wanted it for so many reasons . . . and for no other reason than that she wanted to see him happy. Wanted to see him smile again, the way he had just minutes ago in the bedroom. And if she had to take some risks to do it, then she would. Emotional worries aside, she was willing to take a whole hell of a lot of them.

Because there was something undeniable inside her that said he was worth it.

8

BRIT LOOKED AROUND THE SPACIOUS HOTEL ROOM AS ALEX LOCKED THE
door behind them, still in a state of shock. When he'd said they
were staying in Miami overnight, she hadn't expected anything
this beautiful. But Alex had spared no expense and put them up at
one of the tropical, five-star resorts right on the city's coast.

They'd stopped by an upscale shopping center once they'd
reached the vibrant town, and she watched Alex set the multitude
of bags with her purchases on the foot of the room's sprawling
bed, still a little piqued that he'd refused to let her pay for anything. His generosity had been completely unexpected, and she'd
found herself wondering more and more today about the circumstances of his divorce. She knew from Ben that the divorce had
been ugly, but other than Ben's insistence that Judith Hudson was
a raving bitch, they'd never gone into specifics about why Alex had
taken the end of his marriage so badly.

And *badly* was putting it lightly. He'd not only lost his career as an Orlando homicide detective, but he'd gone on to nearly kill himself with alcohol poisoning.

A shudder swept through her, and Brit pressed a hand to her chest, trying to hold in the panic those words instilled. *Gone on to nearly kill himself* . . . God, she felt so much more than just this churning anxiety when she thought of what was so very nearly a harsh reality for the Hudson family. There was also anger, fear, frustration—and above it all, an overwhelming sense of relief that he was still there with them. And while he might not be the care-free, always ready with a smile guy that Ben claimed Alex had been before his marriage, every day she spent getting to know him better, learning more about him, made it clear that he was so much more than she'd ever realized.

She knew he felt their chemistry. That much had been made pretty clear. But did he feel the connection building between them like she did? One that went even deeper than the mind-melting sex?

And if he did, was *that* why he was leaving her there at the hotel by herself while he went to meet with his old detective buddy, instead of taking her with him?

"You going to be okay while I'm gone?" he asked, jiggling his keys in his hand.

"Yes, of course. I'll be fine."

He'd explained on the way up to the room that he would need to head out for a bit, to meet up with the cop he'd come to town to see. She'd wanted to ask for details about what they were work-ing on, but had bitten back the questions, not wanting to pry. She was well aware that Alex was the kind of man who would share when he wanted, and not a moment before. It was a characteristic that'd been ingrained in his DNA, and while it might be frustrat-ing, the last thing she would ever try to do was change him.

He locked her in his piercing gaze, and his deep voice had a harder edge to it as he said, "You don't leave the hotel, Doc. Shep-

herd might not know where we are, but I still don't want you taking any chances."

"Don't worry. I promise I won't go anywhere but the pool."

"I won't be gone long," he murmured, looking as if he very
much wanted to cross the room and do things to her on the hotel's
massive bed that would have her screaming and begging for more
by the time he was finished. But he didn't. Instead, he headed for
the door, looking back at her only after he'd wrapped one of his
big hands around the handle. Then he said, "I'm glad you came."

"So am I," she whispered, completely stunned by the husky
tremor she'd just heard in his voice.

He left before she could say anything more, and as the door
closed behind him, Brit let out a deep breath and climbed onto
the middle of the bed, her arms splayed wide as she stared up at the
ceiling. She let the day roll through her mind, working back to
the moment when she'd awakened in a panic, and found herself
shaking her head. She simply couldn't believe what she'd told him
that morning. She'd never shared what had happened with Jason
with anyone. Not her family, or her friends. So why Alex? Could
she blame it on being half asleep? The stress she was under because
of Shepherd? Or was it something else?

You know exactly what it is . . .

Shoving those knowing words away, she focused instead on
why she was so comfortable with the usually dark, broody PI.
Alex was the polar opposite of Jason in temperament, which she
supposed could be one of the reasons his quiet intensity didn't
unnerve her as much as it should have. There was a kind of comfort in knowing that with Alex, what you saw was what you got.
He wasn't interested in wearing a mask to please you. He didn't
give a damn about pleasing anyone other than himself. And even
then, she knew he didn't live his life in the pursuit of pleasure.

In truth, he was one of the most complex, intense, arousing

men she'd ever known. If not *the* most. It was driving her crazy, this incessant need working through her mind to figure him out. She knew, deep down, that her "issues" with Alex weren't going to be found in her professional experience. There was no therapeutic solution to their problems. They were born in emotion, steeped so deeply in that confusing, terrifying swirl of maddening desire she felt for him that she couldn't find her way through to any kind of answer or plan.

She should run if she wanted to keep from getting hurt. Even though she knew he would never physically harm her, this was a man who, if she let him, could easily wreck her. And yet, she couldn't just walk away. Not without at least trying to break through to him. She'd made the decision that morning to give this weekend away with him everything that she had, and damn it, she was going to do exactly that.

Suddenly deciding that she could mentally talk herself to death while lying out by the pool as easily as she could right there in the room, Brit changed into the new black one-piece Alex had bought for her, threw on the matching cover-up, grabbed her bag, and headed downstairs.

She found a lounger by the side of the beautiful, palm-tree-shaped pool, and ordered a mojito. Then she read on her e-reader for a while, talking to a few people who stopped to make casual conversation, and simply enjoyed getting away from everything, the way Alex had said he wanted her to. But when she caught sight of a young man who reminded her of Clay, tension crept back through her muscles. Draining the rest of her drink, she set the empty glass on the small table beside the lounger, hoping the alcohol would help calm her nerves. But it didn't.

Despite everything that had happened since Wednesday, there was still a part of her that had trouble accepting it was real. She was angry at Clay for messing with her life, but she still hurt for him, too. For the boy he'd once been, and the troubled man he'd become. Did it mean she wanted him roaming the streets? No, she knew that at this point that wasn't possible. Somewhere along the way, Clay had lost his control or perception of reality, and now everything was so twisted up in his scarred psyche, he was no longer the same young man she'd met in that Miami hospital room three years ago. Instead, he'd become a troubled adult who Alex Hudson was determined to protect her against, even though it was playing havoc with his own life. And the *why* of Alex's choice could too easily drive her mad trying to figure it out.

She winced at the direction of her thoughts, deciding she was done with alcohol for the afternoon. It wasn't helping her think clearly, and it sure as hell wasn't helping her to relax. If anything, it was increasing her tension, and that was the last thing that she needed.

The heat eventually became too oppressive, and the constant chatter from other guests annoying, so she made her way back up to the room. She took a long, luxurious shower, enjoying the marble enclosure's multiple showerheads, and had just walked back into the bedroom wrapped in nothing more than a towel when Alex returned.

Flushing beneath the heated gaze he swept over her, she clutched the knot at the front of the towel and asked, "Did your meeting with your friend go well?"

"Yeah. I just need to get a file from him tomorrow, before we leave town." He pushed his hands in his pockets as he stepped toward her, his expression curious. "Why did you come back to the room? I was going to put on my swim trunks and catch you down by the pool."

She lifted her hand, gesturing toward her pink nose and cheeks. "Little too much sun."

The corner of his mouth kicked up in a sexy grin, and she loved the crinkles that fanned out at the corners of his eyes. "You look adorable in freckles."

"They're cuter on Reese," she said with a small, wry laugh. "She has the coloring for them. I don't."

He'd come to a stop when little more than five feet separated them, but now he came even closer, until he stood only inches away. As she tilted her head back to hold his gaze, he gave her a deep, measuring look. "Brit?" he murmured, his husky voice pitched soft and low. "Are we okay?"

"Of course we are." She sounded breathless, his warm scent making her mouth water. "I'm . . . I'm glad that I came."

He looked as though he wanted to ask her about twenty different questions, but only said, "You feel like going out?"

"What did you have in mind?"

"I thought maybe dinner and then we could hit the club they have here for some drinks."

"Drinks?" She tried not to frown, but God, she hoped she wasn't driving him back to the bottle.

Instead of getting pissed, he laughed at her expression. "It's okay, Doc. I'll stick to water. But that doesn't mean you can't indulge."

She could feel the heat rising in her face. "Alex, that would hardly be fair."

"You let me worry about what's fair, okay?" A devilish glint entered his eyes, and there was something in his expression that she couldn't recall ever seeing before. Something almost playful, and undeniably arousing, that made her bare toes curl into the carpet, her body responding so quickly to this man it made her pulse thrash in her ears.

"After all," he drawled, looking younger than she'd ever seen him, "I plan to thoroughly debauch you once you're tipsy. So it's a win/win situation, Doc."

She bit her lip as she tried hard not to smile, knowing damn well that he could read the lust in her. This sexy, easygoing Alex was even more dangerous to her equilibrium than his surly counterpart, but she was drawn to them both. And as much as she wanted to crawl into that massive bed and spend the weekend doing all that she could to get her fill of him, she was too curious about what dinner would be like not to say yes.

Feeling as if she were in an alternate reality—one where she and Alex Hudson were a blossoming couple—she agreed to his plans for the night. There was every chance it could blow up in her face at any second, but she didn't care. For this one stolen moment in time, she was going to be fearless and take what she wanted, to hell with the consequences.

They took turns in the bathroom to get ready, and Brit was still tingling with anticipation an hour later, as the hostess showed them to their table. The reaction she'd gotten out of Alex when she'd stepped out of the bathroom dressed in the little black dress he'd purchased for her that afternoon had been priceless. The strapless dress was made of a soft, clingy chiffon that flirted with her curves and revealed a lot of leg, while still looking classy. She'd smoothed her hair into soft waves that spilled over one shoulder, and she loved how she kept catching him staring at her body. Not just her cleavage, but the tops of her shoulders and the hollow of her throat. Her arms and her collarbone. If he hadn't already proven his attraction to her during the mind-blowing sex on his dining room table the night before, there would have been no denying it now. The feeling was incredibly heady, and she basked in the heat of his gaze, feeling like an innocent going up against the most intensely sexual male she'd ever come across.

"So are you a born and raised Florida girl?" he asked, leaning back against his side of their booth as they waited for their entrees to arrive. The restaurant was gorgeous and incredibly busy, but they had a booth near the wall of windows that overlooked the sea, the high backs of the booth affording them more privacy than she'd expected.

"Not at all," she said in response to his question, loving the way he looked in his white dress shirt, the top button undone and his cuffs rolled up on his masculine forearms. She wanted to reach across the table and run her fingertips over the thick veins that pressed beneath his dark skin. Wanted to trace them across the hard lines of corded muscle, trailing them over the powerful shape of his wrists, but forced herself to stay focused on the question. "I lived in the suburbs of Atlanta until I graduated. Then I came south."

"What made you move to Moss Beach?"

She laughed as she reached for the glass of white wine she'd ordered, after Alex had refused to let her have an iced tea. "I wasn't chasing your brother, if that's what you're thinking."

A smirk curved his sensual lips. "Then why?"

Brit noticed a group of women at one of the other tables eyeing Alex with appreciative gazes and whispering about him behind their martini glasses, and knew it was the kind of attention he most likely drew wherever he went. His dark good looks and potent masculinity were *that* intoxicating, making a woman long to be the one who captured him, body and heart and soul, and she had to take a moment to remind herself that this weekend was only about the now, and not forever, before she could answer his question.

"I, um, didn't live in Miami," she murmured, after taking a drink of her wine. "Just north of it. But after what happened with Jason, I wanted a fresh start. I was still trying to decide where to go, when Ben invited me over for a weekend after his move, and I ended up falling completely in love with Moss Beach. It just . . . it felt as if that was where I was meant to be. So I looked around at jobs, then landed the one with McNamara." Setting her glass down, she asked, "What about you?"

WITH A SHRUG, ALEX REACHED FOR HIS SODA. "AFTER ORLANDO, I needed a place that was mellow, without being in the middle of fucking nowhere. Mike was close by, Ben wasn't too far away, and our cousin Gary is there. I guess it just made sense."

He watched the way the soft glow of light from the overhead lamp played over the auburn strands of her hair as she looked down, her fingers fiddling with the edge of her napkin, and knew she was thinking something through. "What is it?" he asked.

"Nothing," she said too quickly, a small smile on her lips as she lifted her head and locked that stunning gaze back on his.

"Bullshit." His voice was quiet. "You're wondering about my divorce, aren't you?"

She immediately winced. "I am. I'm sorry. It's none of my business."

"I'm actually surprised you don't already know all the sordid details. I would have thought you had the whole story from Ben."

"Just that it was rough," she offered softly. "But he's loyal, Alex. He doesn't gossip. I just know that he was really worried about you."

"Yeah, well, when I self-destruct, I do it right." The moment the bitter words left his mouth, he shook his head, wondering what the hell he was doing. Was he really going to talk with her about this? And why did it feel so . . . right, as if she was the one person in the world he actually wanted to share this story with, instead of grudgingly coughing it up?

Shaking off the silent, confusing thoughts, he took a drink of his soda, set the glass down, and got the hell on with it. "I came home early one day from work and found my wife in our bed with one of the other homicide detectives I worked with. They were going at it so hard, they didn't even realize I was there until I pulled him off her and threw him through the bedroom window." A low, humorless laugh burst from his chest. "Good thing the master bedroom was on the ground floor of our house, or it probably would have killed him. As it was, he spent two days in hospital."

Her eyes were wide, brimming with questions, but she didn't say anything. She simply waited to see if he would share the rest of the story with her, and he heard himself saying, "After that, I learned that he wasn't the first detective she'd fucked. I lost my shit and confronted one of them at the precinct. We fought until he begged me off. I got control and walked away, but still lost my job. Can't really say that I *lost* my wife, since I was the one who told her to get her ass out." He exhaled a hard, deep breath, then said, "The rest you know."

He could tell by her gentle expression that she thought he'd turned to alcohol after his divorce because he'd been heartbroken. But that wasn't the reason why. He'd turned to drowning himself in liquor because of himself. Because of how fucking disappointed he'd been in how he'd handled the entire situation. Staying when things between him and Judith had started getting bad and he should have left. For not seeing things for what they were, then self-destructing when he'd let his anger get the better of him, going after the men his wife had fucked and beating the hell out of them. Losing his career because of it.

He'd been in a fog for a long time after he'd left Orlando, not really understanding anything, simply lost in his rage. But once he'd finally made the realization that he was angry at his own choices, and not with Judith, he'd been able to look at a bottle of Scotch without wanting to drown himself in it. That had been one of the best damn feelings in the world, and he'd started to get his life back on track, though he knew there'd been a part of him that he kept locked down because it was safer that way. It was the same part that shuddered with awareness every time he set eyes on the woman sitting across from him, and he knew the odds were strong that it wouldn't lead to anything good. But right now, he just didn't fucking care.

"So you became a private investigator," she said in a low voice, finally breaking the heated silence that'd settled between them. "Was that something you'd been interested in before?"

"When I was younger. But my dad had other ideas, and so I joined the force."

"I've heard that it's really difficult for a cop to pass the PI test," she said, just as the waiter arrived with their food. They talked about the test and its difficulties while they ate, the conversation easily flowing from one topic to another, and before he knew it they were done with their meal and he was signing the bill.

Impatience to get her upstairs and alone with him burned through his veins, but he'd promised her a fun, relaxing weekend away, and felt compelled to live up to his words. So instead of tossing her gorgeous body over his shoulder and getting back to their room as quickly as possible, Alex heard himself saying, "You like to dance?"

She blinked at him, looking curious about where he was going with this. "Do you?"

"Oh, I'm full of surprises, Doc." A warm flush spread across her cheeks as he moved to his feet and reached down to take her hand. The startled look in her beautiful eyes made it clear that this was the last thing she would have ever expected of him, and he was glad that he'd decided to do it. He had a feeling there weren't many things in this world that caught a woman as sharp as her by surprise, and he liked that he was one of them.

Heads turned their way as they walked from the restaurant, across the hotel's lavish, palm-tree-filled lobby, and into the upscale club that opened out onto the main pool area, the night sky lit by burning torches, their orange flames reflected in the still surface of the water. The band was good, playing a sultry song with lots of sax, and Alex led her onto the crowded dance floor, then pulled her into his arms, flush against his body. When they started to move, it came as natural as breathing, and his body responded with a will of its own, the way she fit against him more perfect than anything he'd ever known. It was so good it was goddamn unreal.

She looked up at him as she pressed closer, rubbing against his denim-covered erection in a way that should have been fucking illegal. "Alex," she panted, her low voice only just audible over the music, "what are we doing?"

"We can't keep our hands off each other, so we're going to enjoy it. In the middle of all this bullshit that's happening, we're going to take something good from it."

She caught her plush lower lip in her teeth for a moment, then asked, "Do you think it's smart?"

Something hot and thick was firing through his veins, his hands flexing as he dug his fingers into her hips. "I won't let anything happen to you, Brit."

"That's not what I meant."

He studied her through his lashes, and quietly asked, "Then do you care?"

The muscles in her pale throat shifted as she swallowed. "I should."

Pulling her even closer, Alex put his face right above hers as she tilted her head back. "Just enjoy it, Doc."

"For as long as we can?"

He lowered his mouth to her ear, flicking his tongue against the tender lobe. "That's right," he rasped, breathing in her mouthwatering scent. "Starting now."

She shivered in his arms, her soft voice husky with emotion. "All right."

Satisfaction poured through his veins like a drug, and he spread his hands low on her hips, loving the feel of her beneath the gauzy dress. He was imagining how she was going to look when he got her upstairs, the black dress pooling on the floor at her feet as he went down on his knees and buried his face in her slick, succulent cunt, when a loud male voice said, "Hey, buddy, can I cut in?"

Alex immediately stilled. Then he turned his head and scowled at the good-looking thirty-something standing beside them. "Who the fuck are you?"

"Alex, this is Tom," Brit replied, speaking in a nervous rush, her grip tight on his arms, as if she wanted to keep him from facing off against the guy. "We met today when I was at the pool."

"Great." His voice was little more than a guttural snarl. "Now tell him to get lost."

"Alex!" she gasped, sounding shocked by his rudeness.

"Asshole," the guy muttered, before turning and heading over to the bar.

When he shifted his focus back to Brit, Alex found her gaping up at him. "What on earth was that about?" she demanded, her face red with embarrassment. "All he did was ask me to dance!"

He wanted a hell of a lot more than that. In his mind, he already had you spread and fucked," he bit out, struggling to hold on to his temper. "If that's what you want, then go after him. But there's one thing you should know before we go any further." Shoving his hands in his pockets, he worked his jaw, trying his best not to sound like a caveman. But from the look on her face, that ship had already fucking sailed. All he could do now was say what he needed to say, and wait for her to make her choice.

Sucking in a sharp breath, Alex ran his tongue over his teeth, then forced three hard, gritty words past his lips: "I. Don't. Share."

9

BRIT STARED BACK AT ALEX IN A DAZE, UNABLE TO BELIEVE HE WAS reacting this way. She wanted to shout at him that he couldn't talk to her like that, and yet, she knew this had more to do with what had happened to him with his ex-wife than it did with him not trusting her. Using every bit of patience she possessed, she said, "I don't want him, Alex. Of course I don't."

"You're just too damn beautiful for your own good," he muttered, gripping her hip with one hand, while the other fisted in her hair, pulling her head back.

"What are you doing?" she whispered, as he put his face over hers again, so close their noses were nearly touching. His heavy gaze smoldered, burning with dark emotion while the music pulsed around them, sultry and rhythmic, and she shivered, unable to believe this was happening in the middle of a crowded dance floor.

After hearing the story about his cheating ex-wife, she wasn't surprised that he had jealousy issues. She just hadn't realized that kind of possessiveness would apply to *her*. Maybe she should have, after his reaction to McNamara on Friday morning, but she'd seen that as two alpha males posturing for rank. Though McNamara's power came across as pathetically weak when compared to Alex's. One was superficial, and the other ran so deep it struck a primordial nerve. A kind of raw strength that was ancient, feral, and animalistic, belonging to a predatory male in his prime.

He flicked a quick look over her head, and his gaze narrowed. "Ol' Tom is watching you, Doc. He can't take his eyes off you."

"I don't care about Tom. He's no one."

"Good," he muttered. "Then let him look."

She moaned, her knees shaking, as the hand on her hip drifted lower. His fingers spread, his thumb sweeping across the gauzy fabric of her dress, stroking the crease between her thigh and groin. "Alex? What are you—"

Her words broke off in a breathless gasp, her nails digging into his muscular shoulders as he quickly swept his thumb between her legs, where she was already melting for him. The thin material left little to his imagination, and he groaned low in his throat as he put his mouth close to her ear. "Fuck, that's sweet, Doc. You're always so wet for me. So ready."

She opened her mouth, but before she could say anything, he'd covered her lips with his. And, *ahh . . . God*, she'd been waiting for this. Despite everything they'd done together, he hadn't kissed her since Thursday morning in his kitchen, and she'd missed it. Missed his incredible taste and his almost savage intensity. This wasn't some tepid sliding of tongues to pass the time until they could do other things. This was a claiming. A carnal, explicit act of possession that said he *owned* her mouth in that moment, and it made her knees weak. The way his tongue stroked across hers, so deliberate and aggressive, while his hand curled around the back of her neck, holding her in place, created an ache between her legs that was going to have her melting into the middle of the dance floor any second now if she didn't put an end to it.

"Alex, y-you can't do this here," she stammered, turning her head to the side as she struggled to catch her breath. "Please, take me up to the room now. I need . . . I need to be alone with you."

He didn't say anything, his jaw tight as he grabbed her hand and pulled her along behind him through the crowd. When they reached the elevator, he pressed the button for their floor, keeping her hand gripped in his. A few other couples joined them before the doors closed, and Alex moved them both into the far corner, pulling her back against him as he buried his face in the curve of her shoulder, his legs on either side of hers. He was fiercely erect, the broad shaft nestled between the globes of her ass. She couldn't help but wiggle a little, the corner of her mouth curling when she caught the choked sound of his quiet curse near her ear. She was almost feeling like she had the upper hand, until the other couples stepped off on the fifth floor. Before the doors had even closed again, he started running his hand up the inside of her thigh.

Trembling with too many conflicting sensations to name, she somehow managed to say, "I've been waiting for you to touch me all day, and *this* is where you decide to do it?"

"This is just a preview of what's to come when we get to our room," he growled, sliding his hand so high he was able to slip his fingers beneath the drenched gusset of her panties. Heat filled her face as she realized just how telling her body was, her center already creamy and hot, her tissues swollen with arousal. "Trust me, Doc. It's only going to get better when I've got you alone."

"Alex, stop," she whispered, when he started tugging the soaked panties over her hips. She grasped his powerful wrist as her gaze swept over the mirrored walls around them, her wide-eyed, flushed expression reflected back at her again and again. "There could be a camera in here."

"I'm betting there isn't," he rasped, his soft lips moving against the sensitive skin just beneath her ear, "but I wouldn't care if there was."

Her head fell back like a flower on a wilted stem, thumping against his muscular chest. "You wouldn't care about some security guy getting a shot of my crotch?"

"You're beautiful. Why not let him look?" he asked, his low voice edged with a hard note of need, while he swirled one calloused fingertip around her clit in wet, maddening circles. "He doesn't get to touch it. Or taste it. He just gets to eat his heart out, wishing like hell he was the one playing with your juicy little snatch."

There was something there, beneath the hunger vibrating through those rough words. Something important that she couldn't quite put her finger on, like those damn games where you shifted a plastic case and tried to get the tiny metal balls rolling around inside into the holes. Each time she almost had it, it slipped right out, speeding away, leaving her with nothing.

He moved suddenly, and the next thing she knew he had her pressed into the corner while he knelt on the floor in front of her. Using one hand to hold her dress up, he used the other to rip her underwear, and within a second he had her panties falling away in pieces, leaving her lower body completely exposed. "God, Alex. Are you crazy?"

"Shh," he soothed, his dark eyes gleaming as he flicked his tongue over his lower lip. "I just need a taste. A quick one to hold me over."

She nearly screamed when he leaned forward and covered the most sensitive place on her body with that wicked mouth, sucking hard and hungrily, before licking his way to her tight opening and penetrating it, pushing inside her. He fucked her with a few lush, provocative thrusts of his tongue, growling against her tender flesh, then pulled it out and licked her voraciously. Long, hungry swipes from her vulva to her clit, and she knew she was wetter than she'd ever been, her body creaming with moisture simply because he was showing her how desperate he was for it. How much he wanted it. How much he enjoyed it.

Through passion-hazed eyes, she watched the numbers climbing on the digital display above the elevator doors, and somehow managed to groan, "Alex, *stop*. We're almost at our floor."

He growled something guttural against the moist cushion of her sex, then licked his tongue into her one last time, before jerking away. He was breathing hard as he stood and put his rugged face close to hers, and she could scent herself on his warm breath, the musky smell striking her as incredibly erotic. His green eyes burned into hers. "I don't want them touching you. And I don't want them talking to you. But I like the way other men look at you," he scraped out, his ragged breaths coming hard and deep. "You should take that as a sign that I trust you, Doc. It's not something that I do easily, but I do. I trust you to be straight with me. If you want to fuck someone else, you'll tell me. You won't go behind my back. Which means I can enjoy showing you off, making those jealous bastards eat their hearts out."

"I don't," she whispered, barely able to catch her breath. "I don't want to fuck anyone else."

His grin was deliciously cocky. "I know."

"How?"

"Like I just said, Doc. You wouldn't be here with me if you did."

She didn't wait for him to kiss her this time; she went in for it herself. His admission touched her more deeply than anything they'd done together to this point. It was one of the few glimpses into the inner workings of his mind that he'd given her, and she was drowning in it, loving that she'd earned this small bit of trust from him. He might not be spilling out his heart and emotions to her, but he'd opened up that first crack and given her something. Hell, he'd even told her the story about his divorce tonight, which had been heartbreaking to hear. And now it was her turn to give. To trust him and give herself over to this night with him. To stop worrying and overthinking everything and just enjoy him.

The moment the elevator doors slid open for their floor, he grabbed her hand and pulled her along behind him again, his long strides nearly impossible to keep up with in her heels. As soon as they were in their room and the door was locked behind them, he released her hand and moved into the center of the carpeted floor, then turned to face her. He unbuttoned his white shirt, leaving it hanging from his broad, hard shoulders, and said, "Come here."

Brit walked toward him, the heat of his gaze so intense it felt like a physical touch. Something tangible and real, warming her skin, awakening her senses. Without waiting for direction, she reached behind her back and started inching down the zipper on her dress. His heavy-lidded gaze moved hungrily over her body as he undid his belt, then unbuttoned his fly, and her breath caught when she saw that he'd gone without boxers. One second he was covered, and the next he was *there*, his cock rising up from the dark nest of hair, thick and engorged, the heavy, plum-sized head already slick with pre-cum.

Feeling bolder than she ever had before, Brit let the dress slither to the floor, then reached back and unhooked her strapless bra. Seconds later, she'd dropped the bra to the floor, the tiny black pair of panties she'd been wearing left behind back on the elevator floor. She stood before him now in nothing but her sexy heels, the light shining from the bedside table little more than a muted glow as it washed over her. But it was enough to make her feel the exposure of every tingling inch of skin that she'd bared for him.

"You are so fucking beautiful," he growled, the look on his

rugged face one of pure male need, deliciously primitive, hard with aggression.

"Thank you," she whispered, her throat shaking. "I think you're beautiful, too."

His mouth twisted on one side, as if she'd embarrassed him with the compliment. She wanted to say it until he finally believed her, but was distracted by the sight of him wrapping one of those big, powerful hands around his cock. He was shockingly hard, the thick veins pressed up tight beneath the dark skin, and she blinked with feral fascination as she watched his hand tighten around the burgeoning club of flesh, the veins on the back of his hand becoming more prominent as he squeezed. His heavy cockhead glistened now, darkening in color, so succulent looking it made her mouth water. She needed to taste it so badly she could feel the craving coiling through her body, a violent rush of hunger and heat. Needed to know what it felt like to hold all that raw, masculine power in her mouth, her senses overcome with his scent and texture and taste.

Lips tingling, she moved toward him with single-minded intent and started to drop to her knees, but he shook his head and stepped back. "*Don't.*"

Her brows pulled together as her jaw dropped, her disappointment palpable. "What? Why?"

"Because there's no way in hell I'd last more than two seconds in your mouth right now, and I have other plans for this hard-on," he grated, pulling on his erection with a rough, brutal-looking stroke that had to be painful. Then he let go, the long shaft springing up against his ripped abdomen so quick and hard that it made a slapping sound, the slick tip leaving a wet spot on his happy trail.

Sweet, shivering chills ran over her body as she drank in the sight of him, everything inside her going molten and hot and ready.

She could feel her juices slipping down the insides of her thighs, and she squeezed them together, her desperation mounting to an unbearable pitch. This was uncharted territory, needing a man this badly, and she wanted to throw herself at him and get on with it before she lost her nerve and ran for cover.

He pulled his shirt off those broad, sink-your-nails-into-them shoulders, dropping it on the floor before walking over to the edge of the room's exterior glass wall and grabbing the cord for the blinds. Brit blinked a few times, her mind going blank as she watched him pull the cord, yanking the vertical blinds to the far side of the room. She fought the immediate urge to cover herself as she stood before an entire wall of glass in nothing but her high heels, feeling like the world was out there in the glittering darkness, staring back at her.

He turned his head, his gaze heavy-lidded and dark, the irises like smoldering chips of ocean green. "Hands against the glass, Doc," he commanded in a firm, husky slide of words. "I want your legs spread and your ass in the air."

Her heart was racing, but she was too intrigued to see where he was going with this to refuse him. There was no one out there who knew her. No crazed patients or spying coworkers. There was just a moonlit stretch of beach and the endless sea, and with a deep breath, she did as he'd told her.

"Good girl," he murmured, coming up behind her. Then he dropped to his knees, his hot, calloused hands landing on her ankles as he tugged them farther apart, and she could feel the blistering intensity of his gaze heating her skin.

"Alex," she gasped, her palms going damp against the glass. "This is making me nervous."

"The window?" he murmured, stroking his hands up the outside of her legs.

"No," she whispered. "It's you. You're . . . you're staring at me. I can *feel* it."

"That's because I can't help myself, Doc." She could hear the wicked smile in his deep voice. "This pink little cunt down here is too beautiful not to stare at."

She snickered, her shoulders shaking. "That's such a raunchy compliment."

"Maybe," he admitted, his warm breath coasting over her skin as he shifted closer. "But it's the honest to God's truth. If you had any idea of the shit I want to do to it, you'd run screaming."

"I doubt that," she whispered, shocking herself when she arched her back a little deeper, pushing her backside closer to his face. For a woman who always thought she could afford to lose a few pounds through her ass and thighs, she apparently had no problem flaunting them in front of this particular male. But then it was easy to feel sexy when the man you were with made it his mission to ensure you knew exactly how attractive he found you.

"Jesus, Brit. I want to fuck you so hard," he breathed out, his hands flexing around her thighs.

"You already have."

A raw, thick sound rumbled deep in his chest, and she could feel him shake his head. "Not like that. I want you harder than before. I want to tie your gorgeous ass down and fucking own you. Drench you in me, in my sweat and my cum, until I seep into your pores." He brought his hands higher, rubbing his thumbs over her slick folds, and she could actually hear how wet she was as he touched her. "I want this pussy, Brit. I want to lick it, suck on it, cum on it, spank it, kiss it, tongue it, penetrate it, violate it, worship it, and fuck it. I want to do every single one of those things, and more."

"*Alex.*" Her knees trembled, legs teetering on the ridiculously high heels.

"Mmm. And you're pretty here, too," he told her, stroking a blunt fingertip up through her cheeks, until he was touching the puckered, sensitive ring of flesh there. "Pink and tight."

She moaned, her hands slipping across the glass, her body so hot it was like burning with a raging fever.

"I know a lot of women aren't into ass play, but damn, Brit. This beautiful little asshole was just made to be played with." She felt the tip of his tongue suddenly glide over the tiny hole and gasped, shocked by how good it felt. Dirty and illicit and embarrassing, but impossibly *good*, her clit sizzling with heat. He nipped her right cheek, then licked her again, harder this time, and she leaned forward, bracing her forehead against the glass as her pulse roared. When he slipped two long fingers into her pussy and moved to his feet, kissing his way up the trembling length of her spine, she was so overwhelmed, so lost in the moment . . . in *him*, she thought she might pass out.

He pumped his fingers inside her with devastating skill, reaching deep until he was stroking her G-spot, and she started chanting his name like a prayer, over and over. He buried his face against the side of her throat, pulling in her scent with his ragged breaths, and then he licked her, running his tongue from her shoulder up to her ear. Easing his fingers from the tight clasp of her body, he nipped her earlobe, and growled, "Brace yourself, Doc. I'm going to put my dick in you now, and you know it isn't gonna be easy."

She drew in a deep breath, clenching her teeth when she felt him notch his fat cockhead against her vulva, a scream spilling past her lips as he slammed forward, giving her every thick, brutal inch. His fingers dug into her hips, jerking her back against him as he ground against her cushiony flesh, and all she wanted was *more*. More of this feeling, of him, of being with him, getting lost in him, for as long as she could have it. It made no sense, feeling like this, but there was no sense in trying to deny it. The only thing that made it tolerable was that he seemed as wrapped up in it as she was.

"That's good, baby. Take it deep," he groaned, stretching her narrow sheath as he pumped his hips against her backside, feeding his cock into her in a hard, but steady rhythm.

"Hurry, Alex. Please. Just hurry."

He put his mouth to her ear. "For God's sake, don't beg me. Not now. I'll lose it if you do that, and I don't want this to be over too quickly."

"I don't care," she panted, sounding frantic. Desperate. "You can have me again. As many times as you want. I just . . . I need to come with you inside me. I need to feel you inside me when I lose it."

"You will," he rasped, nipping the side of her throat, his breathing harsh as he kept up the slow, hammering pace, hitting her deeper inside than any man ever had before. "You're gonna feel me everywhere," he vowed, sliding one of his thumbs into the crease between her ass cheeks. "You ready?"

"Ready?" Her voice was strangled. "Ready for what?"

He skimmed his teeth along the trembling edge of her jaw as he rubbed against that virgin opening. "Just my thumb tonight, Doc. You okay with that?"

She trembled, her muscles like taffy, but somehow managed to nod her head.

"I need to hear the words, Brit. You gotta tell me if you want this. Do you trust me?"

"Yes, I trust you," she whispered, her heart damn near pounding its way into her throat. She was nervous about trying something new, but undeniably excited. She might not trust this man not to break her heart, but she trusted him to know what he was doing with her body and to make it good for her. "Do it, Alex. I'm okay with it. I want to know what it feels like."

"That's my girl," he purred in her ear, just as the blunt tip of his thumb started to push inside the tight ring of sensitive flesh. It felt strange as the strong, snug muscles stretched around him, but she could instantly understand why lovers liked it. There was a dark, searing eroticism to it, her nerve endings firing with little electric pulses of shock that were racing through her body, before settling between her legs, burning in her clit.

"More. I need *more*," she gasped, pushing back against him. He grunted with satisfaction and shoved his thumb deep at the same time he rammed his cock in on a breathtaking downstroke, and that was it. She came, *hard*, convulsing in a mind-shattering climax that would have sent her crumpling to the floor if he hadn't wrapped his free arm around her, keeping her on her feet. She spread her hands against the glass, trying to brace herself as he quickened the pace, fucking her through the lush, tight orgasm until it went on and on, the almost savage thrust of his hips driving her wild. She hadn't thought it was possible for her body to feel more pleasure than she had on his dining room table, but it was happening. Maybe it had been the sensual night of foreplay leading up to this moment. Or the way he'd finally started to open up to her over dinner. Or hell, maybe it was just her growing addiction to his magnificent body and the unbelievable things he could do with it.

He came right on the heels of her own devastating orgasm, his big body slamming against her as he pulled his thumb from her ass and gripped her hips, nearly yanking her off her feet as he blasted into her with searing, violent bursts of cum that flooded her womb. The raw intensity of his climax shot her into another one, and this time Brit couldn't help but scream as her body got caught up in the crashing waves of heat and sensation, until she was so overwhelmed she couldn't even make a sound. For endless moments, everything was dark and primal and silent, and when she finally blinked her eyes open, she was surprised to find the front of her body plastered against the glass, Alex's muscular form slumped heavily against her back.

Holy hell. Did I pass out? She bit her lip to hold back a giggle, then sobered as something occurred to her. The man had nearly killed her just now with intense sexual pleasure, and he hadn't even touched her breasts or her clit. She swallowed, her head spinning with the realization that he could quite possibly take her even further. Steep her in even deeper, devastating ecstasy. It was as terrifying a concept as it was exhilarating, and she pulled in a slow, calming breath, refusing to let her nerves and insecurities take hold of her. She didn't want anything spoiling this moment— especially not her private fears that had no place in a weekend meant to be about nothing more than having a good time.

With a low groan, he shifted behind her, taking his weight off her as he carefully eased himself from her tight clasp, and Brit managed to peel herself away from the window. Then she looked down, mesmerized by the sight of his cum dripping down her thighs, splashing onto the floor beneath her.

"Jesus. I drenched you again," he rumbled through his ragged breaths.

"Mmm. I know."

Placing his hands on her shoulders, he turned her around to face him. Then he steadied her with a hand at her waist while he reached down with the other and rubbed the thick fluid slipping over her thighs into her skin. It was another sign of his possessive nature, and she knew he'd read her thoughts when he slowly lifted his gaze, locking that smoldering green with hers. One of his dark brows arched as he trailed his wet fingers up the center of her body, and he asked, "You ready to run yet, Doc?"

"No." Licking her lips, she stared up at his flushed, gorgeous face. "I can handle you, Hudson."

"I'm starting to see that," he murmured, the look in his heavy-lidded eyes dark and unreadable. But his body was telling her exactly what it wanted, his cock thumping against her belly as it lengthened and hardened. *Good grief.* Considering Alex was nearing forty, his recovery time was beyond impressive, and she couldn't help thinking again that his ex must be the biggest freaking idiot on the planet.

"Again?" she choked out, as they started to move in a half circle, trading positions, their gazes never once losing contact as he ended up with his back to the glass. Then she started backing away from him, toward the bed that was directly behind her.

His eyes narrowed as he watched her sex-flushed body move in the fuck-me heels, and she caught her breath at the look on his face. God, she loved him like this, when he was raw and in need. Loved watching his big, naked body move, the bunch and flex of lean muscle beneath his tight skin as he started to come toward her the stuff that fantasies were made of. He was like a lethal predator on the scent of its prey, perfect and sinuous and so intensely sexual it made her weak in the knees. Made her pussy flood with moisture, her breasts heavy, her skin tingling in anticipation of his touch.

When the backs of her knees hit the edge of the bed, she crawled onto it backward, knowing she was playing with fire as she struck a provocative pose, her body braced on her elbows, knees bent and legs spread at her sides, letting him see every part of her. And he didn't waste any time coming for her.

"By the time the sun comes up," he scraped out, coming down over her, "you won't be able to take a breath without remembering what it's like to have me buried deep inside you, fucking you raw."

"You're so romantic," she said with a laugh, swatting his shoulder as she fell to her back.

"Time and place, Doc." A deliciously wicked grin curled his lips. "Time and place."

"This isn't the time to be romantic?"

"I'll give it to you slow and romantic when I'm exhausted. Right now, I just want to keep making you scream. You okay with that?"

Grabbing him behind the neck, Brit pulled his beautiful mouth down to hers, and gave him her answer.

10

THE MOMENT BRIT OPENED HER EYES THE FOLLOWING MORNING, SHE had to admit that Alex had most definitely meant what he'd said. She could feel the echoes of his possession in every cell of her body, but it was a sweet, satisfying ache. One that brought a wistful smile to her lips. She knew, without any doubt, that she could be happy waking up like this *every* morning, for the rest of her life. Lazy with pleasure. Deliciously sore. And gifted with the most incredible view in the world.

She sounded like a sap, but it was true.

He lay on his back beside her, his face turned toward her, the white sheet draped low over his hips, barely covering his "junk" as she'd heard him and his brothers refer to their goods. Resting her head on her hand, she spent unknown moments simply watching him sleep, her heart pounding as she took in his deliciously masculine beauty. He was so hard and rugged and hot. Dark hair sprinkled his long, muscular limbs, but it was the perfect amount.

Not so thick that it made him look like an ape, but not so thin that you could miss it.

His strong jaw was dark with silky stubble, his sculpted lips parted for his even breathing. There was a relaxed quality to his gorgeous face that she'd never seen before. One she instinctively knew went deeper than the mere fact that he was lost in sleep at the moment. He was different here, in this vibrant city. She didn't know why, but he was . . . more accessible here. More open.

Loving the feel of his skin, she trailed her fingers across the sculpted ridges on his stomach, his abs packed hard and tight beneath his tanned flesh, and couldn't help but smile when he gave a husky rumble of laughter. Ohmygod, he was ticklish! The sound of his laughter and the smile curving his lips were too freaking adorable to resist. It reminded her of how he must have looked when he was younger, and she felt something inside her go gooey and soft with emotion.

"Ooh, someone's ticklish," she teased, leaning close and rubbing her nose against his.

Without opening his eyes, he spoke in a low drawl. "If you try to tickle me, Doc, there's gonna be hell to pay."

She gave a mock gasp of outrage. "Is that a threat, Mr. Hudson?"

"Nope." His deep voice was deliciously rough, and she was pretty sure that the way he looked at her as he lifted his long eyelashes was hot enough to make her melt. "Just consider it a warning, sweetheart."

"Hmm, okay, then," she murmured, quickly straddling his hips. "I've been *warned*."

Ignoring his narrowing gaze, Brit settled her fingers against his ribs and started tickling him like crazy. He bucked beneath her as he let out a soft growl, and the next thing she knew she was on her back with over two hundred pounds of badass male on top of her.

"You little minx," he bit out in a playful snarl, catching her wrists and pinning them to the pillow above her head. "Now you're gonna get tortured."

She squealed with laughter when he leaned down and used the soft stubble on his chin to tickle her ribs, while his hands tickled under her arms and behind her knees. He even found the horrifically ticklish spot just under her ass, at the tops of her thighs, and she laughed until tears were pouring over her cheeks as she begged him for mercy.

Thinking he was a devilish fiend, Brit was still caught in the midst of an almost painful fit of giggles, when he suddenly opened his mouth over one of her sensitive nipples, the strong suction he applied making her back arch, just as his fingers slipped between her thighs, sliding and dipping into her, stirring her into a froth of need. Too busy moaning to laugh, she lost all concept of time beneath his knowing touch. It could have been minutes that passed . . . Hours? Days? All she knew was that both her nipples were tight and wet from his wicked mouth, and she was hot and slippery between her legs, melting down the insides of her thighs, when he finally levered himself up and worked his heavy morning erection inside her. His hands found hers, lifting them by her head and pressing them into the pillow again as he pushed deeper, giving her every thick, delicious inch of him, until their groins were pressed tight together and she could actually *feel* the pounding of his heartbeat inside her.

Then he rubbed his lips against hers, giving her the sweetest, softest kiss, lifted his head, and locked that sleepy morning gaze with her own. And as a slow, steady rain began to pelt against the room's glass wall, he just held there for an endless moment, sharing her breath as he stared down into her eyes like he wanted to fall into them. Just slip right inside her, brushing against her thoughts and emotions, until he could fight his way to her heart.

"*Alex,*" she breathed out, feeling the burning sting of tears begin to fill her eyes again.

His beautiful mouth spread into an awed, heart-stopping smile, and he said, "You are the most perfect thing I have ever seen, Doc. You take my damn breath away."

And with those husky words, he started to fuck, their bodies moving together in a rhythm that was slow and raw and seductive, each plunging thrust of his hard length making her writhe. Making her moan. She came on a lush, slick wave of ecstasy, the shattering pulses of molten heat rushing through her, burning her from the inside out as she wrapped her legs around his lean hips, holding him to her as tightly as she could, both inside and out. Her lips trembled with emotion as he lowered his face over hers, his heavy-lidded gaze locked with her tear-filled eyes as his breathing grew harder, deeper. She held that burning gaze as if her life depended on it, willing him not to turn away from her. And this time, he didn't. He kept his gaze locked tight on hers as he went over, letting her see the pleasure shatter him as he spurted hot, powerful blasts of semen into her, working his cockhead against the mouth of her womb with short, jabbing strokes that made her gasp and cry out.

Brit stared up at him as if she needed that shockingly intense connection to live and breathe, and it was the most beautiful thing she'd ever seen, watching him get lost in her . . . in the way she could make him feel. Pulling her hands free, she wrapped her arms around him when he finally collapsed against her with a heartfelt groan, his body wrung out and trembling, her eyes hot with the tears still spilling over her cheeks. She wanted to stay like this forever, but knew they would eventually need to move, and so she simply held him tighter, desperate for every moment that he was in her arms.

"I'm crushing you," he eventually murmured against the side of her throat. "Sorry."

"Don't be sorry. I'm good. I'm wonderful."

"You most certainly are," he rasped, pressing a tender kiss to her lips as he pushed himself up on his elbows. Her body resisted as he pulled out, struggling to hold on to him, and she could tell by the look on his face that he didn't really want to leave her. With a rough groan, he collapsed on the bed beside her, his big hand landing on her hip. He gave her a possessive squeeze, before rubbing that warm hand over her stomach, higher, until he cupped a sensitive breast. Then he just held her as they both struggled to catch their breath, his thumb stroking her nipple, and she loved that he enjoyed touching her both before *and* after sex. That it wasn't just a lead-up to getting what he wanted.

When they were finally able to drag their damp bodies from the wrecked bedding, he carried her into the shower and proceeded to wash her with a sensual tenderness that made her just want to wrap herself around him and never let him go. And when he carefully washed the tears from her face, kissing each sensitive eyelid, her throat shook with so much emotion she didn't know how she managed to choke back all the words she wanted to say to him, but knew that she couldn't. Not if she didn't want to send him running from her as fast and as far as he could.

They had breakfast delivered to the room, then packed, and Brit was sad to be leaving. She'd hoped they could spend a bit longer at the hotel, but Alex explained that his friend had to head out that morning, but was leaving a file for him at his house, and they were going to drive by to pick it up before making the journey home.

"What's the file on?" she asked him, once they'd checked out and had climbed into the Range Rover.

"A special case that needs some pro bono work," he replied, starting the engine and then reversing out of the parking space.

As he pulled the Rover into the light morning traffic, she sat quietly and simply waited, wanting him to go on. When he finally got the hint, he blew out a short breath, shoved his fingers through his close-cropped hair, and said, "It's a domestic violence case. Some asshole who liked to beat up on his wife found a new woman. Normally that would be good news for the wife, but the fuckhead cleared out her bank accounts when he took off. She's been left with nothing, and has three kids to feed."

"So you're going to help track him down and make him accountable?" she asked, blinking at his profile in surprise.

"Hopefully. The fucker deserves to be behind bars." They drove in silence for a moment, both of them lost in their thoughts. But when he stopped at a red light and turned his head toward her, catching her expression, he asked, "What's that look for?"

"I don't know." Her shoulders lifted in a shrug. "I guess I just didn't see you as the kind of man who would do something like that."

He cut his attention back to the road as the light changed, and even though she couldn't read his face, she could hear the stifled edge of bitterness in his low voice. "Because you think I hate women?"

"No. I know you don't hate them. You just . . ." She struggled for the right words to say. "I just don't think you have a lot of respect for them these days."

He grimaced, and she rushed on, hating that she'd ruined the fun, relaxed vibe they'd had going. "I'm not judging, Alex. I mean that. After what you told me about your ex, I can't say that I blame you for feeling the way that you do."

He didn't say anything in response, and Brit silently berated herself for not keeping her mouth shut as they pulled into the driveway of a house that was so incredible, it pretty much left her jaw hanging. The irritated set of his mouth twitched into a lopsided grin when he noticed her dumbstruck expression, and he jerked his chin toward her door. "Come on."

She followed along beside him as he made his way around the

four-car garage to a beautiful wooden gate that was set in a high
Spanish-looking wall. She watched him punch a code into the
alarm panel set into the wall, and then the gate clicked open and
they went through, walking into a garden that was like something
out of a freaking movie. Palm trees and wrought iron arches covered in colorful flowers spread out around them, making it difficult to tell exactly how large the garden actually was. Alex grabbed
her hand, pulling her down one of the cobblestone paths that cut
through the flower beds, and it was obvious that he'd been there
before and knew where he was going. A moment later they came
to a secluded patio area with a beautiful outdoor table and chairs,
and Alex grabbed the thick file packet that'd been left on the tabletop. The file had been wrapped in a blue waterproof folder, since
everyone knew it could rain on the drop of a dime in Miami, even
when the sun was shining.

"So there's actually a file," she mused, wincing when she realized she'd just said the words out loud.

Alex turned toward her with a scowl. "What's that supposed
to mean? Did you think I was lying?"

"No," she said quickly, shaking her head, and feeling like the
biggest idiot on the planet. She could no doubt learn a thing or
two from Alex about the benefits of keeping one's mouth shut,
instead of blurting things out that were better left unsaid. But now
that she had, she owed him an explanation.

Blushing and stammering, looking anything but the educated
professional, she locked her gaze with his. "I, um, guess there was
a part of me yesterday that thought you . . . well, that thought you
might have taken off when we got here not for a meeting, but just
because you needed some space. I figured I'd talked too much on
the way over or something."

"No. Not at all," he muttered, looking as if he didn't quite
know what to make of her. Which wasn't surprising, since she

wasn't making any sense. "I wouldn't have talked to you if I wasn't enjoying it, Brit. I would have just asked you to shut up."

She laughed as she buried her face in her hands, working hard to get control of her jittery emotions, then forced herself to stop hiding.

"What was that about?" he asked, when she'd lowered her hands and met his gaze again.

"Your honesty." She tried to make herself smile, but ended up just blushing and blinking at him, instead. "It's, um, pretty refreshing, that's all. Painful sometimes, I'm sure. But at least a woman doesn't have to worry that you're feeding her some line."

He held her gaze for a moment, then seemed to shake himself out of a daze. "Come on," he murmured, grabbing her hand. "I want to show you something."

"Um, okay," she said, wondering where the sound of running water she could hear was coming from.

As they made their way deeper into the garden, Brit could only gape at the beautiful landscaping and design. When they passed through another flower-covered wrought iron archway and found themselves standing beside a rock-faced waterfall that fed into a massive black-bottomed swimming pool, she realized this was what she'd been hearing. Looking at Alex, she asked, "What is it your friend does again?"

"Believe it or not, he's a narcotics cop. He spent a few years down in the Keys, but now he's at the same precinct where Ben worked."

Her brows lifted with surprise. "And he can afford this place on a cop's salary?"

"Hell, no," he said, shaking his head. "Diaz comes from family money."

"Ah," she murmured. "That explains a lot."

He shot her a wicked grin. "It's fun to rib him about it."

She couldn't help but laugh at his mischievous expression. "Which means you do it every chance you get, right?"

"Well, yeah," he drawled. "That's what friends are for."

She was smiling like an idiot as she moved her body in front of his, facing him with her head tilted back. Reaching up, she threw her arms around his neck and pulled him down so that she could reach his mouth. Then she gave him a kiss that started out as a tender press of her lips against his, until the soft, sweet flavor of the exchange shifted into something hungry and erotic and raw, their tongues tangling and sliding as she tried to tell him without words what was happening to her.

"What was that for?" he rasped, his heavy gaze smoldering with lust when they both had to break away so that they could come up for air. He had his free hand on her hip, his fingers gripping her in that way that made her feel exceptionally needed.

"I just . . . I just wanted to say thank you," she replied a little breathlessly, loving the way he flicked his tongue over his bottom lip, as if to taste the lingering flavor of her mouth.

Something in his gaze went soft and warm. "What are you thanking me for, Doc?"

She kept her hands on the back of his neck, stroking her fingertips against his hot skin. "For bringing me here, to Miami. I needed it, and I've . . . well, I've had a lot of fun. Which, to be honest, hasn't happened in a long time."

For a moment, he simply watched her in that heavy, silent way of his, while his incredible, masculine scent went straight to her head. She had no idea what he was thinking, his dark gaze impossible to read. Then he surprised the hell out of her by asking, "You want some more fun right now?"

She blinked, trying to figure out what he meant. "You mean back in the Rover?" She'd never had sex in a car before, but she was willing. There was actually very little she wouldn't be willing to try with Alex Hudson, and she could feel the warmth of another blush building in her face.

"Not in the Rover." His eyes started to glint with a sinful heat as he tossed the thick folder onto a nearby table. "I was thinking right here."

She could hear her pulse rushing in her ears, her breaths quickening with sharp, almost painful excitement. "But we're . . . outside."

He shrugged those broad shoulders as a corner of his mouth kicked up. "No one can see us. No one will come back here. It's private property."

"*We* came back here."

"Only because Diaz asked me to."

"Where is he again?" she asked, biting her lip as she turned her head, scanning the pool area. The surrounding foliage was so thick, you couldn't even see the house from where they stood. But she knew it was there.

"I told you, baby. He's out of town."

"You're sure?" There was no mistaking the uneasy note of skepticism in the quiet words.

"Yeah, I'm sure." He caught her chin, pulling her face back to his. "Stop worrying, okay?"

"But . . ."

"Do you trust me, Brit?"

There was that damn question again, driving her crazy. Did he even know how intently he watched her when he asked it? How dark his eyes burned, making her feel as if he was looking right inside her, beneath her skin, down to the woman that so few had ever taken the time to see?

"Yes," she heard herself whisper. "I trust you, Alex."

Lowering his hand from her face, he took a step back, pulling out of her arms as he jerked his chin toward her and said, "Then get naked for me."

His voice vibrated with that low, husky tone of command that stirred her on some deep, visceral level she'd never even known existed inside her, and she couldn't resist. Standing beside the rippling pool of water, in the bright Florida sunshine, she reached behind her back and started lowering her zipper.

Heart thundering, she said, "You like ordering me to take my clothes off." It wasn't a question, but a simple statement of fact, and it made his eyes turn even darker, until they looked more gray than green.

"Damn right I do," he muttered, that dark, hot gaze moving over every vulnerable inch of skin she exposed, until the yellow sundress she'd put on that morning was lying on the ground at her feet, and she was standing before him in nothing but her heeled sandals, panties, and bra. "If I had my way," he added, "you'd always be naked. Now lose the rest of it."

Biting her lip, she reached behind her and unclasped the bra, letting it slip down her arms until it fell against the slate gray tiles along with the dress. Then she hooked her hands in the sides of her panties and shimmied them down her legs, carefully stepping out of them since she would have to put them back on when they left. Her sexy new sandals were all that was left on her body, and she started to reach down to undo an ankle strap, when he said, "No, leave them on."

"Hmm," she murmured, sliding him a flirty look through her lashes as she straightened. "You've also got a thing about having me in nothing but shoes."

"Right again," he growled, reaching out and gripping her hips. He pulled her with him as he took several steps back, then positioned her between his knees as he sat on one of the black, backless wooden benches that ran along a heavily scented wall of bougainvillea. Stroking his thumbs over her hip bones, he looked up at her, squinting against the sunlight as he said, "You are so fucking beautiful, Brit. Every inch of you."

"Um, thanks."

The corner of his mouth quirked, and she knew he'd picked up on her uneasiness in the throaty words. "You're going to learn how to take a compliment from me, Doc."

Bracing her hands on his shirt-covered shoulders, she playfully arched one of her eyebrows. "Is that another threat, like the tickling one you gave me this morning?"

"Could be." He cocked his head a bit to the side, studying her with those incredible eyes. "You ever been spanked?"

"What? No! Of course not. I'd probably slap any man who tried it."

"Hmm. That's too bad." He slid his hands behind her, squeezing the curvy globes of her bottom. "Because I'd love to turn this pretty little ass pink."

"You like spanking women?" she whispered, more than a little shocked at how . . . excited she sounded, as if the idea were turning her on. Hadn't she just said that she'd slap any man who tried to do that to her? And now she was aroused? What the hell was going on in her head?

"I'd like spanking *you*," he murmured, his smoldering gaze flicking over her with amusement, as if he was reading her thoughts. "And unless you tell me that you're beautiful, that's exactly what I'm going to do."

"Um, no."

"Yes. Right here. In broad daylight." He grinned up at her. "What's it gonna be, Doc?"

Her throat worked, the words he wanted to hear stuck. She turned bright pink. "I . . . can't."

"Sure you can. It's easy. Just look in my eyes and say 'I know my pussy and ass are beautiful, Alex. That I have sweet thighs and gorgeous tits.'"

"That's ridiculous!" With her face burning, she suddenly had trouble keeping up with everything pouring from her lips. "My ass and breasts are too big, and so are my thighs. And I'm okay with that. Really, I am," she blurted, in a rush to convince him. "It's why I still dress the way I do. There's no sense in not embracing it. But I'm not going to stand here and say that I'm beautiful. Not when I'm with someone who looks as incredible as you do."

ALEX STARED UP AT HER IN A MILD STATE OF SHOCK, HIS LIPS PARTED, unable to believe she'd just said those words to him. "I'm fucking far from incredible, Doc. But it's the perfect word to describe you."

Without giving her any warning, he suddenly flipped her over his lap, her surprised yelp blending with the soft roar of the nearby waterfall. "And before we're done here, those words are gonna be tripping off your tongue, baby girl."

With his heart pounding, he watched her skin turn pinker as he stroked his hand over her feminine curves, soaking up the creamy softness. "This ass is as prime as it gets," he groaned, torturing himself by taking it slow. But he had a point to prove, damn it. He wasn't going to rush this. Slipping two fingers between the lush cheeks, he trailed them over the sensitive little hole there, laughing when she jolted.

"Shh, stay still," he murmured. "I just want to touch you here. That's all. I won't put my thumb inside you like I did last night."

"*Oh.*"

His mouth twitched at the note of disappointment in her breathless voice that she didn't quite manage to disguise. He loved that she'd enjoyed the ass play in the hotel room, and was determined to take it further once they were back at the condo. But that wasn't the lesson he wanted to teach her right now.

Turning her over, he lifted her against his chest and shifted to the side, throwing his leg over the bench so that he was straddling it. Then he rose up a little and laid her down against the dark wood, before sitting again at her sandal-covered feet.

She lay with her arms at her sides, her knees pressed together and bent, so that there was room for him on the bench. "Spread your legs for me, Doc. Show me that pink little pussy."

She gave a breathless laugh. "You really do have such a dirty mouth, Alex."

He shot her a cocky smile. "Dirty, but talented, right?"

She shook her head as she tilted it back, the crooked grin on her lips making his chest tight. He didn't know how it was possible, but she got more beautiful every fucking time he looked at her. It wasn't normal, but he wasn't complaining. Not when he had her laid out before him like a fucking bounty. His breaths were getting deeper . . . rougher, his blood chugging thick and heavily through his veins. He was just about to repeat his command when she finally did as he'd told her to, letting her legs fall open. Soaking in the sight of her spread wide open for him, he drew her soft thighs over his muscular ones and scooted forward, so that she was within easy reach.

She looked like a goddamn goddess, naked in the lush green garden, dappled in sunlight, and he reached up, closing his hands around her mouthwatering breasts. He massaged the firm mounds, stroking her velvety nipples with his thumbs, before running his hands lower, over the sexy curve of her belly and around her hips, gripping her so tightly for a moment that she gasped.

"Sorry," he scraped out of his tight throat, immediately relaxing his grip. His chest started to rise and fall a little harder.

"'S okay," she murmured dreamily, lifting her head so that she could look at him as she trailed her fingertips over the backs of his hands, her touch soothing and light. "You didn't hurt me.

I'm just . . . oversensitive right now. You've got me feeling like a live wire."

A breathless laugh rumbled up from his chest. "Me, too, Doc. Me, too."

He leaned over her then, pressing his open mouth against her navel as he ran his hands down her soft thighs, loving the way she felt against his palms. Her head fell back again as he pushed her thighs a little wider apart, then drew his hands back up their insides, until his fingertips were stroking the smooth, glossy lips of her cunt. Pushing two fingers inside the tight little hole nestled there, he watched as he stretched the pink, tender flesh open, thinking she was the most perfect thing he'd ever seen.

"You're staring again," she said with a soft catch in her voice. "I can *feel* it."

No, he was memorizing. Committing it in detail. Tattooing the sight before him into the very fabric of his brain, wanting it to seep into his blood and sweat and tears. Into every part of him, so that he couldn't ever lose it.

Pulling his fingers free, he loved the way her plush, cushiony muscles clenched down on him, trying to hold him inside. She had such a sweet, hungry cunt, and he had a feeling that no matter how many times he had her, he would always want more. She was simply that addictive. That intoxicating.

"Eyes open," he growled, pushing his fingers in his mouth and sucking them clean before slipping them back inside her. He pushed them deep, undone by the feel of her. "I want you to watch me fingering this sweet pussy. See how wet you get for me? How bright and pink? Jesus, Brit, you drive me fucking crazy."

She panted, biting her lower lip, her heavy eyes wild with need as she locked her stormy gaze with his.

"I know. Trust me, baby, I know," he groaned, pulling his fingers free again. He ripped his shirt off, tossing it on the ground. Then he grasped her hips, his head already dipping as he lifted her lower body off the bench. At the first touch of his tongue to that slippery flesh between her thighs, he made a hard, thick sound of hunger deep in his chest, and buried his face against her. She was so fucking exquisite, melting into sweet, hot liquid, and he couldn't get enough. He could have eaten Brit Cramer out for the rest of his days with a fucking smile on his face, happy to keep tonguing and licking and sucking on her juicy pussy. And the fact that she had no idea exactly how incredible she was only made her that much more wonderful.

"Lift up on your elbows," he grated against her drenched folds, the lower half of his face already wet with her cream. "I want you watching what I do to you."

He didn't just want it, he *needed* it. Needed her to see every intimate detail of what he was doing to her. See the way his tongue swirled around her pulsing clit, over and over. Watch it penetrate the tiny, quivering hole before he sank it deep. He needed her to see how desperate he was for it. How badly he craved it, because it'd *never* fucking been like this for him before, and he needed her to *know* that, damn it. And since he could never find the right fucking words to say to her, he was going to show her instead.

Damn near shaking apart with everything that was running through him, utterly destroying him, Alex suddenly reared up and grabbed her, scooping her against his chest, where his heart was beating like a fucking freight train. "I need you on my dick. *Now*," he snarled, too far gone to control the harshness of his voice as he ripped his jeans open and notched his broad cockhead against her, then slammed her down on him so hard it made her cry out.

"Shit, I'm sorry," he gasped, pulling her tight against him with his arms wrapped around her back, his face buried in the curve of her shoulder. "I didn't mean to hurt you. I just . . . Damn it, I just needed . . . just needed to . . ."

"Shh, it's okay," Brit whispered in his ear, curving her hands over his wide, muscular shoulders. She could sense the crisis in him, feel it burning against her, but wasn't sure what had caused it. Whatever the reason, she was thrilled that he held her like she was the answer, something hot and tender melting in her chest, the sensation so sweet and sharp it made her eyes prickle with tears.

God, she was such an emotional wreck these days, crying at everything that happened, but there was no controlling it. She felt as though a dam had been broken open inside her, and now years' worth of pent-up longing was rushing out, impossible to contain, the feeling only growing more intense as he started to lift her up and down, moving her on his impossibly thick, textured shaft, his hips pumping in a counter rhythm to her own that was sharpening the sweet, piercing ache inside her.

Sniffing to hold back her emotional flood, she kissed her way up the strong, corded side of his hot throat, loving the power she could feel coursing beneath her sensitive lips. It filled him, thrumming through his blood and bones, in every part of him. Visceral and raw and wild. His chest moved like a bellows against hers, his hands stroking down her back, only to stop and clutch at her, squeezing her to him until her breasts were crushed against his heat-glazed chest, before resuming their almost frantic touches across her skin, as if he wanted to both hold and pet her at the same time, all the while keeping up his powering rhythm into her body.

"I love the way you feel against me . . . *inside me*," she told him, trailing her lips along the hard, stubbled line of his jaw, then up to the corner of his mouth. The broken groan that burst from his chest was almost . . . mournful, his arms tightening around her as he turned his head and caught her mouth with his, sinking his tongue inside to claim that breathless space for his own. It was a deep, drugging, deliciously scalding kiss, and she completely lost track of time as his mouth worked over hers, ravaging her, eating at the breathless sounds that she made. She could taste herself on his lips, salty and rich, and it only made her burn hotter for him, her inner muscles clasping his beautiful cock so tightly it made him gasp.

"Brit," he growled in a choked, throaty voice, pressing his forehead against hers. "Christ, you're killing me, baby girl. Fucking destroying me."

"I feel the same way," she whispered, shivering when she felt the change in the air, and she knew what was coming. One second they were moving in this raw, powerful rhythm in the bright, brilliant sunshine, and in the next it started to rain with a soft misting of drops, the way it could only do in Florida. The rain steamed against their skin, heat layering on heat, the sun somehow shining even brighter through the clouds, while the air became moist and thick with emotion as they stared deep into each other's eyes, their bodies moving with perfect timing. A voluptuous give-and-take that felt as natural as breathing.

Something was happening. Something . . . powerful. Deep. And scary as hell, as much for her as she sensed it was for him. But they didn't turn away from it. She knew he would eventually, and she would try to be ready. To protect herself. To be prepared. But right now, in this heady, sensual moment, he was right here with her, completely lost in her, and that was all that mattered. All that she cared about.

She came first, the deep, rhythmic pulses of her orgasm milking his heavy cock until he'd followed her over, crashing hard and thick inside her, giving her every drop. She loved staring into his face and watching him come, his pleasure so visceral and raw, evident in the rigid line of his jaw and the wild, smoldering intensity of his gaze, while his body poured itself inside her again and again and again.

Leaning forward, she touched her trembling lips to his, and he fed his guttural groans into her mouth as he took control, his arms crushing her against him as he devoured her, sliding his tongue inside her as though she was the most necessary, delicious thing that he'd ever tasted. They kissed until their hearts had slowed, completely lost in each other. And she had a strong feeling they would have stayed like that for untold hours, if the skies hadn't decided in that moment to fully crack open.

"The rain!" she gasped, blinking against the lashing sting of raindrops that were pelting her face. "It's coming down harder!"

"We better hurry," he said with a deep-grooved grin that was unbearably beautiful, and they were like fumbling teenagers as he tried to help her with her dress. He snatched his T-shirt from the ground, wrapping it around the folder to keep it dry, then grabbed her hand and pulled her along behind him. They laughed as they ran to the car, soaked to the bone. He pulled a few beach towels that he kept in the back of the Range Rover out for them to use to dry off as much as they could, before slipping his shirt back on. Then she grabbed two extra towels to place on his seats so that they didn't destroy the beautiful leather.

Using the brush she had in her purse to work out the tangles in her wet hair, Brit leaned toward the vents he'd set on a low heat to chase off her chill, a goofy grin on her face as she thought about how much fun they'd had. She hated that the weekend was already over, but refused to ask him to stay longer, knowing he had responsibilities he needed to get back to. And as hard as she'd tried not to think about it while they'd been enjoying themselves, there was still the Clay Shepherd issue that they had to deal with. From what

Alex had told her on their way over, she knew Clay was still in hiding. He hadn't returned to his dorm room since trying to kidnap her on Wednesday night, and although the Volkswagen that was registered in his name was still parked at the university, the sheriff's department suspected that he'd purchased another vehicle secondhand, since bank records showed that a large sum of money had been withdrawn from his savings account on Wednesday morning.

Was he living in whatever car he might have bought? Had he hurt anyone else? Had he harmed himself? Her head ached as the troubling questions pressed in on her, and she shoved them from her mind, knowing there would be time enough to worry when they were back in Moss Beach. Right now, she just wanted to enjoy the simple pleasure of having Alex sitting beside her, a sexy grin on his lips whenever he took his attention off the road to glance her way. Which he was doing often enough to make her blush like a schoolgirl. *Gah!* It was embarrassing, and she knew Ben would have been teasing the hell out of her if he could see her like this, but she was too freaking happy at the moment to care.

They grabbed some lunch to go from a nearby Miami Subs, chatting easily about simple things like movies and their favorite beaches while they ate in the car, the rain now little more than a light patter against the windows, the air flowing through the vents set to cool as the inside of the cab heated from the sun. She had thought the plan was to head straight to the highway and home once they were finished with lunch, but was surprised when she realized he was driving toward Ben's old precinct.

Confusion creased her brow. "What are we doing here?" she asked, as he parked the Range Rover in a visitor's space near the wide front steps that led up to the modern, glass-fronted building.

"I told Ben I'd take care of something for him," he replied, leaving the car running as he opened his door.

"For Ben?" she asked when he turned her way after climbing out. There was a wary note of suspicion in her voice that she knew he was purposely ignoring, which just made her even more apprehensive over what he was doing here.

"Won't take a second," he told her with a quick smile. "Just wait for me here."

He shut the door before she could get another word out, and Brit watched through narrowed eyes as his long legs made short work of the steps before he disappeared inside the building. She knew he wouldn't have any trouble getting past the department's security, given that everyone there knew him as Ben's brother, which only heightened her nerves. He had friends in this place, which meant he could get away with a hell of a lot, and her imagination ran wild.

Needing to see for herself that everything was okay, she started to open her door, then stopped, half convinced that she was being ridiculous. Yeah, the stop by the precinct was unexpected, but that didn't mean Alex hadn't spoken to Ben before they left Moss Beach and was actually here to do a favor for his brother. Just because she and Alex hadn't talked about it didn't mean the brothers hadn't spoken. And, really, wasn't she being a bit presumptuous to think that Alex would go out of his way to confront one of her exes? Wouldn't that imply that he felt something more for her than mere lust?

Before she could make heads or tails of her jumbled thoughts, Alex came back through one of the two sets of double doors at the building's entrance, and her eyes shot wide with shock when she saw him shaking out his right hand. *No!* It wasn't possible . . . Was it?

"What the hell did you do?" she demanded the instant he opened his door.

He flashed her a sharp smile, but didn't answer the question as he climbed in and shut the door, then put on his seat belt.

"Alex Hudson, you didn't," she wheezed, her lungs locking down on her when he curled his right hand over the steering wheel and she saw the blood smeared across his knuckles.

"Didn't what?" he asked, acting as if nothing was wrong as he reversed out of the space. He'd just put the Range Rover into drive when the far set of double doors were flung open and Jason came charging out of the building, blood dripping down the lower half of his face from his swollen nose.

"Holy shit!" she squeaked, gripping her seat belt so tightly she was surprised she hadn't wrenched it loose. Jason's furious gaze landed on the idling Rover, and he took one stunned look at her sitting in the passenger's seat, stumbling to a stop at the top of the steps, before his dark eyes cut sharply toward Alex.

"Come on, you son of a bitch," Alex muttered under his breath, and she knew he was ready to get out and give Jason the fight he'd come looking for. "You want more?"

Jason licked his lips as he looked from Alex to her and then back to Alex again. He was still lean and in good shape, though she was happy to see that he didn't strike her as being as handsome as he once had. But then, he didn't look too great with blood dripping from his nose. In fact, he looked pissed . . . and, if she wasn't mistaken, more than a little scared. His Adam's apple bobbed in his throat, and then he suddenly turned around and headed back inside, running like a dog with his tail between his legs, and she knew why. He'd finally realized that Alex's attack hadn't been unprovoked. It'd been for *her*. Because of what he'd done to her.

"I know you asked me not to mess with him," Alex murmured in a low voice, sliding her a worried look. "But I *needed* to do that, Doc. Diaz knows him and was able to tell me where and when I could find him. He even had a few of the other detectives making sure the jackass didn't leave before we got here, because he understood why I needed to do it." He kept his gaze locked on hers. "You forgive me?"

"Of course. There's actually nothing to forgive. But . . ."

He worked his jaw. "But what?"

"It's just that . . . I can't help thinking that you got in trouble for doing something like this before." A worried frown tightened her expression as she rubbed her palms over her thighs. "After the thing with your ex, you went and got in a fight at the precinct. It's the same thing all over again."

She doubted he would have been able to convince her otherwise with nothing but words. But he gave her more than that, the warmth in his eyes and the lopsided grin on his beautiful mouth beginning to loosen the knots in her stomach before he even started to explain. "You're wrong," he said with firm conviction. "I get how you might think that, but you can't compare the two, Doc. What happened five years ago—that was for *me*. For my . . . Hell, honey, it was for all the *wrong* reasons. But this was right, Brit. I wish it hadn't been necessary, but it was, and there's no way in hell I'm ever gonna regret it."

Her lips trembled with a wobbly, emotional smile and she nodded, letting him know she understood. Neither of them said anything more as he finally gave the car some gas and they pulled out of the parking lot, heading back to the highway. She leaned her head back against the headrest and closed her eyes, fighting a sudden rush of tears that had nothing to do with being upset. No, they were the vibrant, happy kind that came when something that felt unbelievably good or satisfying happened. It might have been a completely caveman kind of move that Alex had just pulled, but she'd have been lying through her teeth if she said she hadn't enjoyed it. What was that saying? *If there's one thing a bully understands, it's a bigger bully.* It was true, even though she knew that wasn't where Alex had been coming from.

He hadn't gone after Jason as a bully. He'd gone after him as a man who wasn't willing to stand by while another man treated women like shit, and it made him all the more incredible in her eyes. Maybe that was mercenary of her, but she didn't care.

What she *did* care about was Alex. And she was going to keep on caring, till the bitter end.

Was it going to hurt when he walked away? Of course it would. After the time that she'd spent with him this weekend, it was going to hurt like a freaking bitch.

But would it have been worth it?

All she could say was that in the end, whatever happened, whatever pain she might have to learn to deal with, she would have no regrets for taking a chance on him.

No matter how things turned out between them, Brit was going to remember this trip as one of the best she'd ever had.

11

WHILE A PART OF BEN HUDSON WAS GLAD TO BE HOME, SO THAT HE could do his part in making sure that Clay Shepherd was apprehended and put behind bars, there was a big part of him that missed having his beautiful wife all to himself on the secluded beach where they'd vacationed. They weren't meant to have come home until Monday night, but both he and Reese had felt that heading back early was the right thing to do, given the circumstances.

Not just because Ben was the sheriff. No, their decision had more to do with the fact that Brit Cramer was their friend and they both cared about her well-being.

Scott Ryder had the investigation well under way, and even though it was proving to be a frustrating one, the deputy was doing a great job, just as Ben had known he would. Alex might be bitching about their progress, but Ben knew Ryder was doing everything that could be done. The former special ops soldier could have easily gone into business for himself, providing exceptional personal and technical security to the wealthy elite, but he'd chosen to remain a deputy in the sleepy little beach town where he wanted to raise a family with his wife. Ben was thankful as hell to have him, and he understood where Ryder was coming from. When a man had the right woman by his side, a meaningful future, and a job that let him go to bed each night knowing he'd made a difference, nothing else mattered.

He and Ryder were currently sitting in Ben's home office, waiting to hear back from the department's tech guys, who were working on a phone trace for a call that had come through on Brit's office number just that morning. A rambling, ugly message had been left with the McNamara Clinic's answering service, which Ryder was already monitoring. A possible sighting had also been made at one of the local campgrounds, confirming their suspicions that Shepherd was either living rough or in a vehicle. Although an initial search of the site hadn't landed them Shepherd, they were hoping they could place him at the campsite through its pay phone once the trace came through.

Sitting with his hip perched on the edge of his desk and his arms crossed over his chest, Ben shook his head as he looked at Ryder. "I still can't believe Alex dragged her off to Miami."

"It makes sense, him wanting to get her out of town. We both know he's had a thing for her for a long time," Ryder drawled, lacing his fingers behind his dark head as he sprawled against the back of his chair. "Yeah, he's been fighting it, but we knew it was there." Lifting his brows, he added, "What you can't believe is that she willingly went along with him."

A wry smile tugged at the corner of Ben's mouth. "True."

"He really turned down your offer to put some personal security on her?" Ryder murmured, sounding intrigued.

"Oh, yeah. He was adamant about it." Which still made Ben want to shake his head in confusion. After he'd finished that call with Alex and Mike on Thursday morning, he'd wondered if maybe all the hours he'd spent down on that Caribbean beach, baking beneath the tropical sun while he fucked his beautiful wife's brains out had fucked his brains out as well, because he couldn't think of a single reason why Alex would purposefully put himself in this situation. Yeah, he knew that Alex had been secretly hung up on Brit, like Ryder had just said, for a long time now. But insisting she stay at his condo with him? Then taking her away to Miami for a weekend getaway?

Who was that guy and what the hell had he done to his brother?

The entire situation was surreal, and despite Reese's optimism that things were finally going to work out for their friend and his brother, Ben couldn't help but have his doubts. He loved the guy, but he cared too much for Brit to just stand by and let Alex use her to get his rocks off. And as much as he hated it, he knew there was a good chance that's exactly what this would turn out to be.

Ben had first noticed Alex's interest in Brit last summer, when all that shit had gone down with Reese and her psycho stalker. He'd been ready to step in if he'd needed to, worried Alex would do something stupid, like fuck her one night and then dump her. But nothing had ever happened. Alex had continued to watch Brit with that hungry, feral gleam in his eyes whenever she wasn't looking at him—but the guy never made a move. All he did was snarl and snipe at her. And that was when Ben finally started to see the light. Well, he might have had a little nudge from Reese, who helped him put it all together. But he gave himself credit for falling in love and claiming such an incredible, insightful woman. And the point was that they both understood what was happening. That Alex did his best to push Brit away because she wasn't just some woman he wanted to fuck.

No. She was a woman he wanted to fuck . . . and then do it again. She wasn't a toss aside, and since his brother was scared shitless of taking another chance on a relationship, after his marriage had crashed and burned so spectacularly, he'd taken to doing everything he could to make Brit think he was a jackass. It was a reflexive, knee-jerk reaction, and Ben understood exactly why Alex acted that way.

While growing up, he and his brothers had been witness to their mother's endless affairs, and their father's depression every time he took her back, and they'd each dealt with the fallout in their own way. Mike had become the serial womanizer, but with a good heart and a ready smile, and Ben had spent years shying away from commitment, until he'd finally found Reese. Alex was the only one of the three who had had the guts to take a chance early on—but it'd been on the wrong woman. When it blew up in his face, he'd retreated and dug in, and almost died trying to drown his failure at the bottom of a bottle, just like their father had so often done.

As badly as he wanted this thing between Brit and Alex to work out, Ben was worried his brother wouldn't be able to shake off his past and move forward. But that was something that would have to be faced later, after they'd dealt with Clay Shepherd and the havoc he was wreaking on Brit's life.

When the phone on Ben's desk started to ring, he and Ryder shared a look, both of them hoping like hell this would be the break that they needed.

"What'd you find?" Ben demanded, after hitting the speaker function on the phone so that Ryder could listen, as well.

"We've got the trace," Toby, his head IT guy, said over the line. "Instead of a burn phone, he used a campsite pay phone this time."

"The site over by North Beach?" Ben asked, referring to the campground where the possible sighting of Shepherd had been reported.

"No, if he was ever there, he's moved on. The call came from the Sunset Shores campsite, located south of us, at the edge of the county line."

"Got it. Thanks, Toby."

"No problem."

Ben ended the call, then looked at Ryder. "We're going to need as many bodies down there as we can get to canvass the area. Even if the bastard has moved on, someone had to have seen something."

Ryder nodded his agreement as he leaned forward in his chair, elbows on his knees. "I'll put in calls to our neighboring counties. See if they can send us some help."

"Good idea," Ben said, reaching for his cell phone. "I'm going to call Mike and see if he can round up some of his DEA buddies to help us."

"No answer?" Ryder asked a moment later, when Ben set the phone back down on his desk.

Shaking his head, he said, "Went to voice mail."

"I saw his truck in front of his place on my way over," Ryder told him with a frown. "Maybe he's sleeping."

Ben snorted. "More like fucking some beach-bunny and completely ignoring the rest of the world." Irritation roughened his tone. "I told him to stay in touch in case we needed him."

"Everything okay? Who are you having trouble getting in touch with?"

At the sound of his wife's voice asking those questions, Ben turned his head and found her standing in the doorway to his office, her beautiful gaze worried as she waited for his reply.

"We've finally got a good lead on Shepherd, but we need everyone we can find to help out. Mike is home, but not answering his phone."

Reese's shoulders sagged with relief, her worried frown curving into a knowing grin. "He probably just hasn't heard his phone because his headboard is banging against the wall too loudly."

Ryder laughed as he moved to his feet. "That's exactly what your husband was just saying."

"Great minds think alike," she teased, winking at Ben. "If it would help," she added, "I can head over to his place to let him know he's needed while you guys get over to the station."

"You sure?" Ben asked, making his way toward her. "I don't want you tiring yourself out." They'd been trying hard for a baby, and had hopes that it'd finally happened. And while he'd always been protective of her, he was even more so now. Hell, he was fucking terrified. When she was finally pregnant, if anything happened to her or the baby, it would kill him, plain and simple. "I want you taking it easy now that we're home."

She rolled her eyes at him. "Ben, I think I can handle driving over to Mike's."

He knew better than to outright forbid her to do anything, since the little hellcat would have him by his balls if he did. But he wasn't going to give in that easily. "Reese, it's going to be a pain in the ass. Whoever goes over there will probably have to help him get rid of whatever poor girl he's got in his bed, and you know what they're like. Mike's fuck-buddies *never* leave easily."

"I can handle it," she assured him, eyes twinkling as she pressed her hands against his chest and stared up at him with a smug grin. "You just go and do your thing with Ryder."

Ryder choked off a laugh behind him, and Ben couldn't help but smile as he teased her. "I'm afraid I only do *my thing* with you now, Mrs. Hudson. And Ryder's got Lily. I don't think he's interested in me that way."

She blushed as she realized what she'd said, then burst out laughing. "That's not what I meant," she giggled, smacking him on the shoulder as she hid her face against his chest.

Leaning down, Ben put his lips to her ear and whispered, "When I get home, I want you in bed. Naked. Wet and ready for me. Then I'll do *my thing*."

Ryder cleared his throat. "I'm just gonna head out and give you two a moment. Ben, I'll meet you out front," the deputy said with a smile in his voice, moving around them as he left the room, his footsteps echoing against the hardwood floor in the hallway as he headed toward the front of the house.

"Sorry if I embarrassed you," she whispered.

Ben grinned as he wrapped her up tight in his arms. "You could never embarrass me, angel."

She tilted her head back and caught his gaze, a wry grin on her lips. "I'm sure that's not true." Leaning up on her tiptoes, she rubbed her mouth against his, the feel of her soft lips making his breath catch as she quietly said, "What you whispered in my ear just now . . . I'm glad. I was worried you might have gotten enough of me while we were away."

"I'll never get enough of you," he growled, gripping her head in his hands as he took control of the kiss, sliding his tongue past her lips with greedy hunger, as undone by the taste of her now as he had been at the beginning of their relationship. It still took him by surprise, how being with her never lost its edge. Instead of leveling off, his need only grew more intense, and he knew it was because he was head-over-ass in love with her.

And he wouldn't have it any other way.

As he lowered one hand down the front of her body, covering the soft curve of her belly, he couldn't hide his excitement. "I have a good feeling about this," he murmured, his breath rough as he lifted his head.

Her soft smile made his chest warm. She was so goddamn beautiful, and she was *his*, and he was going to do everything in his power to get a baby inside her, if he hadn't already done it. He hoped they had a girl first. A chubby little angel who had her mother's dark eyes and hair and adorable freckles.

"I'm meant to start my period tomorrow," she told him, her voice husky with emotion. "If I still haven't started by the end of the week, let's do one of those early pregnancy tests."

He started to smile in response, his heart doing a funny flip behind his ribs, until she killed his good mood by saying, "Now what do you want me to tell Mike?"

"I don't want you—"

"Ben, I can do this," she argued, cutting him off. "I'll be careful, I promise. But you know I can't stay coddled up in this house all the time, even after I'm pregnant. It would drive me crazy."

He sighed and shoved a hand back through his hair, feeling like an idiot. "I know, baby. I just . . . I hate to let you out of my sight."

"I feel the same way about you, you know." She smiled again as she lifted her hand and cupped his cheek. "But the sooner you catch the bad guy, the sooner you can come back home to me. So let me do this."

Knowing she was right, he told her what to say to Mike, then gave her a hard kiss before letting her go to get her shoes on and grab her keys. Just before she disappeared into the hallway, she suddenly turned back to him, her dark eyes shadowed with concern. "I'm so worried about Brit. You will find him, right?"

"You know we will," he said with conviction, hating to see her upset. "And Alex isn't going to let her get hurt. He'll do whatever it takes to protect her."

She nodded, then started to frown again. "I just hope he doesn't blow his shot to keep her around after she's no longer in danger."

Ben held her gaze, wishing he could make a promise about that, as well. But they both knew that when it came to Alex and commitment, the odds weren't in Brit's favor. Hell, she probably had a better chance at winning the fucking lottery or living on Mars.

But because they wanted to see him happy, they were going to hold out hope, just the same.

12

ALEX SCOWLED AS HE WATCHED BRIT RUMMAGING THROUGH HER closet, taking out work clothes that she'd insisted they stop by her house to pick up before heading back to his place. The drive from Miami to Moss Beach had taken longer than he'd planned, thanks to some idiot drunk driver crossing into oncoming traffic and causing a hell of a pileup on the highway. Now it was almost time for dinner, and instead of having her secured in his condo, they were wasting time at her house. A place he wasn't comfortable with her being at.

Deputies had been taking turns watching the house, so there weren't any ugly surprises waiting for them when they arrived, but being there still made him edgy. For all they knew, Shepherd could be watching the place, though it certainly seemed as if he was currently busy evading arrest. Ben had called on the drive home and brought him up to date on their lead at the Sunset Shores campground. But Alex didn't want to take any chances. Shepherd was messed up in the head, which meant he wasn't thinking clearly, which meant you couldn't apply logic to his actions. And that made him damn difficult to protect against.

As he watched her pack yet another pair of sexy heels into the bag on her bed, Alex rolled his shoulders. "Hurry up, Doc. I want you out of this place."

She slid him one of those sexy sideways looks through the fall of her hair. It always reminded him of a forties starlet when she did that, and he felt his body stiffen with more than tension as she said, "Alex, relax. There's still a deputy waiting outside. We're fine."

He grunted in response, hating that she could sound so cool and composed when he was the polar opposite. Of course, he knew much of her calm demeanor was just an act. He was learning that the calmer she became, the more worried she was on the inside. It was probably some therapy technique she'd taught herself, and while he appreciated that she wasn't one of those women who ran around pulling her hair out in a frenzy of nerves, her "cool and controlled" spiel was putting *him* on even more of an edge.

That's just because you like the idea of her clinging to you, begging for the big, strong man to protect her and keep her safe.

He scowled, wondering when the voice in his head had become such a fucking asshole. But he couldn't argue with it. Damn it, he loved keeping her safe. Protecting her. Avenging her fucking honor.

He flexed his hand, enjoying the dull ache from where he'd slammed his fist into Jason Moore's nose. God, that had been satisfying. Even if the detective decided to press charges against him—which he didn't think had a chance in hell of happening—it would have been worth it. Maybe the next time the asshole wanted to raise his hand against a woman, he'd think twice before he acted.

Brit placed another pair of shoes in the bag, then finally zipped it closed. Alex started to reach out for it, but stopped when she turned her head to look at him, the uncertainty in her hazel eyes making him brace for something bad. "You're sure this is what you want?"

He cocked his head to the side, caught off guard by the question. "You mean having you at my place?"

She licked her lips, then swallowed, those beautiful eyes swimming with emotion. "Yes."

"If I didn't, I would tell you to take Ben up on his offer to get some personal security guys over here. But that's the last thing I want to happen, Brit. I want you with me."

"All right," she murmured, and there was no disguising how much relief he felt at the fact that she wasn't ready for it to be over between them, either. He stepped closer with every intention of kissing her until she couldn't even remember her own name, when someone started knocking on her front door. Who the hell was that going to be?

She paled as she stared up at him. "You don't think Clay would—"

"Naw," he murmured, cutting her off. "Don't worry, Doc. It's not him. There's still a deputy parked out on the street, remember?"

They went downstairs, and while Brit hovered near his side, Alex peeked through the peephole in her door . . . then ground his jaw. *Son of a fucking bitch.* He couldn't believe this guy's audacity. Who the fuck did he think he was? Pulling the door open, he kept the handle gripped in his fist, ready to slam it at a moment's notice, as he locked his narrow gaze on Ray McNamara. "What the hell are you doing here?" he barked, not caring that he sounded like a belligerent asshole.

Brit gasped beside him. "Alex!"

"Answer the question," he snarled, keeping his attention focused on her boss. "What makes you think it's okay to show up at her house?"

Ignoring him, McNamara turned his pale gaze on Brit. "I'm

sorry for just showing up, but I was planning on leaving you this note if you weren't at home," he said, holding up a white envelope. "I know that Dr. Chin is taking your calls right now, but I wanted to let you know that your office has been cleaned and everything is back in its place. And I give you my word that this breach in security will not happen again."

"My office?" she whispered. "What happened to my office? What breach are you talking about, Ray?"

McNamara's brows lifted. "You don't know?"

"Know what?" she demanded, sounding panicked now.

Alex wanted to use his fist to wipe the smug expression off the bastard's face when McNamara slid him a gloating look. It was clear the pompous ass thought he'd just been handed the keys to the kingdom because of Alex's screwup. Turning those icy blue eyes back on the doc, McNamara said, "I'm so sorry, Brit. If I'd known he was keeping it from you, I would have made sure I found a way to contact you."

Her posture was stiff. "Keeping what from me? What's going on, Ray?"

"It's nothing," Alex muttered, hating that she wouldn't look at him. "I'll tell you everything when this jackass gets lost."

"What happened?" she snapped, completely ignoring Alex as she posed her question to McNamara.

"Clay Shepherd managed to sneak past the security guards on Friday night and break into your office," McNamara told her, pushing a hand through his sandy-colored hair. "He went through the computer files he could access without your password, and he vandalized your things."

Her head whipped in Alex's direction, her beautiful face pinched with angry disbelief as she stared up at him. "Alex, is that true? Did you know? Is that why . . . ?" Her voice trailed off and she blanched, her gaze narrowing. "What the hell is going on?"

"Tell him to get lost," he grunted, jerking his chin toward McNamara.

Her breath left her lungs in a sharp, angry burst. "That's your response? Seriously?"

"We need to talk, but not in front of him."

She shook her head a little as she closed her eyes, clearly trying to get control of her emotions. Taking a deep breath, she lifted her thick lashes and looked at McNamara. "I appreciate you stopping by, Ray, but I think it might be best if you left now."

Sliding the envelope he'd been holding back into the inside pocket on his sports jacket, the asshole said, "I just wanted you to know that the building is secure. I've doubled the security staff. You'll be safe there, Brit. I can even arrange for additional security." Lowering his voice, he added, "There's no need for you to keep hiding out with this low-class bastard."

"Don't!" she said loudly, at the same time Alex snarled, "Get the fuck out of here, McNamara. Now!"

BRIT DREW IN ANOTHER DEEP, SHUDDERING BREATH, SO ANGRY SHE wanted to scream. Somehow, she choked it back and managed to find a calmer tone as she addressed her boss. "I really do think it's best if you leave now, Ray. I'll be in touch with the department head later to let them know when I'll be returning to the clinic."

A muscle jumped along Ray's jaw, but he accepted her choice with a muttered request for her to call him the next day, then turned to head back to the Mercedes he'd left parked on the street. The deputy watching her house was standing near the car, a curious look on his face. She watched Ray make his way down her front walkway until the front door slammed shut, then cut her angry gaze to the man turning toward her with his powerful arms crossed over his chest. Alex's eyes were hooded, his mouth a flat, irritated line within his stubble-darkened cheeks.

Pacing away from him, she fisted her hands at her sides, then spun back around to face him. "You had no right to keep that from me, Alex. This whole damn weekend was a freaking lie!"

"Like hell it was. I just didn't want you worrying about Shepherd any more than you already did while we were gone. You needed a break. You needed some time to just get away from it and relax."

"That wasn't for you to decide," she snapped, hating that she'd been so blind. She felt like an idiot for the stars she'd had in her eyes the past few days, her pathetic heart going pitter-patter every time she thought about Alex wanting to get away with her. God, she could be so stupid when it came to men! Especially this one! He didn't care about spending time with her. He simply hadn't wanted her being at her office, where she would have more than likely been given Ray's help while dealing with things.

Completely misunderstanding why she was upset, Alex said, "Damn it, Brit. If you would just calm down for a minute, you'd realize that you're overreacting for no reason. We've had protection in place for your parents since learning about the information he accessed during the break-in."

What? Her parents? Her thoughts spun so quickly she felt dizzy, and she had to reach out and grab hold of the back of a sofa. "Wait a minute. Are you telling me that my parents could be in danger, and you kept that from me?"

"Brit, we—"

"Jesus, Alex!" She pressed a fist against the center of her chest, where her heart was pounding so hard it ached. "My parents and I aren't close. I hadn't even called to tell them what was happening with Shepherd, so that must have come as a hell of a shock when the cops showed up to protect them. They're probably so furious they won't even talk to me now!"

He frowned, looking as if the idea of her parents being so cold troubled him. Then he shook it off, and muttered, "No one is in any danger, Brit. Your parents might be feeling a little . . . inconvenienced, but they're safe. Shepherd isn't getting anywhere close to them."

"And what about my friends?"

"We've got that covered, as well. And Ben has the entire department on the search, as well as help from neighboring counties. We're going to find this guy, and soon. Then everything can go back to the way it was."

To the way it was . . .

There was something about the way he said that simple phrase that had white-hot pain ripping through her chest. She felt as if something she'd thought might finally be within reach was slowly slipping out of her grasp, too slippery to hold on to.

Damn it, why was it so fucking difficult for men to love her? Sure, Jason was an ass. But he hadn't destroyed her. Hadn't turned her into a hater, like Judith had nearly done with Alex. She'd been able to see Jason's issues for what they were, once she'd removed herself from the situation. But it didn't mean that it didn't hurt, knowing she hadn't been enough for him. That she'd never been enough for *any* man.

She wasn't vain or full of ego. She knew there were more talented women out there. Smarter ones. Prettier ones. Skinnier ones. Women who were wittier, sexier, funnier than she could ever hope to be. But, damn it, that didn't mean she was unlovable. And if she was, then by God, she wanted to know why! She wanted to know why this one man, who she wanted to feel at least *something* for her, no matter how small, couldn't. She wanted him to look her in the eye and give her the honest to God's truth. To just come out and tell her why she didn't touch him any deeper than his surface. She needed it. Because if he didn't make her understand, there was a strong chance she was going to walk away from this permanently scarred by the experience.

Swallowing her pride, Brit stepped toward him and nervously licked her lips. "What was Miami really about, Alex? Was that just your way of keeping me away from McNamara? Or was it . . . was it your way of saying good-bye?"

"Neither," he grunted. "I just wanted you somewhere safe. Even if it was for only a few days. I just wanted you to have a break from it all."

She had to fight to keep her voice from shaking as she searched his closed expression. "Was it all a lie?"

His eyes narrowed to piercing slits, his deep voice little more than a guttural rasp. "Was what a lie?"

"The way you were there. The way you looked at me. The way you touched me. Was any of it real?"

She could see a muscle begin to pulse in his lean cheek, his jaw clenched so hard it had to be hurting his teeth. He took two deep breaths, then ground out, "It was real."

"And now that we're back?" She sniffed, fighting hard not to completely lose it. But it wasn't easy. Especially when she could see the fear and dread etching themselves onto his features, his body drawn so tight with tension he looked like he might crack.

"What are you asking me, Brit?"

She licked her lips again, and whispered, "If I have to ask, then I guess that's my answer."

He worked his jaw, but he didn't comment. She knew he'd understood exactly what she'd been asking him, and his silence was answer enough. Now that they were back, they were back to the real world. The one where they were just fucking each other because it felt good and for the moment it was convenient. Something they'd needed to get out of their systems for a long time, and once Shepherd was caught and in a psychiatric hospital, where he belonged, things would go back to the way they'd been. Maybe they would manage to act a bit friendlier toward one another, but nothing more. Honestly, she didn't know if that was something she could even manage, after the two days she'd just spent with him, but she couldn't worry about that now. That would be a decision she made later, when she was thinking more clearly.

And if she decided that space was what she needed, she wouldn't let fear hold her back. She might try someplace like San Francisco or Seattle, just for a change of scenery. Someplace where she wouldn't have to worry about running into him every time she got together with her friends or was out in town. Someplace she could put this all behind her, and try to find a way to start over. Start new.

Without a word, she moved past him and climbed the stairs, heading back up to her room. She wasn't even aware that he'd followed her until she went to grab her bag off the bed and he touched her arm.

"I've got the bag," he muttered, picking it up.

Brit shrugged to let him know she didn't care who carried the bag, grabbing her purse before she headed out of the room and back down the stairs again. She grabbed her keys from the small table in the entryway, and was about to turn away, when she caught the blinking light on her phone cradle from the corner of her eye. When she had a message, a tiny red light blinked on the unit, letting her know.

With a sick feeling in her stomach, she pushed the play button, and Clay's troubled voice began playing through the small speaker.

"Will you get this?" he asked, the quiet words shaking with emotion. "I know you're not at home. You're hiding from me, but you have to come back eventually. And when you do, I'll make you understand. He's poisoning you—that asshole you're hiding with—but I can help you see the truth. That you are perfect for me. That we can be perfect together. I'll find out who he is. And when I do, you'll be *mine*."

He broke down at that point, his sobbing making her insides twist and knot. Then he cursed, clearly trying to catch his breath, and went on. "I can make this happen, Dr. Cramer. Do you know how easy it would be to set a fire? Or to poison his food in a restaurant? You can't hide forever. All I need is to get him out of the picture. Then you'll fall right into my hands. I don't understand why you keep fighting it, when it makes so much sense. When it's so perfect. So—"

The phone beeped, cutting off the message because he'd run out of time. Pressing a hand to her churning stomach, she turned and looked at Alex, who had been standing beside her while the message played. "This came through on my actual home number," she told him. "He must have found it when he searched my office."

He jerked his chin toward the door, his expression grim. "Come on. I want you out of here."

With her emotions in chaos, Brit set the alarm and locked the front door behind them. Then she followed Alex over to her driveway, where the Rover was parked, and climbed inside. It seemed like a lifetime ago since they had pulled into the driveway so that she could run inside and grab some clean clothes. Tugging on her seat belt, she tried to blank her mind and find a measure of calm, silently wondering if Alex was doing the same. Or maybe he was simply being quiet because he was pissed that she'd put him on the spot with her questions. Which was hardly fair. After what he'd done, she was the one with the right to be pissed. Not him.

They'd been driving in silence for a few minutes when he glanced in his rearview mirror and growled, "Motherfucker!"

"What's wrong?" She twisted in her seat, but couldn't see anything to warrant his reaction. Just a few cars behind them.

He hit the gas, barreling them down the wide two-lane road. Luckily, the traffic was light. "Get down as far as you can," he snapped, still accelerating, his narrow gaze switching between the road and his rearview mirror. "We have company."

His words gave her chills. "Is it Clay?"

He turned his head and pinned her with a hard look. "Get your fucking head down, Brit! Now!"

"Is it Clay?" she asked again, sinking lower in her seat. She sent up a fervent prayer that he would say no, but wasn't so lucky.

Grinding his jaw, he said, "Yeah. It's the son of a bitch." His eyes flicked to the rearview mirror again, and she knew the other car must be close when he growled, "I recognize him from the photographs that were in his file."

"Ohmygod," she whispered, unable to believe this was happening.

"Here we go," he said, his voice gruff, and she braced herself for whatever was coming. She wanted to squeeze her eyes shut, but knew that was a cowardly move. Instead, she forced herself to look through Alex's side window, her eyes shooting wide when she saw a haggard, disheveled-looking Clay behind the wheel of an old, beat-up silver Suburban. For a split second, time seemed to stand still, and then the silver SUV slammed into Alex's side of the Range Rover in a horrific, deafening crunch of metal against metal. Terrified they were going to crash, Brit braced herself against the dashboard as Alex rammed back against the Suburban. "What are you doing?" she screamed. "Stop the car!"

"If I do, this bastard will either ram us or get away." She could hear the deadly rage in his voice, and knew it had more to do with the fact that Clay was trying to harm *her* than it did with his own life being in danger. "Just hold on, Brit. I won't let anything happen to you."

"Don't let anything happen to you, either!" she shouted, raising her voice to be heard over the screeching of metal as the two vehicles scraped against each other again. The Range Rover was the more powerful car, and Alex was clearly well trained in dealing with this kind of situation, having already managed to push Clay's vehicle across the center divide. Brit was just thankful there wasn't any oncoming traffic on the road. "What's your plan?" she asked, wondering how much longer this was going to last.

"Either force him into hitting something, or if I can get him in the right position, slam into his rear bumper, spinning him out."

Oh, God, both of those options sounded dangerous. She was sending up a breathless stream of prayers that Alex didn't get hurt, when their luck ran out and a yellow truck came speeding around the upcoming bend, heading straight at them, since both vehicles were now in the wrong lane. Alex cursed as he was forced to swerve, just as the truck did the same, and he ended up having to take the Range Rover up onto the sidewalk, which was thankfully empty. But he had to slam his brakes on before driving straight into one of the town's covered bus stops, while Clay accelerated down the road, the Suburban's tires screeching as he swerved to miss another car, before disappearing out of view around the bend.

"Fuck!" Alex snarled, whipping his head in her direction. "Are you all right? Are you hurt?"

She blinked back at him, filled with a cold, burning rage. In that moment, she knew she would have killed Clay herself if she'd been able to get her hands on him. He'd tried to hurt not only her, but Alex as well, and that was something she simply couldn't forgive.

"Brit, answer me. Are you all right?"

"Y-yes," she stammered, her throat shaking. "Are you?"

"I'm fine," he grunted, checking the road before steering the

Rover across the lanes and pulling onto the verge. He flicked on his hazards, then pulled his phone from his pocket. "I need to call Ben."

He punched in the number, and it was so quiet in the cab that she could hear Ben's voice when he answered the call. "Hey. You back from Miami yet?"

"Yeah, and we've had some trouble," Alex said, his deep voice hard with anger. "We stopped by Brit's house to pick up some things and once we were back on the road, Shepherd tagged us before I could spot him. We made contact a few times, and I tried to drive him off the road, but another car got in the way and he took off."

"Shit! Are you both okay?"

"Yeah, we're fine." His fingers tightened on the phone until his knuckles turned white, and she could all but feel the frustration rolling off him. "But you need to find this fucker. *Now*."

"We're on it, Alex. We're doing everything we can. You know that."

Blowing out a tired sigh, he dropped his head back and pulled his free hand down his face. "I know you are, Ben. Let everyone know he was driving an old, silver Suburban, but I couldn't see the license plates. They were smeared with mud."

"Mud is good," Ben muttered. "With all this rain we've been having, it could well be from one of the campsites. I'll check to see if any vehicles matching that description have been seen in the Sunset Shores area, as well as the others."

"What about the meeting I asked you to set up with the detectives in Westville?"

"I should be hearing back from them first thing in the morning."

"Okay, let me know what you hear. I need to go now and get Brit out of here."

Ben told him to be careful, and Alex ended the call.

Clearing her throat, Brit forced herself to say what she knew needed to be said. "I think I'd like for you to take me to the sheriff's station now."

He turned his head, his dark brows pulled into a scowl. "What? Why?"

She kept her gaze locked on his hostile one, and tried to keep her voice from shaking. "Because I can wait there until Ben can get one of his private security friends over."

His nostrils flared as he sucked in a sharp breath. "No. In fact, *fuck* no."

"I'm serious, Alex. I'm done," she snapped, her fear manifesting itself in a hot surge of emotion that felt remarkably similar to rage. "This isn't a risk you need to be taking. I won't let you. End of story!"

13

He didn't say anything as he studied her with that piercing gaze, and Brit could actually see the moment when he figured out what had her so upset. "I don't need you worrying about me," he told her, his calm tone setting her teeth on edge. "That's the *last* thing you need to waste your time worrying about, Doc."

"Don't you get it?" she shouted. "You could have been killed! I can't stand by and watch that happen. I *won't*."

Shaking his head, he said, "He's not gonna get either one of us."

"I'm serious, Alex. I should go. Stay with friends."

He pinned her with a knowing look. "And put Ben and Reese in danger? Or Lily and Ryder? Is that what you want?"

"No! I can't go to either of them. Obviously," she said as she pressed her fingertips to her pounding temples, knowing damn well she was rambling. "I need to go . . . somewhere else. I don't know."

"Well, I do know," he grunted, flicking off the hazard lights and checking his mirrors, before turning his head and locking his hooded gaze hard on hers. "I know you're staying with me, and if you do something stupid and try to leave, I'll just track your little ass down. So don't waste our time. The safest thing you can do for both of us is to stay put and just do as you're told."

"God, you're infuriating."

He made a rude sound in the back of his throat. "Yeah. Just another alpha asshole, huh?"

"You've got the asshole part right," she muttered, then felt like a jerk. Turning toward him, she reached out and grasped his hand, holding it in both of hers as she said, "Alex, please don't joke about this. You're putting yourself in danger for no reason."

"You're one hell of a reason, Doc. And as for the danger, I don't care."

"Of course you don't," she choked out, letting go of his hand. She was so frustrated she wanted to scream. "You don't care about a lot of things."

He cursed under his breath as he flicked the hazard lights back on, then twisted in his seat and leaned forward, getting right in her face, his eyes burning with a hot, angry glow. "You're right," he snapped, his voice little more than a snarl. "I don't care that you're probably smarter than me. Or that you're way classier. I don't care that you make more money than I do, either. What I *do* care about is that you're safe, and happy, and *very* sexually satisfied. And I can and will make those things happen. So come home with me, Brit." He paused, the grim look in his eyes softening as he said, "*Please.* You're safe there, and I need you close, where I can keep an eye on you."

It was so hard to say no when every part of her heart wanted to say yes. But she was still so scared for him. Searching his beautiful eyes for the reassurance she needed, she said, "What if he finds out where you live? You just pissed McNamara off royally. Who knows what he might let slip to the wrong person?"

"He wouldn't risk your safety that way. He's an asshole, not a psychotic bastard. And not even McNamara would be able to learn my home address. I keep myself covered, Doc. It's all good."

"Tell that to your poor car," she grumbled, knowing the damage on his side of the Range Rover had to be extensive. The thought made her cringe, and she decided that one way or another, she would trick him into letting her pay for the repairs.

Staring back at him in the thickening twilight, cool air still blowing softly over her body from the vents, Brit thought that it was simply mad, how much things had changed in just a matter of days. How feelings she'd tried to keep from growing for so long now refused to be ignored or denied.

Their time in Miami had been a beautiful dreamland, but they were back to reality now. And at this moment, that meant a danger that she couldn't just ignore, no matter how badly she wanted to. To just pretend it didn't exist. All she had to do was get out and look at the side of his car, and she could see just how real it was.

As if he could read her troubled thoughts, he said, "Brit, listen to me. Cars can get fixed. It's no big deal." Before she could argue, he pulled her close, cupping her face in his hands, and went on. "Don't worry about me, babe. I mean it. I'm hard to kill."

"Before, I thought it was just me. That I was the only one in danger," she whispered through trembling lips, her throat burning with emotion. "But this changes it, Alex. It changes everything. I just want you to be safe."

"And I just want to keep *you* safe. Don't you see that? If you try to go, I'm just gonna follow you and protect you from the outside, where it's even more dangerous."

A wry smile twisted her lips. "We're a pair, aren't we?"

"Stubborn to the core," he drawled, stroking his thumb across her lower lip before muttering something under his breath about "time and place" and letting go of her. Putting the Rover into drive, he flicked off the hazard lights again as he pulled back onto the road, and she didn't say anything more, knowing his attention was focused on making sure they weren't being followed.

They grabbed fast food, eating it at the dining room table when they got in, while a ball game played in the background on the TV. She was no longer angry at him, because . . . well, it just wasn't important, after what had happened. There was so much that didn't seem important now. His silence about her office. His silence about so many things. How could she hold a grudge about any of it when he was risking his life for her? What could be more telling than that?

"About McNamara," he murmured, shoving their empty wrappers into the trash can in the kitchen.

She'd followed behind him with their empty soda glasses, setting them in the sink as she asked, "What about him?"

"I don't like you working for that prick. You should find another job."

Ohmygod. Was he serious? Had he lost his mind? Or . . . or was this just his way of taking his mind off what had happened? "He's never acted like this before," she said, hoping he would just let it go. "It's not his usual behavior."

He leaned back against the counter and crossed his powerful arms over his chest as she turned to face him. "Maybe he's never seen you give another man the time of day. And now that he has, he doesn't like it."

She blinked at him in surprise. "I've dated. You know that."

Shrugging that off, he said, "Now and again you have. But you've never gone out with any particular guy often enough to catch McNamara's notice. They bore you too quickly."

Her eyebrows lifted. "And what exactly do you know about the men that I've dated?"

He looked as if he was trying hard not to laugh at her, which made her suddenly want to kick him. "We've known each other for a few years now, Doc, and I have ears. I might not talk a lot around the group, but I know how to listen."

"Are you saying that you've eavesdropped on me talking to Reese and Lily?"

Closing the distance between them, he put his face right over hers. "I'm saying that I know more about you than you seem to think."

"Including what's right for me?"

"*I* want to be right for you," he said in a quiet rasp, shocking the hell out of her. "I'm not trying to fuck you over, Brit. I swear that's not why I didn't tell you about your office, or why I was a dick to McNamara. I just . . . I'm just trying to protect you."

He was suddenly shaking with a fine tremor of emotion, and she could actually *feel* his fear. "Okay. All right," she murmured, hoping to soothe him. "I get it, Alex. I'm not happy that you didn't just tell me what had happened, because I hate being left in the dark. But I get it. I understand."

"Then lose the clothes for me," he said in a low voice, jerking his chin toward her dress as he stepped back.

With her hands pressed to her warm cheeks, Brit gaped at him. "Are you serious? You want to pull your caveman routine *now*?"

"You heard me," he said, reaching down to open his jeans. He had that look of intense determination in his eyes again, but she could have told him no if she wanted to. No matter how dominant he was, she knew he would always respect her choices. Even when he was in this possessive, over-the-top, alpha caveman mode.

Not that she actually wanted to deny him. No, she just wanted as much of him as she could get. Wanted to glut on him through-out the night, knowing this was closing in hard and tight on the end.

If it was going to be about nothing more than sex, then she

wanted to get her heartbreak's worth now, so that she could use the remembered pleasure to soothe her wounds later on.

"All right," she murmured, reaching behind her to undo the zipper, before sliding the straps of her dress over her shoulders. Then she reached back for the clasp on her bra.

"Get on the table," he told her, when her bra and panties had joined the yellow sundress on the floor.

"What is it with you and tables?" she murmured, arching one of her brows at him as she hopped up on the table in the breakfast nook, sitting with her legs hanging over the edge.

ALEX GAVE HER A SLOW, HUNGRY SMILE. "I LIKE GETTING YOU ON ANY horizontal surface. Tables just tend to be close by," he said, forcing her legs apart as he stepped between them. He told her to lie back, then ran his hands down the insides of her thighs and lifted her knees, opening her up completely as he pushed her knees down to the tabletop. "Oh, God, that's so beautiful." Grabbing her hands, he brought them between her legs. "Now hold it just like that for me. I want your pussy spread wide open."

She started shaking her head, but he leaned over her and caught her lips, kissing her hard and deep, his tongue sinking into her mouth. "Yes," he breathed against her soft lips, flicking them with his tongue. "I need this, Doc. I need you to feel comfortable with me."

She trembled, but exhaled a long breath and allowed him to place her fingers where he wanted them. When he was done, her fingertips were pulling her outer labia wide, revealing all the juicy pink bits inside, her tender flesh already glistening with her lube.

"Fuck, that's perfect," he groaned. "Just . . . hold it, don't move."

"I'm—"

"Do. Not. Fucking. Move. Brit."

She gave a breathless laugh. "Fine," she huffed. "I won't move."

"Christ," he scraped out a moment later, running his tongue over the edge of his teeth as he drank in the stunning, provocative sight she made, all laid out before him like a gift. "I need to be inside you so badly, but I can't stop staring at how fucking gorgeous you look."

She had a dark red, luxurious bush, trimmed up all nice and neat. And below that, a hot pink little cunt that contrasted sharply with the creamy paleness of her skin. It was so incredibly beautiful, and he honestly couldn't seem to get enough of it. That wasn't bullshit. Each time he had her, it didn't matter how long or how hard he fucked her or tongued her, the hunger in his gut just grew more intense.

Ripping his shirt off, Alex finally leaned down and started suckling her clit, determined to make her come so hard she forgot all about McNamara and Shepherd and any other bastard who wanted to mess with her life. Licking his way down to her vulva, he took her with his tongue like a man starved for the taste of his woman, plunging in and out of that sweet little hole while he shoved his jeans down over his hips.

Unable to wait any longer, he ripped his mouth away from her, straightened, and notched his cockhead against her opening, more than ready to thrust deep and fuck the hell out of her. But then he . . . stopped. Lowering himself over her, Alex braced himself on his elbows and dropped his forehead to hers, his muscles twitching as he tried to make sense of the chaotic messages firing through his brain. She'd been through hell tonight, and the last thing she needed was to get nailed to the hard surface of the table. She deserved something soft and giving, and though it was probably going to kill him to wait, he forced his hips back.

"Alex?"

"Shh," he whispered against her cheek, gathering her in his arms. "Put your legs around me, baby, and hold on."

He picked her up and carried her into the living room, snatching at the soft throw Reese had hung across the back of the sofa the last time she and Ben had been over. Thankful for it, he laid the blanket over the leather cushions. Something inside him felt compelled to make this as comfortable for Brit as possible, knowing she deserved to be treated like a fucking goddess.

Lowering them both to the long sofa, he lifted her knee and pushed inside her voluptuous body. And, oh, Christ, that was so fucking perfect. For a moment, he couldn't do anything but hang his head over hers, his eyes squeezed shut, biceps bulging as he braced his upper body on his arms. Then he slowly lowered himself against her, crushing her beautiful tits against his chest, buried his face in the warm, fragrant curve of her throat, and started to move.

With his hips working between her shapely thighs, their heat-glazed bodies slipping and sliding, Alex placed his hands on her sides, then ran them over every silken inch of skin he could reach, soaking in every part of her. All the smooth, satiny curves. She was lushly feminine, the smell of her skin so good it made his mouth water, her taste even better when he parted his lips and licked her. He ran his tongue up the sensual column of her throat, fastening his lips around her earlobe and nipping it with his teeth.

"It's unreal," he groaned, grinding himself against the hot, moist cushion of her pussy. "Nothing's ever felt as right as being inside you. I fucking love it, Brit. Won't ever get enough of it."

Whoa . . . Did he really just say that? What the hell was he thinking? That wasn't . . . him. Not now. Not the man he'd become.

Before she could respond, calling him on the crazy words, Alex pulled out, flipped her over, and pushed back in, fucking her hard and fast, his mouth all over her as he licked and nipped at her shoulders, trying to lose himself in the physical moment so that he didn't have to think about . . . anything. She was tight as a fist, her sweet ass cushioning his hammering thrusts as he powered into her again and again, the wet, suctioning sounds filling the room, and it didn't take long before they were both shaking and groaning with release, their bodies straining in a pleasure so violent and dark it nearly left them destroyed.

As the fog slowly cleared from his brain, Alex braced himself on his arms and stared down at the trembling length of her back with a dawning sense of horror. There were red splotches on her hips from where he'd gripped her too tightly, the smooth skin on her shoulders and upper back covered with marks that he knew had been made by his stubble, and even his teeth.

"Shit," he grunted. "I was too rough."

"No. I'm good." Her voice was deliciously husky, almost slurred with pleasure.

He worked his jaw, then clenched it, his throat tight. "I left marks, Doc."

"Hmm." The crazy woman actually sounded like she was smiling. "I'm sure I've left a few on you, as well. You didn't hurt me, Alex. So stop worrying."

"You're okay?"

"I'm fine. I swear."

He dropped his head forward, eyes screwed tightly shut as he tried to make sense of the chaos going on inside him. He was too off balance, his insides churning, so twisted up in knots he had to grit his teeth to keep from groaning like a pussy.

"I hate that guy," he eventually muttered, trying to convince himself that her bastard of a boss was the reason why he couldn't get his thoughts straight, since it was easier than facing the truth. And he really did despise the smarmy asshole.

"Who?"

"McNamara. I don't want him coming anywhere near you."

She turned her face to the side, her cheek pressed against the soft throw, and he could see that her languorous gaze was focused on something distant as she said, "Alex, you know that you can trust me, right? I mean, I don't know exactly what it is . . . what's between us. I don't know where your head is in all of this, but I'm not the kind of woman who sleeps with one man and flirts with another. I never have been, and I never would be."

"He wants you," he forced from his tight throat, hating the way the words tasted in his mouth.

"Maybe. I . . . I don't know. I think he's reeling from his divorce and trying to find his way through the fallout. But even if he does, it doesn't matter. I'm not interested in him. I never have been."

"You weren't interested in me, either," he pointed out sourly.

"If you really think that," she said, and he could tell that she was trying not to laugh at him, "then I'm a better actress than I thought."

He took a deep breath as he carefully pulled himself from her body, then lifted her and turned her over. He searched her expression in the golden light spilling from the lamp at the end of the sofa. "What are you saying?"

She lifted her gaze to his, looking at him through her lashes, her voice soft as she said, "I'm saying that I've been interested since I met you."

"No. You hated my guts."

Her lips twisted with something caught somewhere between a grin and a frown. "Not really. I hated that you didn't support Ben when he met Reese, but I've never hated *you*. I just didn't let on because it was pretty clear that you *really* weren't interested in having anything to do with me."

He swallowed thickly, a strange buzzing in his ears as he heard himself say, "I wanted to fuck you the first time I ever set eyes on you."

Her eyes went wide and her jaw dropped. "Seriously?"

"Oh, yeah." He grinned a little. "I went home that night and had a hell of a fantasy about you while jacking off in the shower."

She laughed as she socked him in the shoulder. "Nice."

"Not nearly as nice as this," he murmured, leaning down and pressing his lips to the sensitive place beneath her ear. Pulling in another deep breath, he felt something stunning and huge roll through him as he took in her familiar scent. *Familiar.* Christ, he'd been obsessed with that warm, womanly smell for months now, trying to get his fix whenever they were around each other without getting caught. It was ingrained in his system, a part of him, like tree roots digging their way deep into the earth, and the rightness of it was as shocking as it was terrifying.

She wasn't just some casual hookup. He *knew* her, damn it. Her laugh. Her smile. He respected her . . . was protective of her. Enjoyed her. And the more he had her, the more he wanted from her.

Shit, he wanted so much he no longer even recognized himself, and in that moment, Alex understood exactly what had driven him so hard when he'd had her in Miami. Taking her away hadn't only been about her safety. No, it had been his way of giving himself a chance to claim her outside of the life he'd made for himself in Moss Beach. Away from the man he'd become here. The one who didn't commit or do relationships or let a woman mean anything to him other than a hard fuck.

But it only worked when they'd existed in that alternate paradigm. Now that they were home, back in the "real" world, he didn't know how to reconcile the man he'd been there with the one he was here. He didn't even think it could be done.

More importantly, he wasn't even sure he wanted it to work.

Not when he knew how destructive the fallout could be. Damn it, he'd learned his lesson. Learned that there were some things it was better to shy away from, before they tore you down so far you no longer even recognized yourself, than to take a chance on them.

He couldn't afford another hit. So he had better make sure he was prepared for what was coming. Which meant putting some distance between them when distance was needed.

Pressing a kiss to her forehead, he moved to his feet and hiked up his jeans, buttoning them closed before heading into the kitchen and bringing back her dress. The scene was strangely reminiscent of Friday night, when he'd taken her in the dining room. It was like watching himself in motion from behind a wall of soundproof glass. No matter how hard he banged the shit out of that thing, he couldn't reach the dumbass son of a bitch standing there getting ready to give her the brush-off again. She studied his closed expression as he handed the dress to her, and he figured she didn't need to be a therapist to know that he'd just taken another wrong turn in his head.

With a soft catch in her voice, she said, "I'm going to go and grab a shower. Want to join me?"

"I would, but I need to get some work done. I'll be up in a little while."

"All right." She gave him a small, close-lipped smile that was clearly forced. He wouldn't be surprised if she was already getting tired of his shit, and the thought made his chest feel like someone had just taken a hammer to it. He felt cold, but there was a trickle of sweat slipping down his spine, and he shook his head. What the fuck was wrong with him?

"We still need to talk about what I'm doing about work this week, but we can do that in the morning," Brit was saying as she smoothed her dress back over her beautiful body, her gaze focused on her task instead of him. "But I thought I could make dinner tomorrow night, so I'll need to go by the store at some point."

He frowned. "You don't need to cook. We can pick something up, like we did tonight."

"I can only eat so much fast food," she said with a wry twist of her lips, shifting her gaze to his, "and it's not a big deal. I like to cook when I'm at home."

He flinched before he could stop himself when she referred to his condo as *home*, and knew that she'd noticed. He instantly felt like a dick. Seriously, what the hell was he doing?

He deserved to have his ass kicked, for acting like such a child, but she didn't even call him on it. She just stood there for a moment, her luminous eyes swirling with emotion. So many he couldn't quite catch them all. But the pity was coming through too loudly to miss, and he swallowed against the rise of bile in his throat.

In a move that was becoming frustratingly familiar, she took a deep breath, then looked away from him and went upstairs to take her shower.

And that time, she didn't ask him to join her.

14

Twenty-four hours later, Brit was still trying to figure out what was going on with Alex. He hadn't touched her since the telling encounter on his sofa the day before. In fact, he'd barely even spoken to her. Instead, he was keeping himself busy in his home office, working in conjunction with Ben to locate Clay, while trying to keep up on his other cases.

And he was doing a damn fine job of making her feel like she wasn't even there.

After what had happened with Clay on the road, Brit had decided that it was safer for everyone, especially her patients, if she took some personal time away from the office this week and stayed at home. Well, at the condo. Alex had one of Ben's deputies bring her laptop over from her office, so she'd been able to stay busy with some work. But it'd still been a long, lonely day. When Reese had phoned to check on how she was doing that afternoon, she'd offered to come over and keep her company. Now, in the early evening, Brit found herself curled up in one of the chairs on Alex's patio and pouring it all out to the petite brunette who had become one of her closest friends.

"I think he's just really worried about you," Reese murmured, leaning forward to set her coffee mug on the small patio table that sat between them. "Ben said that when you guys got back last night, Alex started calling in every favor owed to him so that they can find Shepherd. I think the danger you're in is driving him crazy."

"Maybe," she said with a worried sigh. "Or maybe he's just pulling back because we . . . I don't know. Got too close or something."

"What exactly happened in Miami?" Reese asked, her tone curious as she lifted her feet onto the edge of her wicker chair and wrapped her arms around her knees. Her dark hair was shot with glints of gold from the Caribbean sun, the freckles sprinkled over her nose even more prominent than usual, making her look adorable. And she had that disgustingly happy glow that said she was completely and utterly in love. It was a good thing Brit liked her so much, or she would have been green with envy.

She thought about Reese's question for a moment, and then she said, "He's always been so closemouthed about himself, but while we were away, he finally started opening up to me, telling me about his past. About his marriage to the bitch-face who cheated on him. Even about what happened with his career. And he was . . . I don't know. More at ease. At times even playful. It just . . . it made everything between us seem so much deeper. I'm wondering if that freaked him out."

Reese nodded in understanding. "For a guy like Alex, what you two have going on is probably not only unfamiliar, but forbidden territory."

Brit frowned. "It's fairly unfamiliar to me, too."

"But you're a woman, which means you're genetically programmed to handle the emotional stuff better than he is."

A quiet laugh fell from her lips. "God, that is so screwed up."

"Tell me about it." With a smirk, Reese added, "But you're the one with the psych degree, so you should already know this."

"It's funny, but I'm a lot better at sorting out others' emotional situations than I am my own."

"Well, I'll just take this opportunity to remind you of the little pep talk you once gave me about Ben. The one where you said you placed a lot of importance on the type of *connection* that can exist between a man and a woman. And let me just tell you that a person would have to be blind not to see that you and Alex definitely have one, Brit. He might not make it easy, and it's probably scaring the hell out of him, but there's no doubt that the two of you share something intense. It's been there for as long as I've known both of you, even though neither one of you wanted to admit it, or accept it."

Pulling in a deep breath, she realized Reese was right. Brit *had* been the one to coax her friend into taking a chance on Ben . . . and to give credence to their connection. But was she brave enough to take the advice and apply it to herself? Why was it so freaking hard to figure these things out when they pertained to her own life, and not to one of her patients?

Sliding Reese a wry look, she said, "You know, one of the reasons I've been so pissed at Alex is because of how he treats you."

"I know," Reese murmured, tilting her head a bit to the side. "And that makes you a great friend. It really does. But you need to stop and take a look at how he is with me now."

"What do you mean?"

"I mean that Alex and I have been good for a long time, Brit. Really good."

An uneasy sense of disbelief had her sitting up in her chair, but she could tell that Reese was being serious. Jesus, how had she not seen this? Had she been walking around with her head in her ass when it came to that man for so long that she no longer even saw him clearly?

Or had it been a simple safety reflex, since she'd known there was a good chance he could break her heart if she ever got too close to him? Had she been seeing what she wanted to see, because she knew it was safer to keep her distance from him?

"I feel like such a douche," she blurted, which made Reese laugh.

"You're not a douche," Reese said gently. "And trust me, it wasn't something that changed overnight. It took months before Alex and I warmed up to each other, but I can't fault him, because I know where he's coming from, and I know he was just looking out for his brother. But things are better now, and I don't want you to think badly of him because of me. He's a good man."

"I know he is," she sighed.

"So maybe you just need to do something now to remind him of how good the sex is between the two of you. You know, do something to really rock his world. Get in his face and don't let him get away with ignoring you."

Her lips twitched with a nervous smile. "Maybe. I've never really been the instigator." No, she was always just swept up in his intensity, letting herself get wrapped up in his raw, aggressive sexuality, going along for the ride.

Giving her a wicked grin that definitely had a little bit of Ben in it, Reese said, "Well, there you go. Give him a chance to let off some steam and unwind."

She nodded, her mind already buzzing with ideas . . . her insides churning with excitement. Oh, she knew she'd be nervous, but she wasn't afraid to give it a shot. If anything, her time with Alex had taught her that she was woman enough to handle him. That he really *did* see her as someone who was sexy and worthy of his interest.

And, damn it, she wasn't going to just let him slip away from her without a fight. Screw that. They could be over when this nightmare was finished, if that's what he wanted. But until then, she was going to get as much of him as she could and at least know that she hadn't held back from him. That she'd given it her all.

A half hour later, Mike showed up to bring Reese to the station, where Ben was waiting to take her out for a late dinner. Alex came out from his office to talk to his brother for a few minutes, scowling like an idiot when Mike gave Brit a good-bye hug. They walked them out to Mike's truck, and as they came back inside, there was an eager, determined smile curving her lips. She was about to do something tonight that she never would have had the confidence to do a week ago. But now she was actually looking forward to it.

Heading into the kitchen, Brit started the dishwasher after loading up her and Reese's coffee mugs, and thought about her plan of attack. She figured she would have to go and track Alex down when she was ready, assuming he'd headed straight for his office again. But he hadn't. When she turned away from the sink, she was surprised to find him standing in the archway to the kitchen, his expression partly in shadow. She hadn't turned on many lights when she and Reese came inside, the muted track lighting in the living room giving the space a soothing ambience that she hadn't wanted to disrupt.

He watched her with a dark, hooded gaze. "Why the hell did you guys talk for so long?"

"Why?" she murmured, a small smile playing at the corner of her mouth as she moved toward him. "Did you miss me?"

He grunted at her teasing, shoving one of those rugged, masculine hands back through his short hair. His posture was tense, as if he'd been walking around carrying the weight of the world on his wide shoulders. She could sense the darkness swirling around him, through him. It was so much a part of him, she didn't think that he would ever completely shake free of it, and it made her heart hurt. She cared about him to the point that she truly hoped he would one day find a way to be free of his past.

Even if it was with a woman who wasn't her.

Oh, she wouldn't be happy about it, because it would hurt like hell, and she'd probably have to move just to keep her sanity. But there would be a peace in knowing that he was happy. That he'd finally given himself the chance to live again.

Holding his shadowed gaze, she stopped a few feet in front of him, and decided to be direct and to the point. "So, are you done ignoring me?"

His lashes lowered a bit more, shielding the look in his eyes. "I wasn't ignoring you."

"Then prove it," she said softly, walking around him and heading straight for the stairs. By the time she was halfway up, she'd already pulled her white T-shirt over her head and let it drop to the steps behind her.

When she reached back to undo her bra, his deep voice came from the bottom of the stairs. "What the hell are you doing, Doc?"

"You wanted me here." She put a little extra sway in her hips as she climbed the last few steps to the upstairs landing. "Wouldn't hear of me going anywhere else. So here I am."

She walked into his bedroom without looking back at him. If he wanted her, he could come and get her. She wasn't going to chase him.

When he came into the room, she was already pushing her unbuttoned jeans over her hips, taking them off along with her panties. His color was high, and she'd never seen his thick-lashed gaze so sharp and hot, the pale grayish green reminding her of molten silver.

"You want to fuck?" he grunted, sounding surly. Wary, even. "Is that what this is about?"

"I want to fuck *you*, Alex." She lowered her gaze to the front of his jeans, where his cock had already thickened into an impressively long, thick ridge. "Looks like you want the same thing."

He snorted as he shook his head. "I get hard whenever you walk in a room."

"Then there's no telling how you'll react when I do this," she drawled, crossing the space between them and dropping to her knees. Her hands shook as she yanked at the buttons on his jeans, desperate to get them open before he could stop her. His cock sprang out as if it'd been trapped in there against its will, pulsing against her palms as she wrapped her hands around the thick, vein-ridged shaft and pulled it toward her mouth.

"Let's see if I can get more of a reaction out of you than your neighbor did," she breathed, rubbing the engorged head against her lips.

"Damn it, Doc. You don't— *Fuck*!" He shuddered from head to toe as she flicked her tongue over the tip, taking his warm, salty taste into her mouth. God, she couldn't get enough of him.

"You're wrong. I do fuck," she murmured, deliberately misinterpreting his words. "I fuck *you*, when you let me. Now take your shirt off. I want to look at you while I have your dick in my mouth."

"Son of a bitch," he groaned, ripping the shirt over his head and tossing it on the floor. His legs and hands were shaking, and she felt drunk on the thrill coursing through her veins, pumping through her blood.

Driven with the need to make this something he would never forget, she greedily sucked on his cock like it was her newest, most favorite thing in the entire world, growing addicted to his taste. To how he felt on her tongue and how he stretched her mouth as wide as it would go. The heady scent that filled her nose each time she sucked in a deep, desperate breath. She'd gone down on lovers in the past, but she'd never been all that turned on by it. Not like this. Never felt like she might scream if a guy didn't let her keep sucking on him, licking him with her tongue.

"You taste so good, Alex."

"You goddamn little tease," he growled, his hands fisting in her hair as he thrust himself deeper. "You're driving me crazy on purpose."

She smiled, loving that his initial resistance had vanished in the face of his pleasure, and he'd taken over in typical Alex fashion. Not that she was complaining. She loved the feel of his hands on her head, tangled in her hair, controlling her movements. Loved the way he fucked himself into her mouth, setting the pace, careful not to go too deep and gag her, but definitely flirting with her limits.

"That's it," he choked out, the tendons in his strong neck pressing against his skin as he flung his head back, his muscular body sheened with sweat. She stared at his abs, mesmerized by the way they rippled beneath his skin as he fucked her mouth like he owned it. "Keep doing that, baby girl, and I'm gonna come all over your tight little throat."

She moaned, loving it when he talked to her like that, and sucked him harder, letting him know how much she wanted exactly what he'd told her would happen. Her lashes drifted closed as she focused all her concentration on making this good for him, but she could feel the scorching intensity of his gaze focused on her face, on her mouth, as he lowered his head and looked down at her. He made a thick, guttural sound, his hands tightening, and she nearly gagged as his next thrust sent that massive cockhead bumping against the back of her throat.

"Fuck, I'm sorry," he gasped, shaking as he quickly retreated.

She let him know it was okay by sucking him even harder, her mouth wet and voracious, refusing to let him pull her off when he snarled that he was going to come. It happened just seconds later, a harsh curse on his lips as he gripped her head, his body rigid as he started pumping his cock over her tongue, the thick, heavy spurts of cum filling her mouth. She swallowed . . . and swallowed, determined to keep up with him, their heavy-lidded gazes locked hard and tight on each other the entire time.

When his grip on her head finally gentled, she pulled back, surprised by how rigid his thick shaft remained. The broad crown was still ruddy and swollen, and she licked her lips as she wrapped her hands around him. "You're still hard," she murmured, sounding a little hoarse.

"As long as I have you naked and wet, I'm staying that way." He got rid of his jeans, then reached down and lifted her into his arms, turning and pressing her against the nearest wall. His mouth covered hers, moving over it in his greed, his tongue sliding against hers in a slow, carnal rhythm that she would never get enough of.

"Put me in," he growled against her lips, nudging himself against her slick, swollen folds.

She reached between them, wrapping both hands around his rigid length again, but she didn't notch him against her. Instead, she rubbed the wet tip against her clit, teasing them both. He made another raw, thick sound deep in his chest, and she knew she was playing with fire, which only made her burn hotter. So many times now, he'd asked her if she trusted him, and she did. Which gave her the freedom to play with him in a way she'd never been able to do with a man before, and it felt incredible.

"Stop teasing me and put me in that tight cunt," he bit out, nipping her shoulder with his teeth. "Now, damn it."

"Say please," she whispered, licking his ear.

He drew his head back, locking his narrow, burning gaze on hers, his breaths coming rougher now . . . sharper. "You know what you're doing, Doc?"

She lowered her lashes, and caught her lower lip in her teeth. "All I'm asking for is one little word, Alex."

"God, you drive me crazy," he growled, dropping his forehead against hers.

"You want inside," she whispered, rolling her hips so that her wet folds rubbed along the underside of his shaft, "then carry me to the bed. I want you underneath me."

His chest heaved as he lifted his head, his intense stare deep and measuring, and she waited to see what he would decide. Which way he would go. All the while hoping he'd play along.

When he tightened his hands on her ass and started walking backward, toward the bed behind him, she lowered her head, an excited smile on her lips as she nuzzled the silken skin at the side of his strong, corded throat. Kissing her way to his jaw, she ran her lips against the rasp of dark stubble as he tumbled them back onto the sprawling mattress, his long legs hanging over the end.

Eager to feel him filling her, stretching her deep inside, Brit braced herself on her knees, holding his cock upright as she placed the fat head against her wet opening. Then she covered the hands he had curled hard around her hips with her own, and forced her body down, until she'd taken every massive, delicious inch of him.

"That feel good?" she asked breathlessly, tightening her inner muscles as she pulsed her hips against him.

"Hell, yes," he hissed, using his hold on her hips to lift her up and then slam her back down on him, before trailing one hand up her spine, then gripping the back of her neck. He had her under his complete control as he pulled her over him, until he could take her mouth with a raw, aggressive hunger, and she loved it. *Oh, dear*

God. In that shining, blinding moment, Brit suddenly realized that she loved *him.*

It was probably the most foolish thing she'd ever done, but somewhere along the way, she'd gone and fallen in love with him. With the dark, brooding, wary Alex Hudson.

And now there was going to be emotional hell to pay.

She knew she might never get the chance to tell him, because it might never be the right time for them, and she had too much pride to put herself out there just to be shut down. But that didn't mean she couldn't show him how much this meant to her. That she couldn't give him every part of her love but the words.

Reaching behind her neck, Brit took his hand, holding it as she sat up, the move pushing him even deeper inside her. He stared up at her glistening eyes with a cautious awareness, as if he'd suddenly sensed the change in her. She lifted his other hand from her hip, then placed both on her heavy, aching breasts. Pressing his hot palms against the full mounds, she started to pulse her hips in a slow, grinding rhythm, and he groaned deep and low as he arched his head back, squeezing his eyes shut. "Jesus, you're trying to torture me with pleasure tonight, aren't you? Is this some kind of twisted payback for me acting like a dick today?"

"No. I just . . ." She swallowed against the burning knot of emotion lodged in her throat. "Alex, if you could do anything you wanted to me, what would it be?"

He opened his eyes, giving her a sharp, curious stare. "Seriously?"

She nodded, loving the way she could feel him throbbing inside her as she trailed her hands down his powerful arms, his muscles flexing beneath his hot skin.

"I'd fuck your sweet ass," he growled, palming a breast in a possessive hold with one hand, while his other reached around her hip and gripped her right butt cheek.

"That's it?" she asked with a smirk.

Snorting, he said, "You make it sound like a walk in the park, Doc."

She lowered her lashes, and took a quick breath. "I just . . . I was wondering if you'd like to get a bit . . . *rougher* with me?"

ALEX FROZE, WATCHING HER CLOSELY FROM BENEATH HIS BROWS, HIS lips parted for the harsh breaths jerking from his chest. "What are you talking about?"

She stilled, but he could still feel her muscular sheath pulsing around him, his damn heart pounding like a bitch as she said, "I know that you're careful with me."

"I wasn't last night." Hell, he hadn't exactly been gentle *any* of the times he'd touched her. Including tonight. Including right now, the way he had her plump nipple trapped between his thumb and forefinger probably more than most women could handle. But he could see how much she liked it. Feel it in the way her slick cunt got even wetter, hotter, clasping him so tightly it damn near had his eyes rolling back in his head.

She pushed her breast harder against his hand, and her red hair shimmered over her shoulders as she tilted her head. "I told you I was fine last night, Alex. I loved the way you were. And even though you don't think so, you were still careful not to hurt me." Her slender brows knitted together, while her beautiful eyes burned with determination. "I think you're always a little worried about pushing me too far. But you don't have to be. I trust you."

"To do what?" he heard himself ask, his lust-dazed brain trying to figure out what was going on with her, in her head, while his body just demanded that he get her on her back and fuck the living hell out of her.

She licked her lips. "Whatever you want." She pulled in a quick breath, her voice a little huskier as she said, "Tie me up. Spank me. Fuck me really hard and let off some steam."

His lungs heaved, his voice like gravel as he snapped, "Stop. Just *stop*. You don't know what the hell you're asking for, Brit."

"Wanna bet?" she whispered, her pink lips twitching with a provocative smile that he felt all the way down in his damn balls.

"This isn't a fucking game," he growled, gripping her hips. He knew damn well where she was pushing him, and was scared shitless it would be too much for her. Send her running.

Her hair fell like a veil around their faces as she leaned over him, bracing her delicate hands on his hard shoulders. "Come on, Alex. You know what I'm like. I wouldn't say it if I didn't mean it. If it wasn't something I wanted. But it is."

Fuck it. He couldn't fight this. Not when it was Brit, the woman who turned him inside out. Who he wanted more than any other. Who he would have kept for-fucking-ever if he'd been a different man.

With a guttural sound ripping up from his throat, he suddenly reversed their positions, putting them in the middle of the bed with her voluptuous little body trapped beneath him. He pulled his hips back, his hooded gaze locked tight on her wide one as he slowly fed his broad shaft back inside her, his mind churning with the possibilities, his dick somehow getting even harder when he was already hard as a fucking rock. Lowering his head, he gave himself a moment to suck on those mouthwatering tits that tasted like sweet, honeyed sin on his lips, his hands pushing the mounds up high, the throaty moans she gave as he sucked and tongued her plump nipples driving him wild.

From the corner of his eye, he spotted a flash of metal, remembering he'd left his handcuffs sitting on his bedside table after taking them from his belt the last time he'd carried them, and he knew exactly what he wanted from her generous offer. He didn't deserve it—sure as hell didn't deserve *her*—but he was taking it anyway.

Bracing his weight on one arm, he leaned over her as he lifted his other hand, pushing the damp strands of auburn hair at her temple back from her flushed, beautiful face.

"You sure about this, Doc?"

"Mmm," she moaned, her lashes fluttering. "I want you. I want it all."

Gritting his teeth, he pulled his dick from her succulent hold, the flushed rod drenched in her cream as it sprang up against his stomach. Kneeling in the middle of the bed, he jerked his chin toward her, and said, "Then roll over and put your ass in the air, hands behind your back."

She didn't waste any time doing as he said, and Alex scrubbed a rough hand over his mouth as he took a moment to stare at the provocative picture she made, kneeling on the bed before him with her ass presented to him, the side of her pink face pressed to the sheets, hands exactly where he'd told her to place them. Reaching over, he snagged the cuffs off the table, hearing the small catch in her breath when she realized what he was going to do. He couldn't stop his damn hands from shaking as he clicked the metal cuffs around her slender wrists, his heart pounding like a fucking jackhammer.

Bondage games weren't something he ever messed around with, because it wasn't something he wanted. Not from the women he'd been wasting his time with. Women like Chloe. Good women who deserved a hell of a lot more than what he'd given them. He didn't care about earning their trust on a deeper level. Didn't care about pushing the limits with them or taking them to a higher level of pleasure than anything they'd ever known.

But the doc . . . Fuck, she was different. He cared about so many different things when it came to her, he was afraid to look too closely at them for fear of what he might find.

With the cuffs clicked into place, he trailed his hands up either side of her spine, the feminine length of her back arching into his touch. He'd expected her to be tense at first in the restraints, but if anything, her reaction was the exact opposite. She relaxed into them, into the moment, her body soft and perfect beneath his hands as he stroked his way back down her back, curving his hands over the gorgeous globes of her ass. She was peachy and firm and soft, a delicious handful as he pulled her cheeks apart, opening her up so that he could see her pretty little pink asshole and the plush, glistening seam of her pussy.

Another rough, guttural sound rumbled up from his chest, and his fingers tightened. "Christ, Doc. Do you have any idea what the sight of you like this does to me?"

She shivered, pushing her ass up into his hands as she pressed her knees a little wider, and his dick pulsed so hard he was surprised it didn't burst. He slid two fingers through her drenched folds, getting them wet, then touched his slippery fingertips to that tight ring of muscle. "I'm giving you two fingers in your ass tonight," he warned her, applying steady pressure until she opened and took the tips of his fingers inside her.

She was panting, her entire body rosy with a blush—but she didn't try to shy away from his hand or tell him to stop. Instead, she arched her hips a little higher, taking his fingers even deeper, and Alex couldn't stop the primitive growl that shot from his throat.

"That is so fucking sweet," he grunted, pulling his fingers back a few inches and then pumping them back inside, the erotic sight of her taking the thick digits in that pink, puckered hole making him so hot he had to shake the sweat from his eyes.

When he finally slipped his dick back inside her, he thought he might have had a religious experience. It was that . . . shocking. That . . . life changing. She gave a raw, keening cry, panting hard as he pumped into her, grinding himself against her juicy cunt, her inner muscles holding him like a fucking vise.

He knew he was a big man, both his overall physical size and the size of his dick. It wasn't bragging or ego, just fact. And he knew he was more than a little jagged and rough around the edges. But he'd never, *never*, felt as primal and male as he did when he had Brit Cramer's lush little body beneath him. She was so soft and feminine and sweet. So pale and smooth and impossibly perfect.

What he didn't know was why she worried about the size of her thighs or her ass or her tits. They were fucking works of art that brought him to his knees. He wasn't a spiritual man by any means, but he worshipped *this* woman. Her sheer existence made him believe in things that were beyond his grasp and experience. Did he like it or welcome the way he felt? Hell no. It scared the living shit out of him, being drawn to a woman this way. But he couldn't walk away. Not anymore. He just . . . he just needed to find a way to control it. To measure his reaction to her. To somehow master it, though now was clearly not the time to figure out how. There was no way he was finding any measure of control right now. She'd stripped him of it completely the moment she gave him more trust than any other woman had ever done. Even the one he'd been married to.

The doc was a goddamn miracle, stubborn and smart and so selflessly giving, and he wanted to bury himself so deep inside her that she felt him for days. For a fucking lifetime.

Shoving that staggering, terrifying thought from his mind, Alex gritted his teeth and let go.

Loving that she couldn't control how hard or how deep he took her, he pulled his fingers from her backside and curled that arm around her hips, fisting his other hand in her silky hair, and laid his big body over hers, her hands trapped between them as he buried his hot face in the curve of her shoulder. Then he cleared his mind of everything but the stunning feel of his hips pounding against her sweet ass, his cock ramming into her snug heat again and again, while he licked and softly bit at her smooth skin like an animal.

"Alex!" she cried, her fist-tight cunt starting to convulse around him as she climaxed, and he pulled her with him as he went up on his knees, her head falling back to his shoulder as he held her in a tight hold and shoved himself into her, pounding into her so hard her knees left the mattress. He came in a powerful eruption of cum and heat and pleasure that felt so intense it was almost agonizing, the sounds he made raw and rough and pained.

"Oh, Jesus . . . *Oh, God*," he gasped, dropping his head to her damp shoulder as he clutched her against him, never wanting to let her go. "That was fucking incredible."

"Mmm," she slurred, and he forced himself to lay her down and leave her body, knowing he needed to get the cuffs off her before her shoulders became sore. Using the extra key he kept in his bedside table, he unlocked the metal cuffs and tossed them aside. Then he gently massaged her shoulders and arms while she lay on her front, her body boneless and flushed with heat. But there was a small smile on her sensual mouth as she turned her head to the side, and he couldn't resist lying down beside her, drawing her into his arms.

"You okay?" he asked, tilting her face up to his with his fingers beneath her chin.

Her smile spread, beautiful and blinding. "Perfect," she whispered, reaching up to stroke her fingertips across his stubbled jaw. Keeping her drowsy gaze locked with his, she asked, "So what now?"

His arms tightened around her, and he pushed one hairy thigh between her legs, loving the way he could feel his cum slipping out of her as he pressed up against her swollen pussy. "I want you in here with me," he said in a low voice. "All night. In my bed."

"Are you sure this is what you want?"

"Yeah. I'm sure, Doc."

She touched her fingertips to the dark smudges he knew were under his eyes. "You look tired."

With a snort, he said, "That's because I couldn't sleep for shit without you last night."

She looked at him with a question in those big, beautiful eyes, and he heard himself saying, "I wish I could explain, but I can't. Just . . . let it go, Brit. Please."

He could feel her waiting for more, but that was it. He had nothing more to give her. He already felt scraped raw just from making such an uncharacteristic confession. Reaching behind him to turn off the bedside light, he pulled the sheet up over them, then pulled her close again, until he could feel her against the heavy pounding of his heart. "Stay with me," he murmured against the top of her head, the husky words like a plea. "All night. Let me hold you."

"And when it's over?" she whispered, her soft lips moving against his chest.

He swallowed thickly, and closed his eyes. "Just sleep now, baby. Let's not borrow trouble."

LET'S NOT BORROW TROUBLE . . .

It was probably good advice. But as she burrowed closer to his heat, breathing in his heady scent, Brit had a feeling she was already neck-deep in trouble.

And wrapped up tight in his arms.

15

AFTER A HECTIC AFTERNOON SPENT UP AT THE WESTVILLE POLICE STAtion, talking to the detectives who were working Clay Shepherd's case—the case which dealt with the attack against Shepherd himself a few weeks ago—Alex came through his front door, expecting to set eyes on Brit. He hadn't been happy about leaving her at the condo with one of Ben's deputies for protection but hadn't had a choice. It was too important that he talk to the detectives himself, and he was glad that he'd gone, the conclusions they'd come to shedding a grim light on the situation.

Now that he was home, he was trying hard not to think about how excited he was by the prospect of seeing her . . . or how much he was looking forward to it.

But Brit wasn't anywhere to be seen. Instead, the only person waiting for him in his living room was Ben.

Scowling at his brother, who was looking tanned and a bit

tense as he sprawled in one of Alex's leather chairs, he asked, "Where's Brit? Upstairs?"

He hadn't had much of a chance to talk to her that morning, and though she'd seemed fine, he was still worried about how she was feeling after what had happened between them. Not just the bondage, but the *other* things that had taken place in the middle of the night. Things that had probably had her sweet ass cheeks feeling a little tender today, like his palm.

And one thing was for damn certain: the doc didn't just like having her ass spanked—she *loved* it.

Alex hadn't been able to stop thinking about her, and everything they'd done, all day, which had made concentrating during the meeting with the detectives hard as fuck. But he didn't have a clue what *she* was thinking . . . or if she was feeling all right. God only knew she'd probably had trouble walking after the way that he'd ridden her, and he had to shake his head before he got wrapped up in the heated memories all over again.

Forcing his attention back to his brother, he watched as Ben leaned forward in the chair and tossed the sports magazine he'd been reading onto the coffee table. "I know you're not going to like it," Ben said, "but there was an emergency with one of her patients and Brit needed to go to the hospital to see the woman."

He stood there and stared, unable to believe what he was hearing. "You let her leave? What the fuck were you thinking?"

"She's with Mike," Ben murmured, his green gaze steady and direct. "Which means she's okay. So why don't you try staying calm?"

"Calm?" he muttered, his insides knotting with tension. "Fuck, Ben. The asshole already tried to shove her off the road *once*. You don't think he'd try it again?"

Moving to his feet, Ben said, "He still doesn't know who you are or where you live, so he couldn't follow them from here. And just so you know, there was no stopping her. This is about more than her work, Alex. She's been patient, taking your advice and not going out, but this was someone she cares about. No one was going to keep her from doing it."

"You should have," he bit out, his deep voice thick with frustration. He glared at his brother from beneath his brows. "If it was Reese, you would have."

Ben started to respond, but cut off whatever he was going to say when Reese herself came out of the kitchen carrying a glass of iced tea. She offered Alex an apologetic look, as if she knew he didn't want her there. Not when he'd been getting ready to lay into his brother some more for acting like a know-it-all asshole.

Damn it, he should have been here with Brit. If he had been, he sure as shit would have been able to stop her from setting foot outside the condo. He'd have done whatever was necessary, even if it meant tying her little ass down, to make her stay put, where she was safe.

Pulling his keys from where he'd shoved them in his pocket, he said, "I'm going to the hospital."

"There's no need," Ben argued, hooking his thumbs in the front pockets of his jeans. "They won't be much longer. You'd probably drive past them on their way home."

Fuck! It was going to kill him, sitting here waiting when he knew damn good and well that she'd put herself in potential danger by going out there, where Shepherd could all too easily get to her.

"I'd tell you to have a drink," Ben drawled, cutting into his thoughts, "but I don't think that would be a good idea. Wanna play a game of gin rummy while we wait, instead?"

Choking back the words he *really* wanted to say, since Reese was there, he curled his lip and muttered, "Piss off."

"Um, I'm just going to use the restroom," Reese murmured,

setting her tea on a coaster on the table before quickly making her escape.

Alex noticed the warm look in Ben's eyes as he watched his wife disappear down the hallway, and let out an explosive curse that drew his brother's attention. "How the hell do you survive it?" he grunted.

"What? Being in love?" Ben asked, as strangely intuitive as he'd always been.

Alex jerked his chin in response.

His brother sat on the arm of the sofa and grinned like a cocky jackass. "It's pretty much paradise on my side of the pond, brother. You should stop fighting so hard to tread water and just come on over."

"Fuck you."

Ben sighed in response. "You'd listen to me if you were smart, Alex. I know what I'm talking about."

He ground his teeth together, saved from having to listen to any more of Ben's bullshit relationship advice when Reese came back into the room. Changing the subject, his brother asked him how things had gone with the detectives up in Westville, but Alex was too furious to get into it then. He muttered something about needing to do some work, telling Ben that he'd fill him in on everything later, then left the room. Once in his office, he left the door open so that he'd hear when Brit came in, and paced the floor, listening to Ben and Reese murmur to each other.

Christ, the glow on those two these days was so bright it was blinding. He kept waiting for it to wear off, but if anything, they looked more in love now than they ever had. And they'd already been nauseatingly head-over-ass for each other right from the start of their relationship.

Pacing from one side of the small room to the other, Alex pressed his fingertips to his temples, feeling like his damn head was splitting in two. Or maybe that was just his fucking personality. What the hell was happening to him? He was so goddamn angry and on edge, he wanted to put his bloody fist through the wall.

He pulled off his shoulder holster, setting it on his desk, then tossed the pack of cigarettes in his shirt pocket down beside it. He'd been surprised when he'd reached for a smoke while on the drive to Westville and found the pack he always kept tucked behind his visor still half full. He hadn't realized until that moment how little he'd smoked since Brit had come to stay with him. He normally would have already been through several packs by this time of the week, and there he was, with the same damn pack from the week before.

Taking his phone from his pocket, he started to call her, then stopped and tossed the phone on his desk along with the other things. He didn't want to yell at her over the fucking phone. What he wanted was to put her across his knee and spank her beautiful little ass for scaring the hell out of him.

Flicking a dark look at the clock mounted on the far wall, Alex continued to pace, counting down the seconds until she was finally back where she belonged.

EVEN IF SHE HADN'T ALREADY SEEN HIS BATTERED RANGE ROVER parked out on the street when Mike had dropped her off, the minute she came in through the front door and saw Ben and Reese's expressions, Brit would have known Alex was home. She tried to mentally prepare herself to deal with him, but was still stunned by the look of fury on his hard face when he suddenly came in from the hallway, a muscle pulsing steadily in the grim set of his jaw.

Oh, shit. He was seriously livid.

Taking a deep breath, she fought to stay calm, knowing her

own temper would have been gearing up for an argument in defense of her actions, if it weren't for the stark worry in his hooded gaze that he hadn't quite managed to conceal. Instead of making her defensive, it just made her feel like crap for not calling him and at least trying to explain why she'd had to go. She knew she should have, but she'd simply been too wrapped up in her own worries, after dealing with her suicidal patient, to talk to anyone. Much less the man who was playing havoc with her heart.

"You, I'll deal with later," he told her, before turning away from her and glaring at his family. Shoving his hands in his pockets, he said, "You two need to get lost."

"Nice," Ben murmured, his tone resigned. "Being a dick is just your go-to behavior, isn't it?"

Alex ground his jaw, but didn't bother arguing. Brit knew he knew he was being a jerk. At the moment, he was just too angry to care.

She cast the couple an apologetic smile as they walked past, hugging Reese back when her friend threw her arms around her shoulders.

"You didn't have to be a dick to them," she murmured, the moment the front door was closed behind them. She locked it, then turned around to face him. "I'm the one you're mad at. Not them."

"I'm pissed at everyone right now," he countered, the gruff words ominously soft. "But that's not what I want to talk about. What I *want* is to know . . ." His breathing roughened, his deep voice lashing with anger. "Christ, Brit. I want to know what the *fuck* you were thinking!"

She swiped her tongue over her lower lip, and tried to keep her voice steady. "I'm sorry I didn't call you. But I had a lot to . . . deal with."

He stared back at her, waiting for more, and she knew that as far as explanations went, that one wasn't going to hold water. But what else could she tell him? Certainly not the truth. That her patient had turned suicidal after her boyfriend left her for another woman, and that she'd been profoundly affected by the woman's pain. By her tears and the wrenching heartbreak that was ripping her in two.

How could she tell Alex, the man who never wanted to talk about his emotions and what he was feeling, that the only way she'd been able to deal with tonight was by taking a step back and giving herself some time to think? Yes, she should have called him—but she *couldn't*. Not then. Hell, she barely knew what to say to him now.

And, to be honest, he didn't look like a man who wanted to talk at the moment. No, he looked like a man who was ready to put his woman over his knee and spank her ass until it burned with a hot, rosy glow.

But she wasn't his woman. He'd made that clear last night, when he'd refused to give her an answer about their future. She knew, with every fiber of her being, that there was a strong connection between them. One that was as beautiful as it was unique. One of those once-in-a-lifetime kind of things. But that didn't mean that anything would ever come of it. Didn't mean that he would ever be able to accept it. Be happy for it and thankful, instead of looking at it as a curse.

"You had a lot to deal with," he muttered, shaking his head. "You know, you're not stupid, Brit, so why the hell are you acting like it? Going out like that without me . . . Fuck, I can't even begin to understand what you were thinking."

"Alex, this was a legitimate call."

"You didn't know that!" he roared. "When that call first came in, you didn't know that! Shepherd could have targeted that woman and set the whole thing up. You could have been walking right into one of his sick, twisted fantasies!"

Seeing precisely how terrified he'd been, her frustration and worries simply faded beneath a heavy wave of remorse that made her feel even crappier for doing this to him. "I'm sorry," she said quietly, walking toward him. "I really am, Alex. I didn't mean to worry you."

"You didn't *worry* me," he muttered hoarsely, scrubbing his hands down his face, before shoving all ten fingers back through his hair. The look he gave her was stark, and filled with pain. "You scared the ever-living hell out of me."

"I didn't mean to." She stepped closer, and put her hand on his hard chest. "How can I make it up to you?"

His nostrils flared as he pulled in a slow, deep breath, his strong throat working as he swallowed. "Considering I'm about two seconds away from spanking your little ass raw right now, Doc, I'd be careful what you say."

She flicked her tongue over her bottom lip. "If it'll make you forgive me, then do it, Alex. I couldn't get enough of it last night. And I can't imagine I'd feel any differently now. So do it. Do whatever will make you feel better."

His eyes went heavy as his body stilled in a tense, predatory way. "You want to make me feel better?"

Her voice was soft, breathless. "Yes."

She watched as his pupils dilated, the turbulent black nearly drowning out the pale, angry green. "Anything I want?"

She nodded, wondering what on earth she was getting herself into. Every time she should be smart and take a step back, she found herself rushing headfirst into another carnal sexual encounter with him, each one binding her even deeper under his spell. But, damn it, she wanted this, too. Wanted it too badly to turn away from him, even if she *was* like the proverbial moth flying closer and closer to the flame.

If she were Icarus, her wings would have melted long ago. And the scary thing was, she just didn't give a damn.

"What do you want, Alex? Tell me."

His eyes burned with a hot, possessive glow. "I want you up in my bed, naked, begging me to take you in the ass."

"All right," she somehow managed to reply in a steady voice. "Then come with me." Taking his hand, she pulled him along behind her as she headed up the stairs, her heart pounding with each step. She could feel the heat of his stare burning against her, *into* her, his hand hot to the touch, as if he were raging with fever, and she shivered in response, knowing they were no doubt going to set the sheets on fire.

Needing to grab something from the guest room, she left him standing by his doorway, and his eyes darkened when she came back to him with a small bottle of baby oil in her hand. He followed her into his room, which was silent and still but for the soft whoosh of the cool air spilling from the air-conditioning vent.

"I'm sorry I scared you," she murmured, looking up at him when they were both standing at the foot of his bed, where she'd tossed the bottle of baby oil. Unbuttoning the top button on her blouse, she went on. "But I didn't have a choice. I needed to make sure she was okay."

His breath left his lungs on a deep exhalation. "I get that you felt you needed to be there, but the way you handled it was wrong, Brit. You should have waited for me. Hell, at the very least you should have called me and talked it over with me."

Dropping the blouse to the floor, she stepped out of her shoes and reached back to the zipper on her skirt, pulling it down. "When I first got the call, it was right in the middle of when you were scheduled to be in your meeting with the detectives and I didn't want to interrupt you."

His dark brows drew together. "And then later?"

"I . . . um, it's complicated," she murmured, hoping to distract him as she let the skirt slip down her legs. And it worked for a moment. His searing gaze moved over her body with avid appreciation, taking in her lacy bra and panties. He ran a hand over his mouth roughly, sighed, then lifted his searching gaze to hers.

"What kind of answer is that?"

Her lips twitched as she tried not to smile. "The same kind you usually give me," she said lightly.

He grunted, the harsh sound thick with frustration, then lifted a hand to the back of his neck. "You sure you want to do this?" he asked, watching her carefully.

"Why wouldn't I be?" she countered, tilting her head a bit to the side.

His lashes lowered, but not before she caught the flash of something dark and visceral in his eyes. "Because if you get on that bed, I really am going to put every hard, thick inch of my cock up your ass. And then I'm going to fuck it like I own it."

She sucked in a sharp breath at the low, gritty statement of intent, and her pulse quickened.

Reading her expression, he slowly arched an eyebrow. "You sure you don't want to run now, Doc?" he murmured, and she could tell by his tone that he expected her to do exactly that.

But I'm no coward. Like hell am I running.

"Does this look like I'm scared?" she asked him, reaching behind her and unclasping her bra. She almost smiled at the look of surprise he tried to conceal, then found herself shuddering with a powerful wave of desire when his surprise bled into raw, primitive hunger. He watched her strip out of her panties like a predator might watch his evening meal, his breaths deepening as his body seemed to expand, all those acres of hard, lean muscle flexing beneath his tight skin.

Without a word, Brit crawled onto the bed, then turned over, bracing herself on her elbows as she slowly bent her knees, opening her legs so that he could see every part of her. She didn't need to touch herself to know that she was already sopping and swollen between her thighs, her tender folds tingling with anticipation as he visually claimed every inch of her. He turned away, walking over to his dresser, where he laid his wallet down, along with some loose change. Then he leaned over, giving her a great shot of his tight ass as he took off his boots and socks. When he straightened, he pulled his shirt off, dropping it as he turned back to her, his hands slowly undoing his belt and fly as he walked back toward the foot of the bed. Shoving the denim and tight black boxers over his hips, he let them drop as he climbed onto the bed, so freaking gorgeous she was pretty sure she'd been watching him with her mouth hanging open.

She wasn't quite sure of what to expect from what they were about to do, but she'd have been outright lying if she'd said she wasn't excited about it. She was curious . . . and yes, a little apprehensive. But mostly she was eager to see just how far Alex could go with her. How deep into the raw, emotionally intense, blisteringly hot connection they shared he could take her.

Chills swept over her heated skin as she watched him fist his cock in a brutal grip, the veins on the back of his hand pressing against his skin as he pumped the engorged shaft a few times, the head already dark and wet. "On your hands and knees," he said in a low voice as he dragged his hard gaze up the trembling length of her body, lingering on her pussy, breasts, and mouth, before finally locking it tight with hers.

Taking a deep breath, she rolled over and got into position, a violent tremor of remembered pleasure rushing through her when she thought about how he'd cuffed and fucked her from behind the night before. Her throat was still a little hoarse from how hard she'd screamed, her insides tender. But, God, it had been worth it.

And the way he'd held her in his arms throughout the long night, during those quiet hours when he hadn't been inside her, had been so sweet she'd nearly burst into tears that morning when she'd opened her eyes.

But this wasn't the time to think about the things that had already happened. It was time to focus on what he was about to do to her *now*, and as she curled her fingers into the sheets, Brit felt him move up behind her, the press of his hands against her inner thighs forcing her to open her legs wider, her ass presented to him as she went down on her elbows and arched her back.

"That's fucking perfect," he scraped out, his big hands squeezing her ass, and then pulling the cheeks apart, opening her right up. "Your cunt's already dripping, Brit. You have cream sliding down your thighs."

"I know," she whispered.

"Are you excited about what's coming?" he asked in a dark rasp, stroking his thumbs along either side of the sensitive opening buried there between her cheeks. "About what I'm going to do to this tight little hole?"

She shivered, arching her back even deeper. "I am," she breathed out, moaning low in her throat. "You make me want everything with you, Alex. So just do it. Stop making me wait."

"Not yet," he muttered, reaching over to the bedside table and taking something from the drawer. For a moment, she thought he was getting the handcuffs again. But then she heard the sound of a foil wrapper being opened, and realized he was putting on a condom. It made her wonder if he was planning on fucking her pussy after he fucked her ass, but then she forgot all about asking him for an explanation when he notched the broad head of his cock against her vulva. He pushed into her slow and deep, parting her swollen tissues with his thick penetration. "God, Brit." He barely moved his hips in a brief back and forth motion, but it was enough to make her writhe. "You have the tightest, sweetest little pussy. It's always so fucking hot and ready."

Because of him. Because he made her that way.

"What are you doing?" she asked. "I mean, other than the obvious?"

"The baby oil is great, but nothing's as good as your lube." He ground against her, giving her every inch, groaning when she tightened her inner muscles, squeezing him inside her. "Fuck, that feels good."

"Are you wet enough yet?" she gasped, her breaths quickening as she felt him rub the tip of his thumb around her drenched vulva, the tender skin stretched tight around the thick root of his cock. Then he pressed the slick digit against the puckered ring of muscle where she was waiting to take him, briefly pushing it inside, and she all but shouted, "*When*, Alex?"

"Now," he muttered, carefully pulling from her sheath. She was still swollen enough inside that he could have hurt her if he wasn't gentle, and the way he handled her just made her trust him all the more.

"Good . . . that's good," she moaned, shocked by how greedy she sounded. How desperate. Her heart raced, pounding hard and fast in her chest, as she heard him pop open the top of the small baby oil bottle, then felt the wet trickle of oil as he drizzled it between her cheeks. A quick glance back showed him rubbing more of the oil onto his already glistening, latex-covered cock, and she bit her lip as she closed her eyes, trying not to think about how freaking big he looked.

"Push out for me," he said a moment later, pressing his wide cockhead against the sensitive hole. "It'll make it easier for you."

Oh, *wow*. Her eyes were shocked wide, her heart damn near climbing its way into her throat as she felt him start to push inside. "You're kidding, right?" she wheezed, her chest jerking with a breathless laugh. "The only thing that could make this easier for me is if *I* was the one doing it to *you*!"

"Yeah, but that wouldn't be anywhere near as much fun," he rumbled, his big hands gripping her ass. He spread her cheeks, and she knew he was watching what he was doing to her as he pushed a little more of his veined shaft into the tiny hole. Voice even rougher than it'd been before, he said, "And anything worth having is worth some hard effort, Doc. Don't you preach that to your patients?"

"Are you saying you're worth it?" she asked, as he sank in another thick, steely inch.

He froze at her words, and she couldn't even hear him breathing. Then he blew out a hard breath, and muttered, "The pleasure'll be worth it."

She was panting too hard to even talk now, her pulse roaring in her ears as he dipped two fingers into her empty sex, swirling them around to get them nice and wet, before slicking her juices onto the inches of cock he hadn't worked inside her yet. It was getting easier, but was still . . . intense, and even a little painful. She started focusing on pushing back as he went forward, determined to make it work, and somewhere in the middle of all the searing, bone-melting sensations, she realized she was nearly taking him all the way to the root now.

Oh, holy hell. It was . . . She grit her teeth, unable to think of how to describe it as he started fucking her ass with short, jabbing strokes. Powerful, but controlled, as if he had to leash himself as tightly as possible to keep from losing it. Sweat glistened on her skin as he gripped her hips in a greedy, biting hold, the warm drops slipping into the hollow at her lower back. She was taking him a little easier now, his thrusts getting a bit harder as he read the signals and cues from her body, and she got lost in the onslaught of raw ecstasy and pinching pain, the two sensations so intertwined she could no longer tell one from the other. She was bombarded with maddening pulses of heat and fullness, intense pulling and stretching, her body so lost in the devastating chaos she was making sounds and screaming things she didn't even understand. All she knew was that she *loved* it. Fucking loved it. Loved how carnal and intimate it felt, as if he was driving himself into the very heart of her. But that wasn't even the best part.

No, the best part wasn't what was happening to *her* body. It was what was happening to Alex's. The way she could feel him trembling behind her as she started pushing back against his thrusts, slamming her ass against him. The strong, possessive grip of his big hands on her hips as he started yanking her against him, struggling to go slow as hoarse, guttural curses spilled from his lips in a violent rush. The urgency of his breaths and the pumping, pulsing strokes of his hips as he tried not to lose control and give her too much, too hard, too soon. He was coming undone, and she wanted just to push and shove and force him over that edge, even knowing she would be weathering the storm right along with him. But he suddenly pulled out before she could act on the dangerous impulses, her body left aching and empty as she looked over her shoulder just in time to see him ripping the condom off and tossing it on the floor.

What was he . . . ?

"I couldn't hold it," he growled, braced on his knees as he grabbed her and turned her over. Then he jerked her up against him, her legs on either side of his muscular thighs. His arms were like steel bands around her, his body shaking as much as his voice. "Damn it, baby. Are you okay?"

"I'm fine," she breathed against his hot skin, nuzzling his chest with her mouth. "You didn't need to stop. You weren't hurting me."

"It was too good. Too fucking incredible. I was terrified I was going to lose it and hurt you," he scraped out between his hard breaths. He held her even tighter, crushing her against him as he panted against her temple, still fighting for control, and the next thing she knew she was on her back on the bed and he was coming down over her, a cry of surprise on her lips as he rammed his massive cock deep in her pussy. He started fucking her before she'd even taken her next breath, and the rhythm was too hard, too fast, after everything that they'd done during the previous night, but she didn't care. She was unraveling, beyond desperate for him, his weight pressing her deep into the mattress as he buried his face in the curve of her shoulder, his open mouth pressed to the heat of her skin. With one hand fisted in her hair, and the other gripping her ass, he hammered himself into her like their lives depended on how wild and hard and fast he could fuck her. She could feel his knees digging into the bedding as he braced himself, using his muscular ass and abs to drive himself into her even deeper, with even more power.

She came almost instantly, her husky cries and the clasping spasms of her inner muscles only making him wilder . . . *greedier*, as if he couldn't get enough of her. She was breathless and stammering, telling him how much she loved the feel of him inside her, choking back the truly important words she knew she couldn't say. They burned on her tongue, poignant and hot, as he gripped her ass with both hands and wrenched her lower body off the bed, pulling her against him as he drew up on his knees and crashed into her. He pulled back, then crashed into her again as he came in a scalding burst of pressure, burying his strangled roar against the side of her throat. He kept pumping into her, again and again, his body spilling in thick, sharp pulses, until she could feel his cum being pushed out of her sheath every time he lunged back in.

He collapsed against her fully when he was finally spent, pressing her back into the mattress. The move pushed him even deeper into her swollen, tender tissues, and she gasped.

"Shh," he murmured, pressing his lips to the sensitive skin beneath her ear. "I'll make it better." A deep groan rattled in his throat as he wrapped his arms around her and rolled them to their sides. "Just as soon as I can fucking move, I'll take care of you, baby girl. I promise."

Snuggling against his chest, Brit couldn't help but smile, loving the way he talked to her. She probably would have ripped into any other man who tried to say something like that to her, calling her *baby girl*, but it was different when coming from Alex.

"You sore?" he whispered, stroking his palm down her spine, and then back up again.

"A little," she admitted.

He started to pull out, moving so carefully it took him nearly a full minute, and she groaned, hating the loss of him, wanting to keep him inside her forever, which was madness. Dangerous, heart-destroying madness. As if he sensed her restless emotions, he cupped her slick folds in his hand, holding her. His fingers moved, stroking across her labia, and she gasped when she realized what he was doing. That he was pushing the thick wetness slipping from the tiny hole back inside her, as if that was where it belonged. It was earthy and raw and breathtakingly erotic, knowing that he wanted her drenched in him. That he wanted her wet and filled with his cum as they lay in the wrecked, tangled bedding, their bodies damp and hot, breaths still rough from exertion. He'd fucked her with so much wild, visceral passion that she didn't know if she'd ever breathe normally again, the violent intensity of his hunger making her desperate for him even now, when her tender flesh was so swollen and used.

"You okay?" he asked, still stroking her softly.

"Yes." She lifted her hand and placed it against his powerful biceps, loving how he felt against her palm. So solid and perfect and warm. "I might be a bit tender, but it was worth it."

ALEX COULD HEAR THE SMILE IN THE DOC'S SOFT WORDS, AND HE wrapped both arms around her, holding her tight against his chest. He'd never lost it the way he just had with her, his need to somehow bind her to him with pleasure pushing him to a place where he'd lost every fucking ounce of his control. It'd simply been obliterated, leaving him with nothing but hunger and craving and instinct. His head was still spinning as he tried to make sense of what had happened. But it was too hard to concentrate when he had every inch of her silky skin pressed against his, her soft breaths feathering against his chest as she burrowed against him.

"You haven't told me what happened today in Westville," she murmured, stroking the hand on his arm up to his shoulder, his skin tingling in the wake of her touch.

It took him a moment to get his brain in the right gear, and then he realized that he still hadn't shared what he'd learned with Ben, either. Deciding that he could wait until the morning to call his brother, he said, "After the detectives and I talked, we all came to the conclusion that the attack Shepherd said took place at that frat party was a sham."

She stiffened against him, and he knew she was frowning as she worked through the implications of what he'd just told her. "But there was . . . physical evidence of an attack."

Running his fingers through her silky hair, he let out a tired sigh. "I know, Doc. But we think he planned it. That he paid someone to do it."

"Ohmygod. That's so awful!"

"I just wish I knew what set him off."

Shaking her head, she said, "Sometimes there *is* no reason.

Sometimes people just can't handle life and it breaks them. Or shit stockpiles on them and they can't hold it together. The loss of their job or a failed class. Even a bad relationship."

He grunted, and she immediately pulled back a little, looking up and locking her worried gaze with his.

"I didn't mean it like that. I wasn't casting any judgments, Alex."

His mouth twisted. "Don't worry about it."

Moving her hand to his face, she cupped his cheek as she softly said, "You tried to self-destruct, yes. But you didn't try to hurt anyone else."

"Except for the jackasses that I beat up," he rumbled.

Her slender brows drew together. "Yeah, well, it may sound barbaric, but I think they had it coming."

With a quiet, grateful laugh slipping past his lips, Alex lowered his head and gave her a soft kiss. Then he placed his hand on the back of her head and pulled her face against his chest again before he could get carried away, since he knew she needed some downtime.

He closed his eyes, holding her close, and had no idea how much time had actually passed, seconds or minutes or hours, when he suddenly said, "Brit?"

"Hmm?" came her sleepy reply.

"What did I say to you that night?" His tone was low, thick with concern, since he wasn't really sure that he wanted to know. But he couldn't stop himself from asking the question.

"What night?"

"A few weeks ago, when we were standing on Ryder and Lily's patio and everyone else had gone inside."

When she didn't immediately reply, her body stiffening against him again, he said, "Don't try to tell me you don't remember. You slapped me across the face that night, Doc."

"You don't remember what you said?" she asked in a muffled voice.

"I'm afraid not."

She drew her head back, looking up at him with a wary gaze. "Were you drunk?"

"On lust, not alcohol," he explained with a regretful smile.

Her lips parted with a soft gasp. "What?"

He lifted his hand, pushing her lovely hair back from her even lovelier face. "You're always beautiful, but that night you were wearing some slinky little green dress that clung to your curves, and your hair was flowing down your back in a riot of curls," he explained in a husky murmur. Then a wry smile twisted his lips. "You had me so horny I damn near swallowed my tongue when I saw you. And I was pissed as hell that I couldn't do anything about it."

She blinked up at him, looking stunned. "I wish I'd known," she whispered.

"Why?"

"Because I would've done my best to really make you suffer," she said hotly, smacking his shoulder. "You were such an ass that night!"

Alex laughed at the teasing he heard in her throaty voice, then quietly sobered. "Seriously, Doc. What did I say?"

Lifting her brows, she shrugged as she said, "Just something about how you weren't surprised I was still single, because a woman like me was never worth the time or effort."

"Jesus, I'm an ass," he muttered with a scowl, his insides churning. "I can't believe I said that to you. I'm such a motherfucker."

She lifted up and pressed a sweet, brief kiss to his lips that he felt in every fucking part of his body, then looked into his eyes. "It's okay, Alex. You were just . . . angry."

Curling his hand around her nape, he said, "I didn't mean a word of it, Doc. You know that, right?"

"I know," she murmured, snuggling back down against his chest, and he pulled her closer, rubbing the back of her neck, wondering if, like him, she felt too exhausted at that moment to deal with the confusing emotions that were pressing in on them, making it difficult to breathe. Closing his eyes, he tried to let it all just drift away, and simply enjoy the moment. Enjoy having her right where he needed her.

He didn't think much time had passed when he suddenly jerked awake, his heart nearly pounding its way into his throat as he tried to pull in a deep enough breath. He'd had the dream again. The weird as shit one where Brit was caught up in the churning ocean waves and kept getting pulled away from him, while he struggled to draw her closer . . . *closer* . . .

Trying to calm his rapid breaths, he wrapped his arms around her, one hand digging into her hair, the other at her lower back, holding her so tight . . . probably *too* tight, but he couldn't make himself let go.

"Hmm . . . Keep me closer."

"Brit? What did you just say?" he gasped, the husky words nearly tripping over themselves as they fell from his lips.

He waited, his chest tight, but she didn't respond.

Then he realized she'd already fallen back asleep.

16

THE MOMENT ALEX OPENED HIS EYES, HE FELT LIKE HE WAS LIVING ON borrowed time. The heavy weight of something approaching pressed in on him, and his blood fired with an urgency that he couldn't explain.

The sun was only just rising, slipping through the slanted blinds on the far window, painting the room in muted, golden colors. Brit slept soundly beside him, no doubt exhausted from the long night, since he hadn't been able to keep his hands off her. He'd let her sleep for a few hours after that first shattering encounter, and then he'd woken her up so that they could go down to the kitchen together and eat. They'd filled themselves up on fresh bread and slices of cheese and salami that came from a little local gourmet deli, and then he'd carried her back upstairs and made love to her until they were both too exhausted to move. Despite how furious he'd been with her for going to the hospital without him, and that strange dream he'd had, the night had turned out to be incredibly satisfying. And now he wanted to get lost in her lush little body all over again.

He *needed* her, damn it, as quickly as he could get her, that ticking clock getting louder in the back of his head. But he forced himself to take it slow. Not to rush.

Rolling to his side, he took his time looking at her, his hungry gaze roving over her beautiful form. She lay on her side, facing him, and he slowly pulled the sheet a little lower so that he could watch the way the soft wisps of morning light played over her creamy skin. The gentle breeze from the air-conditioning vent was making her nipples pucker, and his mouth watered with its need to warm them. Taste them. Hold them against his tongue and suckle on the sweet tips until she came.

Christ, he loved her body. Every plush, delectable inch of it. But he was fascinated by her mind as well. By her intellect and her quick wit.

And then there was her heart. Her warmness and caring and sense of compassion. She was so many things he wasn't used to, and didn't think he deserved, wrapped up in a mouthwatering, gorgeous package. There'd been times during the night when he'd awakened, and simply watched her in the silvery streams of moonlight, almost afraid to believe she was real. That she was there, with him, in his bed. That she wanted him. *All* of him. Even as fucked up and difficult as he could be.

Lifting his hand, he curved it around the feminine slope of her shoulder, then trailed his palm down the elegant length of her arm, her pale skin cool to the touch. He needed to turn the air conditioner up so that she didn't get too cold at night. Or . . . he could just keep her body under his, his dick buried deep in that cushiony pussy, keeping her warm from the inside out.

His cock shot even harder, more than interested in the idea, and he'd just started to lower his mouth to her slightly parted lips, intent on kissing her awake, when the cell phone he'd left on his bedside table started to ring.

Choking back a sharp curse, Alex rolled over and threw his legs over the side of the bed as he sat up, reaching for the phone. When he saw Ben's name flashing on the screen, he thought, *Shit, this is it. I'm out of time.*

"You got him?" he muttered, already knowing what the answer would be.

"Yeah." Ben's deep voice filled his ear. "We've got him, Alex."

"When?"

"Less than twenty minutes ago. A guy called it in from a camp-site over by Ridgeway. He was camping there with his family, and when he got up to take his little girl to the bathroom, he spotted Shepherd coming out of the men's restroom. Recognized him from an appeal we'd put in all the local papers. He put in the call, then kept an eye on Shepherd's Suburban until we got there."

Alex could tell by the tone of his brother's voice that there was something he wasn't telling him. "What?" he grunted, shoving his free hand back through his hair. "You might as well go ahead and say whatever it is you think is going to piss me off."

Ben exhaled a sharp breath. "The bastard had the back of the Suburban fitted out like a torture chamber. We're talking hand-cuffs, pliers, blowtorch, scalpels, saws, rope, and a fucking five-foot coil of barbwire."

Fury scorched through Alex's veins, pulsing in his head like a guttural roar. He slowly curled his free hand into a fist, his chest jerking as he sucked in hard, deep breaths. "Where is that sick motherfucker?" he snarled. "I want to know where he is, Ben. *Now.* I want to know what the fuck he planned on doing to her."

"His ass is already headed to jail, where you can't reach him. And you don't need to be driving yourself crazy, thinking about what he had planned. He isn't getting anywhere near her, so it's over. It's done."

He didn't say anything, the muscle at the side of his jaw ticking as he ground his molars, and Ben dropped his voice. "Alex, seriously, man, you need to be happy about this. She does not need to be dealing with any of your shit right now. So don't fuck it up."

"I'll call you later," he muttered, disconnecting the call. He set the phone back on the bedside table, braced his elbows on his spread knees, and dropped his face into his hands. Ben was right. He needed to get his shit together. He was so damn relieved that sick fuck hadn't gotten his hands on Brit that he could have cried. But at the same time, he couldn't manage to swallow down the fury ripping through him, or the fucking fear crawling over his skin.

And his heart was thudding with an unmistakable beat of dread, because he didn't know what the hell was going to happen when he told her that the nightmare was over.

Before he had time to get any of it figured out, he felt the bed shift as she sat up, her sleepy voice rough with worry. "Alex? What's wrong?"

"Nothing," he replied in a low voice, twisting so that he could face her. "It's good news, babe. Shepherd's been caught."

She blinked, her big eyes filling with a powerful swell of emotion. "Oh, God, that's so wonderful," she whispered, but she was pale beneath the bright flush spreading across her cheeks, and he'd have given his left nut to know if it was worry for Shepherd that was upsetting her . . . or the same thing that was eating at him.

He watched her slender throat work as she swallowed, her hands clenched in the sheet that had fallen over her lap, her upper body completely bare to him, and he cut her off before she could speak, saying, *"Don't go."*

Her eyes went wide at his husky demand. "What?" she mouthed.

"Don't go back home," he rasped, forcing the words past his tight throat. "Don't leave."

She caught her lower lip in her teeth. "You want me to stay?"

"*Yes.*"

Auburn waves of hair spilled over her shoulders as she tilted her head a bit to the side, her eyes bright as she studied him through her lashes. "In what . . . capacity?"

He jerked his head back as if she'd just clipped him on the chin. Maybe he wasn't thinking straight, but he hadn't been expecting the question. "You want me to define it?"

"Yes," she said calmly, pulling the sheet up over her breasts and clutching it against her chest. "I *need* you to define it."

Fuck. Rubbing his hand over his mouth, he struggled to find the right words, but couldn't. He couldn't even explain what he wanted to himself, so how the hell could he be expected to explain it to her?

At his silence, she gave him a small, sad smile that made his insides twist and ache, because he knew what was coming. "Alex, as much as I would love to keep staying here with you, I . . . I can't. I need to go home, where I belong. But we can . . . we can talk about things when you're ready."

"I don't want to talk," he growled, surprised by the way his throat burned. Unable to sit still, he surged to his feet and grabbed a pair of boxers from his dresser, yanking them on. Then he turned around and crossed his arms over his chest, pinning her with an irritated glare. "I just want you to fucking accept what I'm saying and stay with me."

She lifted her shoulders in a helpless shrug. "You want it all your way."

"And what is it you want to talk about?" he snarled. "Our *feelings*?"

"Yes."

He worked his jaw while his heart thundered, so frustrated he wanted to roar. "Jesus, Brit. We've been together for the fucking blink of an eye. Why are you pushing this?"

BRIT STARED BACK AT HIM, FIGHTING HARD TO CHOKE BACK HER SOBS. Licking her lips, she clutched the sheet tighter against her chest, and said, "I'm not pushing anything. I need to go home, Alex. I need to regroup. And we might not have been together long, but we've known each other for a long time. I know more about you than I ever realized. So just give me some space, because my emotions . . . they're apparently a lot more involved in this than yours are."

The rhythmic tick in his taut cheek told her he was beyond furious. "This isn't a contest. You don't get to measure it in degrees."

Very softly, she said, "I do when I'm the one whose emotions are on the line."

"*Fuck,*" he bit out, scraping his hands back through his hair as he started to pace across the floor at the foot of the bed. Locking his fingers behind his neck, he kept his raw gaze focused on his pacing steps, his words punching from his lips like a hammer. "I don't know what the hell I'm feeling. I can't even think straight right now."

He looked stricken, almost ill, his breaths leaving his lungs in sharp, angry bursts, and she wondered if he was having a panic attack. Or was he simply so used to shutting down his emotions that he didn't know how to react when he no longer had them under control? Either way, Brit knew this was the right move. Nothing would be accomplished or solved by her staying.

She started to swing her legs over the side of the bed, intending to get dressed, but he was suddenly right there, looming over her, and she had to crane her head back to see his face. His chest was rising and falling like a bellows, the look in his beautiful eyes almost too heartbreaking to endure. "Christ, Brit. Why do you have to make everything so goddamn complicated?"

She forced herself to hold that pain-filled gaze, took a deep breath for courage, and gave him the truth. "Because I love you."

His eyes shot wide as he paled. "*What?*"

Her throat shook, melting, while her mouth trembled. But she somehow found the strength to keep her voice steady. "I love you, Alex. So much. And I need more from you."

For a moment, he only stared, looking down at her as if he didn't even know her. Then he shuddered, pulling his hand over his mouth, and quietly muttered, "I didn't expect this kind of crap from you. From other women, yeah. But not from *you*."

Confusion creased her brow. "Why?"

"Because you know what I'm like! You know I don't . . . that I don't do this *shit*."

"Is that why you took me to Miami?" she demanded, needing him to give her something that was honest and real and from his heart, even if it wasn't his love. Needing him to at least *try* to open up to her. "Was it to give us a moment before it ended, because you knew it was going to come to this? Because you were different there, Alex. You *were*. So is that why? You could show me yourself there because you knew it wasn't going to last when we came back?"

His gaze darted over her face, revealing his nerves, and he licked his lips. "Yes. Maybe. I . . . I don't know."

Holding the sheet with one hand, she pressed the other over the rapid beating of his heart. His muscles tightened beneath her touch, and she could feel the telling tremor of emotion rushing through him, shaking him from the inside out. "Talk to me. *Please*," she begged, sniffing as hot, salty tears spilled over her cheeks. "Give me something, Alex. *Anything.*"

"I didn't think at all, okay? I just knew that I wanted you!"

"And now you don't?"

Desperation filled his expression, carved into the rugged, hard-edged lines of his beloved face. "I'm not asking you to leave, Brit. I'm telling you that I want you here. Badly. Isn't that enough?"

Swiping the tears from her cheeks, she choked out a heartfelt, "No. Not anymore. Not after . . . everything. I need more than that. More than sex."

"I don't have any more than that to give you," he said thickly. "Not now."

"You're wrong. You just don't want to risk it."

He looked so angry and broken right then, so *lost*, that Brit knew she wasn't ever going to reach him. That his shields were too strong, too entrenched into the fabric of his soul, for her to smash her way through.

"You're being such a manipulative bitch," he rasped, the soft tone so at odds with the painful words. "I didn't expect that from you, either."

"There's probably a lot you didn't expect. And I'm sorry you feel that way. I'm not trying to make you do something you don't want to do. But I can't pretend that I'm not in love with you."

"Stop!" he growled, the harsh command sharp with anguish. "Just shut up and stop saying that!"

Ignoring his outburst, she kept going. "I love you, Alex. I'm not just saying it. They're not just words. I mean it, with every part of me. I love you. I am *in love* with you. It might not be easy for you to hear, but it isn't any easier for me to say. It's . . . terrifying. But I won't lie to you. Not now. Not ever. I just . . . I love you."

He roared as he stepped back from her, his hands on his head, the awful sound ripping up from his chest as guttural and stark as a wounded animal, and she flinched.

"Goddamn it," he choked out, the instant he caught the look on her face. Slowly lowering his arms, he relaxed his shoulders, exhaling a shallow breath. "Jesus, Brit. Don't look like that. No matter how angry I am, I would never hurt you."

"I know that," she whispered. "I'm not afraid of you, Alex. I just hate to see you like this because you mean so much to me."

He tensed all over again at her words. Stepping to the edge of the bed, he grabbed her by the arms and yanked her up against him, then lowered his hard face over hers. "I don't want to hear how you *feel*," he ground out, the look in his eyes full of pain and devastating longing. "Who the fuck cares about feelings that come and go at the drop of a hat?"

"Mine don't," she argued. "Don't compare me to the other women you've known. I'm not them!"

Shaking, he bellowed, "Why can't it be enough for you, damn it? What we have, physically, isn't something you just walk away from, Brit. Why the fuck can't that be enough for you?"

His mouth was on hers before she could respond, and it was clear that he'd decided to convince her another way. That he'd abandoned his argument with her mind, and had now begun his siege against her senses.

Before she even realized what had happened, he had her pressed into the middle of the bed with the heavy weight of his body, the sheet gone, as well as his boxers. They were wound together, skin against skin, their mouths locked in a hungry battle for dominance when he shoved her legs apart and she grabbed his ass, his cock slamming inside her so hard he had to swallow her scream.

The moment he was packed in deep and tight, grinding his hips until she'd taken every inch of his hot, burgeoning flesh, he lifted his head and locked his gaze with hers. His eyes were wild and damp, the pale green burning with raw emotion. She could *see* the love shimmering there as if it were a neon sign blazing at her. Sense it with every part of her body. In every cell. In every spasm of pleasure that he made her feel.

But she knew he wasn't going to admit it. The beautiful jackass. He was going to use every ounce, every element, of his sexual skill—and God did he have it in spades—to get her to keep saying it. To keep telling him she loved him. Even though he hated them, she could feel his feral desperation for the words in the hard, primal movements of his body. But she wasn't going to give in. She'd put herself out there, and he'd answered with *this*. With sex.

He would fuck her, and happily. But he would never allow himself to be vulnerable enough to give her his heart. Even if she already owned it.

I love you . . . I love you . . . I love you, she cried silently, wrapping him tight in her arms and legs, while he begged her with his powerful, magnificent body.

But she refused to say the words out loud again.

ALEX KNEW SHE WAS GONE BEFORE HE EVEN OPENED HIS EYES. His internal clock told him it was midafternoon, which meant he'd slept for several hours. Rolling to his side, he cracked his eyelids a fraction, staring at the indent in the pillow where her head had lain. There was a vibrant red hair curled across the white cotton, and he reached out for it, winding it slowly around the blunt tip of his finger. Round . . . and round . . . and round.

He didn't want to think. He just wanted to find a way to turn off his thoughts, but the only way he knew how to do that was with a bottle, and he grimaced, unwilling to slip into that particular hell again.

Her warm, womanly scent filled his head as he pulled in a deep breath, the shuddering exhale full of a thousand memories he didn't know how to deal with. The morning had been . . . decadent, to say the least. Raw. Greedy. He'd made her come so many times, over and over, until her cries were hoarse and she was limp with pleasure. But it hadn't been enough. She'd still gotten up and walked away from him.

He rolled onto his back again, staring up at the ceiling, and realized he stank of sweat and self-loathing. But it wasn't like there was anyone here to care. No, he could just lie in bed and wallow in misery for as long as he wanted, and no one would be the wiser. Which was why he needed to force his ass up and into the shower. This was the way pathetic sons of bitches were made, and he refused to give in to that shitty outcome too easily. He might not have any reason for getting up, but by God, he could at least fucking fake it.

Climbing out of bed, he headed into his bathroom and set the shower to scalding. He managed to turn off everything in his head while he stood under the roar of the water, but the instant he stepped out into the steam-filled bathroom, the silence started pressing in on him. Heavy, weighted, like a physical thing waiting to pounce.

"Get a grip," he muttered to himself, heading into his bedroom and grabbing a pair of shorts to pull on. He leaned over and braced his hands on the edge of his dresser, breathing hard as he struggled to pull his shit together, but he fucking hated this sterile, empty quiet. This vacant, hollow nothingness. He felt like all the goddamn air had been sucked out of his lungs, of the room, his muscles bulging across his shoulders as he gnashed his teeth. He heard a low, serrated sound tearing from his chest, and the next thing he knew he'd turned and picked up the chair sitting in the corner and flung it clear across the room. It slammed into the far wall, making a huge-ass hole in the plaster, scattering dust and Sheetrock all over the place in a white, diaphanous cloud.

He blinked, and thought, *Well, fuck*. That was going to be a bitch to fix.

"Dumbass," he grunted, feeling like an idiot. What the hell was he doing? Throwing a tantrum like a child? Jesus. He could be such a stupid prick sometimes!

He sank onto the foot of the bed and dropped his head in his hands, squeezing against the pain in his skull. Every part of him hurt, like he'd been put through twenty rounds in a cage fighting ring. He could hear the fucking knocking of his brain inside his skull, over and over, until he finally realized the jarring noise wasn't in his head, but coming from his front door.

"Fuck," he snarled, knowing it wasn't going to be Brit. And she was the only person he wanted to see. The only one he wanted to be around.

"You look like shit." That was Ben's opening comment after he'd opened the door, and Alex knew damn well that the conversation was only going to go downhill from there. He was tempted to just shut the door in his brother's face, but knew he wouldn't be able to get rid of the jackass that easily. Ben was stubborn that way.

He snorted, thinking the character trait was one that definitely ran in the family. "It's funny, but I don't recall asking for your opinion," he muttered, as Ben came inside.

His brother cast him a curious look. "Who pissed in your Wheaties this morning? I thought you'd be celebrating. Taking the day off to spend with Brit. Instead, you look someone who's just been through hell."

"Yeah, well, waiting for you to catch that bastard wasn't exactly a walk in the park," he snapped, rubbing his jaw as he walked past Ben, heading toward the kitchen. He needed coffee if he was expected to deal with the good sheriff today. A fucking gallon of it.

Ben followed behind him, bracing his shoulder against the side of the archway into the kitchen, thumbs hooked in his front pockets, as he watched Alex put on a fresh pot. When Alex leaned back against the counter with his arms crossed and looked at him, Ben said, "Shepherd's been booked and we're working on getting bail denied."

When he didn't respond, just stood there glaring, Ben raised his brows. "Brit at least has to be relieved that it's over."

"Yeah," he grunted, the knot in his stomach getting tighter.

"Speaking of your little roommate, where is she?"

Voice flat, he said, "She's gone."

Ben frowned. "What do you mean *gone*?"

"I mean she ran out on me." He didn't shout the words, though he wanted to. Instead, they came out quiet and tightly controlled.

"Shit." His brother pulled a hand over his mouth, and muttered, "That's bad news, man."

Alex made a thick, bitter sound in the back of his throat that was meant to be a laugh, but didn't come anywhere close. "You fucking think?"

Green eyes burning with concern, Ben asked, "Do you know where she went?"

Lifting his arms, he locked his hands behind his neck. "Home. She went home."

Ben shook his head, his dark brows drawn together. "Fuck, that sucks. I thought, hell . . . I thought you guys were onto something together. Even though you were pissed off last night, I hadn't seen you look at a woman that way in years. Truth be told, I don't think I've *ever* seen you look the way you did when you were with her."

Lowering his arms, Alex pushed away from the counter and

turned to pull down a mug. For a second, he thought about getting one down for Ben as well, then changed his mind. This wasn't a *let's sit down and share a cup of coffee* kind of moment. Not even close. And all he wanted was to get this over with so he could be alone.

Filling his mug, he said, "I might be angry, but it was going to end eventually anyway. Might as well be now, before she got hurt."

When he turned back around, holding his mug by the handle, Ben was staring at him like he'd lost his mind. "Did you honestly just say those fucking words to me?" he growled.

"You don't like what you're hearing, you can leave. No one asked you to come here."

The seconds stretched out, a silent, raging argument taking place between them, conveyed with nothing more than their speaking, telling stares. "I can't believe you're not even going to fight for her," Ben finally muttered, his deep voice thick with disappointment. "Mike's right. You really are a chickenshit."

Lifting his eyebrow, Alex gave him a mocking smirk. "And you weren't?"

"At least I pulled my head out of my ass and owned up to my feelings." With a challenging look, his brother asked, "Do I need to remind you of how that happened?"

He knew Ben was referring to the way Alex had prompted him into finding the courage to tell Reese that he was in love with her—but this was different. Damn it, *he* was different. "I can't admit something I don't know, Ben. You want me to lie to her?"

With a frustrated snarl, Ben pushed away from the archway, the look in his eyes almost pleading as he said, "Just . . . take some time to think about what you really want, Alex. Don't do anything stupid that you can't take back."

Ben turned and left then, leaving him alone, which was what

he'd wanted. But it sure as fuck didn't make him feel any better. He dumped the coffee into the sink, no longer wanting it. What he wanted was something a hell of a lot stronger, but then, he didn't think there was enough alcohol in the world to handle this shit situation.

Shoving both hands through his hair, he stalked from the kitchen into the dining room, and stopped dead in his tracks, as if he'd smacked right into an invisible wall, his narrow gaze locked in hard and tight on the table. *The goddamn fucking table.* Christ, she was everywhere. Imprinted on his life and in his mind. Tattooed into his fucking veins.

It was a mark Alex was beginning to realize he wouldn't ever get rid of. No matter what he did, or how hard he tried.

Walking to the sliding glass doors, he braced his hands against the glass as he leaned forward, pressing his forehead to the cool surface, and closed his eyes, one single burning thought churning its way through his mind again . . . and again:

So what the hell am I meant to do now?

17

THERE WEREN'T A LOT OF PROBLEMS THAT A MARGARITA COULDN'T FIX. Unfortunately, a broken heart was one of them.

Seriously, what was this? How in God's name had she gotten to this point?

Well, all right, she knew the answer to that one. Brit just couldn't believe she'd let herself be so stupid.

It'd been hours since she'd walked away from him, the spring sun gradually making its descent toward the horizon, but she still felt as if she'd only just walked away from his bed. She'd taken a taxi home from his condo, then called Lily to see if she could have Ryder bring over her car when he had the time. He'd shown up with the Audi later that afternoon, and Lily had followed him over in his Jeep. After seeing how upset Brit was, they'd both insisted she get out for a while, and had brought her home with them.

Now she was sitting out on their patio with Lily, drinking margaritas while listening to the waves crash against the shore, thinking about Alex, and trying to figure out how she could have let herself get so in over her head with the stubborn ass. Maybe it'd simply been a matter of needing to focus on something other than the disturbed young man who'd been screwing with her life. In the face of Clay's overly emotional obsession, Alex's straightforward, no-frills desire had been exactly what she'd needed. Or maybe it was simply Alex. He was the kind of man it was damn easy to lose your head over.

Just not the kind you wanted to steal your heart.

But now that it'd happened, there was nothing she could do to change it. All she could do was hold her head high and keep going, showing him that she could survive. It was inevitable that they'd run into each other in such a small town, but running wasn't going to solve anything. She wasn't going to be one of those whiny bitches who turned her back on her friends just so she wouldn't have to face the jackass who'd broken her heart. She would suck it up and survive. And hey, at least it wasn't like she would have to see him parading around with some random beach-bunny on his arm. Despite worrying about it before, she knew that wasn't Alex's style.

Beside her, Lily murmured, "I hate seeing you like this, Brit. You look so down."

She took a long sip of her drink, then lifted her gaze to Lily's concerned one. "Men suck."

The pretty strawberry blonde smirked as she laughed. "Tell me something I don't know, honey. Do you have any idea how long it took before Ryder would admit that he cared about me? I waited *years* for that big lug. And even then, I was the one who had to come after him." Smiling, she said, "I'm not saying it wasn't worth it—but he sure as hell didn't make it easy."

Ryder came outside to make sure they were okay, planting a possessive kiss on his wife's lips before heading back in to do some work, and Brit tried not to turn green with envy. But it wasn't easy. When Lily asked her if she wanted to talk about what had happened, Brit heard herself saying, "I told him that I love him."

Lily blinked. "Oh, um, and what did he do?"

"He pretty much freaked."

Lily's eyes went wide. "He got angry?"

"Yeah. He got angry about that . . . and because I refused to hang around as his fuck-buddy."

"Double ouch. What a bastard!"

"Tell me about it," she groaned, taking another sip of her drink. But it wasn't doing anything to help. The alcohol was only making her tired. Staring out at the turbulent Gulf, she swallowed the knot of emotion in her throat, and said, "I don't know what I'm going to do now, Lily. I . . . I think he's ruined me. You know what I mean?"

She turned to her friend just in time to catch Lily's wince. "He was that good?"

She swallowed again. Nodded. And after another drink of her margarita, she blurted out, "There's something in the way that he moves. He fucks with *every* part of his body. Every single beautiful part. I don't even need his fingers on me. I come so hard just from having him inside me, against me, around me, that I almost pass out."

Lily fanned her face. "Wow. No wonder you look so crushed."

She nodded as she set her drink down, thinking that she'd probably had enough, if she was going to start talking about her orgasms. "But it's more than the amazing sex," she said, her breath hitching as she fought back a fresh spate of tears. "I thought we were finally starting to develop that kind of connection that . . . ugh, I don't know. That crazy connection you read about in books. Like you and Ryder have. And Reese and Ben."

Lily gave her a gentle smile. "Just remember how hard we had to fight for those men, Brit. Like I said before, there was a time that I honestly didn't think Ryder was ever going to let himself admit that he cared about me."

After that depressing bit of news, Brit stayed for another hour, then decided she should head back home and let them enjoy dinner without her moping presence. They tried to argue with her, but in the end Ryder finally agreed to take her home, and Lily made the drive with him. They made plans to meet up together sometime over the weekend, and then Brit waved good-bye and made her way inside, punching in the code to her alarm before setting her purse down. She was no longer buzzed, but was glad she hadn't had that third margarita. In her current emotional state, there was no telling what kind of drunk she would have been. The only given was that it wouldn't have been pretty.

Empty silence surrounded her as she locked herself in, away from the rest of the world, and she choked back a sob, her body trembling.

God, she was going to miss Alex. Miss waking up to his face. Miss the way he held her so tightly in his sleep, as if he was trying to imprint himself on her skin. She was going to miss just looking at him, watching him when he hadn't even known she was doing it, soaking in his dark good looks and raw masculinity as if she needed the sight of them to breathe.

Turning away from the door, she walked across the living room, into the kitchen, moving by rote, lost in her thoughts as she headed toward her coffeemaker. She reached for the pot to fill it with water, then suddenly stopped. A prickle of awareness lifted the hairs on the back of her neck, but she figured it was probably just going to take her some time before she got used to being alone again.

Getting on with her task, she'd just filled the back of the machine and set it to brew, when she realized someone was standing behind her. She could smell him, *feel* him, and a sharp cry of fear ripped up from her throat, her voice still hoarse from her pleasure-cries the night before with Alex . . . as well as from that morning. It'd taken everything she had to keep from telling him she loved him again during those heated hours. She'd felt as if he was driving for it, pursuing those words with single-minded purpose, but she'd fought them back. Now, though, she wished she hadn't been so stubborn. Wished she'd used the time they'd had to keep telling him everything that was in her heart.

Because it was suddenly too late. Somehow, they'd been wrong, because she knew who was behind her before she even heard the chilling sound of his voice.

"Hello, Dr. Cramer," he whispered near her ear. "I've been waiting for you."

ALEX WAS SLOWLY DRIVING HIMSELF CRAZY, BUT NO MATTER HOW HARD he tried, he couldn't stop thinking about Brit. He'd tried calling her a dozen times that afternoon, just needing to talk to her, to hear her voice, even though there was nothing new he could say to make things right. But she wasn't answering her phone.

Not that he blamed her. If he were Brit, he wouldn't want to talk to him right now, either. Not until he had something more meaningful to say than an invitation to dinner. Which he was pretty sure she would refuse.

Going stir-crazy in the condo without her, the subtle whiffs of her scent he'd catch every now and then making him feel like a knife was stabbing him in the heart, he finally grabbed his keys, locked up behind him, and headed down to the beach on foot. He didn't live as close to the shore as Ben and Ryder, the walk taking him nearly fifteen minutes, but he needed to be out in the fresh air, hoping it could help him clear his head.

By the time he'd kicked off his sandals and made it onto the sand, the sun was a burning smear of crimson and orange on the distant horizon, melting into the Gulf. A few families had bonfires already going, and he walked for a while at the foamy edge of the surf, pulling in deep breaths of the salty air, watching the others around him. He'd walked maybe half a mile when he noticed an older couple coming toward him, walking in the opposite direction. As he drew closer, Alex could see the way they clasped hands, the man tall and gray, the woman still beautiful, with long silvery hair and bright blue eyes. He felt like a voyeur, studying them as closely as he was, but he couldn't look away.

What they had, it was tangible. You could physically *see* the love between them. As a strong breeze blew in off the water, the woman shivered, and the man drew her closer to his side, holding her like she was . . . precious. Like she was his *life*. He realized they'd stopped to watch some kids playing up the beach, the little ones waving down at them, making him think the kids were probably their grandchildren. You could fucking feel their satisfaction and happiness as they watched the children playing. Their commitment. Their joy. It made his damn eyes sting, which made him feel like a pussy.

Fuck. He didn't want a drink . . . or a redo on his past . . . or to never have gone through any of the shitty stuff that had happened in his life. In that moment, standing like a statue in the surf, Alex realized that he just . . . he just wanted Brit Cramer, pain in the ass, best fuck of his life, most beautiful, stubborn woman that he'd ever known, who could make him laugh and smile and . . . *Christ.* Who made him *feel.* Everything. All of it. She'd scared the shit out of him, with how much she'd changed his existence in such a short amount of time. She'd hit him like an emotional storm, and he was still reeling from the effects.

Somehow, he found himself out of the water, his ass in the

sand, eyes burning from the salty air as he stared out over the sea, and he saw it all play out before him, across the canvas in his mind. Saw how it could be, if he would just own up to what was happening. To what had happened to *him*.

Damn it, he didn't need time to figure out how he felt. What he needed was a fucking spine, because sitting on that beach, watching a storm roll in on the distant horizon, Alex knew *exactly* what he felt for Brit Cramer. And it wasn't simply like or lust or respect. It was love.

He loved her.

He was *in love* with her.

He was in love with the doc.

And he'd fucking blown it!

Shit. He was as bad as his idiot brother had been. Why hadn't he just told her this morning? Just admitted that he needed her for more than sex? That he enjoyed every damn beautiful, incredible thing about her? Maybe then she wouldn't have run. Maybe then he wouldn't be prowling around like a fucking zombie, with no idea how he was going to get her the fuck back. It wasn't finding her that would be the problem. No, it was what the hell he was going to say to her once he did. Would she believe him if he told her that he had feelings for her? That he'd just needed time to figure out what they were? That they'd been buried behind a fucking wall he hadn't been able to get through? Or would she be her typical stubborn self and think he was only trying to tell her what she needed to hear? Would she think he was just trying to find a way to make her come back?

And, Jesus, would he blame her if she did? So many times, he should have spoken, should have just talked to her, but he never had.

Scrubbing his hands down his face, he groaned long and low as he thought of how she'd told him she loved him, and he'd just thrown it back in her face. He was such a dick. But he was a deter-mined one. So goddamn determined he'd get on his fucking knees and beg her, if that's what it took, because there was no outrun-ning this. What was the point, when he would just run himself in a circle . . . right back to her?

It was about damn time that he pulled his head out of his ass and started embracing it. Embracing *her*. Because she was the absolute best thing that had ever happened to him, and she deserved a man who made her proud. Who did whatever it took to make her happy and fucking fought for her, no matter the bat-tle. Even if it was against himself.

She might not like it, but he was bringing her home with him. The last thing they needed right now was distance. That was only going to pull her further out of his grip, when he needed closer. As close as he could possibly get.

Filled with purpose for the first time in what felt like a lifetime of just going through the motions, Alex surged to his feet and started making his way home. He made it back to the condo in record time, buzzing with nervous energy as he grabbed his wallet, and was just about to head back out his front door when someone knocked on it. Hoping like hell that Ben hadn't come back to give him a hard time, since he was in a fucking hurry, he was relieved, and a little confused, when he found Reese standing on his doorstep.

"Is everything okay?" he asked as he stepped aside to let her in, worried that something might have happened to Ben or Mike.

"Uh, yeah, everything's fine," she murmured, pushing her hands in the pockets of her jeans as she gazed up at him with her big blue eyes. "I was wondering if you had a moment to chat?"

Jiggling his keys in his hand, Alex knew he was being rude, but he was too impatient to get to Brit to sit around and talk, even to someone he liked as much as his sister-in-law. "I was actually just on my way out. I—"

"It won't take but a minute," she cut in, her sharp tone taking him by surprise. "I just wanted to tell you what an idiot asshole I think you're being."

Rubbing his hand over his mouth to cover his sudden grin, Alex lifted his brows and asked, "Did Ben put you up to this?"

She shook her head and glared up at him. "He told me about the talk he had with you earlier, but that's it. He doesn't even know I'm here. He thinks I'm at Lily's."

"So you decided to come over here and bully me all on your own?"

"I'm not here to bully you into anything," she muttered, stepping closer and jabbing him in the center of his chest with her finger. "I just want you to face reality. You love this woman, Alex. If that means you have to crawl after her on your hands and knees, then you find some fucking kneepads and get to it!"

She was so adorable when she was furious. No wonder Ben always got such a kick out of riling her. "Reese," he murmured, his mouth twitching with a smile. "You're right. I love her."

She blinked, then grabbed two handfuls of his T-shirt and shook him, yelling, "Then go after her, Alex!"

He was grinning like an idiot. "I am."

"Good!"

"It will be," he said, his low voice rough with conviction.

"So if you're going after her, then why am I still yelling at you?" she demanded, blinking up at him again.

"Hell if I know," he drawled, a sudden burst of laughter rumbling up from his chest.

Reese shook her head a little as she let go of his shirt and stepped back, her expression hopeful as she tucked a strand of hair behind her ear. "Okay, let me see if I've got this straight. You've realized you were a flaming jackass, and now you're ready to go and make it right with her, but I'm holding you back. Is that right?"

"You hit it on the head, sweetheart."

Rolling her eyes, she said, "Then get the hell out of here!"

Alex gave her a hard hug, then left her to lock up the place as he ran out and jumped into the Range Rover, breaking about twenty different traffic violations as he drove to Brit's house. By the time he pulled onto her road and parked in her driveway, beside her Audi, his smile had been replaced by a terrified look of nervous tension, his heart damn near pounding its way through his chest. And while he was all about laying his heart at her feet, he figured she'd enjoy it more in a figurative sense, rather than a literal one.

Wishing he'd taken the time to change into something other than his ratty T-shirt, shorts, and sandals, Alex climbed out of the Rover. He could tell there was a light on inside, but the house seemed unusually quiet as he made his way up to her front door, considering he knew how much she loved to have music playing. But if she'd been feeling anything like he had today, then she probably wasn't in the mood. Hell, she might have just crawled into bed and slept the miserable day away.

Taking a deep breath for courage, he lifted his hand and knocked on the door. He waited a few moments, thinking he heard someone moving around on the other side, then knocked again. Finally, he just shouted, "I know you're in there, Doc! You might as well open the door because I'm not leaving without getting a chance to talk to you! I'll stay here all damn night if I have to!"

Five heavy seconds of silence passed, and then the door cracked open, only far enough that he could see a sliver of her beautiful face, which was pinched and pale. Guilt twisted through his insides, burning like acid, and he realized that he might have screwed up so badly she simply would never forgive him.

No . . . no . . . no . . . please don't let that be true.

He opened his mouth, ready to start begging her for that second chance he so badly wanted, when she spoke first. "What the hell are you doing here, Alex?"

He swallowed the knot in his throat, and braced his hands on either side of the doorframe as he leaned forward, getting as close to her as he could with the fucking door between them. "I need to talk to you, baby. Please let me in."

Her eyes went wide with shock, then narrowed, her nostrils flaring as she sucked in a sharp breath. "I can't do that. *I won't.* I think you need to face reality, and see that it's best this way."

"Face reality?" He wanted to howl like a lunatic, but somehow choked it back. Instead, his voice was almost painfully soft, little more than a whisper. "Open your eyes, Brit. Reality was you ripping my fucking heart out and walking away from me this morning."

"I'm sorry you feel that way," she said flatly, "but I can't do this right now. Please, just go."

"No," he croaked, digging his fingers into the doorframe. "Jesus, Brit, I'm *begging* you. I know I was a jackass, but please, just give me a chance to explain. I need to tell you that—"

"I gave you everything," she snapped, cutting him off. "And you made it clear that you didn't want it, Alex. Now it's too late."

He stumbled back a step, unable to believe she wasn't even going to give him a chance to talk to her. "So that's it? You don't even want to hear what I have to say?"

Her expression was so cold it looked glacial, and he wondered for a moment if that was how he always appeared to other people. Like a cold-ass bastard who didn't give a fuck about anything or anyone.

He opened his mouth, no idea what to say to her. He was lost, drowning in regret, until a desperate spark of hope suddenly flared in his chest when he caught a vibrant, anguished flash in her eyes. It looked as raw and sharp and powerful as his own raging need was for her—but then it was gone in an instant, wiped out of existence by a blink of her lashes. She lifted her chin, and with her low voice completely devoid of emotion, she said, "I'm sorry, but I won't let you destroy me the way that you let your ex destroy you. I'm getting out now, before you can do any more damage. I'm just not brave enough to take any more risks with you."

Uh . . . yeah. He opened his mouth again, but was no more successful getting words out this time than he'd been a few seconds ago. He was fucking dying inside, but what the hell could he say to *that*?

Nothing, you idiot. You blew it.

Rubbing at the center of his chest, Alex turned around and practically staggered back to the Rover, only distantly aware of her shutting the door behind him. He was dizzy with heartbreak, his fucking chest feeling like it was caving in. He couldn't believe he'd had something so wonderful just that morning, but had lost it. Just shit all over it and destroyed it. He'd survived emotional blows before, but never one like this. He truly didn't know how he was going to pick himself up now that he'd found the one woman he fucking knew, with every part of his being, was meant to be with him, and lost her.

Opening his door, he started to climb behind the wheel, sucking in shuddering breaths, trying not to bawl like a jackass in the middle of her driveway. He just . . . he just didn't fucking get it. Yeah, he knew there was a chance she would kick his ass out after he'd said everything he'd come to say. But he hadn't reckoned on her not even *giving* him a chance to talk to her.

I'm just not brave enough . . .

Standing there braced in the open driver's side door, Alex ran his tongue over his front teeth, letting those words work deeper into his head. There was something that just wasn't . . . right, damn it. Because Brit Cramer wasn't a coward. She was a damn goddess. An Amazon. One of the bravest fucking people he'd ever known. So then what the hell was her problem?

He turned his head, staring back at the silent house, and a

trickle of unease started to slip its way down his spine as he thought about her last words . . . and that devastating look of need that had flashed on her pale face before she'd killed it. *Oh, God. Oh, shit*, he thought, as his worst nightmares started crashing into his head with the force of a hammer. Working on autopilot, he reached across the center console and grabbed his spare gun from his glove compartment. Tucking the gun into his waistband at his lower back, he carefully shut the door on the Rover and made his way into the thickening shadows by the garage. Taking his cell phone from his pocket, he scrolled for Ben's number, then started making his way around the side of her house, careful to duck beneath the windows, as he waited for his brother to answer.

When he did, Ben's deep voice was rough with worry. "Alex, I was just getting ready to call you."

"Where the hell is Shepherd?" he quietly snarled, careful to keep his voice low as he made his way toward the French doors he knew would give him his best view inside the house.

"You're not gonna believe this shit," Ben muttered. "Shepherd started complaining of chest pains, and an ambulance was called. The medics said he needed to go to the hospital, and the fucking thing was involved in an accident on the way. In the middle of the chaos, Shepherd slipped away and got a gun off one of the deputies who was riding with him."

Leaning against the back of the house, Alex closed his eyes for a moment and silently cursed like a motherfucker, so furious he wanted to . . . to . . . Shit, he didn't want anything in that moment but to know that Brit was safe. He hoped to God his instincts were wrong. That she was fine and just severely pissed off at him, instead of in trouble.

"Alex, you there?" Ben asked.

"Yeah, I'm here," he muttered, opening his eyes and edging closer to her French doors.

"I've already got two deputies on their way over to Brit's place. I know this sucks, but we'll pick him up fast, Alex. He won't get near her."

"Too late," he growled, his stomach plummeting as he peeked around the edge of the French doors. "I'm looking at him, Ben. Get your ass over to Brit's *now*. He's already inside with her."

"Fuck!"

"Just hurry," he grunted, ending the call and slipping the phone back in his pocket. He was careful to keep far enough back that he couldn't be spotted by the asshole standing in Brit's living room with a fucking gun in his hand, while she stood just a few feet away from him, bleached with fear.

Reaching for the gun at his lower back, Alex focused on breathing in and out in a slow, deliberate rhythm, fighting against the terror and rage coiling through his insides, knowing he couldn't let them take hold. He needed to be numb, damn it. Cold. Or he was never going to make it through this. Anger and fear were only going to make him stupid, and he couldn't afford to make any mistakes. Not when her fucking life was on the line. Which meant he would have to wait until later to lose his shit over the way she'd just purposefully tried to send him away. He didn't have any doubt that she'd done it in order to protect him, and it made him want to shake some sense into her until she promised to never do anything that crazy again.

Getting as close to the glass as he dared, he could just make out what they were saying to each other.

"How did you get the code to my alarm? Was it in my office?" Brit asked, her soft voice rough with fear.

Shepherd's voice, on the other hand, was cocky with confidence, as if he'd finally gotten exactly what he wanted and couldn't wait to enjoy his spoils. "No. It was even easier than that, Dr. Cramer. I just stood in your backyard the other night and used a pair of binoculars to watch through your French doors as you came inside and punched in your code."

"Which night was this?"

"Sunday night," Shepherd muttered, "when you came here with that cop bastard you just sent away."

"He's not a cop, Clay. He's a private investigator."

"He's an asshole."

"You don't even know him," she snapped, and Alex was glad to see the rush of color burning in her cheeks. He didn't want her doing anything to antagonize her former patient, but he'd rather see her angry than afraid.

"I know he's a dumbass and that I hate him." Shepherd's voice got eerily quiet as he stepped closer to her, making it difficult to hear him. But Alex could just make out his chilling words as he said, "I almost hate *you* for letting him touch you."

Alex exhaled in an audible rush, knowing damn well that the safest thing to do was wait for backup. But he didn't know how long he would be able to hold back while she was in there with that raging psychopath.

Shepherd's next words made it clear he wouldn't be able to wait long at all.

"Enough stalling, Dr. Cramer. I've waited long enough. Take off your clothes for me."

Alex's fingers tightened around his gun until he was surprised the metal didn't give way under the pressure. He had to go in *now*, without the others, and hope to God he could get her out without her getting hurt.

With his free hand, he reached for the door handle, listening as Brit said, "No, I won't do it."

"You'll do it or you'll die," Shepherd argued.

"Then you'll have to kill me, Clay. Are you really willing to do that? You want to watch me bleed out from a bullet wound?"

"No, I don't want you to die," Shepherd said unsteadily, sounding confused . . . and distressed. "I just want your tears and your pleasure. I just want you to look up at me and truly see me for what I am. Your perfect partner. The devil to your angel. Hell to your heaven. Sin to your salvation. You are so perfect and I love you! Don't you see this is the only way I know how to show you?"

Sending up a silent prayer of thanks that the door was unlocked, Alex slowly opened it until he could squeeze in, the heated argument taking place in the living room keeping Brit and Shepherd from noticing his entry. He left the door ajar as he aimed his gun at Shepherd and eased toward them, making his way around her dining table.

"Shepherd," he said in a firm voice, when no more than fifteen feet separated them, "I want you to step away from her."

They both swung toward him with expressions of shock, but while Brit's was edged with soul-shredding terror, Shepherd's face had a maniacal cast to it that said the guy had lost his grip on reality long ago.

Now that he was standing in the same room with him, Alex could see that the asshole wasn't what he'd expected. He also could see why Brit had held such empathy for the young man. When you looked at Clay Shepherd, with his slight frame and shaggy hair, you could still see the shattered teenager who'd had his life stolen from him so cruelly by the ones who were meant to protect him. An adolescent who had been twisted into something even Shepherd himself didn't know how to handle. He was hurting, and in his pain he was trying to find relief. But it was just too fucking late.

Still, that didn't mean that Alex wanted to have to kill him. He could see now that the best place for this guy was a high-security psych ward, where he couldn't hurt anyone else . . . or himself.

Inching closer to where they stood, he said, "Shepherd, I need you to put the gun down. If you do that for me, then everything's going to be okay."

"Alex, what are you doing?" Brit whispered. Her beautiful face was stiff with fear as she stared at him, tears running unchecked from her glittering eyes.

"Shh. Just stay calm, Doc. I swear it's going to be all right."

Shepherd's gaze was darting between them, and Alex wanted to fucking roar when she said, "Clay, just ignore him. Just keep your focus on me, okay? We can work this out."

"No!" Shepherd shouted, his arm trembling as he tried to keep the gun trained on her in the middle of his breakdown. "He's just going to try and take you away from me, but I won't let him. I'll never let him have you!"

Forcing his words through his clenched teeth, Alex said, "I don't want to shoot you, Clay, but I will if I have to. I can't let you hurt her."

"But I have to," he cried, shaking. "I love her! I have to show her!" Swinging the gun toward Alex, he said, "I won't let you take her. I'll blow your fucking brains out before I let you take her!"

"No!" she gasped, holding her hands up, as if she were surrendering. Alex's insides froze when he realized that's exactly what she was doing. "I'll go with you," she choked out. "Are you listening to me, Clay? I'll go with you and do whatever you want. Just don't hurt him."

Turning his head toward her, Shepherd blinked in confusion. "You care about him that much?"

Trying to get Shepherd's focus back on him, hoping like hell that Ben and the others hurried up and got there, Alex started talking in a calm, even tone. "It was a setup, wasn't it, Shepherd? The thing up at your school. It was your way of getting close to her again. Am I right?"

Shepherd shook his head as he looked at Alex again, as if he

was trying to quiet something raging inside his skull. Then he
laughed. "Bet you think you're smart for figuring that one out."

"How did you do it?" Alex asked, hoping he could keep the guy
talking.

Shepherd shrugged his slender shoulders. "It was surprisingly
easy. There are so many people willing to do horrible things for
money. You just have to make them the right offer."

"I'm sorry you feel that way, man. But you know Dr. Cramer
only wants what's best for you, right?"

Shepherd's brown eyes gleamed with his madness. "She will,
once I'm done with her."

"She isn't yours to hurt, Clay."

Still holding his gun on Alex, Shepherd slid his calculating gaze
over to Brit. "She will be. I love her, and so it's up to me to fix her."

Brit's voice was steady as she held Shepherd's stare. "Those
aren't your thoughts, Clay. Those are your mother's."

He went on as if he hadn't even heard her, his eyes going glassy
and wild again. "Don't you see? Hurting you is the only way to
break through the masks so that you can truly see. Pain is the most
pure form of emotion that exists in our world, so easily created . . .
and manipulated. And with the right person, it *can* make us new.
Enable us to transcend all this earthly shit and chaos that doesn't
mean anything, until we find a plane where the only thing that
matters is me . . . and you. Where we can be together, for always."

"Clay," she said softly, "when you care about someone, it isn't
natural to want to hurt them."

"Isn't it though? You were upset when you came home tonight."
He swung his wild gaze back to Alex. "Is that because you hurt her?"

Oh, Christ. Alex felt like someone had just reached into his
chest and ripped out his heart. He knew he'd just gone as pale as
Brit, and Shepherd laughed as he glanced her way, a knowing smile
curling his lips. "Open your eyes, Dr. Cramer. People are always

hurting one another. Man is flawed. We can't help our true nature. All we can do is try to accept it, and make it beautiful."

"No," she whispered. "I refuse to believe that, Clay."

Narrowing his eyes, he said, "Then I'll make you believe it," and his finger started to tighten on the trigger of his gun. Left with no other choice, Alex fired into Shepherd's shoulder, the impact of the bullet jerking the young man to the side, but he amazingly kept hold of the gun. Brit was screaming, and Alex was ready to fire another shot, when she threw herself at Shepherd's gun arm, trying to wrest the weapon away from him.

"No!" she screamed, clawing and hitting his arm. "I won't let you hurt him, Clay! Don't you dare fucking hurt him!"

Alex shouted for her to get the hell away, so that he could get a clear shot, just as Shepherd jerked the gun up, slamming it into Brit's temple. She staggered back, dazed, but stayed on her feet, still standing between the two of them. Alex shifted to the side, ready to take another shot at the guy, but Shepherd had lowered the gun, his shocked gaze locked in hard and tight on Brit.

"You're bleeding," he whispered, glancing at her gashed temple, before looking back at her eyes. "Why would you do that? Why would you risk yourself for him that way?"

"Because I love him," she said, at the same time Alex barked for her to get behind him—an order she ignored. He didn't know what she'd been thinking, but he was going to spank her beautiful ass for putting herself at risk like that—because of *him*, no less— just as soon as this was over.

"You love him?" Shepherd asked in a broken voice, while tears streamed from his eyes, his body shaking with bone-jarring tremors.

"Clay, I'm sorry," she said softly . . . gently. "I know you're hurt- ing, but it's the truth. I love him, and if you hurt him, it will kill me. I won't be the same person you've known. I won't be. I'll be dead inside."

Blinking against the tears in his eyes, Shepherd said, "I didn't know. I thought you were just fucking him. That it was all in your head. It's always all in a woman's head. How can you love him?"

"Because he's mine," she told him, making pride surge through Alex in a dizzying rush. "And he's so many different things that I need. That I can't live without."

A sob broke from the guy's throat. "This changes everything."

"Clay," she started to say, but he cut her off.

"I hope you know how lucky you are," he whispered, looking at Alex. Then he lifted the gun to his temple and fired, his body slumping to the ground as what was left of his head bled out over the floor.

Fuck, Alex thought, lunging toward Brit. She swayed, nearly falling to the floor, and he knew she was in shock. Scooping her boneless body up into his arms, he clutched her against his chest as he carried her outside, away from the gore and the stench of death.

Sitting on the edge of a patio chair, he cradled her against his chest as he rocked her back and forth, the side of his face pressed to the top of her head. His insides ached, and he knew he was going to be shredded for God only knew how long by what she'd tried to sacrifice. By the way she'd actually tried to send him away, leaving herself at the mercy of that psychopath, just to keep his own ass out of danger. Then putting herself between them and trying to get control of Shepherd's gun. What the fuck had she been thinking? Didn't she know that losing her would have killed him anyway? Gutted him to the bone?

If anything had happened to her, Alex knew there would have been no coming back from it. He would have been ripped open and emptied, left as nothing but a shell, and the churning desire he still felt to spank her little backside for taking such an ungodly risk with her own life was almost too much to control. Only the fact that she was shivering in shock in his arms helped him keep it together.

But when she was better, so help her, there was going to be hell to pay.

Right now, though, he was quickly getting lost in a soul-searing sense of relief that pervaded every cell of his body, pumping through his veins like a fever. He couldn't stop the tears running down his face now that she was safe in his arms, and he didn't even try as he spoke to her in a raw, broken voice that he prayed she could hear through her shock.

"I've got you, Doc, and I love you. Christ, I love you. So much. I love you . . . love you . . . *love you* . . ."

They were still sitting there, those hoarse words still tumbling from Alex's lips, when his brother and the others finally arrived.

18

For three days, Alex had tried to give Brit the time that she needed. Three goddamn painful, miserable, soul-destroying days that were slowly killing him.

He'd brought her home with him the night Shepherd had killed himself, considering there was a hell of a cleanup job that had needed to be done at her place, as well as all the work that had to be carried out by the forensics team. He hadn't wanted her dealing with all of that while she was resting, and so he'd bundled her sweet little ass up once the doctors in the emergency room had cleared her to leave—after stitching the wound on her temple and diagnosing her with a mild concussion—and brought her back to his condo.

He'd hoped they would be able to talk things out after she'd had a good night's sleep, but she'd continued to be withdrawn. He'd known she needed some time to heal, both physically and emotionally, but enough was enough. He'd let his inability to communicate his feelings cause enough bad shit to happen between them. Now it was time to put an end to it.

But first, he was going to sit out here on his back patio, and do something that he should have done a hell of a long time ago.

When things had almost fallen apart between Ben and Reese last summer, Alex had pointed out the simple truth that Hudson men held an inherent flaw when it came to emotions. It wasn't that they didn't feel. They felt deeply. Maybe even too deeply for their damn sanity. But they were shit when it came to owning up to those feelings. To expressing them. To sharing them and letting another person in. Ben had fought against his personal demons and won, thank God, finally admitting to Reese that he loved her.

That was something Alex had never done with Judith. He'd been protective, possessive, and faithful. Had taken his vows of fidelity as seriously as a man could. But as the blow she'd driven against his pride finally healed these past few weeks, he'd started to see things a bit more clearly.

Yes, there'd been a time when he'd loved her as a person. But after seeing how Ben was with Reese, and Ryder was with Lily, Alex had finally taken a deeper look at his marriage to Judith, at his emotional connection to her, and realized a difficult truth: He'd loved her, but he hadn't been *in love* with her. And somewhere along the way, she'd figured it out.

It didn't excuse what she'd done or how she went about destroying their marriage, but it'd lessened a great deal of the blow. Especially now that he knew what it felt like to truly love another person with every part of his body, heart, and soul. Because of that, he needed to move forward, and to do *that*, he finally needed to put his past behind him, where it belonged.

And that's why he was finally making this call.

When her familiar voice answered the phone, he cleared his throat. "Uh, hey, Judith. It's Alex."

"Alex?" she whispered with surprise. "Ohmygod, I'm so . . . well, shocked to hear from you. Did you hear that Pete and I are no longer together?"

"Um, no." He hadn't even known that she and Pete Mannis, the detective he'd put in the hospital, had kept seeing each other after Alex had divorced her . . . and he didn't care.

"Oh." She sounded almost disappointed. "Well, I'm so glad you called. Are you in Orlando? Can I see you?"

"Naw," he murmured, rubbing the back of his neck. Christ, this was awkward. But he was determined to get it done. "That's not why I was calling. I just wanted to, um . . . well, to wish you well."

"Wish me well?" she asked, and he could hear the catch in her voice.

"I'm sorry it's taken me so long to say that, Judith. But it's true. I want you to have a good life. A happy life."

"Oh, Alex." At the sound of her sniffling, he started to cringe. But then he breathed out a silent sigh of relief when he could hear the smile in her next words. "You've finally fallen in love, haven't you?"

"Yeah, I have." He took a deep, cleansing breath of fresh air, then told her, "I know I never said it, but I did love you, Jude."

"I know you did," she whispered. "But you weren't *in love* with me, Alex. I knew you weren't, but I married you anyway."

"Big mistake on both our parts," he offered in a wry drawl.

"God, isn't that the truth." They shared a quiet laugh, and then she said, "I wish . . . I *want* you to be happy, too, Alex. And I'm sorry, for not being honest with you. For the way I . . . well, for what happened."

"I'm sorry, too."

They said good-bye then, and he felt a weight lift. And, damn, did it feel good. He'd known that he needed to do that, so that he could move on and go to Brit as a whole man, and he was so fucking glad that he had.

Heading back inside, he found the little doc up in his guest bedroom, where she'd slept for the past three nights. She was curled up against the headboard, reading a book, until she realized he was standing in the doorway. Then she set the book aside, lifted her head, and looked right at him.

Hoping with everything inside him that he didn't screw this up, Alex said, "It's time for that talk now."

With a gentle shake of her head, since it was still bothering her a bit, she said, "Later."

"No. Now, Doc. I can't wait anymore."

She blinked at him, and he could see her pulse racing in the hollow of her throat. "Alex, please."

He took a deep breath again, this time striving for patience. "Just listen to me, Brit. That's all I'm asking."

"I can't," she choked out. "I don't want to hear you take it back."

What the hell?

Alex stared at her pale face, stunned. Christ, is that what she'd thought he wanted to talk about these past few days? "I'm not. . . . That's not what . . . *Fuck*, Brit. You think I would say I love you and then take it back?"

Tears glistened on her thick lashes, making his chest feel like it'd just been ripped wide open. "Why not?" she asked, her mouth trembling. "I never know what to expect from you."

He came into the room then, because he couldn't stay away, and sat down on the side of the bed, his elbows braced on his parted knees. Then he turned his head and looked at her. "Before, on that morning of our fight, I panicked because I realized how much you mean to me. Realized how deeply it could cut me if I lost you. Not like it did with Judith. That was more about ego and bullshit than anything else."

"But she broke your heart."

Giving her a wry smile, he said, "No, she broke my pride, angel. Big difference."

"Alex. It's—"

"No, just listen to me, Doc. I'm giving this to you as straight as I can. And I want you to know that I called her."

"What?" she gasped, gaping at him. "When?"

"Just before I came upstairs."

"Oh." Concern for him filled her beautiful eyes. "Did it . . . um, go okay? Are you all right?"

"I'm good. And I'm glad I did it. It closed the door on a part of my life that needed to be left behind so that I can move forward."

"Oh," she said again.

He braced himself as he forced out the rest. "And I, uh . . . I even spoke to Chloe yesterday, when I was picking up my mail."

Her eyes went wide, but she didn't say anything.

Clearing his throat, he kept his gaze locked hard on hers as he explained. "I apologized for using her like I did that night. It was a dick move, and I want you to know that that night was the only time I've ever . . . well, that *anything* ever happened between us. And I didn't touch her. It doesn't make it better, but I need you to know that."

"I'm . . . uh, I don't know what to say."

His gaze narrowed. "Well, before you throw some bullshit back in my face about me only feeling like this because I almost lost you to Shepherd, it won't work. I had already come for you. That's why I was at your front door, begging for the chance to talk to you." He paused for a moment as he shifted so that he was facing her, one knee drawn up on the bed, and then went on. "When you walked out on me, it felt like my fucking heart had been knifed. I've never felt anything like it. Not when I found Judith with my coworker. Not when I kicked her ass out. Not when I lost my career and nearly drank myself to death. Those things all kicked me in the balls, but they didn't come close to how I felt when you left me." Shaking his head, he said, "I might be a thickheaded son of a bitch, but I've learned something. When it matters and it's right and it's the fucking best thing in the world that could ever happen to you, then you get down on your knees and you fucking grovel until you get it back. So you need to know that I'll do whatever it takes to make this work, because I have to. Because I want to. You are *mine*, Britten Cramer, and I'm fucking keeping you. Forever."

She stared back at him in absolute shock. "Ohmygod, you said my name."

"I'm a PI," he drawled with a cocky smirk. "You didn't think I was *that* bad at noticing details, did you? I saw it on your medical license the first time I went into your office." Reaching out, he cupped the side of her face. "It's a beautiful name, baby. Just like you."

"You really do love me, don't you?" she whispered, sounding adorably dazed.

"I do, and I swear to everything I believe in that it's not a line I'm using just to get you back. I mean every word, Brit. I love you. I love you so fucking much it's killing me."

"Love is meant to be a good thing, Alex."

"It will be," he breathed out, "just as soon as you tell me we're good."

"Oh, we're good," she said in a rush, grabbing his hand and moving it from her cheek to her lips, where she could press a soft kiss against his knuckles. "We're so good."

Knowing he needed to get it all out, he said, "I really can be a stubborn ass. What I feel for you, it was there all along, Brit. I didn't know what it was, and I wouldn't let myself take the time to figure it out. I just shoved it away, where I thought it couldn't hurt me. But it *was* there. And the moment I realized what I'd lost, what I was letting slip through my fingers, there was no way to keep hiding from it."

Needing her in his arms, he pulled her onto his lap, and then he carefully pushed her hair back from her wounded temple. "I know you could do so much better, Doc. I *know* that. But I guarantee there's no one out there who could ever love you more. I can't change my past or the things I've done, but I can promise to live every day of the rest of my life being a good man for you."

"You already are a good man."

Grinning a little, he rumbled, "If that's so, then it's because of you. Because that's what I want to be for you. And before you say anything, I want it for me, too. I want to be the best damn thing that's ever happened to you."

"Stop, please. You're going to make me cry."

"You're already crying."

"I know." A smile ghosted her lips. "I just can't believe that after everything that's happened, we've actually made it to this point."

"Yeah, well, that's another thing I wanted to talk to you about." She stiffened at his gruff tone, and he knew she'd guessed where this was going. "That shit you pulled by trying to send me away that night," he muttered, tightening his grip on her. "That can't happen again."

She bit her lip as she touched the side of his face. "I didn't have a choice. He said he would hurt you."

"I don't care if someone is threatening to take my fucking head off, you don't turn away from me. *Ever*, Brit. You understand?"

"I understand," she murmured, suddenly looking as if she was fighting back another smile. "But it's natural to want to protect what you love, Alex."

He gave her a piercing look. "It's natural to trust in that love, as well. And trust me when I say that I'll spend the rest of my life doing everything I can to ensure you are never in danger. But if something were to happen, and you got caught up in something," he rasped, gripping her chin, "I want your promise that you would do whatever it took to have me with you. That you would call me closer, instead of sending me away. Because protecting you, being with you, is where I belong, Doc, no matter the situation. Even if you were surrounded by fucking walkers, I'd want to be right in the middle of hell with you, doing everything I could to keep you alive."

"Walkers, huh?" she said with a soft laugh, her eyes shining. "I didn't know you were a *Walking Dead* fan."

"Don't change the subject," he grunted.

"Fine, I promise." Her lips curled up on one side in a sexy smirk. "But could I hold on to Daryl just until you got there to protect me?"

"Don't test me, beautiful." He pressed his forehead to hers, and his voice lowered to a possessive growl. "Even with a guy who isn't real."

She gave another soft laugh, and he took her mouth in a scalding kiss before she could tease him for being jealous over a TV character. But, hell, at least she had good taste. Daryl Dixon was a badass. Of course, that didn't mean Alex wanted her thinking about the guy. No, he planned on keeping her so sated and satisfied, there wouldn't ever be any room in her brilliant mind for any other man but himself—fictional ones included.

Pulling back a bit so that he could catch her expression, he told her, "We're going to have a hell of a life together, Doc."

She gave him a blinding smile, but Alex frowned as he took in the tears spilling back over her lashes. "You're crying again, baby."

She sniffled. "Yeah, well, I do that a lot around you."

"I know," he sighed, his hands tightening on her waist. "And I'm so damn sorry."

"Don't be," she murmured, running her fingers through his hair. "I've had a lot of happy tears, as well as sad ones. I mean, I usually cry when you make me come." She pressed her lips to the edge of his jaw . . . then the corner of his mouth, telling him, "Because it feels so good. So right."

"Get used to it," he groaned against her soft lips. "I'll still fuck you hard and rough and raw, every chance I get. But I'm going to work just as hard to blow your mind and own your heart. Hell, I even want to lay claim to your soul."

"You can do whatever you want, just as long as I get to do the same to you."

"You already own every part of me, Brit." Holding her tight, he pressed his lips to her ear, and growled, "Every. Fucking. Part."

"Then prove it," she moaned, shivering in his arms as she clutched at his shoulders.

"I won't hurt you again," he vowed, lifting his head and staring deep into her eyes. "Not like I did. I swear I won't."

She gave him another beautiful smile. "I know, Alex. I trust you with my heart. And I have so much faith in you."

"Fuck, Ben was right," he said unsteadily. "I don't deserve you. But I'm keeping you anyway. I'm never letting you go."

Studying him through her heavy lashes, she asked, "Isn't this the part where you usually tell me to get naked?"

"No. I want to be the one who undresses you this time. It'll be like unwrapping the best birthday present in the world."

He ripped his shirt over his head, then turned and laid her back on the bed, coming down over her. Taking his time, he kissed every inch of silky skin he uncovered as he slowly removed her jeans, T-shirt, panties, and bra. When he had her naked and soft and deliciously sweet beneath him, Alex opened his jeans, pushed himself deep inside her, and then held there as he spent long, mouthwatering moments sucking on her tender nipples, loving the way she felt on his tongue. And completely undone by the way she felt around his dick.

Braced on his forearms, he looked up at her and growled, "You're mine, Brit. You belong to me. Every part of you. And I'm yours. Forever. You understand?"

She curled her hand around the back of his neck, pulling him to her mouth, and kissed him like she needed his taste to survive. And, God, it was hot. Then she whispered that she loved him, and he lost it, pinning her wrists above her head before taking her mouth with an aggression that surpassed everything that had ever come before. He was raw and unleashed, every barrier broken down and shattered, completely without any shields or restraints. Which was just fine by him, seeing as how he wanted her in every part of him. Wanted his life so entwined with hers they couldn't ever be torn apart.

Lifting his head, Alex caught her shimmering, heavy-lidded gaze, and leaned down, catching her lower lip in his teeth. He gave it a gentle nip, then licked the sting away, their frantic breaths soughing together as he fucked her like a man intent on claiming the hell out of his woman.

Like a man who would *never* be able to get enough of her.

"God, Brit. I love you so fucking much," he groaned, shoving himself deep and grinding against her, against her swollen little clit, and that was it. She trembled and gasped, then let out a keening cry as her body shattered around him, convulsing around his thick shaft so tightly he could barely move inside her, and he followed her over. Still holding her wrists in his hands, he pressed his forehead against hers and came so hard it nearly turned him inside out, his muscles tremoring as he cursed and growled, his seed jetting from the swollen head of his cock with so much force he actually sobbed. And his hips just kept pumping him into her again . . . and again, until he was slick with sweat, so replete with satisfaction he felt drunk on it.

Somehow, he finally managed to drag himself onto his side, his clutching arms bringing her with him as he pulled her against his chest, still struggling to catch his breath. She scooted up so that they could share the pillow, and they both smiled like the lovesick idiots they were. It was sappy and sweet and, without any doubt, the best fucking moment of his entire life.

"I've wanted you forever," he told her, digging his fingers into the soft mass of her beautiful hair. Seeing the question in her eyes, he went on. "It's true, Doc. From the first moment I ever laid eyes on you. And I started falling in love with you during our first conversation a few years ago, when you called me a conceited jackass."

"But the other night you said you'd just wanted to fuck me."

"I did," he rasped, giving her a crooked smile. "But it was so much more than that. I wanted to toss you over my shoulder and steal you away. Keep you forever. Make you mine, in every way. I wanted you so badly it fucking tore me up inside that I couldn't have you."

Placing her soft palm against his chest, over the heavy beat of his heart, she asked, "Then why didn't you ever say anything?"

He gave a dry laugh. "Because I knew *you* knew I was a fuckup. And, well, for a long time I thought you were in love with my little brother. That would be Ben, not Mike."

"Hmm. I don't think I'd call Ben little."

Arching an eyebrow, he asked, "Is that all you have to say about that?"

"Well, it's a bit creepy," she murmured, scrunching up her cute little nose. "I mean, he's like a brother to me, too. I know he's hot and all, but we've just never had that kind of connection."

"I'm glad," he said with a heavy dose of satisfaction. "It would have sucked to have to kill him. I kind of like the guy."

She blinked, looking like he'd just told her he saw dead people. "You would choose me over Ben?"

"You still don't get it, do you?" he said, wanting her to see the truth in his eyes as he put his face close to hers. "I would choose *you* over anyone or anything, Doc. I love you. And one of these days, after I've proven myself to you, you're going to marry my stubborn ass."

Her jaw actually dropped. "I thought you believed that marriage and Hudson men don't mix. Isn't that what you're always saying?"

"Yeah, well, I've been known to say a lot of shit," he muttered against her lips, needing more of her taste. Needing more of everything when it came to her.

Pulling his head back so that he could see her eyes again, he ran his fingers through her silky hair. "I'm so damn sorry for fucking up so badly, Doc. If I hadn't been such an idiot, you would have been home with me that day and he never would have gotten close to you. I'm sorry for so many things. For all the times I said dick things to you, when I should have been seducing you. For not figuring out earlier that I was head-over-ass in love with you, instead of running like a jackass."

"Alex—"

Cutting her off, he said, "I'm sorry that I didn't find you sooner. That I wasn't there to stop every bad thing that's ever happened to you and that I wasn't there to hold and comfort you afterward. But if you'll let me, I promise I'll always be there from this day forward. I love you so much, and I will work my ass off to be worthy of you." Exhaling deeply as he tried to calm his emotional outpouring, Alex shot her a wry grin, then drawled, "And for such a smart woman, you should have *known* better than to listen to any of that shit I said about marriage. That was just stupid."

She laughed as she smacked his shoulder, then gave him a kind of shy, impossibly sexy smile. "You know how you can make it up to me?"

Giving her a heavy-lidded look, he asked, "How's that, Doc?"

"I want you to love me some more."

"I'll love you forever," he told her, the look on her precious face so beautiful it made his chest hurt. It was a face he was going to love not only ten years from now, but twenty . . . thirty . . . fifty. Until the day he fucking died.

"I'm holding you to that," she said huskily, running her hot little hand down the front of his body.

"You do that, baby. Just promise to always hold me tight," he groaned against her lips, rolling her to her back as he came down over her, which was right where he belonged. "And *close*. As close as you can, Doc. For-fucking-ever."

Epilogue

Weeks later . . .

ALEX HUDSON HAD THE SUN, SAND, AND A BREATHTAKING VIEW OF THE woman he loved in a bikini. Life just didn't get any fucking better than this.

The Fourth of July barbecue that Ben and Reese were throwing was proving to be the best party of the year, and as cheesy as it sounded, love was definitely in the air. Or, hell, maybe it was in the water. All Alex knew was that he'd found his own little personal slice of heaven here in the sleepy little town of Moss Beach. He smiled so often these days his family had taken to calling him "Dimples," which was beyond stupid, but he was suffering through it with a good-natured attitude that still had the power to leave them stunned.

It was apparently going to take them a while to get used to the fact that he was no longer a foul-tempered, broody, cold-hearted son of a bitch. But he knew it would come with time.

Alex also knew there were times when his past would weigh him down, fucking with his head. But Brit would be there to see him through. To lead him from the shadows and back into the light.

He didn't deserve her, but he was sure as fuck keeping her. Keeping her as close as humanly possible, until the day he died.

Though the start of their relationship had been as tumultuous as a storm, things were finally settling into a calmer rhythm. No longer comfortable in her house, after what had happened there with Shepherd, she'd sold it and moved in with him at the condo, which he loved. And her old boss, Ray McNamara, was no longer an issue. When the guy had found out they were moving in together, he acted like an ass, and Brit told him she'd had enough. She'd opened her own private therapy practice and was doing great, just like Alex had known she would. He was so damn proud of her, and he made it a point to tell her whenever she needed to hear the words.

In an unexpected twist, it seemed that getting better at sharing his feelings with the woman who owned his heart meant that he was also better at reading her own emotions. And, God, did that come in handy. Especially since there were still times he put his foot in it and acted like a jackass.

He might be in love, but he was still a guy. Which meant he was known to talk out of his ass from time to time. But he'd gotten damn good at saying he was sorry when he needed to. And the doc always did the same. It wasn't hard to figure out that this was how a healthy relationship worked, and Alex knew deep down that he would never be able to thank her enough for giving him a second chance to show her that he could love her.

And loving Dr. Cramer was something he'd become exceptionally good at.

Leaning back in his beach chair, Alex grinned as he watched Brit goofing around down in the water with Mike, Ben, and a still-not-showing, but over-the-moon-to-be-pregnant Reese. He loved watching the doc interact with his family. And later, when they'd all gathered back up at the house, he and Brit were going to tell them their own special news—that they were getting married—and he couldn't wait. Alex had finally popped the question the night before, and when she'd told him yes, that she would be his wife, and kissed him through her tears, it'd been the hottest fucking thing he'd ever known.

And the sex that had followed had damn near melted his brain.

Eager to be close to her again, he was just getting ready to pull his lazy ass out of the chair and join her down in the water, when she left the others and started heading his way. The sight of her creamy skin and lush curves glistening with drops of water was enough to make him have to shift a bit in his chair, and he licked his lips, unable to believe how lucky he was.

"What?" she asked, noticing the way he was staring up at her when she reached him.

A smile touched his lips as he reached up and grabbed her, her laughter filling the air as he tugged her into his lap. Wrapping his arms around her damp, beautiful body, he stared into her stunning eyes and said, "Have I ever thanked you, Doc?"

"For what?" Lifting a hand, she ran her fingers through his short hair, and he could actually *feel* her love whenever she touched him. And it was the best damn feeling in the world.

"For never giving up on me," he told her.

"*Alex.*" Her gaze softened, and he tightened his hold on her.

"I mean it, Brit. You're my life. I'd be so fucking lost without you. If you hadn't given me another chance, I don't . . ." His throat worked as he swallowed. Then he quietly said, "I wouldn't have liked what I became without you."

"I would never give up on you," she murmured, touching her soft lips to his. "I love you too much, Alex Hudson."

He gave a heartfelt groan against her mouth. "Thank God for that."

"You know what I think we should do?" she asked him, her big eyes twinkling as she softly stroked the back of his neck, the tender touch giving him chills.

"What's that, beautiful?"

Lowering her voice to a seductive whisper, she said, "I think we should go home and you should do everything you can to remind me why falling in love with you was such a brilliant thing to do."

"Good idea, Doc. I definitely do my best convincing when you're under me."

"You do your best *everything* when I'm under you," she purred, waggling her brows at him, and he laughed so hard he figured everyone on the beach was probably staring at them. But he didn't give a damn.

Let them see how happy we are, he thought, standing up with her in his arms, then cradling her against his chest.

"Where are we going?" she asked, when he started carrying her up the beach, toward Ben and Reese's house.

"We can't leave yet, and I can't wait. So we're going to lock ourselves in their spare room for a few hours, so I can get you under me again right now." His voice dropped to a husky drawl as he lost himself in her beautiful gaze. "And that's where I'm going to keep you. Every day, Brit, for the rest of my life."

She grinned up at him, her heavy-lidded eyes bright with excitement. "Promise?"

A slow, satisfied smile curved his mouth, and Alex held her closer, burying his face in her silky hair. "You have my word, angel. You have my absolute word."